OF SOUND
MIND

OF SOUND MIND

JAMES WALTZER

MEDALLION

Medallion Press, Inc.
Printed in USA

DEDICATION

To Nicole, Lauren, and Jordan
and their future reading adventures

Published 2016 by Medallion Press, Inc., 4222 Meridian Pkwy., Suite 110, Aurora, IL 60504

The MEDALLION PRESS LOGO
is a registered trademark of Medallion Press, Inc.

Cataloging-in-Publication Data is on file with the Library of Congress

Typeset in Adobe Caslon Pro
Printed in the United States of America
ISBN #9781942546184
10 9 8 7 6 5 4 3 2 1
First Edition

ACKNOWLEDGMENTS

As a structure and a symbol, Philadelphia City Hall captures the imagination. I salute the many men who risked their lives to construct this massive building, and the sculptor of the iconic bronze statue of William Penn that tops it: Alexander Milne Calder.

Literary agent Nat Sobel first saw the potential in this story. I thank him.

Numerous editors and publishers over the years have given my scribblings a home. I thank them.

Foremost, I am indebted to the gang at Medallion Press: Emily Steele and Traci Post for their sharp-eyed and thoughtful editing, Jim Tampa and his art designers for their noir sensibility, Brigitte Shepard for her marketing muscle.

PROLOGUE

*I*t's an old bedsheet that he holds out from his chest, the cotton thinned by many wash cycles, and no match for his veiny wrists and hands. He tears off a strip, and the sound rips through the small, dim room.

Her eyes flare. She whimpers.

Keep quiet.

His voice is subdued, businesslike.

She sits on a wooden chair that has been pulled out from the table. Nylon rope runs across her chest and around the back of the chair, tied tightly so that her arms are pinned to her sides. She recoils and lets loose a strangled scream—more of a sob trying to grow into a scream—when he wraps the strip of bedsheet around her head, forcing it between her lips, then her teeth, then knots it at the base of her skull. He is economical in his movements, and his knot is tidy, expert even. A square knot, the ends frayed where they were torn. Hunched over as he works, he looks at her dispassionately. She sees only forehead sweat crowning soulless eyes.

I told you to keep quiet. I'm not going to rape you.

He takes a new length of the nylon rope and ties her right ankle to a chair leg. Again, the assured knot.

She wriggles for an instant, then gives him her left, eases it toward him as if she were submitting it for a pedicure or a shoe fitting.

Once more, he winds rope around ankle and chair leg.

He stands and appraises his handiwork. A gasp catches in her throat. She whimpers again, a plea suppressed by the gag. When he slides the chair forward a few inches, it scrapes the bare floor. She stops muttering. He pulls up a second chair and sits next to her as if he's going to tell her a bedtime story. Her breathing ceases.

Something inside her ignites.

Her legs thrash against their restraints, the left one summoning enough terrified energy to undo the knot and break free, her head shaking furiously and her foot shooting out, the toe of her running shoe nailing him on the shin. He grunts with the surprise impact, then darts below her flailing leg and resecures the rope, this time binding it tightly enough to threaten circulation. Her eyes water, and her consciousness retreats to this clamp of intimate horror.

He tugs the gag and is satisfied with its tautness. She is motionless, and the room is still and silent. He stands over her and, for a moment, seems to be calculating his next move.

It comes fast.

He forms a fist and strikes her with a short, unerring, right-hand punch, his knuckles cracking fragile cheekbones. She is unconscious.

He shakes his punching hand in one vigorous movement, as if trying to get rid of mud or a landed wasp. He looks at the hand, flexing it several times, each contraction re-forming the fist.

There is more for that hand to do.

No, he is not going to rape her.

ONE

At nighttime, the city is a sprawling showcase of diamonds. No matter that some lights reflect the architect's design, while others serve strictly an industrial utility. To birds on the wing and to passengers on planes in descent, they are all glittering gems.

They civilize the darkness.

The lights define the tall buildings that rise from the floor of the city, for their features identifiable in daylight are unavailable. The structures' relative heights and distinctive shapes are suggested by their contained arrangements of lights that, collectively, offer assurances of life and purpose and stability. Every large city's nocturnal face gives onlookers a feeling of confidence and a sense of order, a belief in tomorrow. Within cocoons of security, the keen-eyed in window seats and the gazers from high floors of skyscrapers mark highways and bridges, towers and spires, the landmarks and boundaries that impart uniqueness and comfort with familiarity.

But many people who inhabit the city often abandon this charm of recognition as they go about the business of living their lives, daytime and nighttime. Theirs is a constant battle of coping, of avoiding dangers that surface with surprising suddenness.

Though they erupt with fierceness, such dangers are often unapparent from a distance.

Some evade detection even when they're right under your nose.

Sounds ruled his consciousness. They unnerved him, enchanted him, woke him in the wee hours, sent him hurtling around street corners to escape, came to his ear as little messengers, singed him like a bullet delivering a flesh wound. He heard things that dogs could not. He had an earful of the planet.

It had been so as far back as he could remember. Kids in the neighborhood said he was strange, freakish. He heard the swish of its tires before a car turned the corner and appeared on his block. Thunder while it was still in the sky's throat. Preternatural: that's what his mother called his hearing. Spooky, his father said.

But they didn't trust him when it mattered most. When he heard it happen. When he was the only one to hear, who *could* hear.

Other than, of course, the little girl herself and her father. They heard it, unless the horror froze their eardrums. Her gasping, her petrified whimpering, came through the walls and permeated his bedroom like steam from a vent. Small sounds muted by inches-thick plaster and wood but loud enough for his ears, those ultrasensitive instruments.

The little girl's sounds invaded the sanctuary of

his room with its wallpaper of cowboys aboard bucking broncos—actually, the same cowboy and bronco repeated several dozen times, each imprint separated from its replica above, below, and to either side by blank beige. He heard the sounds and, at first, didn't know precisely what they meant, but he knew instinctively that something was very wrong. He lay there, paralyzed and smothered in blankets. He heard but did nothing, didn't even wake his parents. Only later, the following afternoon, when the sun had long since chased the night's fears, did he tell them. But by then it was too late, far too late, and the workaday row-house neighborhood had seen evil's nocturnal delivery, the little body sheeted and strapped, wheeled out on the gurney, all the more terrifying in the sanitizing daylight.

And now, more than two decades later, it was a stain that would not yield to the mind's harshest corrosives, a memory that clung like a spider's gossamer stickiness, a trap not to be escaped.

As surely as the eardrum played to the brain, he was caught in this trap.

It is a 3:00 a.m. bugle blast, three nights a week. A delivery truck pulling up alongside the twenty-four-hour convenience store adjacent to his high-rise apartment building, the unloading ramp banging the street, instantly waking him despite the rubber plugs wedged into his ears. Heavy boxes tossed from inside the truck thudding onto the metal ramp. Booted feet trampling in the darkness. A half hour of this and then the motor's rumble and the flurry of warning beeps, a high-pitched piercing staccato that seems injected into his ear.

Richard Keene will be wide awake, flinging back the bedcovers, standing and looking out the window, as if his gaze could do anything, could reverse the disturbance that has taken place, or preclude any future such disturbances. Twenty-two floors up, he can see nothing of his tormentors at the foot of the sheer drop. But he might raise the micro-blinds anyway and have a look at the vast, spangled city, glittering at this no-man's hour, its towers empty but lit like the backdrop of a stage production. He might look beneath him at squatter buildings, where the racket of rooftop compressors is just as likely to interrupt his sleep. He might listen for sounds emanating from apartments above, below, and beside his. Though the building is a fortress with extra layers of foam insulation, he can hear faint footsteps, coughing, sighing, stubborn drains, beeping microwaves.

Sometimes he remains under the sheets, eyes shut in defiance yet ears straining to defeat the plugs, a triumph of instinct.

When he's up and out of bed, prompted by the noise and something far from the surface, something deep in his gut, he switches on the desk lamp and its harsh light staggers him. The room is spare and ordered. Compact, matching oak bureaus stand side by side against one wall; they've been hewn from one tree, the finish natural, the dovetailing expert and all wood, not a screw or nail anywhere. It reminds him of the knots he learned to make when he was a Boy Scout, all those slip knots, loop knots, and square knots, interlaced cord or twine drawn into tight, perfect nodes.

The desk is by the same hand, a Japanese furniture maker discovered in bucolic Bucks County north of Philadelphia by Richard's style-conscious mother, Evelyn. A queen-sized bed and box springs sit on apartment-standard, dishwater-colored carpet, and the warped shelves of a shiny, black bookcase are filled except for a small rectangle of space at the top. A few volumes of poetry, including Walt Whitman's *Leaves of Grass*, huddle on the middle shelf. Elsewhere, history and crime titles predominate: presidential biographies, thick studies of the Civil War and the two World Wars, and several accounts of small-town murder, the victims' children. Alone at one end of the top shelf, Richard's favorite work of fiction— *The Stranger* by Camus—leans against the varnished wood, its paperback pages billowed from use. He reread it twice during his stay at the clinic.

Richard Keene has just turned thirty, and his world continues to be a fearful place. The milestone passed without notice, except for a card and a phone call from his parents. No acknowledgment from anyone else, but how could there be? Richard long ago lost touch with the few relatives he'd known in his extended family, an aunt here, a cousin there. And he has no close friends, no girlfriend. Sometimes, he's not even sure whether he has *himself*. After the breakdown, after he'd been confined to the room with no mirrors, he would lie on his bed and relive the sensation of facing his image in the full-length mirror that hung on his bedroom door at home. He had discovered the dread in that exercise as a young boy, the out-of-body feeling of it, a fizz of fear like tiny insects inside his skin, the unthinkable notion that he did not exist, at least not as he understood it. He would stand there and stare at himself and feel the desperation come over him. He could not quite recognize the image in that mirror. It would take a forced recitation of familiar things and concepts (his name, his birthday, his parents' names, the fact that the sun comes up in the morning) to stave off total panic and return him to a point where he could function. Nothing scared him more than this sensation, and sometimes he could re-create it—even without the mirror's spell—if he concentrated hard enough.

Richard confessed all this to his doctors, whose designated, mirrorless rooms were intended to discourage more than just imaginary fright. They taught him how to parry his fear through self-distraction, diverting it at or before the onset with unrelated thoughts. It's a technique he has continued to use on the outside. So now, this morning, once the sun has snuck some light into the concrete canyon beyond his window, Richard stands before the bathroom mirror, mouth unhinged, and gives his teeth a thorough flossing. He thinks of his dentist and the pretty technician who cleans his teeth twice a year, her long lashes and sweet breath. No thoughts of the paranormal at present, no worries that existence is an illusion. He rinses and spits into the sink— not a trace of blood, thanks to his daily rigors. He looks up, and active brown eyes in an angular face stare back at him. Sometimes they seem to him like marbles about to pop out and roll down the slope of the sink. He knows not to keep looking into those eyes for more than a few seconds, though he can't help checking the pupils, which tend to shrink and dilate unequally. Below his sharp chin, a columnar neck attaches to a bony torso. If he lingers, the strange fears may rise, so he busies himself with movement. Shaving is quick and electric, his beard narrow and light. He applies deodorant, runs a comb just once through his unruly black hair. He pulls on an undershirt and a short-sleeved Arrow shirt, chinos, a pair of Rockports. Dress is casual at his workplace.

Lastly, he tethers the iPod to his ears. Never leaves home without it. Music is his faithful traveling companion, and he wants no intrusion from an iPhone's jarring ring.

In the pallid hallway, a tame scent rises from the vacuum-stroked carpet. The elevator requires patience, a wait of three to four minutes or sometimes more. He won't make a musical selection from his downloaded iTunes catalog until he leaves the building. Several floors up, muted chimes distinct to Richard's ear signal stops, the subsequent drone a resumption of the elevator's down rush. Now a loud chime fires an embedded light, and the door opens, revealing bodies from any one of the twenty higher floors. Richard tries to find a corner or at least some wall space, some breathing room. They all stare straight ahead and don't notice his jaw ripple as he gnashes his teeth. The young woman wearing a navy suit jacket and a broad belt cinching her matching skirt looks up at the panel of numbers to monitor the elevator's descent. At sixteen, a heavyset man gets on, leading with his stomach. As the others press more closely about him, Richard feels his chest tighten, but with the elevator descending once more and the lobby rushing up to meet them, he knows that release is imminent. When the elevator reaches ground level, Richard bolts off, gulps air.

The polished tile of the lobby floor reflects light beams from bulbs recessed in the ceiling, as do the mirrored wall panels that flank the elevator doors. Richard walks past the front desk, through the automatic sliding glass doors, and into the sunshine of a mid-September Tuesday morning.

Richard's new home, the 42s (fashionably named for the number of stories it rises above Locust Street), races upward toward a docile sky. Summer has only a week to run, but it seems in no hurry to depart. The city is warm and sticky, and Locust Street is crammed with faces expectant, blank, or disconcerted. Cell phones, cupped by hands, bloom out of ears. Richard reaches into his pocket for his iPod and dials up some music, his fingers nimble on the small touch screen; he is a fan of classical in particular, knows all the great names and their greatest works. He turns up Fifteenth Street and dodges trash cans, no-parking signs, and pedestrians too oblivious or arrogant to give way. Through his earbuds he hears the clarion tones of a Chopin polonaise as the city's muffled cacophony swirls about him.

Clamped down in an iPod world, Richard can still hear the outside fury, in nuance and volume, better than most of those unencumbered. His other senses, too, are quite sharp, if not as exceptional as his hearing. The morning's creased light outlines every object he sees. In the alleyway outside a hash house on the corner at Sansom Street, a stuffed Dumpster emits the scent of sour milk. At Market Street, the number of traffic lanes doubles, and Richard moves smartly across when the silvery Walk icon beckons. He's a reflex quicker than everyone else as he strides down the steps to the subway concourse to the busy stop below City Hall.

Once on the underground platform, he spies the light in the distance burning a hole through the black tunnel and braces himself for the onrushing train and its deafening roar. He steps back as it blurs past, closing his eyes, inhaling the dankness. Chopin's crystal notes rain on him, bursting through the train's thunder.

Inside, the seats are all occupied, and Richard stands, grasping a shiny metal pole. At Race/Vine, Fairmount, and Girard, more people get on than off, and the tide engulfs Richard, pressing him against his gleaming pole, his life raft. As the train lurches into motion, he is sweating, the world closing in on him, but he takes two deep breaths and, slowly, convinces himself not to panic. Gradually, he has been learning to cope with this phobia. Sweat evaporates. He settles into himself, feels warmth spreading across his chest. Heroic chords fill his head.

Richard gets off at Olney Avenue and surfaces through soiled passageways leading to a wide, concrete staircase. Preston Medical Tower is directly across a perilous intersection, where multicar crackups are commonplace, participants seemingly encouraged by the convenience of Logan General Hospital on the next block of Broad Street. In the Preston lobby, Richard enters a waiting elevator and retreats to the rear when two uniformed nurses arrive, giving him their backs. He removes his earbuds and stashes them with the iPod in his pants pocket.

Rosen & Wallingford ENT Associates has a suite on the fifth floor. Kathy, the receptionist, wears clinging sweaters, blouses, or T-shirts that showcase breasts too ample for her slender frame. Her forehead is still trying to chase lingering acne. Richard knows about girls; he doesn't need an owner's manual. He's had girlfriends, though not recently. He has thought about asking Kathy out once or twice, but the connection doesn't seem to be there. They're civil to each other;

that's all. He nods as he passes the front desk.

"Morning, Kathy."

"Oh, Richard, there's a change in your schedule. Your ten o'clock, Mrs. O'Hanlon, canceled, so I stuck in Mrs. Campbell."

"Who?"

"Loretta Campbell. Doctor wants a complete work-up for dizzy spells. And Mr. Caracappa can't make it this afternoon at three, so I rescheduled for tomorrow morning."

Richard shrugs. "Thanks." Campbell, O'Hanlon, Caracappa; it's all the same in the life of an audiometric technician. Plug 'em in, turn the dials, jack up the hertz. At first, it was a novel task to run the contraption and let loose the thin, high-pitched tones; he was a kind of Master of the Machine who could exercise dominion over all sounds in the universe, the faintest of which could not escape his astounding acuity. But now, after eighteen months on the job, it has grown routine. Once he gathers a few extra dollars and musters sufficient stamina, he'll study to be an audiologist qualified to administer an electronystagmography and an auditory brainstem response, tests designed to evaluate the balance mechanism and central nervous system, the clumsy terms portentous enough to scare the earlobes off most patients. For now, though, he has to be content with his audiometer and merely assisting on the ENGs and ABRs.

It is ironic—Richard is quick to detect irony—that the boy with superhearing has grown up to be a tester of other people's hearing, as if searching for a fellow traveler. He considered technical training in several medical disciplines and gravitated to audiology. Who better to make the call than

Richard Keene? But, of course, it's the machine that does the real work. The technician's just a recorder, a secretary, like Kathy at the front desk.

This particular workday is uneventful, as most of them are. One woman displays a sense of humor—she professes to have better hearing than her Chihuahua—but the others sit glumly in the booth and raise their hands when they hear something or think they do. On the other side of the glass, Richard reminds himself that the human element in this process does matter. The good technician doesn't telegraph the sounds but varies the rhythm and looks away from the patient to avoid prompting. A raised hand is easy enough to pick up without making direct eye contact; it's surprising to see technicians who don't grasp that. Limited peripheral vision in some cases but mostly stupidity. Richard prides himself on technique and producing reliable results. So he's worth something, after all, as he sits in his mechanized cell and spools out filaments of sound.

This day, in addition to his regular customers, he has a personal health matter that needs attention. During his lunch break, he takes the stairs to the sixth floor to see an osteopath. Dr. Melvin Natrol is rostered on Richard's HMO, and you can't beat the convenience; if he knows what he's doing, it's a bonus. Richard's right knee has been bothering him the last couple of years, and now the dull soreness has become a stabbing pain. Still, he pounds the treadmill nightly in his apartment building's fitness center, driving his weight onto the tender knee, kneading it like mad afterward to lessen the pain.

"Maybe it's time you got an MRI," says Natrol, swarthy

and rather grave as he flexes Richard's leg dangling aside the padded table, the patient seated there in his briefs, pants draped over a straight-back chair. Richard grimaces more at the doctor's suggestion than at his probing hands. Natrol notices.

"You okay?"

"Yeah."

Natrol manipulates the knee some more, thumbs it.

"Can you breathe in those things?" Richard asks.

Natrol looks at him, begins to understand. "Usually."

Richard manages a weak smile, which Natrol returns.

"A little claustrophobia?" Richard's frozen expression provides the answer. "I'll get you into one of the newer machines. It's like flying first class."

The subway ride home is decidedly lower than first class, but Richard is learning to tolerate this cramped, subterranean passage. It is a kind of training regimen as he attempts to blunt his claustrophobia. As the train hurtles through the darkness, he finds a seat smack up against the window and stares at his photographic negative in the tunnel-blackened glass. His iPod parries the sonic insult with soothing strings, the burnished sound of the Philadelphia Orchestra. Richard closes his eyes and floats on the rise and swell of melody, the train's clatter and hollow roar receded to a far corner of the stage.

Six weeks on his own, he's a man of the world now. He's getting the hang of it. His mission is to rejoin the human race. The doctors told him it was high time, and he accepted their recommendations. Time to move out of his parents' suburban home, where he'd been forever, a halfway house following his six-month stay at the mental treatment center, that repository of bruised minds, of beige walls and restful gardens and rooms with shatterproof Plexiglas windows and no mirrors, where he had his books to read and jigsaw puzzles to solve but was denied the rope or string he requested for practicing his knot-making, an old skill, an activity he believed to be therapeutic.

At Fifteenth and Market, the City Hall stop, Richard emerges from the depths into a jamboree world. Skateboarders dodge grim, hard-soled walkers in the plaza dwarfed by the gray Bastille-like tower conceived and built in another era, topped by the city's historic benefactor, William Penn and his Quaker garb memorialized in black bronze. Richard approaches the river of traffic on Market Street, and the blare of car horns bounces off his earbuds, but enough of it filters through to make him wince. When the traffic light signals him to walk, he scoots across the street to the concrete apron at the foot of the high-rise offices of Centre Square. In front of a twenty-five-foot-tall sculpture of a clothespin, a pale, ill-dressed man points to a homemade chart propped on an easel. The circled words *tension* and *peace* and *happiness* claim much of the space on the chart.

"Everybody is looking to get rid of their loneliness," the man says to a clutch of onlookers. Looming above him, the giant chocolate-brown clothespin is pinched at the top by an oversized metal clasp. The small audience is an oasis in the surge, for the sidewalk is thick with the day's work crowd careening for the exits, anxious to escape from the place where they make their livelihood. As center city empties itself of the white-collar horde, it turns the streets over to the twilight people, a mix of stragglers, incense peddlers, and club hoppers.

Richard's refuge, he hopes, is a building a few blocks away on Locust Street, and in daylight, his apartment building, the monolith that is the 42s, arches skyward, poking cottony clouds.

The sliding-glass doors part and Richard is home. He passes the front desk, where chief attendant Frank is speaking with an elderly couple, and heads straight to the mail room. Tarnished-metal slot doors, like miniature crypts, fill the walls. Richard keys one open and eyes a narrow cylinder of space between wraparound catalogs and a large, manila envelope. He tries to remove the whole wedge with one tug, but it stalls on the edges of the compartment. He grips and tries again in vain. Finally, he angrily yanks the mass toward him and, with a small rip, it spurts from its cloister, out of his hand and onto the tiled floor, scattering at his feet. There's a yellow slip among the fallen, telling him he's got a package waiting at the desk.

Richard gathers up his pile, marches back to the front desk, and extends the slip to Frank, a gregarious fellow who has manned this post for several years and likes the idea of running the building's nerve center.

"Twenty-two oh seven," Richard says without expression. He dislikes small talk and is not a big fan of Frank, who seems more concerned with his own image than the welfare of the tenants.

Frank reaches under the U-shaped counter, selects an item, and hands it to Richard. It is a small parcel too rigid for the mail compartment.

"There you go, my man."

Richard takes it, mutters, "Thanks," and moves away

quickly to the elevator, another station in his training regimen to combat claustrophobia. He gets on, moves to the rear as others board, and shuts his eyes, imploring the door to close and set the conveyance in motion. The elevator pulls upward and Richard opens his eyes. The little light on the horizontal panel above the door is on the move, hopping floors. The corresponding side panel shows six floors lit, only one lower than Richard's. When a woman gets off at fourteen, Richard feels the lift in his chest, the readiness to rid himself of this closed-in shuttle. The next chime is his release, and he's off the elevator, into the hallway, and across it at a modest angle to the first apartment on the left, number 2207. Home.

Inside, he sorts through his mail, tosses the solicitations, opens the parcel (a historical documentary titled *Skyscrapers* ordered through Amazon; he has seen it on PBS), and checks for telephone messages. There are two, the first in a familiar nasal voice.

"Richard, it's your mother. Your father and I would like to come over for dinner one night, if you'd be so kind as to extend an invitation. You know, we haven't even seen your place yet—it's been at least a month, hasn't it? We have a birthday present and housewarming gift for you all wrapped up in one. Anyway, call me and let's schedule. Hope you're all settled in and having a ball . . . Lotsa love."

Six weeks, to be exact, since leaving home just shy of his thirtieth birthday. His parents help with the rent (good of them, but not a huge sacrifice since they had to be happy to get him out of the house); center city isn't cheap. Comes the liberation, finally, the doctors' latest and boldest prescription more than two years after the illness. But the cure is not immediate; the same fears have moved right along with him and dwell with him in his new apartment.

"Second message," says the female-approximate computer voice, followed by a prerecorded pitch for a center-city singles group, something about a Friday night bash at a pub on Walnut Street. Richard erases it. There must be a constantly updated file of every newcomer to every place in the world, he thinks. By phone, mail, or Internet, they get you; there's no hiding. But he didn't come here to hide—quite the opposite. He's here to make a new start, join the crowd, reconstruct a life. Still, he yearns for solitude and silence—at least he thinks he does. But he can't trust that impulse either. Which way does freedom lie?

He spends nearly half an hour in the bathroom, dousing his face with cold water, sending streams of saline spray up each nostril, roosting on the toilet and straining to remove the accumulations of twenty-four hours. Must get more bran and roughage and flaxseed into the system. He scrubs his hands with antibacterial soap, orange and fragrant.

He knows he's compulsive, neurotic. Not so easily rectified.

He munches on some garlic crackers, chews a carrot, and makes himself a turkey-roll sandwich with lettuce and tomato on wheat bread. A nectarine for dessert. A good, balanced dinner with no mess to clean up. He mutes the TV evening news and gets the subtitles, then powers on his Bose sound system—the one high-end item he owns—and listens to the New York Philharmonic embroider a symphony by Berlioz.

An hour and fifteen minutes later, Richard changes into

gym shorts and cross trainers and gets back on the elevator, taking it to the top floor—number forty-two—which, in addition to the fitness center, houses a banquet room, an indoor swimming pool and, outside, an expansive sundeck still bright and warm though it's nearly 6:30. Through the windows, Richard sees a lone female form bronzing on the deck in the late-summer sun, coaxing the last coat of pigment before the long, pale winter; he just glances, never lingers. The banquet room is silent, chairs and tables stacked to one side, but from the fitness center comes the drone and squeak of movable parts, mechanical and human. Richard strides to a vacant treadmill at the far left. Of the other four machines in the row, each facing floor-to-ceiling windows, two are occupied. Through the glass, the city's skyscrapers loom like giant rockets.

For Richard, the treadmill is an escape hatch from discomfort. He grips the rubber-sheathed sidebars, extends each leg behind him in turn to stretch the hamstrings and calf muscles, and looks down the row. A hefty guy about his age pads along on the middle treadmill, surprisingly light on his feet. Two over from him, at the end of the row, a woman moves at a fast but fluid clip. Her curves are encased in a cotton sports bra and spandex shorts. Red hair as bright as a flare falls onto bare shoulders. Richard feels that ping, the little jolt that tells him this is a woman he desires but who intimidates him. He sees her up here all the time, it seems, and each time he gets the same feeling. All he can do for now is match her pace.

He drapes his towel over the right sidebar, punches up a starter pace on the electronic monitor, and begins walking, quickly moves to a jog, and soon accelerates to a miler's steady swiftness. The soreness disappears from his knee as his speed increases. He doesn't use the iPod when he works out. His light breathing and the treadmill's hum serve as a sound conditioner and, moreover, he doesn't like sweating into the earbuds.

The big guy two over steps down after another five minutes, and Richard and the redhead are left to match strides, separated by three vacant treadmills. Visible through a glass wall to their left is an adjoining room packed with strength-training equipment, where a weightlifter lets a heavy iron plate fall to the carpeted floor. The thud jars Richard, almost knocking him off his stride. He feels a twinge in the knee, shakes it off, and resumes the pace, glowering toward the offending weightlifter, who is looking the other way; Richard's look of contempt is a safe move with no repercussions.

The woman on the treadmill is aware of Richard, the way any fine-tuned athlete feels the competition without looking at it head-on. Though he doesn't know it yet, her name is Janet Kroll and she's been living at the 42s for about a month now, a short time less than him. She stays on the treadmill for another forty-five minutes and follows with fifteen brisk minutes of resistance work, using dumbbells and selectorized machines. Her shoulders have a small swell of muscle, and her legs are taut as a dancer's. Richard's discreet glances take it all in, and when the two of them pass on the floor, he notices freckles below her eyes, giving her a vulnerability she lacks from a distance. This relaxes him for a moment, but he needs more time to find his comfort zone, to muster the confidence to speak to her. That time is always elusive. As Richard fills a paper cup with filtered water from the cooler and downs it, Janet Kroll and her tumbling, flame-colored hair and well-contoured body stride out of the fitness center.

TWO

On the elevator drifting downward, Richard towels his face and closes his eyes. With no one else on board, he feels secure in the space. The elevator descends, a suspended box humming down a barren shaft. Richard feels like he's floating.

The chime and an absence of movement yank him from his repose. The door slides open and, just as he steps off, a tall woman wearing orange hoop earrings steps onto the elevator. She is a mere passing image to Richard, who is already angling to his left and nearing his apartment across the hallway. He withdraws the single key from the back pocket of his shorts and inserts it into the lock.

When he tries to turn the key, it doesn't cooperate. He wiggles it to no avail, then removes it and tries again, gently, but the key will not go. And just like that, Richard is lost, a man falling through space, as if he were back in the elevator disengaged from its pulleys and plummeting. It doesn't take much to throw him off-kilter; panic is always crouching nearby and ready to spring. He feels the same unnerving sensation as when he stands before the mirror and has difficulty recognizing himself, doubting all of existence. Where am I? Who am I? His heart palpitates as he looks up and finally sees the number above the peephole on the door: *2307.* His apartment's counterpart, one floor up. All of them lined up to the sky, floor after floor after floor, but only one that's his, only one that opens to his special little world.

The woodpecker pulses retreat from his heart and are replaced by three thumps like a heavy-footed man stomping out the front door. Richard shakes his head and looks back toward the elevator, searching for clues. He's got it. Of course. The tall woman with the orange earrings, stepping on as he got off. *Her* floor. On her subsequent way down, a futile stop at the floor just below, twenty-two, which he had pressed when leaving the fitness center on forty-two.

He has taken that postworkout ride almost every day for six weeks now, and this is the first time it's been interrupted. The ride is languid, dreamy and kinetic, and gives him a sense of distance and time elapsed. He has almost always had the elevator to himself for this trip, coming down from the top floor, the day's rush over.

Clean, deductive reasoning. Nice to have a rational explanation for things.

He turns to leave the apartment door but doesn't get a step away before the coarse sound of tearing fabric stops him. To Richard, it is a sound as cruel as a blade slicing flesh. It has come from inside apartment 2307 and is followed by a woman's plaintive cry, then a man's voice saying matter-of-factly, "Keep quiet."

Richard steps back to the door. He hears a shuffling

within, a swishing sound like palms rubbing against one another, then a muffled scream, a woman's howl, but muted and distorted as if she's wrapped in cellophane.

"I told you to keep quiet. I'm not going to rape you."

Richard edges even closer to the door, plasters himself against it. As a gasp becomes a whimper, he concentrates fully, trying to catch every nuance of sound, fighting off the intrusion of his heart, which is racing again. He will store these sounds in sequence in his auditory memory, while his concentration filters out sounds beyond this threshold. What he hears, he will be able to replay in his head as if on a digital recorder. But while he trusts this capability absolutely, he has grown to distrust his state of mind at any given moment. That mind's power of invention. Devilish and unchecked, his mind has a mind of its own. Is he hearing what he thinks he is hearing? Is he standing where he thinks he is standing?

A scraping, wood on wood. Then stillness. But not for long.

Sounds of struggle, choked breathing, a desperate bid to escape a trap. A grunt—male. The struggle abates.

Richard stands there, transfixed. He looks down at his feet, but they seem to have no purchase; then at his hands, the fingers curled and stiffened. He doesn't feel whole. He could lift off and hover in the hallway, or he might sift through the door like a wraith. He hears a rasping, like a drain trying to clear, then a sound that is a cross between a fist pulverizing meat and an openhanded smack.

The rasping is gone, and the silence is unsettling. Movement. The faint strain of exertion. A small crack, like a snapped wishbone. Now a thud with a floor squeak underneath, and—Richard blinks in consternation—a thump, heavy and full, like a ball of wet towels hurled into the dryer, a stack of books plopped onto a desk, a body fallen to the floor.

And then someone breathing.

It's as if Richard is on the apartment side of the door, right in the center of the apparent crime. Committing it. But he can't be; that can't be. The door is still in front of him, a barrier between himself and the horror.

He steps back, distraught, all rigid limbs and frightened eyes, and looks nervously around the empty hallway. This is what he has dreamed of and dreaded almost forever, a crazy happenstance, a signal from *The Stranger*'s universe of benign indifference, from the dark horizon of his future. Richard stands there, muscles coiled to flee, to strike he knows not what. Finally, three jerky strides take him to the elevator and he presses the down button, repeatedly presses it. Sweat that has beaded on his forehead now falls off in droplets. He wipes his face with his towel, which he then jams between his sharp hip and the waistband of his shorts. A fresh layer of sweat surfaces within seconds. When the elevator arrives, its chime is like an air-raid siren.

On the elevator, a heavyset woman in a tentlike dress takes one look at dripping, disheveled Richard and keeps her distance. He makes his way to the rear, turns, braces himself against a metal rail, and sits into the corner. Wants to wrap himself into a small ball.

He is back there, back in the row-house bedroom of cowboys riding bucking broncos across the wall, from beyond which come the muted, disturbing gasps of a young girl. And a man's voice, just a few quiet words. He knows who is speaking and who is gasping, now whimpering. There is no mistaking it. To his ears, sound permeates these walls as if they were tissue paper. He lies there frozen, not sure of what is going on, but he knows where it's coming from and who is involved, and he knows there is something very wrong.

When the elevator door opens, the heavyset woman walks into the lobby, not bothering to look back at Richard, who pauses at the threshold, disoriented. As the door closes, it brushes the back of his damp T-shirt bunching at the waist, and he lurches forward.

He approaches the front desk and Frank, who is dawdling on the phone. Richard passes the desk, stops, puts his hands in his pockets, lowers his head, and flexes his knees in a standstill position. Frank watches as he winds up his phone call.

"You okay, man? You look like you gotta go to the bathroom or somethin'."

Two young guys with baseball caps pass with a "Yo, Frank" on their way out.

Richard tries to stifle his trembling and turns toward Frank, who now looks concerned. Not so much for Richard as for the distraction, a possible problem in the works, an upset to lobby decorum. Frank likes a tight ship.

"Take it easy, man. What's wrong?"

Richard's instinct is that he must talk to someone. This time he must, right away. He steps to the counter. Hesitates. Frank's musky aftershave hits him. "Who lives in 2307?" He is surprised at the firmness of his voice.

Frank is amused at Richard's uncool style and issues a little smile. "Hold on a second. Just relax and tell me what's goin' on before you start runnin' the place."

Richard feels the familiar little sting of put-down. He

must fight through it. "I'm, uh, concerned about something. Can you call up there?"

"Slow down, man. Just tell me what's up. What's got you jazzed?"

They look at each other and Frank waits. Richard takes some breaths. What did he really hear? Tricks the mind plays . . . Wherever this leads, he must speak up. To say nothing, to run and hide, is to swallow a cancer. A second cancer. His lips stick for an instant as he opens his mouth to speak.

"Come on now," Frank says. "I'm all ears."

"Someone may have been attacked."

Frank leans in with "What's that mean?"

"I think someone may have been attacked in that apartment . . . I mean, it's possible." Richard squeezes the countertop ledge with both hands.

Frank is no longer smiling, but he's a long way from believing this tenant, already deeming him to be one shaky dude. "You talkin' 2307?"

"Yes."

Frank tries to situate Richard's apartment. He's given him several pieces of mail in the past few weeks, including one just a couple hours ago. "You're what, twenty-two—?"

"—Oh seven. I got off on the wrong floor."

"Okay . . . and?"

"I heard something."

"Like what?"

Richard looks beyond Frank and sees himself reflected in the gold-leaf mirror behind the counter. He tries to measure the resolve in the image he sees. He could still run away from this, drop it and shrink into the night. "Like maybe a woman being strangled."

Frank deadpans it. "Like a woman being strangled?"

"That's right."

"So you're tellin' me you *heard* this?"

"Yes."

"You sure 'bout that?"

He's damn sure of the sounds that he heard. "I can't be a hundred percent sure that something actually happened, you know, that somebody was harmed."

"Well, what exactly did you hear, man? Was there screaming or—?" Frank pretends to choke himself and makes a few strangulated grunts. "Or what?"

"There was a scream. Well, kind of a scream."

"*Kind* of a scream?"

"It won't hurt to call up there," says Richard, quietly frantic. "That's all I want."

"Oh, so that's all *you* want." This time, Frank's smile fronts a touch of resentment. But Richard won't back down; he rocks nervously on his feet and forces himself to maintain eye contact. He won't let Frank clear him away like a picked-up parcel.

Finally, Frank picks up the phone and punches in four numbers. "What did you hear, again?" he asks as the line rings.

"I think it was a scream. And there were whimpers, then kind of a rasping, then a—"

Frank holds up a hand and speaks into the phone, "Hello, Dr. Braun?" With that, he arches an eyebrow at Richard, signifying the respectability of a man of medicine. Frank oversees a mixed roster at the 42s, but he likes to highlight the professional people.

"This is Frank at the front desk. How are you, sir?" Frank listens, chuckles. "Yeah, I know what you mean. Listen, just checking, is everything all right up there? A neighbor heard somethin', some noises, thought there might be a problem; that's all . . . Oh, don't worry about that, that's nothin' . . . Right, got it. Well, thank you. Sorry for the disturbance."

Frank hangs up the phone and shoots Richard a told-you-so look. "Everything's cool." But Richard stares past him in rapt concentration, seeing something awful on the flocked wallpaper that surrounds the mirror. Then he drifts to his face in the mirror once again and, through the decorative golden cobweb, the old fright shivers him.

"You hear me?" says Frank. "Everything's okay up there. Hunky-dory. You can relax. Thanks for bein' concerned, though. I like that. Makes for a better lifestyle around here. Know what I mean?"

Richard's cheek twitches and his eyes turn frantic.

"Hey, man, you're startin' to freak me out."

"*Brawn?*"

"That's right, Dr. Braun, Davis Braun. Good guy. Know 'im?"

"Is he married? Who's he live with?"

Frank turns and opens the storage-room door behind him. "You takin' a census?"

Richard is back on the elevator and headed to the twenty-third floor. The noises he heard—the tearing and rasping and thudding—dance in his ear. He tries to make sense of them. His instincts guide him and, in the realm of acoustics, they are powerful. Something falls in your lap, and it can be your one chance for redemption. Or, he concedes, assessing it as the psychiatrists who treated him might, it could be a matter of wish fulfillment—how often has he lain awake, straining through the earplugs to hear a muted alarm, a muffled cry for help, among the disparate noises of the night?

Then, of course, maybe it was nothing more than TV, a fake-out, a delusion. But no, there was something very real about this, he thinks, he feels. He must find out.

He congratulates himself on his rationality.

Now Richard stands in the hallway of the twenty-third floor. Sounds jump out of apartments, keen to his ear: laughter, a toilet flushing, a teakettle whistling. He is at once reckless and fearful as he walks past the door to 2307, stops, and cocks an ear toward the wall. He slows his breathing so it doesn't distort other sounds. Still, there is nothing coming from inside 2307. No telltale sounds of panic or improvisation. No television. Nothing at all. Richard stands there for several minutes, poised to dart away should someone come to the door or someone else leave a nearby apartment.

He walks across the hallway to the elevator, presses the down button and waits. Behind him, an apartment door swings open, and instantly he knows that it's 2307; he can tell by distance and direction. He won't betray himself, stares straight ahead at the closed elevator door. Impeccable timing or did the guy see him through the peephole? It will be a guy, of course.

Davis Braun totes an empty pizza box and a small plastic garbage bag as he walks out of 2307 and makes his way to the trash room tucked into an alcove next to the elevator. His muscular arms extend from the short sleeves of a pale-green medical smock. Sandy blond hair feathers his forehead, and an expression of casual confidence reinforces his relaxed gait.

Richard is rooted to the floor.

"How ya doin'?"

Richard forces his voice into the carpet-hushed corridor. "Good . . . and you?" A monotone.

Braun opens the door to the trash room, holds up the pizza box and smiles. "With this diet, how can I miss?"

Richard glances at the evidence. When Braun goes inside the trash room, the door closes behind him, and in a moment Richard hears the creak of the metal trash flap and the whoosh of air rushing up the chute. Braun emerges, unburdened. Now he seems to be in a hurry.

"I live on that stuff, unfortunately," he says, in motion. "Med school doesn't leave much time for cooking."

What about your girlfriend? Richard thinks. Doesn't she cook? *Didn't* she cook?

The elevator chimes.

"Yeah," is all that Richard says, and he steps onto the elevator. As the door closes, he hears Braun's apartment door slam shut.

So that's him.

Impressive-looking guy. Has a relaxed way about him. Implausible to most people that this fellow is a killer, but he just might be.

Back on the twenty-second floor, Richard hears silverware tapping plates, microwaves beeping, snatches of conversation. This time he has the right apartment, and his key opens the door at once. He sits on his garage-sale couch and reaches for the remote sitting on the scarred coffee table. He hits the Guide button immediately after pressing the TV power button, and the FiOS channel lineup appears on the screen. He repeatedly presses the down arrow to see the listings in the current time slot, looking for a possible culprit, a television show or movie—one that has been playing within the past hour.

That could be the answer; his fears might be allayed. Yes, TV sounds might have been it, all of it.

Or not.

Or they might have masked or complemented the live deed in real time. A random synchronicity? Richard knows that murderers can be much more than impulsive; they can be devious, crafty, symbolic. He knows because he has read about them in newspapers and books, has studied them in movies and documentaries and . . . row-house neighborhoods. He knows because he remembers.

And he simply knows this: what he heard coming from apartment 2307 was all live, all in the flesh.

Or all in his mind.

There it is, right in front of him on the television screen: a listing that thrills him—one that he has either desired or dreaded; he's not sure.

He hurries into the bedroom and taps the keyboard of his aging laptop. The monitor brightens, and he Googles the movie title—only clips and a trailer are available on You-Tube. He views the three-minute clips. They're not what he needs. He finds the website for Netflix, which he's heard a lot about but hasn't joined until now, via the credit card his mother has established for him, opting for streaming though he fears he'll have trouble accessing the movie, computer klutz that he is. (How is it that he deftly manipulates an audiometric testing machine but loses that agility around a computer?) Sure enough, after half a dozen attempts, he can't manage to access the movie he needs. Not because of his incompetence, though—Netflix simply doesn't carry it yet. No *streaming* tonight.

He Googles Locust Video, right here in center city and one of the last stores of its kind in North America—they even carry ancient VHS tapes. He sees that the weekday closing time is 9:00 p.m.

A glance at the digital clock radio tells him it's 9:07.

THREE

Frank Grant has worked at the 42s for five years, his first full-time job after numerous stints at convenience and department stores. He knew he could make his mark here, figured he would easily outshine the other jokers. Sure enough, he's top man at the front desk now. He likes being the hub of the operation, the one who coordinates move-ins and move-outs, fetches the fire department, the police, the electric company, the elevator repairman. He sees himself as the man in the spotlight, doling out FedEx and UPS packages, greeting and dispatching tenants as their lives crisscross with his on the polished lobby floor.

Despite a desperate boyhood, Frank grew up to be an intact human being. Life in the projects was a daily battle for survival. At Wendell Homes on Fairmount Avenue, the pushers were as prevalent as litter and break-ins were a more regular occurrence than breakfast. It was just Frank and his mother in their little patch of hell, and he made it through, thanks to her strength and his—well, his innate optimism. He was a little guy with an animated way of talking and a lot of words to get out. His mother used to tell him he had a "happy streak." He also had, from a young age, the ability to think for himself. He avoided the traps that ensnared most of the youth at Wendell.

Now he's a young man with aspirations. Two nights a week, he takes courses at a community college and thinks that someday maybe he'll go into advertising or public relations. Frank likes people, feels he can relate to all types, and the 42s is a perfect forum. He is ingratiating to the elderly, hip to the younger crowd. He's fast and efficient and sometimes a bit too impressed by his own energy. A well-meaning brother, who grew up far from any public housing project, once suggested that Frank could use a career counselor, an advisor—a mentor, in loftier circles—but Frank downplays the importance of such guidance. He has confidence in himself; he's self-reliant and convinced he'll move up in the world on his own. He fancies himself clever and quick on his feet and doesn't hesitate to spar verbally with people. He thinks he has the right touch for that.

When Davis Braun strides through the lobby at around 11:00 p.m., showered and refreshed for either a late-night round at the hospital or something more promising, Frank greets him with "Hey, Dr. Braun, checked out any corpses lately?"

Braun smiles. "Every day at Metro, Frank."

"That's right; I forgot. Didn't mean to cut so close to the, uh, bone."

Braun shuts one eye in mock response to the groaner.

"Listen, sorry for disturbing you earlier."

"No problem. What was it all about, anyway?"

"One of our nuttier inmates thought he heard somethin'."

"Like what?"

"Nothin' serious. Just thought someone might've been stran-gled at your place," Frank says in full-steam entertainer mode.

Braun wrinkles his nose, squinting. "Strangled?"

"Yeah, tell me about it." Frank sniggers. "This cat was really shook up; he's a strange one. Maybe somethin' you had on TV, you know, around the time that I called, a little bit before?"

"It wasn't one of my neighbors, was it? I didn't hear from any of them, the ones close by."

"No, just some guy passin' in the hallway."

Braun stands there a moment longer, then smiles lightly and leans an arm on the counter, takes Frank into his con-fidence. "I didn't want to go into details when you called, understand, but I was kind of busy at the time." He pushes off the counter with a bemused expression. "That's the culprit. I'm gonna have to tell her to keep it down, know what I mean?"

Frank slaps the counter, laughs out loud. "I heard *that*. I dig that kinda stranglehold . . . Hey, didn't I just see your lady leaving here with a suitcase earlier tonight?"

Not two minutes after he had finally dispatched Richard, Frank saw from the rear a woman hurriedly rolling a suit-case through the open exit doors. He had been in the storage room for a moment and, by the time he'd seen her, she was almost out the door. From her size, shape (fine), and hair (long and blonde), he could all but swear she was the doc's live-in. Down to the clothes she was wearing. When he'd seen her, he'd just shaken his head lightly and smiled to him-self. So much for that nutcase Keene.

"Sounds right," Braun says. "She'll be out of town for a

few days. Hard to believe, but she figures she can exist without me—at least for a little while."

Frank rewards him with a knowing, appreciative laugh.

"So I wanted to give her a nice send-off right before she left. Hope we didn't cut it too close for boarding time."

Frank offers a shorter follow-up laugh, but Braun's already on his way out. Muscular, broad-shouldered, the cut of an athlete. Smooth operator, Frank thinks. That Eleanor chick who lives with him, good-looking woman, no doubt about it. Doctors score nicely with the ladies, that's for sure. But the profession is not Frank's style. Too messy, takes too long to get to where you want to be. And too expensive. Way too expensive. He'll do all right—he's got personality; PR man, that's his profile. He looks around the gleaming lobby, takes in the vaulted ceiling, the buff-colored couches, the synthetic tree waxy and shining in the corner, the corridor leading to the mail room and beyond. This is his territory; he runs the shop. He likes that. But it's just a stepping stone, man. He's goin' somewhere, and he sees himself as a decent human being. Treats people right. One brush with juvie court back in the day, minor stuff, nobody got hurt, ancient history. Lot of those kids from Wendell are in prison now. Or dead. But he's a solid citizen. Frank's proud of himself.

Richard sits cross-legged on his bed, the weak dawn light seeping through the microblinds onto a small pile of paper clips at his feet on the pale-blue velour blanket. He interlocks one clip with another, forming an ever-lengthening chain as if he were working on a kids' craft project at summer camp, and as he does this, the disturbing sounds prick him and he sees the closed door of apartment 2307, that maroon door interrupting the flow of the wall's lime green. The sounds strike at random. Or he can summon them, replaying all of them in order or plucking one out of sequence, like a technician editing a movie sound track. He runs the reel over and over again, his own brand of blood evidence of a crime. Sounds as DNA, as fingerprints.

A crime took place there. In that moment. He believes.

Sure, he stepped off the elevator prematurely, but the mistake was not random. Forces are at play. He was sent there.

He believes.

He is certain of what he heard, and on which side of the door he stood. *Outside*, listening. Not inside, *doing*.

Why do such thoughts persist? Hostages of the past.

He shivers.

He empties a second box of paper clips. The skinny wire snake reaches a menacing length before he puts it aside. He removes a new pair of brown shoelaces from their paper packaging and stretches them on the bed, ties and unties knots, slips, grannies, and half hitches, his fingers fastidious. He puts the laces aside. He inserts his earplugs and lies back, loses sense of time, replays the moment, the sounds, over and over. He falls asleep at some point, a thin half sleep somewhere between dreams and sentience. When the mature morning's screeches and rumbles penetrate the plugs and his eyelids spring open to the slatted sunlight, he knows he can't have dozed for more than an hour or so. The paper clips and shoelaces are strewn between folds of the blanket. Richard pushes back the covers and rolls out of his foxhole.

He sits at his desk, affixes a stamp to a plain white business envelope, and prints a name and address on it: Sheila Braun, The 42s, 1526 Locust Street, Philadelphia, Pennsylvania 19102. He copies the PO cancellation on a received piece of mail, using a razor-point pen to ink squiggly black lines and smaller markings. The postwoman comes every day at three. Nice lady.

Riding the subway, iPod earbuds in place, Richard squeezes the metal pole as he stands in a crowd and the train rockets through the tube. Stale air flies in to assault him when the train stops and the doors belch open. He gets off and makes his way across the platform and through a revolving door of interlaced iron bars, then up the stairs to Olney Avenue and the Preston Tower, and then finally up the elevator to the fifth floor for another big day—this one to be shortened a bit—at Rosen & Wallingford.

In the cork-walled testing booth, subjects raise their hands, but today Richard isn't always sure they're coinciding with the audiometer's squeals, because those other sounds, those unnerving sounds, those thudding and tearing and rasping sounds, have taken over inside his head.

At 10:03 a.m., he calls Locust Video. They do have the movie in stock and agree to put aside a DVD for him.

He had Kathy rearrange his schedule so that his last appointment for the day ends at 2:00 p.m. He tells the office manager he's leaving early and, when he walks past the front desk, offers Kathy a routine "Good night. Thanks for your help."

With no warning, no groundwork, she pipes up with "Got a hot date?"

This stops Richard cold and he puzzles over her face, searching for clues. Ah, just a young girl firing off an unthinking line, trying to be cute. Keeping tabs at the receptionist's desk, nothing more.

"No," he says, "just a dentist appointment—you know the drill." He can see that his wit is lost on her; she's already looking away and thinking about some other weighty matter. But Richard is pleased with his cleverness and aware that, for a moment, his mind has been distracted from the parade of grim sounds that have taken hold of him.

Her soiled sack plopped on the floor behind her, the postwoman inserts pieces of mail into the yawning grid of slots, the shiny facade unhinged like an opened trapdoor. The phony Sheila Braun letter in his hand, Richard watches the postwoman go efficiently about her business. She is all nimble fingers and certain movement.

"Excuse me," he says.

She doesn't miss a beat, keeps plucking envelopes and slanting them into their destinations—not rude, just inexorable. "Yes?"

Richard looks down at his letter and silently reads the name and address, convincing just in case she notices out of the corner of her eye. "I received a letter by mistake," he says. "It's for a Sheila Braun. B, R, A, U, N. No apartment number."

He likes the name Sheila, has a second cousin somewhere with that name, remembers they had fun at some family get-together when they were little kids but hasn't seen her since. Somewhere in northern New Jersey it was, a holiday barbecue with mustard-flavored potato salad, heaps of slightly sour coleslaw, and flame-grilled burgers and hot dogs on charred buns and rolls.

The postwoman finishes distributing her handheld pile and turns his way. In her summer uniform of light gray, short-sleeved shirt, and darker gray shorts, she is built like a football middle guard, maybe a Yale Bulldog from the 1930s—Richard knows of high school classmates who went to Yale and wonders now how far life has taken them—but her eyes are less fierce than her physique. Richard holds the letter out for her, but she ignores it and produces a personal digital assistant, which she brings to life with her fingertips.

"Lemme see . . . I got a Davis Braun. What's your apartment number?"

"Twenty-two oh seven."

She touches the PDA. "You Richard Keene?"

"Yes."

"All right, we're lookin' good there. I got Davis Braun in 2307, along with Eleanor Carson."

"Eleanor Carson?" Richard repeats to firm the name in his mind.

"That's right."

"And no Sheila Braun."

"Nope. You get it yesterday?"

"Yes, that's right."

"That explains it; I wasn't on yesterday." She smiles and points at the letter. "I can take that for you. We'll give him a try. Probably his sister or somebody visiting."

"That's okay," Richard says. "I know Davis. I didn't realize he was right above me. I'll just give it to him."

"All right, thanks. I already done that section."

"You bet," says Richard as he walks away. He leaves

the mail room and exits the building by the rear door. On the delivery dock, he leans against the brick wall next to the door to the Dumpster room, unclips a pen from his shirt pocket, writes the name *Eleanor Carson* on the Sheila Braun letter, then hustles down the Latimer Street alley past a parking garage to the next block, where Locust Video should have a certain DVD waiting for him.

The clerk at the counter has a hacksaw haircut and a small, silver earring on one nostril. The other clerk is checking inventory on the stacks behind the counter, singing as he sorts. Too loud for the venue but a decent voice. Musical theater, priming himself for discovery, Richard figures.

"Richard Keene. I called in earlier . . . *Grip of Death*."

"And who might you be, Jack the Ripper?" Nose Ring says with a cockney accent that's not quite the real thing; another actor type, apparently. "Hey, Hugh Jackman, this bloke 'ere sez ee's Jack the Ripper."

The vocalist stills his pipes long enough to shout, "Better call 911."

Richard plays along reluctantly. "I'm not quite that dangerous." Now he tries to apply a touch of charm, something that does not come easily to him. "By the way, your accent's pretty good."

Nose Ring looks offended. "Accent? That's jus' the way I talk, guv'nuh." He breaks into a wide smile of yellow teeth, reaches below, and produces the requested DVD, which he places on the counter. Catch-22: actors need bright-white teeth but must land paying jobs to afford the dentist's bleaching. "Not bad, huh?" he now says in some northeastern extract, not quite Philadelphian.

"Not bad at all," Richard says, grabbing the disc.

Moments later in his apartment, Richard loads the DVD, then sits on his couch and rocks nervously as the player clicks and whirs, a prelude to images appearing on screen. But when the whirring ceases, the screen simply reports *No disc*. Yet there *is* a disc, damn it; Richard removes it and reloads it. Same result. He reaches into the candy tray on the coffee table and, almost spastically, fires a green sourball across the room. It pings the opposite wall and pinballs to the musty, upright piano he never plays and into the kitchen, where it comes to rest in the open strip between the built-in cupboard and the refrigerator, a space far too narrow for human hand or cleaning implement; graveyard of crumbs, bugs, and stray sourballs.

He's on the phone with the Hugh Jackman wannabe at Locust Video.

"We have another copy due back today. Sorry about that, dude. Want me to reserve that one?"

"Will it work?"

"I hope so."

Richard tells him to put it on hold. Maybe the next disc will cooperate. Otherwise, investigation delayed.

Because that's what he intends to mount: a full-scale investigation. No ignoring, no turning away this time. He is thrilled by his conviction that destiny has handed him a chance for redemption. The doctors and the time away helped restore some of his bearings but failed to convince him that he has been flaying himself all these years for no good cause. An eight-year-old is in no position to take charge in such matters, he was told again and again. What can an eight-year-old do, except tell his parents? Which he most certainly did.

But not the police. He didn't tell them. What he heard. What he heard happen. All those years ago. They asked, but he didn't tell.

His guilt is thick as grime.

He tries to run it off on the treadmill. Today, like every day. The row is empty. Sudden rain slashes the tall windows of the fitness center, distorting the city's lights speckling the premature gathering darkness. Richard's knee throbs, but he pushes himself harder, trying to run through that, too; physical pain, psychic scars, maybe you can outrun both.

He notices another runner stepping up, two treadmills down: the woman with the Olympic stride and the red hair that falls onto her shoulders when it's not tied up, which it is right now. Hardly unexpected, as she's a regular. She fits snugly into a pair of Nike athletic shorts, her skin smooth and just a shade lighter than summer tan. The tendons above her knees are like connective cables as she begins to stride. Richard looks at her and forgets all about the throbbing in his own knee.

But she does not seem aware of his presence as her arms pump and her Reeboks pound the rubber tread that races below her. Though Richard says nothing to her and doesn't even attempt to make eye contact, he is drawn to her as if by magnetism. The hypnotic rain slithers down the tall, rectangular windows, and a rising mist envelops the gray-swathed buildings beyond.

In his apartment after the workout, Richard logs on to Netflix, hoping for a miracle: that his movie will materialize and be ready for streaming. He e-mails, live chats, and still comes up empty. He feels helpless. He swears lustily and feels no better.

Absent the stimuli of adrenaline and endorphins and Janet Kroll, he finds that his knee is sore as hell, and he massages it as he sits on his bed, running shoes and socks tossed onto the carpet. He has a rendezvous with an MRI scanner tomorrow, and though Dr. Natrol has promised him one of the newer, wider cylinders, his anxiety about the test vies with his preoccupation with what transpired behind the closed door of apartment 2307. It all builds overnight, so that when he reports to work in the morning, his stomach feels too small for even the small breakfast he ate.

At Rosen & Wallingford, he gives Kathy a tight-lipped "Morning." As he walks past the photocopy room, some-one takes a ream of paper off the shelf and thumps it onto the table, giving Richard a little start, the sound not unlike the one he heard at the threshold of apartment 2307 thirty-six hours earlier. Thumps, thuds, gasps, and cries are very much on his mind—*in* his mind—and he reminds himself that the moment he heard the thump at 2307, he didn't *feel* it. There was no shudder in his shoe tops. Still, he reminds himself that the 42s is a well-constructed building and that the muted sounds may not have come from the room on the other side of the door but from a room deeper inside the apartment. And the victim may not have been in free fall but might have been half caught by her murderer as she landed, only part of her anatomy grounded, a small woman perhaps, not one to shake the walls. A thump heard but not felt.

Richard presses two fingers hard against his forehead

right above the bridge of his nose to try to quell a headache. A hand at his shoulder startles him. He heard no one approaching, so complete was his absorption in his auditory recollection. He smiles at the irony of not hearing a person right next to him.

"You all right?" she asks.

It is Wendy, the office manager, short blonde hair, square frame, creases at the corners of her eyes, her frequent smiles lacking warmth. She's checking up; that's all. Part of the job description. Richard takes a breath and settles himself down.

"I'm fine."

"You don't look it."

"Just a little headache. I'll be all right. I'd better get to work."

As he moves away, she shakes her head. He wonders what that means. Does she think him strange to work a bunch of little dials all day long?

On his lunch hour, Richard leaves Preston Medical Tower and walks a block to Logan General, where the radiology department's two MRI scanners have cylinders that are the standard twenty-four inches in diameter. Richard dons a hospital gown.

"Is this it?" he asks the technician, a shambling oaf with corned-beef breath.

"This is it."

"I thought I was getting the big machine."

"This ain't Disney World, babe," says the technician through horsy teeth with a guffaw to match. "This is all we got. Tell you what, though, I got something for you." He hands Richard a pair of foam earplugs. "Just wad 'em up in your ears and you won't hear a thing."

Where did they get this guy? "What would I hear otherwise?"

"Oh, machine makes kind of a knocking noise. Bothers some people."

"That's not what I'm worried about."

"I know. You're worried about the confinement, am I right?" The guy must be president of Mensa. "If it's too uncomfortable for you, you'll just have to get your doc to prescribe a sedative and we'll schedule again."

"No," Richard says. "I'm gonna get through this. Let's go."

So a double whammy awaits him: rattling noises engulfed by claustrophobia. He plugs his ears and forces himself to enter the narrow MRI bed, lying on his back as if in a coffin. He looks into the tubular nightmare. The mere anticipation of it is overpowering. His eyes dart as sweat rushes to his forehead. He tries to close his eyes but can't keep them shut.

This isn't the subway or an elevator. This is a different animal. This won't work.

He quivers, fights for breath. He doesn't trust anyone to help get him through this, least of all the goofy technician, who peers down at him like a tourist at an aquarium, asking, "What's the problem?"

Richard jerks his torso upward. His face is plum red, and he is gulping air. He has to get himself out of here. "I can't do this."

"What?"

Richard raises his voice. "I can't go through with this."

"You know, these appointments aren't so easy to come by—we got a full boat, even for rescheduling. Hey, what happened to that courage I heard a moment ago? Why don't ya at least give it a try?"

Richard rolls out of the contraption to safety. "I'm sorry," he says, slumped and damp.

The technician is both bemused and irritated. "You wanna use the bathroom or something?"

Richard slinks across the tiled floor and out the MRI chamber. He'll have to live with a sore knee a while longer.

FOUR

Moving smartly about his compact kitchen, Richard doesn't feel much complaint coming from his knee; he's sure he can live with the occasional ache. He's lived with a lot more pain than that.

He tosses a forest of a salad into a large wooden bowl. Strips of tofu and vegetable stir-fry sizzle in a broad pan above the range's electric coils. He is hardly accomplished in the culinary arts, but every so often he rises to the occasion.

The doorbell rings and he's surprised, miffed. Who the hell is working the front desk?

His mother's face fills the glass peephole with a funhouse-mirror bulge. When Richard opens the door, she pauses at the threshold and smiles like a TV hostess.

"You have company," she says, a lilt to her husky voice. Hairsprayed and pearl-necklaced, Evelyn Keene is dressed for a night out, and when she enters, a perfumed scent trails her, as does her husband, Marty. Richard's father is short and unprepossessing, wearing a shirt and tie and clutching a gift-wrapped box. Always a step or two behind her.

"How'd you get up here?" Richard asks his mother.

"We flew." She flings her arms upward. "You do have elevators in this building."

"The guy at the desk is supposed to call me," says Richard.

"Well, I guess we looked respectable enough to let through. Actually, we didn't see anyone in charge down there when we came in . . . You aren't hiding someone in the closet by any chance, are you?"

When Evelyn purses her lips for a kiss, Richard plants a light one on her cheek, then turns to his father.

"Dad."

"Richie."

Marty holds out the box, which is large enough that it requires two hands.

"For the birthday boy and his new fancy apartment," says Evelyn, who strides across the living room to the sliding glass doors that look out onto a small enclosure and the city beyond. "Some view from up here. Very striking. Very romantic."

"Potentially," Richard says, propping the gift box against the wall, in no hurry to open it.

Evelyn follows her son into the kitchen. "I know what that means. Nothing exciting happening, right?"

Richard has pots and dishes to juggle. He wants to put this meal behind him.

"Have you been getting out?" his mother asks.

He doesn't get out much, has never gotten out much. Of course she knows that.

Evelyn doesn't wait for an answer. "People don't just

show up on your doorstep."

"I'm aware of that, Mother." He wields his spatula, and the stir-fry spits as it tumbles onto plates. "I've only been here a month."

"There must be lots of nurses and secretaries at the medical center," she says.

"Some of them are even doctors," he says with irony, setting one plate on the table.

"Doctors want other doctors."

Her remark is innocent—not snide—but Richard feels his stomach jump, followed by the customary heat rising into his throat and, if he's lucky, out the top of his head. He could snort steam like some cartoon bull, but he shows no sign of distress. He keeps the boil contained; all he offers is a caustic "Thanks" as he places the other two filled plates on the table.

"Well, it's true. Isn't that right, Marty?"

Marty takes his turn gazing out the glass doors.

Evelyn moves closer to Richard, who dishes out the salad. "I want your father to get his hearing checked."

"Fine."

"I'm calling Ben to set up an appointment for you with Richard," she says to Marty, who finally turns toward her.

"Ben?"

"Dr. Detrick."

"What about him?"

"He should make the referral."

"My physical's not 'til January."

"Just to get your hearing checked."

"My hearing's fine."

Evelyn rolls her eyes.

"Dinner is served," Richard says.

"Are you in a hurry to get rid of us?" she asks. "No hors d'oeuvres?"

"Didn't want to spoil your appetite."

Richard pulls out a chair for his mother and nudges it with both hands toward the table after she has filled it.

"What a gentleman," she says. "So tell me, what's this you said the other night on the telephone that you don't like it down here?"

"I didn't say I didn't like it," Richard says, sitting down right after his father. "It's just a little, uh, crowded; that's all."

"Well, of course, dear, you're in the middle of the city," she says. "That's the whole idea."

"I know that. That's the trade-off."

"I'll tell you this: If I lived here, I'd be bankrupt. Every night I'd be at the theater. Or somewhere."

"There's all this construction around," Richard continues, though his audience is no longer listening. "And they deliver things at all hours—"

"Marty," Evelyn interrupts. "Speaking of center city, you know we have the Academy Saturday night."

For Marty, the Academy is just another in a series of stops he must make with his wife; he accepts it like cough medicine. He cuts a segment of tofu, wondering what it is, and doesn't even look up at Evelyn, who turns back to Richard and realizes she has been rude, though she can't help it and doesn't really want to. "I'm sorry, dear. You were saying?"

Richard smiles thinly. "Not much."

He picks at his food, soon stops eating altogether. As Evelyn chatters on, something about her publicity work for some suburban, chamber music quartet, Richard braces himself. He wants this to sound casual, wants to keep his anxiety in check, but as he prepares to say it, he realizes he can't control such things. His heart trip hammers away, and he squirts out his words. "Do you ever see Herb Dempsey?"

Evelyn's fork slips out of her fingers, and she looks at Richard with semipanicked eyes and none of the broader affectation that normally shapes her features. As the emotion heightens, her face contracts further. "God, Richard. Where would I see *him*?"

"I don't know. Anywhere."

Now Evelyn seems annoyed, and blood returns to her cheeks. "Well, we're not exactly bridge partners. Why do you ask that all of a sudden?"

Richard pokes the tofu with his fork. "I was just thinking about him; that's all."

"What on earth *for*?" She looks at Marty for support, but he is concentrating on his food and either hasn't heard a word or is pretending he hasn't.

Evelyn firms up. "We're not going through this again." A bid for finality, but the conviction isn't quite there.

Richard looks at her and pauses, forcing her gaze to meet his. "*I* am," he says.

He explains himself. What he overheard. What he believes happened. In apartment 2307. He realizes this is a familiar refrain wrapped up in a brand-new trauma, more than twenty years later.

Marty listens without reaction. Richard wonders about his father's comprehension. Evelyn clucks, shakes her head, and tells her son that other people's lives are not his responsibility. A predictable response.

"You'll get into trouble, you keep on doing this sort of thing," she warns. "You mark my words: this can lead to no good."

A light, quick smile from Richard. "Only if something really happened, though, right?"

"Only if something really happened? What does that mean?"

"Only if something's happened will I get into trouble. The killer will come after me. That's what you mean, right?"

"Richard, you're impossible with this; you really are. You create these things in your mind and drive yourself crazy with them. And me, too, I might add. I don't know what I can say to you."

"What are you talking about?" Marty asks his wife, and her look of exasperation sends him directly back to his knife and fork.

"Anyway," Evelyn says, "what's this got to do with Herbert Dempsey?"

Richard looks at her, through her. "Everything."

"He doesn't live here, does he?" She's being sarcastic.

Richard just keeps looking at her.

"Very tasty, Son," Marty says, and Richard's not sure which part of the meal he's referring to.

"I guarantee you nothing happened here," Evelyn says to her son. "Do you think terrible murders like what you're describing just follow you around wherever you go? You're in a big apartment building with hundreds of people. You're going to hear all kinds of things. Your imagination gets carried away. You know how apprehensive you can get . . . This is all part of the healing process, isn't that what they said?"

Richard has nothing

moment, and they mov

about center-city food n

"Open your presen

dessert and coffee in th

who could wait to ope

"Let me give yo

Richard calls in. He knows ...

with a scoop of vanilla ice cream. Evelyn gets ...

scoop. Black coffee, no sugar, for both.

He brings in the goodies, sets them on the table, and attends to his present, tearing off the wrapping paper and crumpling it beyond salvaging so that his mother is not tempted to reuse it.

"Read the card first," Evelyn says.

Richard plucks a large greeting card out of a red envelope. There's a sketch of a dilapidated house on the front of the card; on the inside are the printed words *The fixin's are great here*, and below them in Evelyn's script, *Hope your new life is a whirlwind*. Evelyn's eyes are alive with expectation. Richard dreads the rest of the scenario. He knows whatever is inside the box will not thrill him, and he will be incapable of pretending that it does. He opens the box, and the first thing he sees are assembly instructions. Slats of wood and metal hinges lurk underneath.

"It's a lazy Susan," Evelyn says. "Get it—a whirl?" She twirls her wrist, hand, and forefinger. "These things are fantastic. Can you put it underneath the counter somewhere?"

"I don't think so."

"Sure, you can. Well, if not, then it can just sit on top."

ichard says. "It's a nice gift." He kisses her

his father. "Thanks, Dad."

shakes her head. "Don't get so excited."

ave the boy alone, Evelyn." Marty moves to the

. "What do you expect him to do, jump up and down?

e appreciates it."

After the coffee cups have been drained, they've exhausted their conversation topics other than the one Richard wants to explore but chooses not to bring up again. Before long, they're all in the elevator, then stepping across the polished lobby tile, then outside engulfed by the mild damp September night and the swarm of the city. Richard walks his parents to the 42s' adjacent parking garage on Locust.

"What level are we on, Marty?" Evelyn asks.

"Three, I think."

She looks at Richard. "He *thinks*. Last time in Atlantic City, we got lost at Harrah's."

"Only for a little while," Marty says. "That lot is very confusing."

"They all are when you don't pay attention," Evelyn says and kisses her son's cheek. "Have some fun, honey bun."

Richard says his good nights, sees them to the garage elevator. "Want me to go up with you?"

"No, we're fine from here, Son," Marty says.

They disappear as the blackened metal door slides closed. Richard is especially leery of garage elevators. They're rickety and unreliable, and there's a good chance of spending the night in them if there's a breakdown. He uses the stairs to get to his car. When it's working, that is.

Now that the evening's mission has been completed and

they're gone, he feels more regret than relief. Regret that he wasn't nicer, over things he should have said or not said.

They still won't talk about what happened that night in the old neighborhood, much less about what's happening now. They don't want to hear it. *She* doesn't.

He walks to the video store on the next block. Jackman and Nose Ring are gone; the girl at the counter has red-purple hair and skin pallor that suggests she's spent all of her twenty years in an attic. She also has Richard's replacement DVD.

After returning to the 42s, Richard reads the label warning against commercial use on the DVD's plastic casing as he waits for the elevator. He is aware of a woman approaching and stopping near him, an elegant scent that takes hold of him, the woman shapely in her tailored business suit.

Janet Kroll, the treadmill queen. It is just the two of them. The elevator arrives and Richard gestures for her to get on first. The gentlemanly thing to do.

Janet presses the button for fifteen. Richard reaches over and presses twenty-two. As the elevator moves upward, Richard rechecks his selection on the side panel. He looks at Janet with a self-effacing grin.

"Got to make sure. The other day, I got off on the wrong floor coming down from the gym."

Good job, he thinks. Making civilized, relaxed conversation. Still, all he gets for his efforts is a small smile. But that's better than a wrinkled brow and a flash of irritation. A girl with her looks gets plenty of uninvited attention, so her defenses must be well fortified.

"Guess I was half asleep trying to keep up with you," he

says. "Coming down from the gym, I mean."

Janet looks at him more closely. "Right . . . you're the runner."

"No, *you're* the runner."

This triggers a more genuine smile, which vanishes when the elevator reaches her floor, chimes, stops, and opens.

"Have a nice evening," Richard says to Janet's retreating form.

"You, too," she says over her shoulder.

All right, not too bad, Richard figures. He watches her walk away as the closing elevator door narrows the frame. Plenty of time to see her at the fitness center. Time to grow on her (like mold—his mother's joke). A hint of discernment in her eyes suggested she prefers lean, cardiovascular types to muscle heads. Well, it's worth thinking about it that way. At least for now.

On to other matters. In his apartment, Richard has the nervous anticipation of a student about to receive the results of a crucial exam. The answers he seeks are in this movie, he's certain, and this copy had better damn well work—tonight's chalk-skinned clerk told him they tested it on a player right at the store. Richard turns on his television and DVD player and inserts the disc. This time, as promised, the images are intact. He sits on the edge of the couch, palms on his knees, rocking gently.

He has not seen the movie, though he knows the title and subject matter—not exactly Disney. He concentrates. He needs to assimilate every sound and movement. Soon enough, he sees a man tear off a strip of bedsheet; a tied-up woman shivers, a soft cry escaping her; he says, "Keep quiet," with no urgency or malice in his voice. They are alone in a bedroom. He forces the thin, cotton strip between her teeth and ties it around the back of her head but not before she tries to scream and manages only a throaty sob.

He looks at her as if disappointed. "I told you to keep quiet. I'm not going to rape you."

Now he uses rope to tie one foot to the leg of the chair to which her torso is bound already. She resists, but only for an instant, and is compliant when he lashes the other foot. But her gasps and whimpers struggle to push through the gag, and when the man pulls up a chair next to her, she erupts in terror, summoning unknown strength from desperation to free one foot and kick her captor. He immediately reties the loose foot, doubling down on the knot, rises and fires a short, sharp punch that connects dead-on with her cheekbone, knocking her out. He flexes the hand, forcing himself not to wince.

He stares at his prey.

The scene is over.

One after another, the sounds have jarred Richard like smacks to the face. Tearing, shuffling, scraping. The woman gasps, whimpers, rasps. Her strangulated scream. *Grip of Death*, a B-movie televised two nights earlier, this very scene, Richard guesses, coinciding with his chance visit to apartment 2307.

This very scene, he believes, and something more.

Richard presses the remote's back button to repeat the scene. He cringes before the blue-white glow of the screen.

He plays it again in its entirety, from the first ripping sounds to the brutal punch and corresponding faint, cracking sound.

He plays it again. And again. Until he turns off the DVD player and the television. He stands there and might as well be quaking. Tearing, shuffling, gasping, whimpering, rasping, cracking.

No thud and accompanying squeak. No thump.

He heard them at the door, but they aren't in the movie scene. They are stored in his auditory memory. Palpable distinctions among sounds.

He takes a book—a thick, hardback biography of Abraham Lincoln he's had since he was five years old—from the shelf above the television, holds it at eye level with both hands, parallel to the floor, and lets it drop so that it lands flush. When it thumps to the carpeted floor, he shivers. It's a different, fuller sound than any movie-doctored punch. He heard something like it that night, that moment at the closed door of 2307. A thump of finality, scripted by real life, a falling book, a sack of potatoes, of laundry, of a body.

And he heard it *after* all the movie sounds.

Richard looks down at the book. He stands motionless for nearly a minute, sorting out the sounds in his head. "What makes you think the thump was a body?" he can hear people asking him. It could have been lots of things.

Sure, it could have. But the exertion and breathing he heard were human sounds. Prosaic sounds turned evil, he is convinced. And the faint snapping, the squeaking floor, the thud, the thump. They all add up.

Yes, a scene from a movie and something more. A coincident murder. Live. Fortuitous or expertly timed. If timed, symbolic or merely strategic. Or both.

His mind races.

Less than an hour later, he is on the telephone with his

mother, stirring up the devil-ghost. Of course, it can't be the same killer. A span of more than twenty years; it's got to be two different perpetrators.

"You never forget your next-door neighbor," he says.

"Don't start," Evelyn says.

"I never stopped."

"Richard, why do you have to ruin things? Why do you keep torturing yourself?"

"Myself?"

"What's that supposed to mean? Oh, is that it—you're torturing *me*? Well, congratulations, that's a fine thing to do. I suppose you are. You're exhausting me; that's for sure. Tell me, what were we supposed to do—make a citizen's arrest? Don't you understand? For the last time, for God's sake, nothing was ever proved, and your father and I were still worried he could be a dangerous man . . . We wanted to keep you out of it."

"What were you protecting me from?"

"That's obvious, isn't it?"

"Not to me."

"Well, a little boy is easily confused and intimidated. The police could have—"

"From myself. Protecting me from myself. That's what you were doing, isn't it?"

"In a way."

"You thought it was possible, didn't you?"

"Thought what was possible?"

"That I was the one. That I made up that story of hearing things. That I was the one who snuck next door in the middle of the night and—"

"Don't be ridiculous."

"Not that you thought I was something vicious and horrible as a rule but that I was nonetheless capable of it because I was essentially . . . out of my mind."

"Stop it, Richard!"

"That was it, wasn't it? Not to protect me from Herb Dempsey but from myself. Pick your crazy out of two possibles, and choose the little boy."

Evelyn sobs quietly. "How can you say something as awful as that? How can you say it? To me, no less. How could I possibly think that an eight-year-old boy . . . ? Have you been taking your medication?"

"I'm no longer on medication, Mother. The doctors suspended it, remember?"

"Are you sure about that?"

"Of course I'm sure."

"Richard, it's pointless to keep bringing this up. Isn't that what they told you? You'll put yourself back in the hospital. You really will."

"You know, when you think about it—"

"Just don't think about it."

"—I guess I should thank you, whatever your rationale was. Because it could've been me, too. I could've been next. After Cindy. I believe that. He did warn me, in a way."

"Enough, Richard. We did what we thought was the right thing. What else do you want from me?"

"I want you to tell me what you think right now. About me. About that night."

"What do you mean?"

"Who do you think was the one?"

"The police could never solve it. There wasn't—"

"Forget the police. I want to know what *you* think."

The two seconds of silence seem much longer than that.

"Richard . . . how could I think that my own son . . . ?"

Her hesitation betrays her. He cuts her off. "Thank you." Oblique and with a touch of finality, the two words are almost a whisper as his hand seems to move on its own, gently placing the receiver back into the pockets of the cradle. Through the creases in the microblinds, he sees office-building lights dotting the blackness. Later he will sleep a jagged sleep. Sounds will fill his unconsciousness and unnerve him, prodding him awake, pushing sweat from his pores, clenching his breath.

FIVE

The thick wooden chair is heavier and stiffer than his seat at school. His legs dangle, shoes swaying six inches above the tiled floor worn colorless and pocked by metal desk legs. He has seen police stations on television, but they seem more exciting than this. He has imagined himself as one of the characters in those shows, working at the station, on the move, at his desk, answering the phone, drinking coffee, though he knows he's too young to drink coffee.

But this room in this police station is dreary and chilly, and the man sitting in front of him seems to surround him, seems to blot out much of the rest of the room, reducing the wall behind to a strip on either side.

Cindy was your best friend, wasn't she?

I guess so, Richard says.

You liked her a lot.

Yes.

You were close to her.

I live next door.

You've been in her house, right?

Yes.

How often?

I don't know.

A lot?

No, not that much, mostly she comes over to my house or we play outside or we go somewhere.

Like where?

The movies, the schoolyard, miniature golf.

Really? Your parents let you go off alone like that?

Only when it's in the neighborhood.

You were at her house more than once, right?

Yes.

How many times? Five, ten, twenty?

Five, maybe.

Were you ever in her bedroom?

Yes, once or twice, I think.

Were you ever in her bedroom at nighttime?

No, I don't think so.

You don't think so?

No, I wasn't.

Did you ever go over there at night? To her house?

Just to meet her to go out for Halloween.

The man leans forward, heavy arms inside the creases of powder-blue long sleeves, beard stubble like three or four ants at the neckline just above the fat knot of his tie. Richard tries to look past him, tries to find some breathing room, but the strips of wall have closed in and are right at the man's shoulders. Richard hates to be a big enough sissy to turn to look back at his mother, but he can't help it and jerks his head around so he can see her standing off to one side. Her eyes and her sudden short breath and the little movement of her nose remind him of what she wants him to *do, to say, to not say. Then he turns back to the policeman, who looks irritated and different—harder—than when he stood in their living room and asked them if they had seen anything or heard anything, and Richard flinched and almost started to speak that time, but his mother had stopped him with her eyes, as she did now.*

Would you mind stepping out of the room and leaving us alone for a few minutes, Mrs. Keene?

Well, I thought . . . I mean, I suppose—

It'll only be for a few minutes. It'll be fine.

He escorts her out of the room, returns in seconds, and resumes his seat in front of Richard. After its momentary expansion in his absence, the room shrinks back to a phone booth.

Do you know Mr. Dempsey?

Yes.

Do you like him?

Richard's eyes lose focus, and a shiver jumps from his spine to his neck.

You're not too crazy about him, the policeman says.

He's okay. I don't see him that much.

Uh-huh.

I like Mrs. Dempsey.

Yes, she's a nice lady . . . Have you ever used the key the Dempseys leave at your house to get into their house?

Richard is ready for this one; he's been waiting for the policeman to bring up the key, been told to expect it. No, Richard says, I've never used it at all. It's only for emergencies, like if they lost their own keys or something.

I see.

The policeman shifts in his seat, large square hands smoothing his pant legs.

And you were never there at nighttime. Is that right?

SIX

The body. How was it disposed of?

Not so easy from the twenty-third floor.

In sections?

He can't go to the police. At least not yet. They'd laugh at him; he knew that from the start. You heard what? Sure, pal.

Frank. It's Friday morning, and Frank might be in an expansive mood. Maybe some more information can be coaxed out of him.

Richard calls in sick. He has sick days coming, hasn't taken a single one or any vacation days in the year and a half he's been at Rosen & Wallingford. He stays healthy, at least by conventional measures. His announcement surprises Kathy. She'll have to reschedule appointments again. The doctors themselves may have to conduct the hearing tests for the ones that can't wait. They won't be happy about that.

At the 42s' front desk, Frank organizes several UPS packages of varying size as tenants drift past.

"Morning," says Richard.

Frank looks up and forces a smile. Since Richard ordinarily is not one to say hello, Frank is suspicious.

"Seen any Boston Stranglers lately?"

A little snake wraps around Richard's stomach and the small of his back. He tries to loosen its grip, parts his lips to say something, but all that comes out is air.

Frank cocks his head. "Say what?"

Richard swallows. "Nothing." Bad idea, trying to enlist Frank's help. He tries to walk away, but his body won't move. "Have you seen Eleanor Carson the past couple of days?" he asks, the words remote and fluttering upward toward the high ceiling. Now he steadies his voice. "Eleanor Carson, 2307."

Frank looks up from his UPS pile. "Now listen to me, my man. We been through this. I don't want you botherin' those people."

"Have you seen her?"

"Can't you just be cool, man?"

"My guess is you haven't, right?"

"I don't know. Is that your guess?"

Richard is hardly the bold type, but there is something persistent and sincere in his expression that won't quit. Frank sees it, can't help but see it.

"You're too much, man."

"Where does she work?"

"You know, you need to increase your medication or somethin'."

"I don't take any medication."

"I'm just sayin' . . ."

But now Richard senses a grudging willingness in Frank, a curiosity despite himself.

"Just tell me where she works. If she's there, that's it. You won't hear another word from me."

Frank thinks about it—it's not a bad deal at that. Damn if he doesn't feel a touch of respect for this guy's determination. Can't hurt to check, just doing his job, no invasion of privacy. He glares at Richard but sits at the computer terminal and pulls up the file on Eleanor Carson, who, the screen indicates, shares apartment 2307 with Davis Braun. Her employment information is right there. Frank smiles to himself, marveling at his efficiency and that of the modern world.

"All right, my man. One time—then you're off my back. That's the deal, right?"

"That's right."

Frank reaches for the telephone, presses the ten digits.

"This is gonna be a waste of time, my man. I saw the girl the night you came to me with that crazy story of yours. Saw her *after* we talked."

"You *saw* her?" Richard does an odd little pivot, as if a dog were nipping at his pant leg. The awful sounds, speeded up in sequence, careen through his head.

"Eleanor Carson, please," Frank says into the phone. "This is the front desk at the 42s on Locust Street, her apartment building." While he waits, he says to Richard, "Saw her walk out of here with a suitcase. She didn't look like she'd been strangled."

Richard flinches, then looks down at the tile and scans the scuff marks. The murderous noises have stopped reverberating within his skull. For the moment.

"Yes, Eleanor Carson, please . . . Oh, is that right?" A big, friendly smile forms on Frank's face. "When did she

73

leave? . . . Uh-huh. When will she be back? . . . I see. She didn't leave word here at the front desk. Well, thank you very much . . . No, that's okay, nothing urgent. Bye now."

Frank hangs up. "She's on vacation, my man. Coulda guessed that. Satisfied?"

Richard is not. "Since when?"

"Wednesday."

"That's convenient."

"Look, man, I saw her walk out this door Tuesday night with a suitcase. Her employer says her vacation started Wednesday. Go there yourself if you don't believe me. Perris and Blumenthal, Twenty-first Street."

"When's she due back?"

"Monday, they said."

Richard believes Frank, but he is certain that the employer's information does not tell the story. More than anything, he trusts the sounds in his head, returning now, swirling and stabbing.

"Perris and Blumenthal?"

"That's what I said."

"What's that, a law firm?"

"That's right. She's a paralegal. Now hit the road; go bother *them*."

In his apartment, Richard calls the firm of Perris and Blumenthal. Eleanor Carson is on vacation, he is told. Her schedule indicates that she'll be back on Monday. The secretary is polite. "I'll reach her then," Richard says. "No hurry."

But there *is* a hurry. Trails grow cold.

After lunch, Richard finds himself walking past a cavernous excavation dwarfed by a towering crane on Fifteenth

Street. At Spruce Street, the music center rises, all planes and angles with an arching, hangar-like roofline, the home of the acclaimed Philadelphia Orchestra, whose lush strings warmed the elegant but antiquated Academy of Music just around the corner the previous century. Richard loves the magisterial sound of classical symphonies, but rather than attend performances, he prefers to listen to recordings, whose volume he can adjust, just as he now tweaks the volume in his earbuds. A Rachmaninoff concerto. Big, stirring, gorgeous melody.

He reverses course and heads north on Fifteenth Street. He wanders several blocks to City Hall, the ornate throwback with its soaring tower topped by the lofty statue of William Penn. Tunneled paths send walkers into the courtyard, the precise geographic center of Penn's original city. Richard enters the building through the Market Street East portal, goes into the gift shop, and buys a six-dollar ticket for admission to the observation deck. He needs time and space to think, and this is an exercise that affords both.

He has taken this elevator ride at City Hall several times, so he's familiar with the confines of this particular elevator and with what awaits him on top. He'll be climbing to a place where he can breathe, like a caught fish thrown back into the water. Where he's freed from tight, suffocating spaces and the waves of sound that envelop him, all the oppressive blare and clang and caterwaul of the street-level depths.

A security guard accompanies him. As the windowed elevator rises through the gizzard of City Hall tower, Richard views the spooky infrastructure crisscrossing in the shadows. It is a nonfunctional tower—the municipal offices are housed in the broad, blocky wing below—save for the large, yellow clock facings high up at each exposure, beacons for the grounded populace.

When the elevator reaches the top, almost five hundred feet above the cluttered courtyard, the door opens and Richard steps onto a circular walkway just below the base of the looming statue of Penn, who seems a giant blackbird commanding its roost. One huge hand is outstretched in a vanished gesture of civility. Join us, the massive figure suggests. Brotherly love.

Wind whips against the windows enclosing the observation deck as Richard looks miles to the south and sees two airplanes inching across opposite trajectories. On the northern side, he surveys the great basilica's oxidized dome, rooftops of crumbling housing stock, the bridge's sweeping suspension arms—the city in its entirety, a curious mix of the grand and the neglected. He feels liberated up here, the wind racing by, the view untrammeled. Like he could fly.

Soon enough, though, the insidious sounds seep back in. Sounds of death. Even here, he cannot escape them.

He needs a plan, and it must include other people. He can't do this alone. Surely there are others who will join him, who have a connection to this matter, a stake in it, information, insight.

He walks around the deck once more, tilts his chin to look up at William Penn. The founder is mute, invariant. If only he could speak, Richard is convinced, he would talk about patterns, about the importance of people connecting, of community. This is, after all, his city, his commonwealth, his creation; the great municipal grid that fans out below is his very concept, sprung from his drawing board. Yes, if giant bronze Penn could speak, he'd tell him to reach out to people. Find someone special.

The sun bounces off of Cindy Dempsey's cheeks as she sits at the edge of the schoolyard sandbox on the brightest morning possible. Richard is near her, sitting on the green, wooden ledge, and as they speak to each other in low tones kept private from the other kids chattering and moving about, they shovel sand with their hands and let it run back into the pile. Beyond them is the broad expanse of schoolyard: sloping, pebbled asphalt stretching toward an L-shaped, yellow-brick school building and surrounded by a chain-link fence. A bound universe.

A few paces to one side of the sandbox, boys and girls on metal swings arc skyward, the boys more reckless in their flight. To the other side, a jungle gym rises from a patch of dirt like tangled scaffolding. The older boys assault the apparatus with muscular grips and thrusts, moving smartly from level to level. The younger ones are more tentative in their movements, assuring themselves of stability before climbing or descending. One of the older ones, a kid who lives on Richard's block, hollers in the direction of the sandbox, Hey, Keene, you scared to come up here?

Cindy glares up at the boy, then looks at Richard, who is sifting sand.

Come on, Keene, yells the boy on the jungle gym. The sandbox is for babies.

He should talk, Cindy says under her breath. The biggest baby of them all.

Richard smiles at her, rises deliberately, and walks to the base of the jungle gym. There are four kids aloft, the challenger smirking at the top. Whoa, look out, here he comes.

Whereupon Richard Keene—the strange boy on the block, the boy they say has supernatural hearing, the freaky kid who makes oddball expressions—scales the bars in rapid fluid progression. He accomplishes a perfect over-and-under maneuvering, an expert alternating of hand grips synchronized with upward knee movement and the purchase of feet, and within seconds he is at the top, forcing his taunter to share that domain.

The bigger boy is none too pleased. Shit, that's not bad, he says, irked that his goony neighbor has shown him up a bit. He takes a swipe at Richard's ankles, trying to upend him, but in the process he loses his balance and, just like that, he's falling, his head bouncing off one of the bars. Only his desperate, convulsive hug saves him, his arms wrapping cold, blackened steel.

Richard treads across the top, as surefooted as a high-wire walker. You okay? he asks, looking down at his clinging detractor.

Rattled and embarrassed, the fallen boy steps down all the way and stalks out of the area into the dizzy scampering of the schoolyard, a hundred little games, a thousand moving parts.

Richard straddles the highest quadrant on the jungle gym and surveys the scene. His limbs feel as light as paper, like dragonfly wings. He looks down at Cindy, and her expression tells him that he need not hurry back down, that he has triumphed and she wants to watch him at that vantage point for a while.

After the allotted fifteen minutes, Richard leaves this perch high above the streets of Philadelphia, takes the elevator down, and walks out of City Hall past Market Street to Chestnut and Walnut and then Locust. The day slips away from him as he walks to Spruce and Pine and Lombard and South, then turns west all the way to Twenty-third before backtracking to Locust. He walks past the old brick town-houses with iron-railed stoops and wallpapered vestibules, just walking and thinking and listening to his plugged-in music as the twilight comes on with a sky pocked by floating blue-black clouds. The 42s seems to sway beneath them as Richard gazes upward. He lowers his head as the sliding glass door opens automatically.

He has a plan.

At least something he'll try.

In his apartment, he retrieves a clipboard and a thin, cardboard shirt box from an undisturbed corner of a shelf in the bedroom closet. He secures a sheet of copy paper on the clipboard, wraps the white box in plain brown paper, then seals it with thick mailing tape and writes a name and address on it with a marker, the pungent smell of the ink leaping up his nose. He puts on a baseball cap.

The elevator takes him up one floor, and once off it, he doesn't go left to 2307 but angles to his right to the first apartment across the hall: 2305. He tilts the visor of his cap two inches downward, shielding his forehead. This may seem a bit on the silly side and may prove utterly fruitless, he concedes, but he wants a look at the next-door neighbors; just a look for starters, but maybe something will come of it.

He presses the doorbell and waits; his heart thumps. He keeps waiting. Presses again and waits. Takes in three rapid breaths. No one there, at least no one inclined to answer.

He walks past 2307 to its other adjacent neighbor and presses the doorbell at 2309. Waits.

Just as he's about to try again, a young woman's voice

from inside, small and sweet: "Yes?"

Richard swallows. "Uh . . . delivery." He hasn't said it with much authority. He's glad a female answered, but he imagines she envisions a nobody, some skinny guy with an oversized Adam's apple. A delivery boy.

A few seconds pass; she must be eyeing him through the peephole. He has bowed his head slightly, and his line of vision hits the knob. Finally, the door opens a crack, restrained by the chain latch. He looks up. Indeed, a small, sweet-looking young woman peers at him through the opening. He smiles at her.

"How come they didn't buzz me at the desk?" she asks. "That's what they always do."

Well, they didn't buzz when his parents came last night, Richard reminds himself. Not exactly Fort Knox around here. "I don't know," he says, wondering what he has initiated, how this is going to play out. "He just sent me up. Are you Eleanor Carson?"

"One door over," she says, keeping the chain latched.

Richard looks at the paper on his clipboard, acting puzzled. "Really? I have 2309. That's what this is, right?"

"Yes."

"But you're not Eleanor Carson."

"Sorry—Ellie's next door."

Richard checks the clipboard again, then the box itself: the name Eleanor Carson is handwritten in large letters on the brown wrapping. He looks back at the young woman. Midtwenties, he guesses; short, brown, shining hair and, he can tell through the narrow opening, a slim figure in her jeans and sleeveless cotton T-shirt. "I'm the one who's sorry," he says. "For bothering you, that is."

She looks at the box. "Since when are you guys coming to the door?"

"What do you mean?"

"We always pick up at the desk."

"Don't know. Maybe because this one needs a signature."

"We always sign at the desk, too. Are you from the post office?"

Richard pauses, then says, "Yes, ma'am, US Postal Service."

"Where's your uniform?"

His planned answer is that it's being dry-cleaned, but now that strikes him as less than believable, and as he ponders this, the young woman steps back with a sudden "I'm calling Frank" and shuts the door.

He could dash away. With his cap tugged low, she didn't get a good look at him. But he doesn't want to do that. He almost presses his lips to the door as the words spill out of him.

"Look, I'm not with the post office, but I'm not a stalker or anything. My name is Richard Keene and I live here in apartment 2207, just one floor below, and I guess . . ." He slows down. "I'd just like to talk to you. It's important, it's very important . . . At least it is to me." He has heard his voice echoing off the walls, cringes at the pleading tone.

A moment later the door opens, still latched.

"What's the name of this building?" she asks.

"Huh?"

She waits.

"They call it the 42s," he says.

"What's the street address?"

"Fifteen twenty-six Locust."

"What's the name of the guy at the front desk?"

"Frank."

"I already gave you that, I'm afraid. What's the backup's name?"

"Mike."

She sizes him up, can't stop a little smile from breaking through. "You're a little weird, aren't you?"

"Yes."

"You'll have to tell me what's in the box." She points at it.

Richard looks at the box like it's something that has just materialized in his hands. He looks up at her. "Nothing."

She removes the latch, opens the door a bit farther, and laughs. "Very inventive, Richard Keene. That's the best pickup routine I've seen in a long while. But is it intended for me or Eleanor?"

"Eleanor . . . I mean—"

"Can't help you. She's already got a boyfriend."

"Davis Braun?"

"You know him?"

"Sort of."

"You know he's pretty tough competition, then."

"It's not that. I think she's in trouble."

Her face tightens. "Trouble?"

"That's right."

Her eyes open a bit wider. "Really?"

"Yes . . . really."

"You're being pretty dramatic."

"I don't mean to be."

"What sort of trouble?"

Richard says it earnestly. "The worst kind."

SEVEN

He heard things that no one else could. Hot water straining the pipes before the awful wail in the walls. Trucks shifting gears on a highway miles away. Unseen animals rustling in the far-off brush, tiny throat gurgles preceding a cough. Often, when he anticipated things, he would tell people—not as a game but as a warning. One time, after he and his parents had visited the Franklin Institute and were walking down Market Street, he yelled, "Watch out!" and, though he was only ten at the time, managed to shove them against the base of a high-rise. Seconds later, a window washer's squeegee hit the sidewalk—not exactly a piano but dangerous enough from thirty stories up. He had heard it whistling down the side of the building.

The sensory gift left him continually distracted, hurting his performance at school, where teachers labeled him a daydreamer. Kids in the neighborhood thought him strange, his expressions and the way he tuned out in the middle of a conversation odd; from an early age, he was excluded from their street games. He grew up a loner.

The little girl next door was the exception in his life. Cindy Dempsey was a year younger but with an intelligence and sensitivity far beyond her age. She and Richard seemed to have an almost telepathic way of communicating. When he'd hear something in the distance and cock his head like a cat getting a neck scratching, she'd try to guess what it was—and often did. He loved her for that. She was his refuge in an oppressive world. His mother treated him like secondhand furniture; his father was kindly but detached. But Cindy was crazy about him. They played Chinese checkers on the patio for hours, finger-tipping the marbles into place as they fastened their eyes on one another, Cindy breaking the spell with a shake of her head or Richard with some observation that would make her laugh, a laugh like a cascade of coins.

"You're a strange boy, Richard Keene," she'd say to him like a sophisticated young woman, and it was that very strangeness she found endearing. She felt an urge to be at his side. She wanted to help this strange boy, whose eyes shrank in fear or shone with excitement, depending on the stimulus that had taken hold.

The kitchen is on the right as he enters apartment 2309, the bedroom to the left. Like a matching bookend to the -07 apartments. The young woman in blue jeans stares at him, her eyes probing. He just wants to talk to someone about what is possessing him, and she could be that someone, a grown-up version of Cindy Dempsey.

"Lori Calder."

She extends a hand toward a puzzled Richard.

"You didn't know my name, right?"

"No, I didn't," he says. Now she seems so polite, almost warm. He takes her hand and releases it. "How do you do? Mine's Richard Keene."

"I know."

Richard looks blankly at her, then shrugs and smiles self-consciously.

"Let me ask you, Richard Keene, why didn't you just knock on my door and tell me what it is you want to tell me without the charade?"

She has a good point, as it turns out.

"I don't know. Maybe I had to see you first, you know, before I made up my mind."

"What makes you think Ellie's in trouble?"

Richard gathers himself. "Do you know her well?"

"Not that well, but we're friendly enough."

"When was the last time you saw her?"

"I don't know. Few days, I guess."

"Can you remember exactly?"

Lori thinks about it. "Tuesday. Tuesday evening. She said she was taking a little vacation or something. We bumped into each other at the elevator . . . So what's up? What is it?"

Richard thinks this over. She never made it to that vacation, he believes. "What time was it when you saw her?"

"First, you tell me what's going on." There are pinpoints of concern in her large brown eyes.

"I think something's happened to her."

"Like what?"

"On Tuesday, what time was it when you saw her at the elevator?"

"Eight, eight thirty. I had dinner out with some girl-friends and was waiting to get on the elevator. She was getting off. In the lobby."

He likes that she said *girl*friends. "Was she carrying a suitcase?"

"I think so . . . Yes, definitely."

"Did she say where she was going? For her vacation."

"No, she was in a big hurry."

"Davis Braun wasn't with her?"

"No. And he's still around. He's fine—I saw him yesterday. Will you tell me what this is all about? What do you mean, 'something's happened to her'?"

Richard wants to exploit the tension further, both to gather information and to explore what he hopes may be some chemistry between the two of them. It's a distraction, he realizes, but he can't deny his attraction to her. "Would she take a vacation by herself?"

"Well, I can't speak for Ellie, but it's been known to happen," Lori says, idly stroking a slender forearm. "Maybe they needed a break from each other."

"Maybe."

"Or she had something special to do, like a working vacation. Why don't you ask Davis?"

Richard doesn't like her familiar use of Braun's first name, the comfort level there. But so what? She's the next-door neighbor; she knows them both, is on friendly terms with both. "He's in med school, isn't he?"

"Yep. He's a resident. Second year, I think, at Metropolitan."

"You know him well?"

"A little better than her; I see him around more."

Richard doesn't like the sound of that at all. Funny, he's just met this girl, but already he feels a need for her and, at the same time, a desire to protect her. She's just the type he wants. Sweet and slight, but with a brightness and strength about her, a sharpness of features and speech. The conspiratorial nature of his intent is a kind of aphrodisiac. He wonders if it has a similar effect on her. Doubts it.

"Look," she says, "you're probably making a big production out of something that's nothing. What's your connection to Ellie, anyway?"

He searches for the right way to phrase it, to keep her interested in him, keep her from thinking him a nut. "Random" is all that he says.

"What does that mean?"

"Well, not exactly random. It's like this: I was supposed to contact her about something, uh, work-related"—he is fumbling—"and we never—"

"Oh, I get it," Lori interrupts with a look that says she knows he's not being honest. Kind of a mischievous look, though. "Work-related, huh?"

"Yes."

"What do you do, anyway, Richard Keene?"

The question reaches him a beat late, as if on a delayed broadcast transmission. There are so many other contending sounds and thoughts inside his skull. "Sorry . . . I'm a medical technician." Sorry about that, too.

"So is she a patient of yours? That's how you met her?"

"Yeah, that's it." Richard reaches in vain for something

to hold on to, like the metal railing in the elevator.

Lori gives him a sidelong glance. "So you're not a private detective?"

He takes her smile as a message. Maybe they are getting along, on the same wavelength.

"No, not a private detective."

"You're not doing a bad impersonation."

"I'm just trying—"

"Are you gonna tell me what's going on or keep me in suspense all night? You really think something's happened to her?"

"I do."

"Have you contacted the police?"

"No."

"Why not?"

"I don't have enough to go on—yet."

"And you're suspicious of Davis, aren't you?"

That stops him. An intuitive girl, this Lori Calder. "I am," he admits.

"Why?"

He must explain himself or leave her alone and . . . *leave* her. They stand there, facing each other. Richard feels like he's in a kid's game of freeze and cannot move. Damn if she hasn't read his mind. "Would you like to sit down?"

He would and does.

"I can't stop it," he says.

"Can't stop what?"

He looks at the ceiling, then back at her. He is very close to choking up, forcing out a tear, and he doesn't know how much is genuine and how much is self-induced. For effect. For her benefit.

"Stop what?" she repeats.

"What I hear."

The townhouses on Spruce Street seem to sag, their red stone steps and walls and doorways defenseless against the hard new light, like a woman of a certain age trying to dial back the years with dabs of rouge. It is Saturday morning, and Richard, as is his custom, is alone on the sidewalk. The 42s looms a block behind him and, in motion, he studies it as it towers over the flat roofs of the townhouses. On the corner of Sixteenth Street, a red brick building housing a telephone company is sealed tight as a bank vault, and in the next block, Coggins Elementary School is an old brick pile fronted by an asphalt yard enclosed by a spear-like, wrought-iron fence above a concrete retaining wall. Two thick, gray-barked, freckled oak trees rise from dirt flats in the asphalt and spread generous branches toward swings and monkey bars in one corner of the schoolyard.

Richard has left his iPod in the apartment and confronts the world with naked ears. He hears the creaking of swings long before the little girl in motion comes into view. Then he stops to watch her as she arcs skyward and then descends to earth so that her small sneakers brush the ruts in the dirt. She heightens the backswing by leaning forward, gripping the hanging chains, a human pendulum in full abandon. As he watches her, Richard sees another little girl on swings, hears the creaking with each reversal, follows the wanton flight, her little body precarious in the seat, dauntless, a clinging confidence, no screams of delight as with most little girls but a look of relaxation, incongruous for one so young and in such a vertiginous state. It is Cindy . . . Cindy swinging into the clouds, floating there and then disappearing, vaporized and eternal. Cindy, taken up by the sky.

There can never be a good-bye, a letting go.

He told Lori Calder his story yesterday—not about Cindy, nothing about Cindy, but about what he had heard three days earlier in the twenty-third-floor hallway, what he hears still. He told her his suspicions—no, more than suspicions, convictions now. The proof is in his head. Exhibit number one is the scene from the movie, and there is more evidence to come. He is on the case and will not get off it, because the sounds will not let him. The sounds have a life of their own. They are the bitter pills of his past and the symbionts of his present. Sounds with a permanent shelf life.

Nor did he tell Lori specifically about *Grip of Death* or his uncanny precision at differentiating sounds—just that he had heard a possible murder being committed behind closed doors. She wasn't quick to embrace his theory. As a matter of fact, she didn't accept it at all. She had seen Eleanor Carson leave the building that very evening (as had Frank at the front desk). Still, Richard believes that, when Lori hears all of it, she'll come around. She'll help him. She'll be his inside track, his pipeline. The next-door neighbor. He's the outside man, the orchestrator, the prosecutor. Second chances rarely come so recognizable. This time, he'll have help.

His answer to the Eleanor Carson sightings in the lobby that night is that she returned to the apartment to retrieve something else after depositing her suitcase in her car or a cab. Lori cannot be sure of exactly what time she saw her get off the elevator, and Frank made up his sighting just to get rid of him, or he's mixed up on the timeline, or the woman he saw wasn't Eleanor at all.

Or someone else was murdered in 2307.

The little girl has left the schoolyard swing, which sways above the worn dirt. Richard checks his suppositions. Why would the murderer, why would Davis Braun, allow Eleanor to walk out the door when, according to the theory, her murder was planned to coincide with a scene in a movie screened on television? The answer must be that he knew she would return to get something else (a second suitcase?) for her trip—he had just gotten out of the shower, say, and could not help her with her bags, as she was in a hurry. Or better yet, they'd had a fight and he was unwilling to help, sending her angrily on her way without his assistance. He knew she'd be back, probably with time to spare.

Or Braun could not count on her return and saw his exquisite timing seemingly slip away, only to restore it-self when she did return. And if the timing didn't work for Braun on this occasion, there would be another. Of course, he could commit the murder without the accompanying sound track, but Richard regards Braun as both monster and artist. This is his extended theory.

Could the victim be someone other than Eleanor Carson? A competing girlfriend? Richard will stick with Eleanor until proven wrong.

His plan is taking shape. The world is your prison only if you allow it to be. Passivity does nothing for the soul—*The Stranger*'s Monsieur Meursault had no soul, and that was his problem. Action, as a direction, is critical; it is the only path to freedom, the way to celebrate yourself, as the poet Whit-man urged. Richard feels he understands this and must not squander the insight.

The weekend consists of two gray days drifting toward

dark, blank nights. Biding time. Late Sunday morning, Richard walks down Locust Street to Eighteenth and across to Rittenhouse Square, where the leaves are dense and still summer green, and pigeons chase peanut shells as if they were gold nuggets. It is a patch of tranquility in the urban landscape, a welcome interruption to the ceaseless surge of intersecting cars and pedestrians. The movement here is unstructured, carefree: the plump, fussy pigeons; young mothers wheeling baby carriages or strollers solo or towing toddlers by the hand, taking in the scenery; bodies lolling on blankets and beach towels. Cisterns perch on pedestals, and balustrades rim a central plaza. Richard eyes the square's adornments, its statuary. He greets his immutable sculpted friends: the graceful, young woman clutching a duck to her side, the fierce lion crushing an openmouthed serpent, the giant frog ready to spring, two Grecian youths hoisting a sundial toward the heavens. He passes a nineteenth-century guardhouse keeping watch at the confluence of two pathways that run diagonally from one corner of the square to the other.

He works his way past benches and across lawns onto the elevated plaza, where college students hunch in concentration as they try to digest philosophy and psychology texts; maybe some of them are lit majors and *The Stranger* is on their reading list. Just outside the square bounded by ramparts of stone, a bus belches black fumes that carpet Walnut Street before dispersing, the sooty smell overpowering the stale scent of marijuana sneaking onto the periphery. On the patios of tony restaurants on the square at Nineteenth Street, patrons eat gourmet omelets and chatter with intensity. From afar, Richard hears solicitous waiters recite the day's specials, hears them as clearly as do the customers seated right at the table. He'd like to order a big breakfast, a pile of eggs and French toast with syrup, but he's mindful of his cholesterol count; he's been fine-tuning his ratio of HDL to overall. He doesn't want to stray even one point beyond the AMA's recommended levels, knows that thin guys, too, can have heart problems.

He circles the square and walks past the Curtis Institute, where symphonic strains float out of a third-floor window and student musicians huddle and smoke greedily on the side steps. If only all the sounds of the city could be symphonies. Two blocks down, a luxury sedan parked in front of Marco's Bistro commands attention. People pause to watch on the sidewalk as a photographer fires off a series of shots of a miniskirted woman posing by the hood ornament. When the flurry is complete, she scans the small crowd, looks past Richard to a middle-aged man with graying hair on his temples and a golf-course tan, and commandeers him with a toss of her raven mane and a flash of teeth. They disappear into the car, her legs settling in nicely as the door closes. The man sits in the driver's seat, but they won't be doing any traveling. She brandishes brochures and a booklet and enumerates the attributes of this new, high-end model. Richard can hear her pitch through the rolled-up windows. Angered a trace when her eyes dismissed him on the sidewalk, he now feels better about it. She's just a salesgirl, a decoration, her middle-aged quarry a far likelier prospect for the purchase of the vehicle on display.

Richard continues on his way. Monday morning can't

come fast enough. Back in his apartment, he reads the Sunday paper—at least part of it. He likes to get the hard copy on Sundays, likes the retro feel of a heap of newspaper. He skips the Review & Opinion section, which is full of dull commentary by executive directors of institutes and nonprofit agencies with unwieldy names. He reads every word in Arts & Leisure, which includes reviews of a couple of books he'll reserve at the library. This section has a piece about a mural painted on a brick wall of an old, center-city building adjacent to a lot where a gas station has replaced an architectural treasure of a church; the image is that of the vanished church itself, as if it were still standing and reflected in the brick wall like a mirror.

After reading nearly sixty pages of a thick biography of Theodore Roosevelt—a man of action if there ever was one—Richard gets through the night by settling in front of the television, a PBS special about the American Revolution, then another look at *Grip of Death*, the entire movie this time, the "keep quiet" scene three times for final confirmation. It's all there; he'll return the DVD tomorrow. He doesn't need to view it anymore; it's all in his head and his ears.

After negligible sleep, tomorrow does come. Monday morning. Richard calls the office, makes his voice sound weak.

"Kathy, I can't make it in today."

"Again?"

He issues a convincing cough. "Sorry. I'm still in bad shape. You know I have a scheduled day off tomorrow, right? I figure I'll stay in and knock this thing out of my system . . . How's today's schedule?"

"You've got a lot of appointments."

"Can Jeff handle them?" What's the difference—a

monkey could handle it. He thinks of Jeff, the work-study student from a local college, eager, energetic, believes his position to be a great career opportunity. Comes in Mondays.

"I guess he'll have to," Kathy says. "Maybe we'll reschedule some of them. I'll tell the docs. Better take some extra chicken soup."

Kathy trying to sound grown up.

Richard puts on a pair of chinos over a striped, short-sleeved shirt frayed at the collar and hits the street. It's a crisper morning, a hint of fall, and the rising fumes of the city smell smoky-sharp until a subway train rumbles beneath Broad Street and the updraft shoots mustiness through the grates. Richard is tethered to his iPod and a concerto by Liszt as he passes the venerable Union League building, a dark-hued eye-popper in the modern city, its twin serpentine staircases and portico brown as battlefield mud. A testament to Lincoln. A bronze Union soldier guards the gates. Richard salutes him.

In the next block, the cut-stone squares of the Land Title building are gray and cool to the touch on the shady side of the street. Office workers on cigarette breaks huddle like lepers near the main door. The lobby clock marks the hours with gold Roman numerals, which Richard stares at as the elevator door closes.

The law firm of Perris & Blumenthal occupies half the eighth floor. Richard opens the walnut double doors and approaches the receptionist seated behind a sweeping, polished counter. She has the icy look of corporate grooming.

"Richard Keene. I have an appointment with Eleanor Carson." He tries to project an air of quiet confidence.

"Thank you, Mr. Keene." Her voice is more human than her looks. She presses a button among the phalanx on her telephone. "Richard Keene to see Eleanor . . . She's not?" She repeats Richard's name and listens to instructions. "Okay," she says and hangs up.

"She's not here yet, Mr. Keene. Are you certain your appointment was scheduled for this morning?" She speaks with precision and wears a tailored business suit, and Richard wonders why she's not smart enough to do better than receptionist, why she lacks the brains to match her voice and looks. Then he catches himself in the realization that, if he is to make any headway in this world, he must refrain from being hypercritical—judgmental, the doctors called it. After all, who the hell is *he*?

"Absolutely," he says. "She told me she was returning from vacation and to come in at eleven."

"Perris and Blumenthal." The receptionist fields another call, sends it to its destination, and returns to Richard, who feigns disappointment and a touch of anxiety, impressions he doesn't have to work too hard to make.

"She is due back today," the receptionist says—no nameplate, Richard notices; high turnover in this job—"but there's no record of your appointment."

"She probably didn't put it in the book," Richard says. "It's a special case."

"Can we reschedule, or would you like to speak with her first?"

"I'm afraid I can't reschedule."

"Perris and Blumenthal."

Richard whispers, "I'll call," then turns and walks out

of Perris & Blumenthal, certain that Eleanor is not coming back to work here or anywhere else, sure about it, though he'll call later in the day to check, a routine procedural move, the mark of a pro. Indeed, at 1:30, he calls Perris & Blumenthal and is told that paralegal Eleanor Carson has not yet returned from vacation. At the end of the day, another call, same result. What he sees that night, what he recalls as he sits on the edge of his bed has nothing to do with Eleanor Carson. Nothing . . . and everything.

As a red-and-white ambulance and a blue-and-white police car sit curbside in a row-house neighborhood, paramedics wheel a gurney slowly down a shared walkway, an opaque white sheet covering a small body on the gurney. At the foot of the walkway, two policemen stand before Herb Dempsey, morning light slanting across their cheeks. One of the officers is big and blocky, the other dark complected, smaller, and trim. Dempsey is unshaven, hair uncombed, clothes hurried on. Neighbors watch from their stoops, keeping their distance, a chilly hush settled over the street. Dempsey speaks to the police in low tones half-strangled in his throat, a word or syllable here and there shrill in the cool, morning air. Richard, standing frozen on his patio, can hear most of it, can hear what other neighbors can't.

I heard something, Dempsey says, arms extended, palms upturned as if in supplication or bewilderment. But it was like in a dream or something, know what I mean? His expression swings from shock to anger. It's not possible, he says. It's just not possible.

The gurney passes them and reaches the sidewalk, but Dempsey avoids looking at it. He looks only at the police, even as they turn to watch the gurney being collapsed and loaded onto the ambulance.

We can't find any signs of forced entry, Mr. Dempsey, Richard hears the smaller policeman say.

An instant later, Richard can hear a woman's sobbing seep through the rain-stained bricks of the Dempsey house. The early morning rotates and spins into space, out of focus. Another car arrives, and a man in a suit gets out and speaks to the two police-men. Collective frowns seem etched in their faces. One word of what Richard hears stands out in its exotic ugliness: strangulation. Now the man in the suit approaches Dempsey, nods, and says, Detective Flagler. Let's go inside.

As the ambulance and police car pull away, Dempsey walks back toward his front door, looking at no one until he sees Richard standing to one side, a lone little boy fixing him with unyield-ing eyes. Trailed by Detective Flagler, Dempsey reaches the top of his stoop and yanks open the screen door. Richard does not waver, and Dempsey, as he grips the screen-door handle with his left hand, draws his right to his lips and presses lightly with two fingers, and only Richard hears the little hiss escaping between them, the sssh like a snake's rustle.

Richard sees it and hears it again as he sits on the edge of his bed, and the city's sounds outside his window provide a backbeat. He is frustrated that he must wait, that he cannot move more quickly in this latest matter, but the deed is done and the evidence cold, so he understands that his task is to mount a meticulous investigation and convince the police to follow through. It's the only feasible option.

He is a rational human being.

He must recruit a partner, a sidekick. That person will be Lori Calder. He feels good about her. More than good—excited.

He calls her after finding her number through an online lookup service.

"You said you'd keep an open mind," Richard says.

"I know I did, but I need a lot more information. A lot more convincing."

Still the sweetness in her voice. He feels emboldened. "Lori, you have to believe me. And I'm not asking you to do anything that's really—"

"Richard, you know I don't think you're some kook. I just think that the mind plays tricks on us sometimes, and maybe—"

"I'm just asking you to keep your ears open; that's all. In a very natural way. You see him, you talk to him . . ."

"You know, I'm not exactly a professional at this sort of thing," she says. "Suppose he *is* guilty, and he picks up something in my voice or my expression. Did that ever occur to you? Where does that leave me?"

"He's too smart to do anything really crazy. You would just keep your distance afterward, stay away from him."

"He's right next door, remember?"

"Of course. What I'm saying is—"

"Richard, this is getting ridiculous. You've got me making Davis into a homicidal maniac."

"No, Lori, he did that all by himself."

"Don't you realize it's dangerous to be so sure of yourself?"

"Is Eleanor from Philadelphia?"

"What? You mean originally?"

"Yes."

"I don't know . . . No, I think she's from Washington or somewhere around there."

"She was due back from vacation today. Have you seen her?"

"Well, I haven't gone looking for her. I could go two weeks and not see her. How do you know she was supposed to be back today?"

"They told me down at Perris and Blumenthal. That's the firm she works for. In the Land Title building at Broad and Chestnut."

"She's a lawyer? I didn't even know that."

"Almost—a paralegal. I went down there this morning. Then I called back in the afternoon. Twice. End of the day, she hadn't come back. They were expecting her."

"Really?"

"Really."

"Well, so she's late getting back. For all you know, she might be in her apartment right now."

"Let's call and find out."

"You call."

"All right, but you listen in."

"At your apartment?"

"No, not from here or on my cell—you know, caller ID. We'll have to find another phone. I want to see you, Lori. I want to explain to you what I heard."

"You already did yesterday."

"No, I mean all of it, every detail. Then you'll understand. Have you ever seen the movie *Grip of Death*?"

"Sounds like a regular chick flick."

Richard is sorry he's mentioned it on the phone. "Never

mind. I'll explain when I see you."

Ten minutes later, Lori exits the 42s by the rear door and walks on alley-like Latimer Street to Sixteenth, then to Locust and across. A quarter of the way down the block is a life-size statue of an urban gent clutching a spread umbrella, and there next to the stationary blackened bronze is Richard Keene, in the flesh.

"This cloak-and-dagger stuff makes me feel pretty foolish," Lori says.

"Thanks for coming. We'll use a pay phone not far from here."

"I don't know about this *we* stuff."

They walk slowly along Sixteenth Street, and Richard tells his story of murder—all of it this time. He dissects for her every sound he heard in that moment, separating the *Grip of Death* sounds from those he believes were happening live. His description is controlled and precise.

"I believe you believe it," says Lori. "But that doesn't mean it actually happened. It doesn't mean a murder was committed."

Richard touches her elbow, and they stop at a red light. "That's why I want to see how the facts add up," he says. "That's why I need help. Isn't that reasonable?"

"That's why we have a police department."

"The police have too much to check out as it is. Things have a way of getting lost in a big city. I can't just turn away from this."

The light is green, and Lori has a little smile for him. The next block offers a pub with fist-thick sandwiches and beer and billiards and that vanishing breed of the modern world: a pay phone. The city's phone hooded in the kiosk on the sidewalk right outside of the 42s is obviously to be avoided for this particular mission. Plus, it takes plastic only. The throwback in the pub vestibule handles coins. Richard inserts two quarters, gets a dial tone, and punches in Davis Braun's number retrieved from the same online locater service that gave him Lori's.

"You know," Lori says, "if he has done what you say, you ought to watch out for yourself, Richard, running around, digging things up. Know what I mean?"

Richard smiles. "I think I do."

"Not that I believe you, understand. About Davis, I mean." Her eyes are alive with curiosity and, Richard believes, something close to affection. For him?

Davis Braun's voice comes through the receiver, familiar to Richard after just the one exposure on the twenty-third floor. ". . . Please leave a message." Richard holds the phone out to Lori. "Looks like nobody's home."

"So that leaves us nowhere," Lori says. "They could be out having a bite to eat. Maybe they're in here." She motions toward the interior of the pub. Richard nervously takes her arm and leads her outside.

They walk slowly back toward the 42s. Misty rain drifts down from the invisible sky, streaking the bronze umbrella-bearer.

"I have something else to tell you," Richard says. Lori blinks away the light rain. "A long time ago, I heard a little girl being murdered." They pause at the corner of Sixteenth and Locust, Richard wary, the front entrance of the

42s coming into view. As Lori looks up at him, expectant and uncertain, she seems a little girl herself.

She waits for him to say more. "And?"

"And I did nothing."

After his rain-slicked meeting with Lori, his apartment feels lonely. A sense of satisfaction fills Richard. He has told her the whole story, past and present. Now that she knows it, she'll come around. He feels sure of that.

Sleep evades him, as usual. The next day will be a legitimate day off from work, scheduled in advance, one due him for the many Saturday mornings he has put in. Richard knows what he will do on his day off.

He will track his man.

EIGHT

She looks at her face in the bathroom mirror: angular cheeks, eyebrows thinned, hair layered and luxuriant and colored. Altered. It still surprises her when she meets it in the mirror, though she grows more accustomed to it every day. The cheeks, and the body, seem natural because they've slimmed gradually, but the brows and hair still startle. Especially the hair. That tumble of red hair.

She has always preferred understated makeup, and that hasn't changed. Indeed, her new look calls for low-key cosmetics: moisturizer for supple skin, a few touches of special serum to thicken the eyelashes, some deft strokes of lip liner, a spritz of perfume behind the ears and on the wrist. The pumps fit just right over her nylons, and her business suit tapers smartly to the waist. Janet Kroll is still surprised by what she sees in the mirror, but that doesn't mean she dislikes it. To the contrary.

When she gets on the elevator, her expensive scent and curved contours wake up a couple of flaccid, middle-aged riders. She faces front, clutching a small briefcase. When the door reopens, eyes follow her as she strides through the lobby; at the front desk, Frank gives her his very best smile.

"Good morning, Frank," she says, in motion.

"Yes ma'am," he says.

The day has come up muggy, a lapse into August stickiness. Janet has some things on her mind as she walks to the 42s' parking garage. She thinks she has a buyer for the three-bedroom condo at The Philadelphian, and she certainly could use the commission. Finances have tightened since she moved into the city a month ago. And anxieties have expanded, even as she's maintained a cool exterior. Yet something has hardened inside of her, a resolve that has changed the shape of her life. Yes, she has some things on her mind. Making a living is one of them, but at the top of the list is why she is here in this building and what she wants to see happen, how she plans to make it happen. And what could go wrong on this dangerous path she has chosen.

Moments after Janet leaves the 42s, Davis Braun is aftershave-smooth in a powder-blue tennis jacket as he walks through the lobby and greets Frank on the way out.

"Hey there, Dr. Braun," Frank says, looking up from a stack of flat envelopes.

Outside, shafts of sunlight dagger street and sidewalk, exposing the age of gray-brown buildings. Braun joins the flow of pedestrians; he's casual and refreshed, a man of calm stature among the frenetic and the disenfranchised. Were he to glance back at the entrance of the 42s, he would see Richard emerging from the shadows, tentative at first, then steady in pursuit.

Richard's iPod sends a Grieg piano concerto into his earbuds.

Braun walks to Twentieth Street and then several blocks north past Market and John F. Kennedy Boulevard, all the way to tree-lined Benjamin Franklin Parkway, Philadelphia's version of the Champs Elysees in Paris. He heads west and passes the Rodin Museum fronted by the sculptor's black bronze *The Thinker* hunched and brooding, all muscular tenacity and weary contemplation. It's a long walk, but Braun's size and natural athleticism propel him at a swift clip. His follower stays in step, well behind and always separated by a few people.

Behind Richard, also comfortably separated, another deliberate follower keeps pace on foot along the city streets.

When Richard reaches *The Thinker*, he wants to spend time appraising the iconic statue, this grounded cousin of William Penn, who looks down from his aerie at the end of the Parkway. But this is not the time to linger. Richard has communed with the statue before; he'll do so again another time.

Braun walks to Twenty-first Street and reaches the police station. It is a two-story, brick-and-glass building, long and lean with a flat roof, a 1950s structure that originally housed insurance offices. A narrow parking lot horseshoes the building, squad cars angled between white-painted slats on the asphalt. Braun opens the glass double doors and goes inside.

Richard watches him from across Twenty-first at Callowhill Street, standing there with hands in pockets, partially shielded by a streetlight pylon. He moves forward as if he'll cross the street, checks himself, ambles over to a vendor's pushcart at the corner for a cup of coffee.

The day is gathering itself, a warm busy hum replacing

the jagged spurts of early morning. Richard paces the sidewalk and sips his coffee, drifts into the adjacent supermarket parking lot, returns to his sidewalk stakeout—not a suspicious-looking guy, just another city character taking in the air. He loiters there for about twenty minutes, until Braun reappears at the front door of the police station. Richard tosses his second cup of coffee into a tall, metal trash can.

Now he parallels Braun, maintaining a suitable distance, moving inconspicuously among the scattered pedestrians. They take Callowhill to Twentieth, then retrace the trip back across the Parkway, the Boulevard, Market, Chestnut, to Walnut and down to Sixteenth and a 1930s neoclassical building that houses a retail branch of Mazer National Bancorp, an interstate behemoth that gobbled up several old-line Philadelphia banks two decades ago. On this leg of the trip, Richard feels another's eyes trained on him and jerks his head around twice in a bid to catch his pursuer off guard. Each time, he sees at various distances several men and women unfazed by his sharp glance. No one familiar.

Richard follows Braun inside the bank building and onto the main floor, where ribbed columns rise to a vaulted ceiling, and the day's brightness comes through arched windows. Braun stands in a teller line restrained by thick cordons as in a vintage movie theater. A security guard watches over things, prodding stragglers away from incoming traffic, routing newcomers to their destinations. Richard plants himself next to a display carrel and fingers several brochures while keeping an eye on Braun. The slotted brochures are benign pieces of modern marketing fluff: IRAs, cash management services, CDs, premium checking, all explained and extolled in neat, bite-sized, meaningless chunks of prose. Richard's heart hops around its chamber as he shuffles the brochures and angles himself in such a way that the carrel hides him from Braun's view. When a nasal "Next" calls Braun to a teller window, Richard strains to hear the exchange. Scattered voices and heels scuffling on the marble floor interfere with the transmission, the sounds magnified in the cavernous space. "I'd like to—" Braun says, his next words swallowed in echo. He slides something small enough to be a check or a deposit/withdrawal slip toward the teller, a young unremarkable guy in a white shirt and red tie.

" . . . form of ID," the teller requests.

"Sure," Braun says and removes his wallet from his back pocket. He retrieves a small plastic card and hands it to the teller, who inspects it and makes a notation before handing it back.

"Thanks."

Simple enough. The teller counts out some cash, making sure that no bills are stuck together, and hands it to Braun, who has completed his business at the window. When he turns to leave, Richard rotates around the carrel to stay out of sight. Braun walks through the revolving door and into a flood of sunshine. Richard holds back a few seconds, then follows him through the door, whose glass is laced with towel smears and sponge strokes laid bare in the sun.

He considers the possibilities. An innocent transaction? Not on your life. Braun has just forged a check and cashed it, or phonied up a withdrawal slip. The dead girl's signature.

No, he wouldn't be that stupid.

Unless he believes that he's invincible. That trumps intelligence and rationality. Catch me if you can.

It's easy to lag behind Braun and stay unobtrusive as others flit in and out of the breach. Richard enjoys this cloak-and-dagger stuff, as Lori put it, though he does want it to remain all cloak and no dagger. He can't dismiss the sensation that someone is following him, even as he tracks Davis Braun. Again he whips his head around and, this time, glimpses a face that may have been among those he'd seen walking behind him earlier. It is the angular face of a man in his midtwenties.

On the 1500 block of Locust, Braun walks inside the 42s. He moves with a taut gracefulness confirming muscles and command, and as Richard watches him with envy rather than fear or distaste, he realizes that Braun's stride has been unperturbed throughout the jaunt, that he has neither hurried nor shown uncertainty but has simply strolled about the city as if on a morning constitutional. No guilty tics.

But no urgency to reach the police station, either. He hardly seems distressed.

Richard decides to use the phone kiosk in front of the 42s this time, as he's in a hurry; again, he does not want this call traced to his cell or landline. He inserts a credit card (his father's) and presses the three digits to reach Information. A man passes, munching on something that leaves a greasy fragrance. Cars dash by; to Richard's ear, they sound like planes on the tarmac, now that he's removed his earbuds. He asks the operator for the number of the police station, and she connects him. His peripheral vision spies the lean, midtwenties face, and he can see now that the man is angling into the 42s. Richard considers hanging up and following the young man into the building.

"Fairmount Station."

Richard stays put. He mimics Braun's mellow voice, which he has sampled only briefly. "Yeah, I was just in—Davis Braun, wearing a blue jacket. I forgot to tell the officer something. Can you connect me?" He bites his thumb cuticle.

"Who'd you see?"

"Uh, sorry, I can't re—"

"Never mind, I got it here. Hold on."

Distant subway sounds rise through vents and, above-ground, the grinding gears of a garbage truck signal that it yearns for the open road. Richard holds a hand to one ear, the receiver to the other.

"Oliver." Gruff but not off-putting.

"This is Davis Braun; I was just there."

"Yes, sir."

Richard bobs his head as he speaks, a little gesture of self-affirmation. "Did I give you Eleanor Carson's work number?"

"We've got it, Mr. Braun."

"Just wanted to be sure. Please let me know as soon as you find something. Thank you." Richard hangs up the phone. Breathes.

In the 42s' lobby, Frank is speaking with Mrs. Levitan, an ancient woman barely taller than the counter. She's expecting something from her granddaughter, a photo album of events surrounding the birth of her first great-grandchild. The granddaughter lives in Minneapolis, where her husband was transferred by Honeywell. It's really something how these young people move around these days, the diminutive nona-genarian tells Frank. She wants him to keep an eye out for the parcel.

"You'll know as soon as it arrives, Mrs. Levitan," he

111

says with a smile, his whitened teeth cousin to the sheen of the lobby floor and the gleaming mirrors. "I never keep my customers waiting."

In walks Richard—his next customer.

"She's missing."

Frank tries to hide in the *Daily News* sports section.

"Did you hear me? Eleanor Carson. She's missing."

"I'm too busy today, Keene."

Frank is busy only with the sports section at the moment, but smart remarks are not Richard's style, though he can think of them as quickly as the next guy.

"She never returned to work."

"Uh-huh." Frank looks up from the newspaper. "She went on vacation, right? So she took a longer vacation. What's the problem?"

"They were expecting her back."

"Maybe you should go to work there and help them run their business."

"Davis Braun was just at the police station. He filed a missing persons report. Interesting, huh?"

"Somebody's gonna smack your ass, you keep this up."

"Think about it," Richard says, his hands gripping the counter, squeezing home the point. "His girlfriend's due back and he reports to the police that she's missing. That takes care of the extended vacation idea, Frank."

"Maybe they broke up—how do you know?" Frank tugs at his collar, scrunches his eyes. "You're prying into people's lives, Keene—it's none of your business. And you're getting on my nerves now, big time." He flips the newspaper onto the desk behind him, and the tabloid pages separate and swim across the flat, hard surface. "I've got a building to run here."

Frank turns away but immediately turns back with enlightenment in his eyes. "Anyway, if he's taking it to the police, he's concerned she's late and all that. Doesn't sound like someone who killed her, now, does it?"

Richard doesn't smile, doesn't fidget, doesn't even change the inflection of his voice. "Sounds like it to me."

Frank slices the air with a dismissive backhand. "C'mon, Keene. Gimme a break."

A FedEx deliveryman arrives with a big box clutched under his armpit. Richard steps aside and watches Frank sign for the package and take it into the storage room. When he returns a few seconds later, Richard is waiting for him.

Frank shakes his head. "You still here?"

"One thing." Richard's voice is almost friendly. "What if I'm right?"

NINE

The skyscraping Comcast Center flickers cobalt blue at the sun. The venerable Bellevue Hotel, now a Hyatt, offers power brokers a moneyed view from its top-floor restaurant. Capping antique City Hall, the statue of William Penn is diminished by distance to a toy soldier that can be grasped and manipulated. Richard pounds his threadbare cross-trainers on the treadmill and shuts his eyes against the glare of the skyline, the soaring buildings' shimmering silhouettes seared onto his retinas. He holds on to the sidebars to maintain balance as the constant thumping takes its toll—a big toe aches, the right knee serves notice that it might buckle. He feels a rivulet of sweat crawling down his collarbone and onto his flat chest and ribs. He keeps his mouth closed and breathes through his nose, even at this accelerated pace.

Running is the release that enables him to cope. It settles his nerves even as it drains his energy, then mysteriously refills his inner reservoir for the next cycle. He must keep his legs and the rest of his working parts healthy enough to perpetuate this daily ritual. Despite the unsteadiness of his knee.

When a clanging weight stack explodes the reverie, Richard opens his eyes and shoots a look toward the adjacent room, where a gorilla in a mud-brown T-shirt and matching pants has risen from the bench. He wears an aggressive, self-satisfied expression as if he has just quaffed a mugful of his favorite brew or popped somebody in the chops. Richard is quick to look away and not catch his attention. He steers clear of confrontation and certainly does not want to tangle with some dumb thug over an irritating noise. His thoughts careen to Braun, who, in his estimation, is neither dumb nor a thug but something far more dangerous.

Afterward, Richard towels his face as he waits for the elevator. When it arrives and the door slides open, Janet Kroll is there, poured into spandex. Richard gets that little kick inside, that jump-start, even before she's in full view. Their paths keep crossing. Something about this girl—a stunner, yes, yet her eyes suggest both reticence and intelligence. It's not automatic that she's after a hard-assed Hercules. He would like to build a bit on their recent brief meeting at the lobby elevator, see if he can give her a reason to be interested in him. "Hi," he says as she steps out of the elevator and their eyes meet unavoidably.

"Hi," she says with a smile, which might be mere politeness or, he hopes, could be recognition of their minimal familiarity. Richard remembers faces and names after the briefest of encounters, and he hates it when the recognition is not reciprocated. In this case, they haven't yet exchanged names.

But her smile is a reference point, he concludes. He gets on the elevator and reaches down to rub his sore knee before pressing number twenty-two.

Got to get her name.

Davis Braun is pumping iron at the Downtown Athletic Club. His thousand-dollar-a-year membership affords him a much wider and slicker array of equipment and women. With beach-boy locks feathering his forehead, wide-set blue eyes, and well-muscled arms and shoulders, Braun tends to flutter pulses among the young, professional females (and some of the males) at Downtown, and the fact that he's a future surgeon doesn't hurt his chances. He's well aware of this. He knows that it's a myth, the psychobabble about women being drawn to the mind rather than the body. Fact is, he's got both qualities working for him: rugged and sensitive, tough and tender. And to showcase it all, he's cool on approach, articulate but off the cuff, very much at ease with himself. In short, rather irresistible. Got to be honest about it.

But he's no pillaging Hun. He *likes* women, and they understand that. Makes him doubly irresistible. Of course, it all goes nowhere unless you have the looks to begin with.

He and Eleanor agreed to an open relationship, but while Davis has seen other women, she has remained loyal to him. They each have free miles to use, but he's been the only one to take advantage. He doesn't lie, makes no apologies, and has treated her well. Like a lady and a lover. That's how he sees it.

The Downtown AC is on the top two floors of a 1920s building that was once a department store and now houses attorneys, accountants, insurers, and consultants of various stripes in the converted offices below. The strength-training and cardiovascular areas encompass the entire top floor, a hangar-like space with no partitions, steel beams crisscrossing the ceiling, and huge arched windows at either end. Braun moves through the cycle of stations, isolating and challenging all of his muscle groups: delts, trapezius, biceps, triceps, chest, abs, quads, calves. He wants the symmetrical look—not like a lot of iron pumpers who build massive arms larger than their legs, which look atrophied by comparison. Those jokers are not athletes, he scoffs, but engorged lummoxes as inert as the barbells they heft. Some of the dummies use illegal juice to further inflate their muscles; that'll work out just fine in a decade or so, when their testicles shrink to the size of walnuts. Braun is an athlete; he swims, bikes, plays tennis, would never touch a steroid. He's the complete package, and this provides him with a well-harnessed cockiness that projects confidence to the world.

As he yanks opposing pulleys downward from shoulder to waist, he sees a blonde bunny three stations down using the inclined chest press with the undoubted aim of increasing her bust size. She has a tight little body and a hard look that functions as repellent for men who bug her. As she finishes a set, a candle-white guy built like a marshmallow with a severe part in his hair and a three o'clock shadow settles in next to her, smiles pleasantly, and says, "Back to the torture chamber." Instead of ignoring him, which would be bad enough, the bunny fires off an annoyed "What?"

The poor guy lurches into his workout so he can justify his reddening face. Braun does an extra set on the pulleys and waits for the bunny to come into his zone. There's no need for that kind of behavior; she gives women a bad name.

But she is a sexy little thing, no question. Soon enough, she's a machine away from him, on the lats rig, which is interesting because girls usually avoid it. She catches sight of Braun, and he can tell right away that now she has a different impulse. He hovers, stretches; she finishes and looks at him.

"Did you want to get on here?" she asks.

The accent is a long way from Braun's native Milwaukee. He can be either amused or disgusted by the torturous Philly sound. He likes female speech to be as cool and smooth as a lake at dawn, with a few suggestive colors in the flow. Autoshop speech out of a pretty face is like bad breath.

But he gives her a conquering little smile and a polite "No, no, it's all yours, thanks," and walks away, no interest shown, leaving her petulant enough to blister through a second set.

It is exactly one week—168 hours—since the deed, since fate handed Richard Keene a chance for redemption. So he believes.

He is in Lori Calder's apartment for an update. His stark tale about Cindy Dempsey last night was the clincher. She seemed to believe him, to feel for him, and reluctantly agreed to find a way to approach Braun and then keep her ears open. She didn't promise immediate action, but a day later, she has some information, and so he has walked up one flight and checked the hallway before hurrying to her door, though Braun, she has told him, is scheduled to work at the hospital this evening. Richard now regards Lori as his field agent, a slim, petite girl with a sweet smile and short, brown hair coifed and framing her face. She can't weigh much more than a hundred pounds. Something special about her. They sit a comfortable distance apart on her plump, hazel-colored sofa, the vertical blinds partitioning the nighttime skyline.

"Why would he do that if he killed her?"

"It's the smart move," Richard answers. He is speaking softly. "It draws suspicion away from him. She doesn't come home; he reports it. He's doing what he should be doing as a faithful, concerned boyfriend. Right?"

Lori has the kind of face that could never turn ugly in anger, Richard thinks, but right now its sweetness has morphed into the sharp edges of a piqued curiosity.

"Could be. Or it could be he really is a faithful, concerned boyfriend."

Richard stares at a piece of sculpture on the coffee table, a naked couple enmeshed in a full-body cling and kiss. Renaissance classicism. "What a nice miniature," he says.

"Yes, it is."

"Michelangelo?"

"I don't know. I think so." She seems distracted, upset.

"So . . ." He doesn't want to press her. "What'd he say?"

The question helps Lori regain her focus. She looks directly at Richard. "Just that she hasn't called and he's worried."

"Uh-huh." No surprises in that. "Anything else?"

"That's it."

"That's it?"

"I didn't want to be obvious."

"I understand. And he seemed perfectly sincere?"

Lori fingers her ear and a small jade earring. "Yes. He did. As far as I could tell. Remember, Richard, I don't know him all that well."

"But you're a perceptive person."

Her eyes open a tiny bit wider, and the corners of her mouth suggest a smile. "You don't know *me* all that well."

"True."

"Maybe *you're* the one who's perceptive."

Richard wants to appear in command, but as he feels himself drawn closer to Lori, the familiar self-doubts fill up inside of him. Stay with the task at hand. "You'll return the coffee maker tomorrow, the Keurig or whatever it's called?"

A little more of her smile. "Of course. Don't want him thinking I'm a caffeine freak."

"Did he believe that you wanted to borrow it for a little party?"

"Why shouldn't he?"

"I don't want you doing or saying anything you're uncomfortable with," Richard says, "but . . . "

"Yes?"

"Can you find out where she went?"

"He could say anything."

Richard jabs a forefinger and shakes his head. "No, he'll play everything straight. The police, a neighbor's inquiry. Consistent. Get it?"

When she stretches her arms behind her head and massages the back of her neck, the sleeves of her T-shirt climb up her arms to her shoulders. It's an erotic stimulus to Richard. But instead of succumbing to self-doubt, instead of running for cover as he usually does, convinced that the impulse is a false lead, he reaches for her, touches her left arm after she lowers it, and lets his hand rest there.

His touch startles her but not sufficiently that she draws back in any way. She looks at him.

His face is all vulnerability. "Do you believe me?"

Her body language says maybe. "Of course I do. Like I said, I believe that *you* believe."

Richard looks away, taken down a peg.

"Richard, you can't expect me to believe in all of this the way you do. The fact that you're here, that I'm doing what I'm doing, is your answer. I still think that, when you get through all this, you'll see nothing's happened. Things only happen when we're not looking for them; I'm convinced of that."

"You're right about that—I wasn't looking for this."

He furrows his hair with his fingers. He's about to step onto shaky terrain, minefield territory. "Do you have a boyfriend, Lori?" he asks, then follows instantaneously with, "I'm sorry, I—"

"No, that's okay." It's so sweet a smile, most of it showing in the eyes. It overtakes him, and as she says, "No, I don't have a boyfriend," he wonders where this rabbit-hole might deposit him, and he knows he has no choice but to yield to its gravity.

TEN

"I see you're among the living."

It is Kathy's greeting to Richard as he enters the reception area of Rosen & Wallingford after a jangled Wednesday-morning subway ride. He thought he had been coping well with the underground roar and confinement, but he has regressed in the past week. Since that night.

He has been absent from work for several days, and Kathy could not resist trying to act sophisticated, though, of course, she missed the mark. Why can't she just be a pleasant, unassuming twenty-year-old?

He decides to show her the face of true maturity. "Good morning, Kathy. How are you?"

He can tell that his warm tone has puzzled her. Finally, she says, "Okay, I guess."

"That's good . . . I guess," and he smiles at her, not too big, just right. Her skin has cleared. Her appearance has a softness that often clashes with her manner. Guess that's her decision; maybe she'll reverse it someday.

Richard strides into the corridor and heads toward his

workstation in the audiology room. He plans to leave early today for another bout with an MRI tunnel—this time at a different hospital—so his appointments are scheduled to conclude at three o'clock. The first customer of the day is Mrs. Kohler, a not-young woman who makes an arduous effort to transport her bulk into the booth, as if she were grappling with a water heater. She smells like she's been sweating under her flower-print dress, her eighteenth-century perfume insufficient to neutralize the human scent.

"Have you been having any problems hearing, Mrs. Kohler?"

"I don't think so; doctor wants to check it anyway. I had a sinus infection—I think that's the problem."

"What kind of problem?"

"I've been a little dizzy"—she holds her hands to her temples—"and my head still feels like it's filled up with something. You know what I mean?"

Richard nods. "Hmm. Well, let's see how the machinery's working inside those ears." He rigs the audiometer for duty. "This will produce several faint, high-pitched sounds with no particular rhythm. Each time you hear a sound, I want you to raise your right hand. Okay?"

"Yes."

"Are you right-handed?"

"Yes."

"Good. That makes it easier. Of course, you could raise your left hand if you wanted to."

He smiles, and that coaxes a smile from her pinched face. He leads her into the cork-walled booth and helps her fit the earphones comfortably over her dyed brown hair, then returns to the audiometer to adjust the volume and frequency dials. He looks at her through the glass, a nod of reassurance, then looks away so as not to prompt or distract. She is motionless in her seat, eyes saucering behind thick glasses.

He raises a squeal on the audiometer, and she lifts her hand.

He hears a woman whimpering, crying, crying out. Then a rasping from the throat. Fabric tearing. A thump. A chorus of death. Death on film, death in the apartment on the twenty-third floor, paying him a visit, swelling inside his head, unbidden, a riot in his head, the cycle repeating, the order changing, the sounds stinging him like thorns. Richard's thumb and forefinger move on their own, and the audiometer's volume dial does a half revolution. He hears nothing but the sounds of death. He shakes his head to chase the intruders, but they recycle and amp up. He sees a fallen body on the carpet of a twenty-third-floor apartment, a woman's body. He sees a little girl on swings, in a sandbox, hunched over a Chinese checkers board, sheeted on a gurney. He sees a riotous kaleidoscope in front of his eyes as each sound pulses a color, searing red and frozen blue, brown like the raging mud of an engorged river, and it's all spinning like some mad, amusement-park ride careening toward disaster, and . . . a savior in miniature, a gnat or stray eyelash finds its way into his eye, and that eye catches Mrs. Kohler through the glass, her mouth contorted in agony, hands clawing her earphones now askew and stuck in her piled-up hair.

The sounds in Richard's head vanish and their absence shatters his equilibrium—the tester becomes the dizzy patient. He reels in his seat, his mouth agape, his fingers glued to the dial, the unearthly frequencies shooting through poor

Mrs. Kohler, whom he knows he must save before it is too late, for he sees her throes in the booth, can hear—faintly, but he above all people can hear it—her shrieking in the soundproof booth. He wills himself out of his paralysis, sees the scorpion pincers of his right thumb and forefinger on the dial, and immediately spins the volume to zero.

Mrs. Kohler slumps, defeated or worse, her heaviness settling to an undeniable center of gravity. All but unconscious, she slides out of the chair, a mass of collapse, hitting the floor like a sack of flour, and damn if the thump of her landing doesn't give Richard a start and spin him right back into the other unreality. A body fallen to the floor. The twenty-third floor.

He rises shakily and stands right by his chair, as if stepping too far away would leave him untethered and discharged into space. He is sweating like the high school harrier he once was: a full-body sweat after a cross-country race, sweating even through his socks. He would run those distance races on the plateau, with the autumn clouds racing overhead and a river of wind streaming past his ears, its sibilance inaudible to the other runners but a tunnel of sound to him, escorting him through the loneliness, masking the clangor of his heart and lungs.

Mrs. Kohler is examined and tested and peered at and pronounced fit for departure, hearing and all inner organs intact. Dr. Wallingford himself does the workup, then asks Wendy for an immediate report—not on Mrs. Kohler's condition but on R&W's legal exposure. Meanwhile, Richard manages to test two successive patients without incident.

Wendy Klein is the office manager and human resources

person for this busy practice of doctors, nurses, technicians, and secretaries, twenty-two employees in all. As her hands join in a prayerful pose and she leans forward on one of the two-seat sofas in her office, her blonde bangs seem to dig into her forehead like a row of scythes.

"What is it, Richard? Something's wrong here."

He sits opposite on the imitation-leather sofa jammed against a squat, flimsy end table supporting a bulbous lamp. "I'm sorry," he says, which is true enough and about all he can say. Now he props an elbow on a knee and presses a thumb onto the bony ridge between his eyebrows.

"You realize this could become a lawsuit," Wendy says.

Richard drops his hand and looks up in alarm. "She's all right, isn't she? She seemed to be fine once she was revived."

"I think so, but that won't necessarily stop her. She has a pretty good case for trauma."

Richard sits back wearily. "I don't know what happened. I just blanked."

"Well, at least you're not blaming the equipment," says Wendy, rising and circling behind her desk. "But this is a high-profile practice, Richard. You understand that."

He's beginning to.

"You've been missing work—that hasn't happened before. What is it, Richard? What's wrong?"

He presses his fingertips against each other. "I guess I've had some things on my mind."

Wendy's smile suggests that's an understatement. "The doctors don't know right now whether they can afford to give you a second chance."

Richard drops his hands as something washes through

him from his forehead to the pit of his stomach, tingling yet calming, a portent of change. He hears some movement and talk wafting down the hallway: a patient leaving with her husband, perhaps; he's trying to buoy her with "Not too bad, huh?" and she's sounding frail, vulnerable. Yes, Richard can feel that it's time for him to leave this insular world of mechanical sounds and pulses channeled to the human ear, thinned at high frequencies, and piercing the invisible air. Time to work somewhere else, a place of visual stimulation perhaps, an art gallery, a museum, a—

"It's a difficult situation, Richard. You've been a fine employee until now."

He nods three times slowly.

"Take the rest of the day off. We'll have to figure this out."

He rises, moves trancelike to the door, opens it, and waits.

"I'll let you know," she says.

He's halfway over the threshold. "You already have."

An ultrasensitivity to sounds has defined him for as long as he can remember. It was one thing to spook parents and classmates with his ability to hear things they could not but quite another to cringe in literal pain at an airplane's sonic blast passing overhead, a clap of thunder on an awful humid night or just ordinary household sounds like a rapping hammer, a telephone ringing out of the stillness (now living on his own, finally, he has set his telephones on a low pulse), even a thick hardcover slammed shut after a satisfying read.

When Richard's hearing was tested in kindergarten, he scored off the charts, picking up sounds beyond the canine range, but neither the technician nor the specialist could explain his gift (curse?) or remediate its painful effects. Some people simply have exceptional hearing, went the explanation, like others have exceptional eyesight, speed, strength, intelligence, or artistic ability. The inexplicable landscape of the brain. Richard's auditory apparatus seemed normal enough: the eardrum, the cochlear canal, and all of its tiny appendages. They asked if he suffered from intense headaches, migraines, which typically heightened the sensitivity to sound. He did get headaches, but they were not debilitating. His condition was not quite dismissed as something he'd grow out of, but the doctors believed that his acuity would level off as he aged, and they offered the sobering assessment that it might be something he'd have to live with. What they really believed was that he was neurotic.

With no relief from the medical community and limited sympathy at home, Richard dealt with his gift/affliction on his own terms. Which meant, to a great extent, withdrawing into his own world through solo excursions and daily perambulations, alone in a crowd because of what he heard in its midst and beyond. He'd dam up his ears with cotton or plugs when things got too bad, but that could make it worse, trapping his pulsating inner machinery, all its disconcerting beats and flutters dancing in his ear. No wonder he reflexively made funny expressions and people found him strange, confused his wonderment with imbecility, his agitation with hostility. He *was* strange: he was possessor of an unharnessed power, one without apparent utility.

When his parents presented him with a Walkman, for Richard it was penicillin, the Salk vaccine, and Prozac all in one. He could go anywhere, anytime, snuff out much of the unwanted sound track in his vicinity and substitute with his favored jazz sounds or classical strains . . . and be socially acceptable. It was a miracle invention, the Walkman, soon supplanted by the Discman, and then the versatile, far less obtrusive iPod. Funny, these most commercial of products becoming godsends for Richard Keene. They gave him the comfort of conformity.

But they have been of no help in the landscape of his dreams, which have a language and sound track all their own and no manmade technology to parry them. The dreams come, even now, like streamers hurled by the wind, some rippling past at high speed, others clinging like crepe and winding about the neck, intent on strangling. Not every night, but often, and always the same feeling if not the same setting: a little boy trapped in sheets and blankets, or drowning just under the surface of the water, or stuck to the tracks and facing the headlong rush of a train, or enveloped by a man in a powder-blue shirt with long sleeves creased and cuffs stiff as slate, the walls closing in.

A little boy with no release. The dreamer trapped as surely as his younger self.

He had an undistinguished record through high school and two years of community college—he had trouble concentrating, paying attention in class. He liked music because it soothed him. He took piano and guitar lessons but wasn't talented enough to pursue a musical career, and so he drifted from job to job, saving a few dollars while continuing to live at home, by that time a nicer home in the suburbs, one with a more spacious bedroom and no bucking broncos on the walls. He tutored children at the neighborhood Y, made tuna fish hoagies at a deli in a strip mall, forced himself to make calls for a telemarketing firm. When Richard trained with an insurance company to be an auto claims adjustor, the sight of a wreck unnerved him; even a battered fender was disturbing. They moved him to the billing department, and there he labored in white-shirted anonymity among the computer-generated invoices, becoming adept at on-screen navigation and mindless processing. He tried to strike a truce with life and with the past by earning wages, handling chores at home, avoiding crowds and noise and unpleasant circumstances. But the past would not be filed away. It returned with increased ferocity, like a hurricane that has idled and gathered strength. Sounds of horror, a little boy immured beneath blankets, the powder-blue long sleeves in his face, the questions jabbing him like little knives, circling him, returning to the same place, that same question of questions. Was he ever there at night? Was he there *that* night? Wasn't he, in fact, there that night, this strange boy who insists that he was in bed and underneath the blankets in his own bedroom?

There was no leashing the past. Still, he tried to slip by it and stay a step ahead. Survival tactics. But then one night the full-length mirror hanging on his bedroom door drew him back as if by magnetism to the awful, reflected reality he had avoided for years. And he looked himself up and down and stared at his face, his brown eyes darker than he remembered, the black pupils swelling like oil slicks. The dormant dread flared: he was an unhinged soul. Who am I, what am I, why this face and form, what if there were no people, no world, no universe, nothing? And the edges of his vision blurred red, and he thought his forehead was vibrating, and a stranger stared back at him from the mirror.

Marty and Evelyn rushed into his room when they heard the screaming. Richard heard nothing. When his parents thrust the bedroom door open, banging the mirror into his nose, he backpedaled to his bed and got under the covers. There he lay awake all night, fully clothed.

His next bedroom was one without mirrors.

The idea of being an audiometric technician had hit him the day he came home from the treatment center, and he was proud and rather relieved that he was thinking in such pragmatic terms. He knew that his special auditory capability was no real asset in this regard—technology did all the work—but the psychological appeal for him was to confront the demon on its home field, a kind of auditory proving ground. And he could offer empathy and counsel to those suffering auditory discomfort, be it sensitivity, deficit, distortion, or otherwise. So he logged the twenty hours necessary for certification and got the job at Rosen & Wallingford. More than a year later, he finally mustered the energy and courage—at the psychologist's urging, and with his parents' financial assistance—to leave home and get his own place, placing him in the big city and much closer to his job.

And now that job is gone.

Wendy calls him at one o'clock. Two weeks' severance is already in the mail.

But when Richard takes the call, he is not thinking

about his job at Rosen & Wallingford at all. His thoughts are on the *case*.

Now he can concentrate on the case. Full time.

Eight days since the murder. No doubt in his mind there was, in fact, a murder. But what he regards as evidence so far would satisfy only him. He must now move to the second stage and identify the pieces of the mosaic. For the first time, he ponders motive. A lovers' quarrel turned violent then deadly, or something more sinister, something planned?

He feels certain that it was planned, premeditated. That it is no coincidence the sounds were masked by the movie scene, but the result of meticulous timing. No, he will not be thrown off the trail—not this time. The matter of motive isn't his concern, really; he's not the prosecutor. But he is curious, naturally, and suggesting a plausible motive might help prod the police. For he will have to enlist the police eventually; he knows that.

He wonders if there's a financial motive. Braun and the transaction at the bank—was it legit?

What became of the body?

An intriguing question. What do you do with a dead body in a high-rise, when you must conceal its disposal?

Medical residents have resources.

He needs more from Lori. He's relying on her—she's his confederate. He hopes she may be something more than that. When she told him she didn't have a boyfriend, she seemed to be opening a door. They looked at each other in silence for a moment. Then back to business.

Business has brought them together. Right now, Richard has some other business: a 4:00 p.m. appointment for another go at an MRI, this one at a site closer to home and, as ordered, in an open machine. His knee remains sore, and it sometimes buckles at high speeds on the treadmill. Something's wrong somewhere.

You lose your job, but the world doesn't stand still, he reminds himself. No reason to sit home and mope. To the contrary, losing the job will be a godsend. Perfect timing.

As he walks to Metropolitan Hospital on Ninth Street, Richard wonders if his path will cross Braun's. This is Braun's turf after all; Lori told him that.

It's a big hospital; chances are slim. Besides, Braun has nothing on him—it's the other way around.

But maybe Braun peered through the peephole and saw him at the door that night—not just later at the elevator. That possibility gnaws at Richard. During this short trip to the hospital, he glances behind him several times to make sure that Braun is not following . . . and to make sure that no one else is following.

He checks in at Diagnostics, then sits in the waiting room with a dozen other patients and a batch of dog-eared magazines. After twenty minutes spent reading two paragraphs of an old *Newsweek* article about unmanned space flights and eavesdropping on snatches of conversation throughout the room, he hears his name called. A plump, pleasant nurse leads him to the interior, mystical chambers. He follows her into the scan room with its MRI apparatus, which reminds him of cold storage, cryogenics but without the frozen steam. Then he thinks of mailing tubes dropped down the postal chute at the building that housed his old job at the insurance company, the same kind of tubes you send winging from your car window to the drive-in teller at the bank, suburban style. Evelyn used to send him on such errands.

This chamber doesn't look any bigger than the last. He takes it calmly.

"I had some trouble the last time I went for an MRI," he says.

"Really?"

"Yes."

The nurse looks at him and tries to move from pleasant to compassionate, but makes it only halfway. "You get uncomfortable?"

"Yes, very. This looks like the same kind of unit I had at Logan. I was supposed to have the open type this time."

"We're getting one in very soon," she says, "but it hasn't arrived yet; I'm sorry. I know we're getting more requests for that these days. But give this one a try. We can do some things so that you don't feel like a sardine."

Nice imagery. Richard casts a wary eye at the tube.

"We have these special glasses that enable you to see behind you and into the room as you're lying down so you don't feel like you're trapped in there, kind of like an optical illusion," she says, handing him a pair. "And we pump in soothing music to relax you. Plus, I'll give you a buzzer to hold in your hand. If at any time you feel panicked, just squeeze it and we'll hear it in the control room, where the technician will be receiving your scan on the computer. That's right over there." She points to a glass-enclosed booth, where a young, sympathetic-looking woman waves from behind a computer screen. "How's that sound?"

So the tables are turned: He's the one under observation,

rather than the detached technician at the controls. Turnabout is fair play. Richard figures he has to try. "Okay, I guess."

"Oh, you'll be fine; you'll see."

But as soon as he climbs in and lies on his back, he starts to sweat and shuts his eyes. "Try the glasses," the nurse says, and he fits them on. They have no optical lens but twin mirrors reflecting the room behind him, wavy, mildly distorted. She gives him a headset to place over his skull and onto his ears, then clamps some sort of coil around his knee. "That landmarks the area we want to focus on," he hears her say through the headset, surf-like sounds already filtering in. He goes with it, tries to visualize the suggested scene, the seashore with a big, blue, restful sky festooned with wisps of cloud, a broad beach stirred by ocean breezes, and the ocean itself stretching in great, sunlit ribbons toward the endless horizon.

She slaps the plastic buzzer in his hand—"Give me a ring if you need to"—and she's gone. He doesn't like the mirrored glasses, so he closes his eyes again and he's at Playtown Park in the Philly suburbs, and Cindy is next to him in the two-seat compartment of the kids' Ferris wheel as it loops skyward in a lazy arc, the open compartments dangling, the ground retreating beneath them. Evelyn and Marty watch from below, and Cindy's mother is there, but not Herb Dempsey; he's nowhere in sight. Cindy and Richard sit side by side, and when they reach the apex of the wheel, the motion torques their bodies so that their arms press against one another, and they look at each other and smile. He can feel her smooth skin. It is a magic moment, but now it's gone in a blink because Richard can't hold onto it, can't keep his eyes shut as he slides into the doom of the narrow tube.

He looks above the glasses, and the metal enclosure is

right on him, as if it would crush down through his nose. The apparatus hums and spits ominous knocking noises like a sick car motor, the magnetic fields dancing, and Richard hears them cut right through the tepid white noise in his headset. Now additional sounds, *the cycle of murder sounds*, join them like an orchestral duo, and he can hear it all distinctly, a world-class conductor who hears every note in the recesses of the stage. He has to urinate. He rolls his shoulders, and the glasses slip across the bridge of his nose. He realizes that, once again, he is not going to make it despite all the accessories. He must get out. He thumbs the buzzer. Hears nothing, figures it doesn't make noise but triggers an emergency light or shows up on the computer screen in the control booth. But there is no response. He presses again, hard, and waits for rescue, time suspended.

He pounds a fist against the side and roof of the cylinder's cold metal, short incessant blows, for that is all the space allows. He pounds as hard and fast as he can, bloodying his knuckles within seconds. He shouts in a voice not quite his own, and the shouting becomes screaming, the effort spraying mucus and saliva onto the metal as if a sudden rain has fallen. He tears off the mirrored glasses and the headset still releasing futile white noise.

Finally, the nurse is there, fetching the tube from its tunnel.

"Oh my God," she says. "Oh my God, I'm so sorry. What happened to the buzzer? Did you press the buzzer?"

As if oxygen has just now reached his brain, Richard bolts up like a reflexed cadaver and spurts out of the contraption. "You're bleeding," the nurse tells him, and he looks down at his bloody hand, aware of its condition for the first time.

ELEVEN

The hell with it, Richard thinks as he walks down Locust Street, his right hand bandaged. If they can't figure out what's wrong with the knee without a damn MRI, then he'll just live with it; that's all. What did they do before MRIs?

His iPod taps into iTunes Radio to play Motown, songs that impress him with their energy and musicality; he understands why this music had such an impact. A passing man wears enough cologne to counteract the fumes emanating from a garbage truck loading up in the alley at midblock between Eleventh and Twelfth. "Nowhere to run, nowhere to hide," sings Martha Reeves and the Vandellas to a driving beat that quickens the walk.

At the 42s, Richard enters the building's adjacent nine-story parking garage. His '98 Toyota is parked in space five on level G, he remembers, secure in the knowledge that he has the vital information written down on a scrap of paper in his wallet, a necessary step since the disabled car has sat there for two weeks already, and locating a parked automobile when you have forgotten its precise location can be a maddening experience in a facility like this, replete with pillars and transverse ramps and levels that replicate each other right down to the puddles.

He approaches the shed where Jay presides over incoming and outgoing traffic. Richard likes the ever-smiling Indonesian, wiry with warm brown eyes and an omnipresent blue baseball cap. In fact, he likes him more than anyone else he has met in the city. Jay's a smart guy. He's about halfway home with the English language and is taking a course to improve his skills. He is determined to go to college. Richard admires that.

Since Richard doesn't use his car that often—and hasn't at all in the last two weeks—he doesn't see a great deal of Jay, but they've developed a rapport based on just a few meetings. For one thing, they know each other's name. Richard is among the few tenants who address Jay by his first name, and they speak about more than just the monthly parking fee.

"What happened to hand?" Jay sees the bandage wrapped around Richard's knuckles, as if the right hand belongs to a boxer getting ready to lace up the gloves.

Richard glances at his hand. "Ah, little accident. Put it through a window—didn't even see it. I should get my eyesight checked, huh?"

Jay looks concerned. "Everything okay?"

"Thanks, everything's fine. Jay . . . let me ask you something; you might be able to help me."

Jay nods and his eyes tell that he'd be happy to help Richard, and he trusts that, if he did, Richard would not put him at risk.

"There's a woman who lives here by the name of Eleanor

Carson—apartment 2307," Richard continues. "Can you tell me if she's a monthly?" He points to the smooth, copper-colored cement at his feet, meaning to indicate the garage itself.

Jay broadens his smile. "Mr. Richard," he says. "Is she pretty?" He reaches out and brushes Richard's sleeve in a friendly way.

Richard returns the smile but turns serious again. "I don't know; I've never seen her. At least I don't think I have."

Jay looks puzzled by Richard's inquiry. He pays attention to rules and regulations, but he's inclined to help his friend. Sensing uneasiness, Richard gives Jay an earnest "It's important," and Jay grabs a PDA from a shelf in the shed. "How spell?"

Richard spells both the first and last names, and Jay punches in the letters.

"Here she is. Eleanor Carson. Nissan Altima. You need license plate?"

Richard smiles, wishes for a moment he were a state trooper so he could run the plate, but what would that get him anyway? He already knows where she lives. *Lived.*

"No, thanks, not now . . . I have one more for you."

Jay has tapped out a four-digit number on the PDA. "Her car's still here."

"Eleanor's?"

"Eleanor Carson." Jay points at the little screen. "It tells me who's here and who's not."

"Very efficient," says Richard, recalling that the magnetic strip on his seldom-used key card raises the gate both ways. "How about Davis Braun, Jay? Does he have a car here? B, R, A, U, N."

"I know that guy," says Jay. "Nice guy. He went out this

morning. Not back yet." He pecks at the PDA.

"A, C, U, R, A."

"Acura."

"Yeah, Acura."

"That's Mr. Braun's car, huh?"

"Yes, that's his."

"Thanks, Jay."

"You're welcome," Jay answers, and his grin shows pride in his work and once again suggests that he trusts Richard. Still, he asks, "Why you need?"

"They're neighbors of mine, and I haven't seen either in a while," Richard explains. "I was getting worried. Glad you saw Davis today." He gives Jay an appreciative tap on the shoulder. "Don't tell him I was asking; he might think I'm being nosy or something."

"Silver Spring, huh?"

Richard and Lori sit on the sofa in Lori's apartment, closer to each other than the last time. Home from work, Lori wears shorts and sits in a yoga position, folded legs pressing calf muscles into prominence. She winced when she saw his hand and heard about his MRI escapade. Richard liked that, figures she's concerned. For real.

"That's what he said," Lori reports. "She was going back to visit her father for a few days."

"Of course, she never arrived."

"He didn't say that."

"He made sure to call there when she didn't return, and the phone records reflect that." Richard is climbing into the criminal's mind, building his case with hypotheticals that he is sure have happened. As he explains, he looks directly into Lori's alert, brown eyes. "By the way, her car is still in the garage; I checked with Jay."

"Who's Jay?"

"The guy at the shed, you know, when you drive in."

"How's he know?"

"He can keep track by computer."

Lori does not seem impressed. "So, she probably went by train and took a cab to the station."

A small smile from Richard. "I bet you none of the dispatchers will have it in their logs."

Lori holds out her arms, palms up, playing devil's advocate. "If that's the case, maybe their records are sloppy." Her eyes open wider. "Or maybe Davis drove her to the station."

"No way—too many things to connect," says Richard. "Did Frank see them walk out? Did Jay see them come to the garage and then Braun return by himself? No, he won't say he drove her. Because, of course, he *didn't* drive her."

"There'd be a credit card payment for the tickets."

"Amtrak?"

"Yup."

"She paid cash."

"Eleanor wouldn't pay cash."

"I thought you didn't know her that well."

"Just an impression—call it woman's intuition."

"What I'm saying is that he suggests to the police that she paid cash. She didn't pay anything, Lori—I'm telling you she never got to the station." Richard rocks on the sofa, inhabiting a murderer's mind, breaking it down cleanly for his listener. "See, she really *was* going to take a vacation. Just like she told you."

"Okay . . ."

"And the law firm had her scheduled for one. Probably was going to see her father, like he says."

"So you're saying he killed her before she could leave, and he planned to do that all along."

"Exactly."

"But I saw her coming off the elevator with a suitcase. She was leaving."

"Are you sure about the suitcase?"

"I told you that before."

"You could be associating it with her vacation. She told you about that, right?"

"Yes, but I saw a suitcase; I remember that."

"Maybe she wasn't leaving just then, just loading the car."

Lori makes a face. "You go to your car in the garage, you're usually ready to go right then and there. She'd have combined or left stuff behind to avoid making two trips.

"Maybe they had an argument, and he refused to help her with a second suitcase."

"Hey, the suitcase would still be in her car, right?"

Richard leans forward, his angular face all sharp planes. "Yes, and that's something to run by the police."

Lori shifts her folded legs on the couch cushion. "But why? Why would he kill her? You need a motive, Sherlock."

There's some chemistry here, Richard is thinking, but he doesn't want this dissolving into a parlor game; the stakes are too high. "You knew them. Any ideas?"

Lori unfolds her legs and stands. Richard takes her in.

She's slim, but there's a nice curve to those legs, and also at the waist and shoulders. "They're like an All-American couple," she says.

"Appearances can be deceiving," Richard says.

"I never heard any shouting, you know, through the walls. Not just that night but any night."

"Slow burn."

"Never a mark on her face when I saw her."

"Uh-huh."

She clasps Richard's hand with both of hers, startling him with a pleasant sensation. "I still think you're wrong about him. Doesn't it occur to you that you could be wrong?"

"Did they have reason to be jealous of each other?"

"What do you mean?"

"Seeing other people, one-night stands—"

"No," Lori says emphatically. She lets go of him and sits. Richard smiles. "You knew them better than you think."

"They just seemed faithful. The way they acted when I saw them together."

"Appearances can be—"

"Yeah, I know, *deceiving*."

"Do you know her father's first name?"

"No."

Richard nods; he didn't expect that she did. "I'll find it. Silver Spring, Maryland, right?"

"Unless he was lying."

"No, why should he? She left for vacation. He reported her missing. That's all he knows."

Lori has a faraway look in her eyes.

"What's the matter?" Richard asks.

She smiles, as if to soften the blow. "Just that you seem so obsessed with this; it's almost as if—"

"As if *what*? As if I was the one who—"

"I didn't say that."

Richard turns away.

"All right, Richard, tell me this. How did he get rid of the body?"

"What do you think?"

"I don't want to think. This is your show."

"He's a medical student, isn't he?"

"Yes."

"Maybe he's creative."

Sunlight at dusk is a golden hue that clings to the Thermopane of the tall buildings and bathes the streets below. Richard walks past the shops on Walnut, turning his head to glimpse his reflection in the windows. At the novelty store Accents, a little snow globe nestled in straw catches his attention. It is a winter scene, a young girl and boy outfitted for the weather, the snow just waiting to be shaken through the miniature, aqueous wonderland. And now he is looking beyond the scene and the store and into a dimension that exists only for him.

There's Cindy in her bright red scarf with matching earmuffs, she and Richard planted on a sturdy sled tugged down snow-banked Airdale Road by a dogged Marty, who grips a healthy length of rope attached to the sled's iron grill. The two kids can't be more than five years old, little people on a glorious ride down the middle of the street, residual snow packed densely on the road surface, polar hillsides plowed against cars sitting silent on a Saturday morning. The agreeably cold air stings their cheeks as they shield their eyes from the sun flaring off of Marty's shoulders as he trudges forward. Cindy's light-brown hair is like silk strands playing about her earmuffs. Up and down the street they're pulled, two round trips, corner to corner, sweet-tempered Marty at the reins. When they pass in front of their row houses, Richard is the only one to see Herb Dempsey hovering behind his storm door, glowering into the morning. Marty concentrates on the roadway, and Cindy purposely looks toward the opposite side of the street.

With a shudder, Richard turns away from the store window and resumes his march down Walnut Street to Rittenhouse Square. A few people slump on benches; fresh from a fashion excursion, a young woman totes a cream-colored shopping bag with black handles. Richard imagines Lori as such a woman on such an excursion, and the image fits.

He does his best thinking when he is in motion. The iPod sends a Debussy nocturne to his ears. He has a phone call to make when he returns home and, on the way back, he will script in his mind two scenarios for the exchange—one congenial and useful, and the other abrasive and futile. Before that, however, he notices the Free Library's small branch across the street from the west side of the square and figures, while he's here, why not check the telephone directories just in case he strikes out later online? Through the turnstile and just past the reference desk is a shelf full of the old yellow directories. Relics but still on hand. In the Maryland section, Richard locates a book marked "Bethesda, Chevy Chase, and Silver Spring." Lots of Carsons in there. He finds a dime in his pocket and photocopies the page, the directory's bulk raising the lid like a lift bridge, the machine's oppressive light forcing him to look away. He takes a tiny pencil from a jar at the librarian's desk and jots down the Silver Spring prefix.

Across Nineteenth Street to Locust and heading home, Richard reaches one of the open-air bistros facing the square. Alfresco diners sit at small pedestal tables below a burgundy awning. Inside, at the bar, the happy-hour crowd gets happy. To one side, a man peers outside from the shadows, drink in hand. As Richard approaches, he can see that the man is looking at him. The face is familiar.

Richard quickly translates the recognition. It is the young guy he twice spotted trailing him on city streets, Davis Braun well in front of both of them. Lean, midtwenties, a probable resident of the 42s. This time, as their gazes meet, Richard studies the angular face, its probing eyes and prominent bone structure and thick, unruly hair—a better-looking version of himself.

As the sharp-featured young man retreats farther inside, Richard considers bypassing him and continuing home on Locust Street, but without breaking stride, he walks past the outdoor tables, under the awning, and into the restaurant. He removes his earbuds and stuffs them into his pocket.

But the one he wants to see has vanished. Richard walks past the bar, circles the interior tables, and pokes his head into the adjacent vestibule, which offers the only entrance when it's cold and the patio is closed. No sign of him. Richard shakes his head as if to say to some future questioner, "No, I did not *imagine* him."

He leaves the restaurant and jogs home, a test that

produces no knee discomfort. Mike is at the front desk; Frank's backup is not too bright but pleasant enough. Richard hurries past him with a hand raised in greeting and a quick "Hi, Mike" as he speeds toward the elevator.

His apartment is backlit by the city's fluorescence. The tensor lamp on the bedroom desk is a spotlight. He prints a sheet of phone numbers from the online locater service and matches against his directory list. He has, at most, eleven Carsons to contact in Silver Spring.

The digital clock says 8:16—prime time for evening phone work.

"Mrs. Carson?"

"Yes?"

"Do you have a daughter named Eleanor?"

"No, I don't. Who is this?"

"Sorry to bother you. I must have the wrong number."

The forefinger and thumb of his bandaged hand pinches a pen, and he lines out *Albert Carson*. City lights peek through the open slats of the microblinds and mingle with the desk lamp's harshness.

"Is this the Carson residence?"

"Yes, it is." Another woman who sounds about the right age.

"I'm trying to reach Eleanor Carson."

"There's no Eleanor Carson here."

"Do you have a daughter named Eleanor?"

"No, I do not."

"Sorry to bother you."

The next two calls produce recorded voices. They sound too young, but he can't be sure, nor does he know what combination of people may be living in the household. He

149

decides not to leave messages.

A fifth call, a man, contentious at the sound of a strange voice. "Yeah?"

Richard tries a different approach, just for the hell of it. "Mr. Carson, my name's Richard Keene. I'm a neighbor of your daughter Eleanor in Philadelphia."

"Well, she's not here."

"She's not?"

"That's what I said."

"I'm sorry. I was told she was visiting you."

"You were told wrong."

"I see. Uh, we live in the same building; I have some important information for her."

"Who the hell are you?"

"Just a neighbor, a friend. Actually, she told me she was coming down to visit you."

Carson eases his tone a bit. "Yeah, she was, but she never showed up."

"Really? Did she call or—?"

"Listen, buddy, tell me what it is you want and if she ever gets here, I'll tell her, okay? Or better yet, tell her boyfriend. You know him?"

"I do."

"Good. Get the message to him." Hangs up.

Richard holds the phone to his ear for a few seconds and listens to the dial tone. "Daddy's little girl," he says to himself.

Cars slash by on Kennedy Boulevard, their beams like broadsides into the night. Richard is on the move again. He waits at the traffic light for the walk signal to flash on Twentieth

Street, canyoned below broad, towering apartment buildings where soft lighting watches over mezzanine-level shops. He moves quickly on the sidewalk, hugging the buildings' granite bases, skirting shadows, veering street-side for a better vantage point when alleys interrupt the pathway, just in case someone or something is lurking. He glances behind intermittently to see if he's being followed. At The Brasserie, a self-consciously hip hangout that boasts the town's widest selection of brews, a couple sit at a two-seat circular table just inside the window, the girl twirling a swizzle stick in her drink and looking up with adoring eyes, the guy with a sleepily smug expression.

Near the Benjamin Franklin Parkway, red-jacketed valets at the Four Seasons Hotel scurry to collect luxury sedans as a fountain spurts over the gray, raised-brick driveway that aprons the entrance. Richard waits for the light, then jogs across the Parkway with its numerous lanes and broad medians. He's retracing his steps from the previous day. The time has come for phase two.

From the outside, the police station looks like an ordinary office with a few people working late, several windows lit. Inside, the desk sergeant sends Richard upstairs to see Lieutenant Robert Oliver. At the top of a ladder that rises a good twenty feet from the base of a stairwell, a wizened handyman attempts to remove the glass globe of a ceiling light fixture; a replacement lightbulb is tucked into the pocket of his overalls. The ladder is unsteady and so is the man who somehow scaled it. After one sway too many, he decides he's had enough. Richard watches as the handyman slowly descends the ladder, the mission having failed.

"No luck, huh?" Richard asks him.

"They got me workin' nights, and I'm kinda shaky these days," the man says. "And that thing up there's a sonofabitch."

"Can I give it a try?"

The man looks at him. "Don't know if the union's got you covered, but go ahead. I don't mind." He hands Richard the bulb.

Richard climbs the ladder, his imitation Reebok sneakers grabbing the rungs, his excellent balance charting the course. Up top, he manages to make the switch and restore the fixture with a minimum of quaking. The handyman and the desk sergeant watch in semiwonderment.

"I got me an assistant," the handyman calls out as Richard makes his way back to ground level.

"Only for today," Richard says when he touches down. He grins as he heads upward once again, this time via the stairs.

On the second level, Richard pads along the tiled corridor. Oliver's office is deserted except for the lieutenant himself standing near the threshold. He's a big man with a round midsection that pushes his belt buckle south. His hound-dog eyes and cheeks betray a weariness that makes it difficult to assess whether he'll tilt toward friendly or nasty when pressed. Richard faces him on the other side of the door. Oliver has him by four, five inches.

"You wanted to see me?" Oliver asks. He notices Richard's bandaged hand.

Richard, his arms crossed at his chest, knows the name and the clipped voice after yesterday's brief telephone conversation at the outdoor kiosk. Same man working both shifts—a good omen. There is no need for Richard to disguise his voice now. "Missing Persons, right?"

Oliver nods. "And assorted other victims. What can I do for you?"

"You had a missing person reported yesterday named Eleanor Carson."

Oliver looks dead at Richard with gray eyes. "Carson . . . Yeah, that's right."

"I have some information that might help."

"Who are you?"

"My name is Richard Keene. I'm a neighbor of hers."

"Neighbor?"

"We live in the same building, one floor apart."

Oliver scratches his considerable ear. "At the 42s on Locust Street, right?"

"Yes."

"She's got a lot of neighbors."

"True."

"Okay, Mr. Keene, whadiya have?"

"She was supposed to be on vacation visiting her father in Maryland, but he says she hasn't been there at all."

"We know that; we've already talked to him."

Richard has figured as much, has counted on Braun to supply all information excluding the fact that he murdered her. He nods at Oliver, one investigator acknowledging another.

"How'd you find this out?" Oliver asks.

"I called Mr. Carson, too."

A smile from Oliver. "You investigatin' the case, son?"

Richard reflexively stares at his shoe tops.

"Better let us handle it," Oliver says.

"How do . . . you handle it?"

Now Oliver's smile is condescending. "We have an

NCIC check out on Miss Carson, so if we get any hits, we follow up."

"What's that?"

"National Crime Information Center. Central database makes a sweep of the country."

Richard wants to act as if this is not new information to him. "Right."

"If she surfaces and law enforcement spots her, we'll be notified."

"How about if she doesn't surface?"

Oliver's smile is not intended to convey warmth. "Well, then, I suppose we'll need a lead or two."

Richard looks right at him. "I think you should broaden your investigation." Matter-of-fact, no dramatics.

Oliver leans into the doorjamb. "What would you suggest, young man?"

He is being patronized—Richard feels it—but it's not the neck-burning variety, just routine. Accordingly, he has nothing smart-alecky in his voice when he answers, "Investigate her boyfriend."

Oliver backs away from the door as he says, "Thanks for the tip."

Richard stops him with an earnest, "Lieutenant Oliver, I know who did it. She was murdered and I know who did it."

Oliver angles his bulk back into full view. "Say again?"

"Eleanor Carson was murdered, Lieutenant, or at least somebody was, yesterday a week ago in apartment 2307 at the 42s building at Fifteenth and Locust."

Richard's faint trembling subsides. Something he had to spill out. The peace, of course, will not last long.

"What happened to your hand?" Oliver asks.

"Banged it against some metal," Richard says, with no hesitation. "Nothing to do with this."

"Glad to hear that," Oliver says wryly; then something changes in his droopy eyes, the suggestion of patience.

"Tell me about it," he says, waving smaller, wiry Richard into the office. Richard sits down opposite Oliver at a gray metal desk whose rubberized top lips the sides. Oliver thuds the desk with the heel of his large hand. "Shoot."

Richard tells his story as precisely as he can, which is to say, with command of all details and no omissions. About the Eleanor Carson case, that is—nothing about Cindy Dempsey. This isn't the time to go into that.

Oliver jots a few notes, leans back, and folds his arms. "Helluva story, son. Tell you what, we'll follow up on that fellow's bank visit. If there's anything irregular, I'll get back to you. How's that?"

Tell the truth, not so hot. Richard keeps still and silent.

"By the way, where's the body?" Oliver asks.

Richard looks at him, not knowing whether to smile or look serious. "I don't know," he says. "But I'll find out."

Oliver's wide face relaxes into a tired smile. "Keep me posted."

He leans forward. The tilt of his head and shifted eyebrows announce that the interview is over.

Richard moves furtively through the night and back home to the 42s. He's feeling good about himself, proud that he has taken the initiative. His investigation is indeed entering a new phase. He needs to show what might have become of the body, as a prelude to determining what did become of

155

the body. It's up to him to develop the hypothesis—nobody else seems to be working on one.

Eight days have passed since the moment, more than enough time to dispose of a body when no eyes are on the murderer and no one else is pressing to know of the missing person's whereabouts.

Braun is a med student and, as such, has access to special resources. Maybe he sneaks the body into the morgue, then on to a crematorium before anyone knows who she is or what's happening.

No, impossible, too many people in the process. Too great a chance for discovery.

He dumps it in the river. Crude but effective. A possibility.

Whatever the final destination, the challenge of removing the body from the high-rise is the first task. Twenty-three floors up.

When Richard opens the sliding glass door and steps onto his balcony, the city's night sounds hit him like a dam break. The building directly across Locust is fourteen or fifteen stories tall, he guesses, and its rooftop compressor below him hisses into the night. He hooks his hands around the top of the metal railing, leans forward, and stares between buildings to Walnut Street, a block north, now glazed by drizzle. A rude car horn seems to leap up the curtain of mist and smack him in the face.

He looks left toward an office building and squints in the effort to pick up any movement in the dim light behind the immovable windows, something as prosaic as a cleaning cart being pushed between cubicles or as prurient as a coupling on top of a desk. All he sees, though, are shadows and barriers and the still life of computers and swivel chairs.

In the hallway outside Richard's apartment, the large bulbs in the light fixtures mounted to the wall buzz like a hive of hornets. Richard stands before the elevators, hands on hips, as if daring the closed doors to spring open and toss him answers. He moves to the end of the hallway and to the door to the stairs. Wire grids the thick glass of the small square window at eye level. Inside, Richard stands on the landing and peers over the railing, downward at the alternately angled flights of stairs that continue beyond his field of vision. It is a long way down to lug a body. But a body in, say, a tall rectangular box (for a floor lamp? a barbell?) could ride smartly down the elevator and then be carted on wheels to a waiting car in the parking garage. A one-man job.

Or a body sectioned in two could make the trip in a pair of large suitcases. Gruesome, the stuff of tabloid front pages and slasher movies, but possible. *Feasible* is another matter, the noise of sawing off body parts, the mess, the time and effort, the potential for being found out by visitors or nosy neighbors.

But that lamp box . . . maybe.

The next problem becomes disposal—disposal that precludes discovery.

Richard returns to the corridor and sees the door to the trash room tucked into an alcove near the elevators. He enters and shuts the door gently behind him. A mild scent of spoil and cinders climbs through his nose and plops onto his tongue. Flattened cardboard and stacked newspapers adorn the wall, opposite a fleet of battleship-gray circuit-breaker boxes and a tangle of cable lines. A metal flap fronts the trash chute embedded in the wall. Richard tugs it open and looks into the blackness, the garbage scent rising from the depths. He lets go of the flap and it snaps shut. He stands there, staring at it, then opens it again. He has jammed some fat trash bags down there; he knows that much.

He sniffs the air, opens the flap again halfway, lets it spring shut.

At the kitchen phone in his apartment, he calls Lori. Tucked under the cabinetry, the soft counter lighting gives the room a soothing, relaxed glow. It is almost ten o'clock.

"Hello?" He loves the smooth, gentle sound of her voice.

"Lori, it's Richard."

"Hi. How's your hand?"

"Fine, it's okay. Listen . . . How about he brought her down in some kind of tall cardboard box, like for curtain rods or something?"

"And then?"

Richard smiles. They're thinking alike. "And then he obviously dumps it somewhere."

"Where?"

"I don't know . . . in the river," Richard says, just making conversation now.

"Hmm . . . awkward. There's a good chance someone would notice, even at 3:00 a.m. He'd be smarter than that, wouldn't he? How 'bout slice and dice?"

Richard cringes in fun, as if she were in the room with him. "Lori, please. Did you really say that?"

"Sorry."

Richard nervously rubs his nose with a forefinger. He warms

to this notion. "Who knows? With surgical instruments . . ."

"Or a good hacksaw."

He wonders if she's putting him on. "You kill me, Lori."

"He doesn't seem like the type."

"What type?"

"A hacker."

"You don't always get what you expect."

"True. Life's full of surprises."

"Exactly."

There's a charged silence between them, delicious to Richard.

"So, Inspector?" she asks.

"Well, whole or not, he needs a way to ship it out of there."

"USPS?"

He can't help but laugh. "Very funny . . . How about this—down the trash chute."

"The trash chute? Come on, too skinny."

"I don't think so; it looks wide enough for, say, a slender woman. You could fit down there, God forbid. Was Ellie slender?"

"I guess you could say that."

"Then down the chute, into the Dumpster, and off to the landfill. No one's the wiser."

"Wrapped in something."

"Nice and tight. Right down into the pile. Stays overnight or he makes the drop early the next morning, timed for pickup. He could have orchestrated the whole thing with that timing in mind."

". . . Richard?"

"Yuh?"

"This is getting scary." She doesn't sound like she's kidding around now.

"It was scarier for Eleanor Carson."

Richard is in the elevator and his senses are on high alert, every fiber taut and pointing him toward the center of this matter. He can feel how attracted he is to Lori, and another part of his brain worries that this will impede his work. He can't let that happen, must control his feelings.

That has never been his strong suit.

He approaches Frank, who is apparently working the overnight shift. Frank stands there by himself, watching Richard step off the elevator and walk toward him. Frank sees the bandaged hand and shakes his head. "Here comes trouble," he says, but the way he says it, it sounds as if he no longer thinks Richard is all that troublesome.

Richard is direct but with none of the uptight mannerisms of earlier go-rounds, his voice relaxed.

"Where's Mike?"

"Had to go. Am *I* good enough for you?"

"Frank, you know this building pretty well, right?"

"Been here six years."

"Structurally?"

Frank settles in; the 42s is his joint. "Well, I'm no engineer, but try me."

"When you drop something down the trash chute, does it go all the way down?" Richard moves his raised right arm down like a lever and points to the floor to underscore his question.

"Straight to the Dumpster," Frank says.

"In one shot?"

"One shot."

"That's what I thought—from no matter where you are."

"No matter where. Same thing, every floor."

"Straight down."

"Straight down." Frank enjoys being the answer man.

"Thanks, Frank."

"Anytime, my man. You think you got somethin' stuck in there?"

"No."

"Good . . . Hey, what happened to your hand?"

"Ah, nothin'."

"You takin' up karate or somethin'?"

"Not yet." Richard chuckles, not because the banter is witty but because he feels good about being one of the guys. He gives Frank a parting smile and walks to the elevator.

Just as he's about to press the button, Richard whirls on his heels like a soldier doing an about-face and marches back to the front desk. "You didn't by any chance see Davis Braun carrying out anything large and bulky in the past week?"

Frank folds his arms. "Now there you go and ruin things, just when we were gettin' to be buddies."

"Can't help it."

"You mean like a body or somethin'? No, he didn't parade nothin' past me."

Richard taps the counter twice and smiles. "That's good news."

Frank snickers. "Yeah, I'd say so. You're an odd duck, Keene—have I told you that?"

TWELVE

Richard figures that Frank knows his business, but just the same, he must test the assertion about the trash chute. He opens the bifold door to his bedroom closet and retrieves a shopping bag embossed with the words *Worthington's Sporting Goods*, the shop on Chestnut where he picked up some socks and gym shorts a couple of weeks back. He dumps his kitchen trash can's contents into the bag, empty tuna and sardine tins and moldering banana peels and crumpled tissues cascading from the plastic liner to a new home. Then he pulls the bag's drawstring tight and ties it into a bowline knot, carries the bag out of his apartment and into the trash room, where he promptly drops it down the chute. He hustles to the elevator, takes it to the lobby and, as he strides to the front desk, calls out, "Frank, can you let me in the Dumpster room for a second?"

"What now, Keene?"

"Just checking on something."

"It's locked after hours."

"I know that. That's why I'm asking you to open it."

"What for?"

"I want to make sure you know the chute as well as you think you do."

A worried look in Frank's eyes. "What'd you drop down there, a mattress?"

"C'mon, let's have a look."

"Keene, you didn't do nothin' foolish now, did you?"

"No, you'll see. C'mon."

Frank gives in and follows Richard past the mail room and through the rear door, outside onto the loading platform. He keys open the door to the Dumpster room. "Hurry up. I wanna get back out front."

Richard steps past Frank into the room and looks back at him. "You don't have to hang around. I'll be fine."

"You know you can't get back in this way."

"I know."

"Suit yourself." Frank sticks his head in the door and looks around. "What're you lookin' for, by the way?"

"I just tossed a little bag of garbage; that's all," Richard says and waves him off.

"Knock yourself out," Frank says and closes the door.

The overhead lights stay on all the time. The huge, green Dumpster sits below the chute opening. Richard moves to the Dumpster, reaches upward until he can grasp the top, does so with both hands, and hoists his torso up and over for a look-see, maintaining his grip so he doesn't fall in. As he does this, several trash bags slide through the chute and onto the Dumpster's asymmetrical pile, at the center of which a volcano-shaped mound of refuse has formed.

Something else is coming down the chute with the whoosh of trailing air and gathering speed. Richard can hear it way up high as it free-falls, and as it draws closer and the rush of its descent whistles through the cylinder . . .

He careens down the waterslide, its sturdy plastic lubricated by a constant flow of chlorinated pool water propelled onto the surface by tiny jets at the base of the curved sidings. As he zooms downward, he likes to focus on a single object: The clock mounted to the clubhouse facade on the other side of the pool is his usual target. He watches that clock all the way down, its hands unmoving within the couple of seconds it takes for him to hit the water. There is something tantalizing about courting the combined danger of height and speed, leaving caution behind, not even following the course with your eyes, secure in the safety promised by an adult world of structure and equipment. Nowhere on earth does he feel safer than on the waterslide, which deposits him in the boundless pool waters that ripple toward the shore of clubhouse and horizon. And now it is her turn, and he waits in the shallow water, moving back a few feet to allow her landing room. She sits at the very top of the slide, where it levels into a seat just above the last rung of the ladder behind it. Other girls scream when they slide down, and their arms and legs fly out with abandon as the bottom drops out from under them, but Cindy pilots her ride, controls the descent, enjoys it but doesn't give in to it. She is an athlete in a young girl's one-piece bathing suit, navy blue and molded to her smooth, sun-carameled skin. She slaloms down the slide on outstretched ski-legs and enters the water with the clean, minimal splash of an Olympic diver and, in that moment, as in many others, Richard is proud of her and feels something of the love he might have for a sister if he had a sister, but something beyond that, too, something he can't quite locate, since he is only eight years old after all, and . . .

A paper shopping bag plops into the Dumpster, contents

spilling out: a red-laced jar of spaghetti sauce, a disfigured TV dinner carton, scattered peach pits.

So many things to dispose of.

The Worthington's bag sits there, sandwiched between a bundle of newspapers and a bulging, oil-colored Hefty jumbo. Richard eases off the Dumpster.

The next step will be to test a body-equivalency down the chute. And then give the results to the police. No guarantee, but they just might pay attention.

Hours earlier, while Richard spars with the MRI machine in the late afternoon, Lori Calder is pruning verbiage from proposed credit card solicitation copy in the Mazer National Bancorp offices on the seventh floor of Two Liberty Center, a dark monolith that years ago joined the ranks of towers dwarfing Philly's former skyline apex, the statue of William Penn on top of City Hall. Penn still looks proud and unperturbed, but no longer so grand, as he holds his perch amid the steel-and-glass forest.

Lori is the designated writer on a five-person crew that develops marketing campaigns for which the department vice president takes credit when they go well and from which he distances himself when they bomb. She's the only person within thirty cubicles who knows an adverb from an adjective; the others crunch numbers, remedy computer program glitches, or devise systems flowcharts with lots of boxes and arrows and jargon. Department VP Dan Stubbleman is an erratic manager and a clunky writer who appreciates Lori's fluid prose and trim, little body. Though she has no plans to have him sample the latter, she's not averse to wearing short skirts, well aware that sweet and sexy is a potent combo in the corporate world, as it is just about anywhere. And someone who can write a complete sentence as well? Suffice it to say she has a bright future at Mazer National.

It's been only five years since she graduated from Villanova University, where she was the brainiest girl on the cheerleading squad, moving adeptly from splits on the hardwood of Philadelphia's creaky Palestra or 'Nova's more modern Pavilion to shunting Bunsen burner flames in chemistry lab and writing mature essays on Romantic poetry and twentieth-century fiction in English lit classes. She didn't, however, have specific career goals, and her bachelor's degree in American studies wasn't a passport to any specific destination. When Mazer National offered her a job after an interview on campus, she liked the salary and the center-city location. Living blocks away from theaters and concert halls is her idea of a lifestyle, as is dancing in late-night clubs like the Boiler Room on Second Street, or Destiny on Columbus Boulevard. There she can transform herself if only for a few hours, put on the cutaway tank top and the leather mini, and do some serious undulating, grinding hips with guys who may not frequent Barnes & Noble but look pretty damn good in their tight jeans. Lori digs life and likes to explore the facets of her personality.

As the afternoon at Mazer National veers toward the golden hour, Lori blue-pencils the hard copy she has been handed by Stubbleman—prose that she originally crafted, only to be manhandled by his mangled syntax and unfortunate word choices. Choosing the right word to appear in print is like taking a good shot in basketball, thinks Lori, a former high school point guard. Most people don't perceive nuance or seek originality; they just regurgitate TV speak or sports lingo or the excruciating phraseology of formal reports.

Still, Stubbleman is smart enough to relax his ego and entrust her with the final draft even after he has dumped his bricks onto the page. When he can't find his way through a tortured explanation, he spits out in the margins, "Something like that," leaving the substance of that *something* to Lori. She feels his pain, the galoot.

"Here are the present-value calculations," says Steve Bettinger, dropping a sheaf of papers onto her desk.

"Thanks, Bettinger."

"Anytime, Calder. How's the writing coming?"

"The usual: I write and he rewrites. Or tries to."

"Tell 'im to get bent."

"I'll try to remember that phrase, come review time."

"Absolutely."

A young guy with a slight build and a well-cultivated mustache, Bettinger likes to act as casual as humanly possible, which is a plus to Lori, but he also tries to be clever all the time, and he's never clever, so that's a minus. Not that she's considering him romantically—he's not her type, plus he's married—but as co-workers, they have a fair amount of interaction, and Lori likes things to crackle, to sing.

"Check those PV figures," Bettinger reminds her, pointing at his stack. "This thing could make us a mint."

"Always looks good on paper," says Lori, clucking her tongue like a schoolgirl. "Anyway, *we* don't make the mint."

"I'm a company man; what goes around comes around. Don't forget to get my name in there, sweets. Compiled by

Bettinger, two *T*s."

"Got it." Lori points her forefinger at him, gunslinger-style. Not a bad sort, this Bettinger, but hardly dynamic. A numbers cruncher saddled with a family at a relatively young age.

After a while she stands and stretches, up and down on her tiptoes to give her calves a little work, and moves to the window. In the distance, the Parkway shoots straight to the Art Museum, and a ribbon of the Schuylkill River curls past upraised train tracks that bank and wind toward the yawning blackness of the Thirtieth Street Station underpass.

While Lori massaged her boss's Mazer National Bancorp Credit Card Department proposal, Janet Kroll was at Philippe for a cut and some color. She has been diligent about masking her natural brunette with an autumn-leaf red—not to satisfy a personal indulgence but to serve an essential undertaking. The hair coloring, along with the eyebrow thinning and the pounds she has shed through rigorous training, have transformed her from plumply appealing (some said voluptuous) to model curvy. All to be sure that she's not recognized, though it is possible she would be safe even with no modifications.

Philippe himself does her hair in his walkup salon on Locust near the Square. Janet likes him; he's a handsome guy, fortyish, Mediterranean, with sensitive eyes and a sweet temperament. His wife, also a sweetie, designed the shop, and she handles the books along with the manes of their few male customers, who choose her to do the honors on a shampoo and cut.

As Janet approaches the red stone steps, she sees through

the tall window that Philippe has just finished with his two o'clock, a woman with hollowed cheeks and coarse, bruise-colored hair that Philippe has coaxed and wrestled (and smoothed and lightened) back to presentability.

"Hi, Phil," Janet says, entering.

"Hello, beautiful."

"Thanks, Philippe," his refurbished customer says, eyeing Janet and looking around as if for a clock that could be pushed back thirty years.

"You very welcome," he says with his Continental charm, opening the door and giving her a wide berth. "You look very nice. Absolutely."

"Thanks again, honey," she says, stepping down. "See you in a month."

Philippe closes the door and turns to Janet with a smile that lights up his face and the room.

"Here she is," he says. "My stunner."

And with her svelte figure, now-prominent cheekbones, and perfectly framed hazel eyes, Janet understands that she is indeed magazine-cover material.

"Honey, look who's here," Philippe calls to his wife, who pokes her head out of the rear-office doorway.

"Hiya, Janet," she says.

"Hi, Chris."

Janet settles into the cushioned, black leather chair and cocks an eye at Philippe.

"So?" he asks.

"How about some blonde highlights? Phil, what do you think?"

He appraises her in the mirror, knits his brows, and

nods. "I like it." He steps toward the mirror and plucks an expensive-looking bottle off the counter. "I've got something new." He offers the bottle to her like a Christmas gift. "The best—from France."

"Foil me, baby." Janet winks at him, igniting Philippe's hearty laughter.

"You hear this, Christina?" he hollers.

"I'm keeping close tabs," she says, slightly nasal, out of view.

Janet looks straight ahead at her image in the mirror as Philippe fastens a black cape around her neck. She was always pretty, wholesome, a kind of healthy sexy, but now the features have become classical and the body contours sculpted. She has been training for months, the last several weeks at the 42s. The new red hair rivets the eye; spike it with some blonde from France, and voilà . . . overpowering. Janet Kroll, erstwhile girl next door.

Her ex-husband would pop his eyes.

She finds that she likes this aroma of intrigue, the element of danger. To a point. She won't let it overwhelm her, seduce her. She's too smart for that.

Sex as weaponry is a new dynamic for her—more so than looks, *brains* were always her prime asset. Karen was the one with the personality and the sly sexiness, the little sister with the rebellious streak, while big sister Janet was stable and a straight-A student, if always battling a tendency to chubbiness. Karen was the one who drew the boys, who embraced the hip fashions then bad-girl duds. Two very different girls from the same suburban upbringing of ease but not opulence, a doting father and a mother who was loving but strict when the situation warranted, a backyard patio and paramecium-shaped swimming pool, holiday barbecues, exchange visits with cousins. Karen was no dummy but was a cerebral match for her sister only in math; she had a terrific facility with numbers, one she would later utilize in her job as a casino blackjack dealer, a job that her parents despised.

This afternoon as always, Philippe works fast, expertly. "I think you rather like this, no?" he says to Janet in the mirror as they both examine the new blonde highlights in her red hair. He has cut it, and it hangs straight and moist, shower-emerged.

"Very cool," Christina says, escaping her ledger in the backroom and walking to her husband's side behind Janet. "Very cool," she repeats, and Janet, too, is taken with what she sees in the mirror, her furtive smile a reflex confirming that this further altered appearance offers even greater protection and that aesthetically it scores.

It is not external noise that robs Richard of his sleep this night but the clatter inside his head, the anticipation of what he must do the next day and the day after that and continue to do without letup until things are set right.

He dozes off just as a glow sneaks into the sky and catches an hour of light sleep before the morning racket jars him awake. A half hour later, the sun has burned off the haze cloaking the skyscrapers, and he searches his short stack of business cards pinched by a rubber band. There it is, Terry Runnels, General Motors, all the way out there in some suburb of Detroit. Terry Runnels, an engineer now, always a whiz in math, a high school and then college classmate, a guy who, unlike Richard, transferred to a four-year college and completed his bachelor's degree. And also unlike Richard, remained breakdown-free.

Terry Runnels, the man to call for a crash-test dummy.

The case must be built piece by piece. Richard intends to construct a plausible scenario for the police, one that he envisions will lead to a court order to dig up a landfill somewhere and produce a body. He will demonstrate how the crime could have been committed—how it *was* committed; the why will follow. He is sure of himself now, sure of what happened, sure of who did it and how. He feels the certainty deep inside, in what spiritualists might call the soul.

Meanwhile, since he is newly jobless, he needs to kill hours between revelations, between breaks in the case, and in the afternoon he is back on the treadmill, sweating, running at a nearly unbearable clip, occasionally wincing from the ache in his knee. He can run through the pain; it's always been his way. Pain in the joints or in the psyche—no different. Just run through it. Somewhere, sometime, he sees himself coming out the other end, to a place where a soothing glow drapes the landscape and the very air is a balm. The pain evaporates and the world relaxes as if it has just rid itself of a muscle cramp.

His day goes by in daydreams. He sees a subway train, brightly lit and postered with public service messages and skin cream ads marred by thick black graffiti, rumbling through its dank underground tunnel, slowing and stopping at a platform backed by green-and-white-tiled walls and thick with concrete columns sturdy enough to hold up a city.

The circus is in town at the huge, aging stadium in southwest

Philadelphia, the high wire strung across its yawning expanse and splicing the clouds hanging like upended mountains in the Sunday afternoon sky; the air soaked by the scents of steaming hot dogs and mustard, salty popcorn, and roasted peanuts; Cindy Dempsey by his side; the trapeze artists' swing flight, the sad prankish profusions of the clowns, and the whip-crack staging of bounding lions and tigers, and the loping rumble of the elephants and their glittering riders almost as pretty, almost as captivating, as Cindy Dempsey by his side.

Dreams and daydreams, the past bleeding into the present, and the panic of not knowing, not being sure, the residue of something disgraceful, the nightmare of chasing yourself through time.

Richard is not dreaming as he finds himself holding a half-gallon jug of filtered water while standing in line at the convenience store next to the 42s' parking garage. One man in line wears unbuckled galoshes and a green army jacket suited for temperatures about forty degrees colder. Young women, early twenties, ask for cigarettes, cartons of them. The clerk is flabby-cheeked and congenial, dispensing death. Richard notices the clerk's wristwatch. It is almost six o'clock. The day has eluded him.

He totes his water back toward the 42s, and as he draws to within fifty feet, he sees two people emerge from the entrance alcove, two people who are immediately familiar to him, but not as a couple. The woman has a spectacular shape in her body-hugging cocktail dress, her sharp, arresting features framed by chin-length, red hair now with blonde highlights like streaks of gold dust. The man is broad and athletic, an easy gait within his blue sport coat and charcoal slacks, blond hair uncombed and looking great that way.

Janet Kroll and Davis Braun are obviously out for the evening, and looking quite pleased with each other, absorbed sufficiently to not notice Richard, who angles past them and into the building, keeping some distance and averting his gaze. Inside, he steps quickly to the front desk.

"Frank, can you watch this for me?" Richard holds up the transparent jug of water. "I forgot something; I'll be back in a minute."

Frank smirks and offers a mocking tone. "Why, sure, my man. That's all part of our twenty-four-hour service here at the 42s."

More evidence that he's winning Frank over gradually, Richard believes—a week ago, the 42s' majordomo would have ignored him or told him to get the water the hell out of the lobby. "Thanks," Richard says simply and is already in motion, headed back out the door. Immediately he has Janet and Braun in his sights: They're at the end of the block and crossing Sixteenth Street. He follows on the opposite side of Locust, the sidewalk busy with two-way traffic. The couple of the evening—they do make one hell of a pair, Richard concedes—cross at Seventeenth and continue two more blocks to Potcheen's and its row of outdoor tables dressed in linen. It is the most formal of the eateries by the Square. Janet and Braun step under the canopy and sit at a table; Richard stays to the other side of the street and keeps walking. He pauses at the steps to the Curtis Institute and sits on a broad concrete ledge. From this distance, he would have no trouble listening in on their conversation, were it not for the intrusive sounds of the city. His considerable powers of concentration are not enough; he'll need to get closer. He boldly crosses Locust, enters the restaurant on the Nineteenth Street side, and slips onto a barstool within earshot of the outdoor tables. When he orders tonic water, the bartender gives him a look. Richard places a five on the bar and turns halfway toward the two people seated twenty feet away, partially shielded by a tall planter.

"A surgeon," Richard hears Braun say to Janet.

"Why?"

"The responsibility. A surgeon holds your life in his hands, delves right into your center, your inner workings—I'm talking organ surgery, of course."

"Open heart?"

"Yes. Lungs, thorax, cardiothoracic surgery."

"Give me your hand," she says, and Braun looks puzzled but obeys the command, extends his right hand across the white tablecloth and she takes it. She sees its size and gracefulness. "You have the hands for it."

He smiles and gives her hand a little squeeze before withdrawing. "I think I have the temperament for it. You have to be cool under fire. Fierce concentration."

"Which you have?"

"I believe so."

"You're probably being modest."

"No, not really. Just not overconfident."

Janet takes a sip of white wine. "Money's not bad either, huh?"

When Braun smiles, there's a flash of white teeth. "You're in real estate," he says, "so I know you don't think money's a bad thing."

"That's certainly true, but I only make it when I produce."

"It's the same, to varying degrees, in any profession."

"You're right, of course. Except real estate's a bigger pain in the ass than most."

Braun laughs vigorously, seeming to forget himself for the moment.

They dine on seafood—scallops for her, crab cakes for him—lubricated by the wine. When their waitress arrives with the check in a leather billfold, Janet reaches for it first.

"I get the commission on that Society Hill townhouse this week," she says. "And you're not a surgeon yet."

"You planning to spoil me?"

Janet slips her credit card behind the billfold's plastic flap. "That's my prerogative."

Richard studies them as he listens, picking up their words and inflections sorted out from the noise—human and otherwise—closer to him at the bar. He has consumed two additional tonic waters and pinned another fiver under the glass. The Braun-Janet conversation has been, in his estimation, vapid and pseudosophisticated, as if each were intent on avoiding feelings and preserving image, performances taken from a shallow script. As Richard rises from the barstool, someone walking on the other side of Locust Street catches his eye. He looks beyond Braun and Janet to see the now-familiar, lean lad who easily could pass as his younger, better-looking brother—whom he saw the previous day at the bistro next door, their vantage points reversed. Richard watches the young man across the street pause at the Curtis steps and then sit, just as Richard did forty minutes earlier.

When the newcomer rises, crosses the street, and approaches Braun's table, Richard retreats into the shadows of the restaurant but keeps his ear tuned to the same spot. He is eager to dispatch the misgiving that his recurring follower is merely a delusion, the equivalent of his own image staring back at him from a mirror.

The answer comes quickly, as Braun acknowledges him.

"How ya doin'?" Richard hears it as casual but not warm.

"Hello," says the visitor.

Braun gestures across the table to his stunning date. "Janet, say hello to Cam . . . Cam, this is Janet Kroll, a neighbor of ours."

"Hello." The word has been swallowed, as if the speaker were nervous or had a speech impediment. So far, Cam has displayed a one-word vocabulary.

The waitress arrives with Janet's receipt, and Braun rises immediately.

"We've got to run."

Even from a distance, Richard believes that Braun's visitor looks crestfallen. *Cam*. Short for . . . Cameron? A resident of the 42s.

On her feet now, Janet smiles at Cam. "Nice meeting you." She and Braun step from the patio onto the sidewalk and move smoothly in the soft light, his hand at the small of her back. Cam watches them, then turns back toward the patio. Richard slips out of the restaurant the way he entered. He wants to know more about this fellow before speaking to him.

His surveillance for the night is over, but he does wonder where Braun and Janet are headed. Their attire and the fact that they didn't linger at the restaurant suggest a concert at the

Kimmel or the Academy of Music. Is that how their tastes run, or is the next stop a private party at a nearby townhouse or perhaps dancing at one of the clubs on Columbus Avenue? Back in the 42s lobby, Richard finds Mike at the front desk.

"Hey, Mike, Richard Keene, apartment 2207. Do you know a fellow named Cam who lives here?"

Mike tickles his graying sideburns to stimulate his recollection. "Cam, you say? I might. Not sure. Tryin' to think."

Richard waits a spell before Mike shakes his head. "Can't come up with it. You need him for something?"

"That's okay, thanks. I'll catch up with him."

In his apartment, Richard calls Lieutenant Oliver.

"Just checking on that trip he made to the bank, Lieutenant. He didn't by any chance cash a check from her account, did he?"

On the other end of the line, pulling another night shift, Oliver has answered with a gruff flatness, but now his voice relaxes.

"Well, I took your advice and interrogated Mr. Braun," he says, tongue-in-cheek. "And as a matter of fact, you are correct. We were on that right away. Braun says Miss Carson postdated a check so he could get the funds in her absence. You guessed that, huh?"

"Yes."

"Well, don't get excited; they'd done it before."

"She didn't disappear before."

"Neither did her money."

"What do you mean?"

"She just closed her account."

"By mail?" Richard rocks in his chair, nodding to himself,

going with it, having anticipated something like this.

"In person."

Richard stops rocking. "In person? So she's back in town—case solved?"

"Not exactly. Braun hasn't seen her. Neither has her employer."

Of course they haven't. "But the bank must have IDed her."

"Not quite, but the signature is her name and it matches other checks."

"It's a phony."

"We're having it checked."

"Well, did their description match Miss Carson?"

"The teller can't really remember what she looked like."

Richard now feels a comfort level with the lieutenant. "Don't security cameras record every transaction?"

"When they're working."

"You mean—?"

"You got it. They were on the blink."

Richard looks at his reflection in a narrow rectangle of darkened bedroom window. "So her car's gone, then?" He imagines Braun driving it out of the garage; Jay might remember. "She drove a, uh, what was it? A Sentra, no, Altima—"

"The car's still there."

Richard jerks back in his chair. "Isn't that a little suspicious, Lieutenant?"

"Everything's suspicious in my world."

"Can you check the car?"

"We plan to."

"See if her suitcase is in there. I think she might have

packed it up and put it in the car, then returned to her apartment . . . you know, that night."

"Why do you say that?"

"Someone saw her with the suitcase. Actually, two people saw her."

"We know that—we've talked to the man at the front desk, the neighbors—"

"You spoke with Lori?" She hasn't told him.

"I believe that was one of the young ladies."

"So you'll be checking the car?"

"That's the general idea. You figure we'll find a body in there?"

Richard knows the lieutenant is toying with him a bit, but doesn't care. "No, that you won't find . . ." Richard is more convinced than ever. "So the security camera breaks down at just the right time."

"It was down all that afternoon."

"The teller could be in on it."

"Let's hold the conspiracy theories for the time being, okay?" Oliver says. "It's hardly out of the ordinary for a store clerk or a bank teller not to be able to positively identify a customer. Could be someone he's seen only that one time, nothing special about the transaction."

"She closed her account. Isn't that pretty involved?"

"Not necessarily. Can be a routine matter."

"Nothing special happened that he remembers? Is it a *he*, by the way?"

"I think we know how to question people in these kinds of circumstances. Hey, you know that superhearing of yours?"

"It's a curse," Richard says softly.

"But you're pretty sure of it, aren't you? I mean, like you told me last time, you trust it."

"Yes."

"All right, that's important. That's a big part of being a witness. If you don't trust yourself, how can we?"

"True."

"Good, we're in agreement."

Richard wants to tell him things. "When I hear stuff that no one else does, I feel like I've been given a weapon that I don't know how to use. Like a gun, I guess, with plenty of firepower, but I can't aim it properly."

"That's a problem, all right."

"So what can I do with it, except *obey* it, know what I mean? When I scale the heights, you see, when I get way up high and out in the open, nothing bothers me. I'm fearless. More than that, I'm *free*. But these things I hear, I get scared and . . . I'm trapped. That's the best way I can describe it."

"What are you, a mountain climber or something?"

"No, not exactly. Skyscrapers, towers, wherever I can get away. I don't climb them—just take the elevator. Oh, sometimes I climb if that's what's intended—like steps at an ancient ruin."

"You know what, son?" Richard hears a change in Oliver's tone. "Your instincts are good."

"Think so?"

"The fact of it is, I did expect that teller to make a positive ID."

That snaps Richard back to business. "But he definitely said it was a woman who made the transaction?"

"That's right, there's no question about that."

"At least he remembers that much."

Moments later, buoyed by a sense of momentum after his call to Lieutenant Oliver, Richard has Silver Spring on the line.

"I didn't want to bother you again, Mr. Carson, but maybe you can help. The police are investigating a check written by your daughter over to Davis Braun, and—"

"Are you with the police?"

"No, sir, I'm not."

"Then what business is it of yours?"

The man's tone irks Richard, who remains polite but will not be less than persistent. "Let me get this straight, sir, it doesn't bother you that—?"

"What bothers me is *my* business."

"I think Braun had the check forged."

"Then the police'll find that out."

Richard pauses. "Don't you care about your daughter, Mr. Carson?"

The man's voice turns ugly. "You got a helluva lot of nerve, kid . . . Look"—the voice suddenly deflated—"none of this is any big surprise. She's always gone off on her own from time to time. She's a hardhead. If you know her, you know what I mean. Tell you the truth, I don't know her all that well, myself."

Richard swallows, squares his shoulders, and delivers the line with the calm certitude of a coroner. "I think your daughter's dead."

"Really?" Now a mocking tone. "And why do you think that?"

"Because I heard her being murdered."

"You are a sick puppy, you know that? What the hell's the matter with you?"

"I'm sorry you feel that—"

"You pissed off at Ellie or somethin'? She shoot you down? What's *with* you?"

"Ask yourself this, Mr. Carson: Why would I bother you about it?"

"How do *I* know? 'Cause you're a nut." Richard hears a sharp crack followed by the unsettling void of a dial tone.

Spanning the Delaware River between Penn's Landing on the Philadelphia waterfront and long-blighted Camden, New Jersey, the Benjamin Franklin Bridge is anchored by great granite piles sunken in the riverbanks like medieval castles with submerged drawbridges. Above the bridge deck, thick cable lines soar toward steel towers painted a gas-flame blue and, on outboard sidings, high-speed trains usher commuters across the river. Old, faded structures near the bridge huddle below the skyward sweep; an aged church steeple once toppled onto the roadway, denting the macadam and displacing a congregation.

Davis Braun coaxes his years-old Fiat—he has explained to Janet that he's weighed down by med-school debt but eventually will have an automobile befitting his station—across the Ben Franklin, heading back from Jersey into Philadelphia, Janet Kroll by his side. Moments earlier, they strolled the Camden waterfront, where the brightly lit State Aquarium etched its reflections on the rolling pleats of the Delaware River, and the late-night breeze off the water both soothed and stirred. The sky sported a honey-dew moon. It was a quick trip, a romantic whim, an evening capper after they'd seen a show—a contemporary drama—at the venerable Walnut Street Theater.

Braun looks at her, and their smiles are a mellow suggestion of comfort with each other, as sensual as the leather contours beneath them. He interrupts the mood by plucking his cell phone—it's been quiet—out of the console between the bucket seats and punching in the Verizon message-retrieval number for the apartment landline.

"Sorry," he says. "Just checking messages—expecting something." He is only five minutes from home, but he likes to get a jump on his messages and ponder the proper response to important ones. He has been receiving offers to join hospitals and surgical practices when he completes his residency next year. He would not mind returning to that hospital near Cape May, New Jersey, where Metro sent him last year for some specialized cardio work. He likes the seashore.

He is thinking about such things, but is not surprised when he hears Dan Carson's voice, the second message. He's not surprised, either, that Carson sounds upset. "Call me right away," the message commands.

He notices that Janet does not seem put off by the distraction. She could be daydreaming as she gazes through the side window. Across the bridge, the city's lights look like a swarm of fireflies. "Well, Doctor, any emergencies?" she asks when he clicks off the phone.

"No, nothing much."

The bridge dumps them onto Sixth Street, and Braun

heads south from Vine to Walnut, past Independence National Park and the steepled hall, where the ghosts of the founding fathers are said to shuffle their quill pens by night. An unbroken string of green lights on Walnut takes them to the left turn on Fifteenth and the right on Latimer. Two more rights, and Braun pulls into the 42s' garage. As he inserts his card and the barrier gate lifts, he points, friendly-like, toward the small shed and Jay, who returns his gesture with a smile as always. Braun and Fiat scale six levels before finding a space. He gets out and, a true gentleman, opens the passenger-side door for Janet. The garage elevator takes them to ground level. Next door at the 42s, it's another elevator and an updraft to the fifteenth floor and Janet's apartment, where a long kiss at the door and then against it ends their night by acclimation, early starts in the morning for both.

"Thanks for a lovely evening," she says, lips parted but not by much.

"Thanks for picking up the dinner tab," he says, just loud enough to be heard, even in the echo-rich hallway. They break and smile and kiss again lightly, and she opens her door, retreats into the apartment, all fragrance and allure and a lot going on in her eyes.

In his apartment eight floors higher, Braun goes right to the landline and listens to the messages again; Carson's is the only one that matters. Braun wants to be helpful, but what can he say to the guy? He makes the call.

"What the hell's he talking about?" Carson asks. "Where's he get all this?"

"I don't know, Mr. Carson. I don't even know him."

"This business about a forged check and he 'heard her being murdered'? What's with this guy?"

"Wish I knew. Maybe he has a thing for Ellie."

"That's what I was thinkin'."

"I'll tell you what, Mr. Carson, I'm gonna introduce myself to this fellow. He shouldn't be bothering you."

"Yeah, have the police get after *him*."

"Right."

"Anything new on your end?"

"No, sir. I wish there were. I'd call you right away. I just don't get it."

Carson issues a sustained, phlegmy cough and lets it run its course with no "Excuse me." He clears his throat violently. "Look, kid, we've never met but you sound okay to me. I seen Eleanor with some real beauts. Appreciate anything you can do here. She don't talk much to me."

"You bet."

Braun hangs up and shakes his head, thinking about what Ellie has told him of her father, how he was never around when she was growing up, how he tuned her out even when he *was* around; thinking also, in fairness, that she's not always the best communicator when it comes to personal matters, that she saves such skills for her legal briefs.

And now Davis Braun turns his thoughts to Richard Keene, to this strange, annoying guy who came from nowhere.

Braun goes online and finds that the phone number is unlisted. He passed Mike at the front desk moments earlier. Mike—a little slow on the uptake, but still have to play it smooth. Takes the elevator to the lobby.

"Hey, Mike, would do me a big favor?"

"Sure, if I can."

"I need a phone number for Richard Keene."

"He live in the building?"

"Yes, Mike, he lives in the building."

"Why don't you just knock on his door or leave a note?"

"It's better to call, Mike—trust me. Anyway, I don't know his apartment number."

Mike doesn't react for a few seconds. "I should really call him first and tell him you want to speak to him. Then I can give him your number, and he can call if he wants to. That's the way they like us to handle things."

Braun leans in. "Mike, it's important that I talk to him right away. He might feel funny about calling me."

Mike looks at him. Finally, "I guess it's okay, Dr. Braun. After all—"

"After all, I'm a good risk, right, Mike?"

"Yeah, that's right." He moves to the computer. "How do you spell that?"

"Try K, E, E, N, E."

"K, E, E, N, E. Yeah, here he is. Apartment 2207." He writes the phone number on a scrap of paper and hands it to him.

"You're a prince, Mike."

In his apartment, he uses his landline to dial the number. "This is Davis Braun. You want to tell me what's going on?" His voice is deeper than usual, the tone menacing.

"Excuse me?"

"Ellie Carson . . . and me. Do you pry into everybody's social life around here or just mine? What's with you?"

"How'd you get my number?"

Now Braun speaks in a voice that is light, airy, and

burnished with a kind of preppy ease. "You want to give her father a heart attack, for Chrissake? He's an old man." Then the anger returns: "What's the matter with you? You're the guy who eavesdropped on me that time, right? Right? Reported some silliness to the front desk? Johnny on the fuckin' spot."

"How do you know it was me?"

"You've got one hell of an imagination, buddy," says Braun. "Nothing wrong with that; you should go off and write a screenplay or something. But now you've become a major pain in the ass to me and to other people, understand that? This has got to stop."

A click on the other end, then a dial tone.

Braun slams his phone into its wall console. He leaves the apartment and moves swiftly to the stairwell at the end of the corridor. One floor down and over to 2207, directly underneath his own pad. His knuckles rap the door sharply, then the side of his fist thuds into the sturdy, shellacked wood.

From inside: Richard's tame "Yes?"

Braun positions himself right in front of the eyelet. "Let's talk."

"We have nothing to talk about." Richard sounds like a man who has just come out of anesthesia.

"I think we have."

"Go ahead, then."

"Face-to-face."

Richard's voice finds some courage, comes alive. "What are you so worried about all of a sudden?"

"You really need help, buddy, you know that?"

"Leave me alone or I'm calling the police."

A nasty chuckle from Braun. "I hear you're keeping

them busy these days. Don't you have anything better to do with yourself?"

A door opens down the hallway, and Braun decides to cut the interview short. It's late, and he doesn't want to wake up the building. It's not like him to lose control, but this little shit really has him upset. He steps back and away from the door, shakes his head, walks away.

On the other side of the door, Richard is frozen, his eyes flitting about as in REM sleep. He had clenched the kitchen phone so hard that his knuckles bulged, stretching the wrinkles on their ridges into onionskin. Confronted by Braun, he all but tasted the fear. Now his upper body trembles and, to stop it, he rams a shoulder into the door, then slides downward until he sits on the floor, hips wedged into the right angle made by the door and the wall, knees up, arms folded on top of them, cocooned, paralyzed.

He closes his eyes and, as he often does or tries to do, forces himself to imagine a scene that will transport him from this nerve-wracking discomfort, from the fear and shame of the moment, to a place of relaxation and confidence and a belief that this world is not only hospitable but an engine of hope and joy—

He is waist-deep in the Atlantic Ocean on a summer afternoon at the Jersey shoreline, and the water runs up his little-boy thighs and underneath the oversized swim trunks to the white webbing. The sun-heated water is warm as it irrigates him, and he dives under a wave and bobs to the surface, a curtain of level water, blue-green and white-flecked and shifting sideways with the wacky current. As he stands, he can feel the undertow on his shins and feet, and he respects it but doesn't fear it; it's a force of nature, commanding and inexorable, but if heeded, a sweet coexistence results—the warm, thrilling feeling of riding the power, living with the earth's elements, and being part of an impossibly vast and detailed tapestry of rise and fall, search and rescue. The lifeguards on their stands behind him are part of that tableau, rowboats ready on the moist sand.

And then he's no longer in the ocean, no longer wet and sloshing about but getting a foothold on limestone steps hardened and flaked by the centuries. The steps are narrow and the ascent is steep, but he climbs without hesitation, no railing to grip, just a wide-open canvas of sky above and whitewashed ruins below, sheared-off foundations and crumbling facades, greenery filling the breach. Up he goes toward the summit of the ancient temple, others tentative and angling their bodies and pausing to sit on skinny steps, but not him—he marches upward on this Mayan pyramid like a prince about to offer a religious sacrifice, as if he has made this trip a hundred times and not merely this first time as a college student intrigued by ancient exotic cultures, by any society not his own. The stairway is like a one-hundred-fifty-foot ladder angled against the side of a building, so steeply is it pitched. He mounts these stairs, unfazed, summoned by a higher order. The fantastical headdresses of the Mayan priests and the buried corpses within lodge in his mind's eye. People interred with their finery and jewelry, servants with their utensils, all for use in the next world. Amid sacrifices, gored animals, bark spattered with human blood. But all that shrinks to a footnote, for when he reaches the peak and takes a panoramic survey of the world around him, a thrill ripples up his arms and across his shoulders to the base of his neck. Here he is unshackled, stoked by the rarefied air, free free free . . .

And now the landscape greens further into farm country below, and he is at the top of the observation tower at Gettysburg Battlefield, the arena of death spread below him, stilled and tagged for modern consumption. The Round Tops, the swath where Pickett charged, where Chamberlain held the line, where they all fell in their deathly hot uniforms, snap-blast of rifles and concussive splintering of musket balls, searing pain and shock and, finally, muggy oblivion. Richard has it all in his sights, the high school history text revisualized, and from up here at the top of the tower, the shrine is quieted by the twin tranquilizers of time and distance, and he is at peace with the world.

THIRTEEN

Once in a great while, a case prods him into action beyond the paperwork. An individual with conviction, with persistence, will reach him in a place that's otherwise quiet these days.

Maybe this Richard Keene is such an individual. If he's not crazy or a murderer himself. His record shows not so much as a traffic ticket. That's a good start, but the six months in a mental hospital do not inspire confidence. Every unraveling starts somewhere.

The intensity in that young man's eyes and his delineation of subtle sounds and their sequence. This business of sorting out the sounds, the real ones interspersed with a movie sound track. A story remarkable in its content and precision, to be sure; unique in Oliver's experience. He can't be certain whether Richard is a jilted suitor, a genius of sorts, a nutcase, or just someone who's seen too many movies. Keep an open mind, his training tells him. More than thirty years as a cop has generated a metric ton of slop and ghastliness, and he's been hardened almost to the point where human discomfort is of no account.

Maybe the boy's elaborate rendering is his way of confessing to an odious crime.

Elbows propped on his desk, Oliver rubs his watery eyes and opens them to a temporary blur. One last horror to decipher? He knows he's been marking time until a year-end retirement from the Philadelphia Police Department, a pension, a party, sayonara, and exit to a cabin near a lake in the Pocono Mountains. Freeze your ass off in the winter, but fishing and true-blue skies when the weather warms. Nice way to play out the string. He figures it'll be a short string.

He is a respected cop after all this time, though he's a husk of the man who walked beats, caught his share of bad guys, and helped innovate community policing in Philadelphia neighborhoods. As an offensive guard on his high school football team several centuries ago, he was an indomitable foot soldier who created daylight for flashy ballcarriers, and his style remained the same when he put on the blue uniform. He thinks Philly top cop Frank Rizzo was too rash back in the sixties, poured fuel on racial fires, though he liked the man's toughness, leadership, charisma. That was well before his time on the force. He had great respect for New York import John Timoney, who hit all the right notes, a capable low-key leader. The two commissioners since are good men.

He worked the long, hard, dangerous hours but always sought some balance between his job and personal life. His easiest assignment was to love his wife. He was also crazy about his kids. Well, at least his daughter.

Balance, he has learned, is a state of mind that can easily become imbalanced.

He has let his body go, let it get soft and bulgy; no use trying to get back in shape, no one on his ear to do so. He has fired his weapon at people and hit some, but he's never killed anyone, not in thirty-three years of service. Took a couple in the body, sheathed by a protective vest, no damage. As he closes out the show on a desk, he tracks the missing, those who run away and wind up floating facedown in a river or decomposed in the underbrush, and those who come home after a seventy-two-hour washout. Kids on a bus to nowhere, vanished housewives and college students, guys fleeing their lives. Perplexing, absurd, sometimes downright silly, sometimes quite ugly.

His wife claimed by cancer. It's been five years.

His daughter is dead.

She would never age beyond twenty-three.

Cassie was the kind of daughter who thrilled fathers, tomboy-tough as a little girl, pretty and athletic in high school, good grades, and good enough on the basketball court to get a partial scholarship to St. Joseph's University and play varsity for four years, running the offense like the kids' tree-house club she founded in her own backyard. Oliver can still see the plywood retreat—by his hand— amid the thick trunk and sturdy arteries of the large oak in the yard; Cassie captained the membership, including kid brother Robert Jr., her leadership gifts such that both boys and girls felt an allegiance toward her. Expeditions to the movies and 7-Eleven, street ball games that developed into full-fledged leagues with teams from different blocks, pretzel sales and car washes, lemonade stands. Cassie's Cavalry, he called the tree-house band of seven: three boys and four girls, including

Bobby and Cassie. She was a throwback, a character out of Mark Twain. Indeed, with her creativity, beguiling smile, and occasional pugnacious streak, it seemed that she had sprung from the pages of a storybook.

But the mature Cassie Oliver was very real and, above all, a woman of character. When her mother got sick, she cared for her with the skill and commitment of a full-time nurse. Aside from the chemotherapy sessions, there was to be no hospital for Libby until the very end, when the cancer shut down her organs one by one.

He thinks all the time about both Cassies, the little indomitable girl and the young woman of strength and promise, the twenty-three-year-old whose boyfriend disregarded a curving roadway and amber caution signs and plowed his convertible and the two of them into an unyielding tree, crumpling the car, crushing Cassie between her bucket seat and the glove compartment, ensuring in the electric blur of an instant that her insides would never have to submit to the same wasting her mother's did.

He has lost them all, including the son who, in his eyes, never measured up, now a stranger living on the other coast, almost as dead to him as the cherished daughter and her mother. His hatred for Cassie's boyfriend—her murderer, he called him—has finally lessened a year or so after the accident. The kid, after all, is dead, too, and it seems self-indulgent to hate a dead man. But his enduring hatred is for a father's helplessness, a feeling so sickening, so infuriating, that only his emotional numbness can prevent it from smothering him with self-pity or rising to some kind of incommensurable fury. And so his instincts to help people have dulled into a clock-puncher's ennui. He musters enough energy and clarity to follow the rules and see a task through, but he lacks the dedication, the extra juice that once made all the difference. *Burnout* is the modern terminology, and he figures he's earned it. Can't ride to the rescue anymore for somebody else's misfortune. His own is too strong.

Along comes this Richard fellow, this Richard Kane, whatever it is, Richard *Keene* . . . something about this boy. Have to admire his doggedness. He's got one hell of a concoction, but he doesn't come across as self-important or completely out of it. Seems to have a strong personal connection to the case but isn't panicky or full of "Why don't you do something?"

So we take some initiative, check things out. Call the missing girl's boyfriend again, make some other calls, maybe send a detective out for a look-see.

Something curious about this case. The father's attitude. And that bank account business. The young lady, Miss Carson, could simply be avoiding this Davis Braun fellow; maybe it's an unhappy situation for her and she wants to break free without seeing him. And maybe she has no interest in seeing her father, either. The guy's no prize; that's for sure. So she disappears on both of them. She takes some time on her own, then returns to get her money.

But if she's clearing out altogether, why are her things still in the apartment and her car still in the garage? And she hasn't contacted her employer at all.

Nix that hypothesis.

The doctor guy's a tough read, too. He could be sincere but unemotional. That's okay; lots of times it seems the more they talk, the phonier they are. Braun seems like a guy who's got it all, so the cynical view is that underneath the contained exterior, he's a psychotic killer. If he is, he's sure as hell not a dummy who would rig this bank thing for a few dollars and hand over a motive on a silver platter. Unless that's the height of arrogance.

Throw Keene and his strange story into the mix, and the boy's right: you have a damn suspicious situation.

Still, returning to square one: the kid could be nuts.

Or a murderer playing with him.

He figures he may not have enough yet for a search warrant on Braun, but he can legitimately have Burnside and Alvarez make an inquiry, try to get more of a feel for things. They're a pair, those two. Burnside slowing but veteran-savvy, Alvarez as eager as a racehorse at the gate. Good combo.

Come to think of it, maybe, with the right judge, there is enough for that warrant. And one for the girl's car, too.

After half an hour in semifetal position, Richard has roused himself. He is on the line with Lori, telling her about his run-in with Braun, and about Eleanor Carson's unmoved car and closed bank account, asking her if she has anything else to report about her next-door neighbor.

"No," she says. "Haven't seen him."

"Good. Don't even think of getting anything more from him, Lori; he may be too dangerous at this point. You've done enough . . . I hear the police spoke to you today."

"They did. How'd you hear that?"

"From Oliver."

"I forgot; you two are buddies."

"You didn't call me."

"It was just routine."

He tells her about his plans to drop a dummy down the trash chute tomorrow as a demo to build the evidence. She sounds less than overwhelmed by his genius.

"Will you witness it?" he asks her.

"Sure, why not."

"Thanks. That helps. Makes it look stronger to the police to have confirmation. Like I'm not a raving lunatic. Know what I mean?"

"Sure, I'm well acquainted with raving lunatics."

"I'm serious."

"I know you are. I'm sorry. You can count on me. Just wait 'til I get home from work."

"I should get it by 10:00 a.m., special delivery. It'll come in sections. I'll have it put together by noon. When will you be home from work?"

"I don't know. Early, about 4:30."

"Want to come over on your lunch break? You're not that far."

"No, no time. What's the big hurry?"

"The sooner the better."

"Well, you can't move any faster than the police, can you?"

"That's the idea—get *them* to move faster."

"But Richard, some little sideshow with a dummy—I'm sorry, I don't mean that, but you know what I mean. It's not going to convince them to call it a murder case."

"I think it helps because it captures the imagination."

"If you say so."

"I'll call you."

"You know, I can't believe he came after you that way. It seems so out of character."

This annoys Richard, as if she doesn't quite believe him. "I told you, guys like this can be very deceptive."

"Listen, if he's guilty—"

"I don't think it's a matter of *if* anymore."

"If he's guilty, he's just trying to intimidate you."

"Ya *think*?"

Lori laughs. "I *think*. But there's no way he's gonna do something drastic to you in a high-rise with a thousand people all around," she says.

"You mean like he did with Eleanor?"

Nothing on the other end of the line, then, "All right, Richard. I get the message."

"Listen, one other thing. He's seeing another woman."

"Really? . . . That's fast." She clears her throat. "I haven't seen anyone around. Of course, I easily could have missed them."

"She lives in the building."

"How do you know?"

"I know her; I've seen her a lot at the gym."

"Wow . . . How do you know they're, uh . . . ?"

"They went out together tonight. I saw them leave the building and followed them. Dinner and drinks at Potcheen's. Didn't look like a first date."

"So? Maybe they're old friends."

"It was too cozy for that."

"What's she look like?"

"Red hair. Attractive, athletic."

"Sounds like you mean kind of sexy." Her voice has a

light, teasing quality.

"Yes, you could say that."

"Where'd they go after dinner?"

"I don't know; I only followed them as far as Potcheen's."

"How come? You've been following him all over creation."

"Something else came up. Do you know a fellow they call Cam, lives here?"

"Cam?"

"Yeah. Cameron, maybe?"

"Not offhand. Who is he?"

"He showed up when they were having dinner and walked over to the table. It was kind of awkward."

"What happened?"

"Well, all he did, really, was say hello to Braun. But I think he followed them there—or followed *me* following them. I didn't tell you this, but I sensed that he might have been following me the time I tracked Braun all around town. I noticed him twice that time."

"Cameron, huh? I'll ask Davis about him."

"No." Richard is emphatic. "Like I said, too dangerous now. Stay away."

"All right, Lieutenant, it's your case. By the way, what's the girl's name, the redhead with the great body?"

"I didn't say she had a great body."

"Yeah, you did. What's her name? Maybe I know her."

"I don't know yet."

"Then you don't know her so well, huh?"

"I've just spoken with her a couple of times, you know, at the fitness center or the elevator. Like that."

"This is major, Richard." Lori catches her breath. "Oh my God, she could be—"

"Yes, she could."

Richard looks at the angry, scabbed knuckles on his right hand now bare of its bandage. He sees a woman's neck turning from red to purple-brown. "Yes, she could," he repeats.

He must speak with this girl. Warn her. Save her.

First, he must find out who she is. After a few brief chance meetings, there has been no exchange of names. He's not much of an operator. No kidding.

Frank. No, Mike's down there now. Try him. Get her name from Mike if he knows it, the dunce. He must have given up Richard's phone number easily enough to Braun.

The elevator pops Richard's ears. It feels like it's rushing downward more quickly than usual, almost like it's falling uncontrolled. It hits bottom harder than it should and recoils. The door stutters as it opens.

Mike is speaking with a sixtyish man who looks like he has time to kill and this is his best option. Their conversation pauses as Richard approaches.

He tries to act casual. "Hey, Mike, you know that real pretty woman with the red hair, lives on fifteen?"

Mike's face goes blank, then comes to life. "Yeah, yeah, I think I know who you mean. The redhead . . . Wow, some looker." His tight jaw forces out a crooked smile. "She's way outta your league, pal."

"Don't I know it," Richard says, thrilled inside that he's grown smooth at this game. "Can't blame me for trying, though, right?"

Mike's conversation partner nods and blinks bloodshot eyes.

"What's her name?" Richard continues. "I've talked to her lots of times at the gym but never got it."

"If it's the redhead on fifteen, it's Janet you're talkin' about," Mike says without hesitation. "Janet Kroll. I always remember the good-lookin' ones. You made a special trip down here just to ask me that?"

"Yeah, it's been on my mind; that's all. You know, I'm trying to get to know people here. Thanks, Mike."

"You know where her apartment is, but you don't know her name?"

"Oh, I just saw her get off the elevator there one time. Thanks again." As he returns to the elevators, Mike says, "Good luck, pal—you'll need plenty of that." Richard picks up a throaty snicker from Mike's buddy.

Moments later, Lori answers the phone. "Will you let me sleep?" she says, but there's no anger in her voice.

"It's Janet Kroll," says Richard, glancing at the digital clock in his bedroom: 12:14. "The girl out with Braun. Janet Kroll—that's her name. Know her?"

"Nope. Guess that's two people for me to find out about. Cam and Jan, right?"

"Lori, please . . . watch your step. I'm the one who got you involved with this and I would feel . . . I don't know how I would live with myself if anything happened to you."

He realizes that living with himself has long been a daunting task as it is.

Janet Kroll lies in bed and thinks about her scheduled appointments. Earning a living is not something she can simply put on hold. Tomorrow, she'll show a couple of properties in Society Hill, one a two-bedroom in the Towers with a river view, the other an Olde City brick townhouse with a private court-yard. She has been told that she's too nice, too principled, to be successful in real estate, but she is hardworking and organized, and she has done all right for herself since the divorce two years ago.

Someday maybe she'll have her own agency. Or get into the commercial market and make more money. Or switch vocations, go into public relations, corporate marketing, or who knows? She's still young enough.

Or maybe she'll get married again. To the right guy, of course. A guy with some of Davis Braun's characteristics.

But only some of them.

In the online directories, he can't find a Janet (or J.) *Krole* or *Kroll* or any other possible surname spelling he conceives. He didn't want to arouse Mike's suspicions by asking for the correct spelling or her apartment number.

When he calls Information, none of his spellings work there, either. It's past midnight. He'll seek her out tomorrow—knock on every door on the fifteenth floor, if need be—and hope that she's in no jeopardy tonight.

He needs a place where he can think clearly, figure things out.

He knows where he wants to go.

Up there, with the night wind ripping across the sky and the darkness like syrup, he can sort it all out. With the available option—simple enough, if the spirit moves—to end it all, dive out of the straitjacket and into the floating sirens of the air.

But he doesn't plan to do that—not at all. That's the coward's way. He has a mission to fulfill. People are depending on him.

Still, it's nice to know there's a way out. The ultimate release. If the noise in his head becomes too great.

He has been up there only in dreams, but he knows he is more than its match. He should have been a construction worker tightroping his way across suspended beams and sky-scraper scaffolds.

Now's the time.

The Ben Franklin Bridge stretches into the night. Smoky-blue lights necklace the giant, cabled suspension arms that sweep up to steel towers on either side. Below and on the Philadelphia side of the river, Interstate 95 bathes in bright yellow light as it races below a concrete overpass. The highway lighting is like artificial sunshine in some laboratory, creating a mini world at extreme variance with the majestic, somber span that arches into the dark sky and traverses water so black it's invisible. Cars sprint across bridge and highway, which seem like conveyor belts at right angles and different altitudes.

There is a coolness at the riverfront as Richard walks through the parking lot of the Hyatt Regency, a converted office building more proletarian than regal. He has walked here from the 42s, half an hour at a brisk clip and no complaint from the knee. The hotel parking lot's downward slant to the river seems too steep, threatening to slide all the cars, massed hive-like, into the depths. Richard notices a BMW and a Chrysler Sebring under a light stanchion. For a fragile moment, he wonders where his car is parked and whether he checked the lock three, four times like he usually does. His heartbeat jumps and his breathing becomes shallow; then he smiles and settles as he realizes that he came here on foot, that the dingy gray Toyota is out of commission and sitting safely in the 42s' garage.

Richard leaves the Hyatt lot and walks along the graveled waterfront, past abandoned docks and pilings, past rancid, soggy shores, past the structures of commerce—the seaport museum, the plaza at Penn's Landing, the restaurants and condominiums—and then inland several blocks in the reverse direction until he reaches the very foot of the bridge, where cars careen off of Vine Street and jockey for lanes sharply curving upward past the massive stone anchorages that loom aboveground and root beneath it.

He steps over a guardrail and onto a skinny road shoulder that turns into wider pavement as the bridge climbs. But before that transition, meant to usher maintenance workers safely away from speeding vehicles, Richard disengages his iPod, steps onto the flattened base of a giant, pipelike suspension beam, and begins to take the skyward gradient, steadying himself on restraining cables that send vibrations up his arms. His ascent will be treacherous without the attaching pulleys and clamps that painters and bridge inspectors typically use, but Richard is fearless in this element. His balance is exceptional, another clinically undetected piece of sensory prowess linked invariably, he once concluded, to his middle ear, those organs tuned beyond a concertmaster's highest standards. Perhaps an autopsy would reveal some structural oddity, he muses, as he grips and climbs, but no one will be likely to look for that. They'll just bury the clues, those subtle, perhaps microscopic, indicators embedded in living tissue, and send the exquisite wiring into the loamy earth, where it will disintegrate into a puff of chalk dust.

The air is heavy, picking up moisture from the river and lifting it up the span, as Richard trudges higher. Fanning out below him and joining him on high with its eruptions of buildings (the yellow clock face of City Hall a beacon, bronze William Penn now Richard's comrade-in-air from a distance), the city seems to be watching him skywalk as oblivious motorists stream underfoot. Richard feels safe here, removed from harm and the clutter and cacophony of grounded life. Free of elevators and subways and congested streets. All the earthbound noises now diffuse and re-gather into a giant cochlear seashell, a muted roar like the ocean's: white noise in the great outdoors. Braun can't get to him here. Even the past with its relentless grasp is at arm's length. Unencumbered and unfazed, he climbs toward the top.

From this vantage point, the past can be laid out bare and studied like specimens. Richard sees with eyes tearless in the wind—floodlights that turn the black curtain of sky into a pull-down movie screen, a gauzy veil behind which shadows play out their dramas among the mustache-like strips of white-gray cloud that float on the pitch canvas. It is there that Cindy Dempsey exists, in this infinite theater of the mind, and it is from behind the cloud wisps that she emerges, radiant as an angel, a hand extended in play, an invitation. Richard's arms and legs move in perfect, weightless rhythm as he reaches the top, the very top of the steel tower, and the cars move like ladybugs beneath him, and the wind embraces him like a dance partner, and the air is a thousand impulses that stretch in one huge loop—like the bridge's suspension arms—toward Cindy, who grows larger and brighter against the curvature of the sky. And in that instant of safe harbor, that seductive offer of release, Richard glances away from Cindy, spreads his arms on the railing like a boardwalk stroller taking a pause, and looks down at the constellation of lights; it's as if the stars were shot down to earth.

He could stay up here forever. Well, maybe not forever but for quite a long time. A week, a month, a year. If he were ensconced in an astronaut's fully equipped chamber to take care of his needs.

But that thought is a distraction because there is an invitation at hand: Cindy's invitation. A giant, spotlit ghost in the sky.

God, what did he do?

The wind is a caress. He could float in the air. Or zoom down a single shaft as if on a giant pool slide, keeping his eyes fixed on the yellow glow of the City Hall clock. He could try it. It feels safe.

Her image seems brighter to him as he feels his muscles relax. Something in her eyes comes through the texture of sky. Fear in those eyes, and panic, yet a kind of love. For him. He sees it. And he shudders.

No. He must not yield.

He inhales sharply and blinks against the coursing air, checks his footing. No, his is not a life that, like *The Stranger*'s, he can allow to flicker out. His life is starting anew. All men are condemned to die; that's true enough, but it doesn't mean you should hasten the process. Especially when you are still learning about that life.

He steadies himself against the guardrail.

The trip down will be easy.

The rest of the night passes for him as it always does—fitfully. Sleep teases him, a promise undelivered.

"What do you mean you lost your job? How did you manage that? God, Richard, what's the matter with you?"

Only the hour, 10:00 a.m., prevents his mother from reaching full shriek. He has finally gotten around to telling her. Friday morning—a good way to start off her weekend.

"Don't bother waiting for an explanation," Richard says. *By the way, I almost jumped off a bridge last night.*

Evelyn isn't listening, is interested only in her own rebuke. "What are you going to do now? I hope you're not under the impression that we—"

"I'm working on a murder case." It just came out of him, naturally, no sarcasm. The truth, as he feels it.

"What?"

"I'm getting close."

A frightened note creeps into Evelyn's voice. "Richard, what is happening to you? It's starting again, isn't it?"

Richard's chin cradles the receiver as he sits at the desk in his bedroom. He doodles on a legal pad on which he has written a checklist of steps he must take to solve his case. "I'm balancing the books; that's all," he says. He's still being honest, but he can't resist being cryptic.

"What does *that* mean?"

"It's long overdue, Mother."

"Richard, I can't talk to you when you're like this. Do you want to talk to your father?"

"No, you tell him."

"Tell him what?"

"Tell him I got laid off and I'm looking for another job; that's all."

"Is that the truth?"

"Sure."

"What about the other thing? Richard, are you still thinking about Herb Dempsey and all that? Is that what you meant when you said murder case? That's making you sick, you know that? It's not healthy."

"I agree, Mother. I'm trying to cure myself."

"You're not talking sense, Richard. You can always call one of the doctors, you know. Who was the one you really liked? What was his name? Dr.—"

"They can't tell me any more than they already have. It's up to me now."

There is silence for a few seconds before Evelyn speaks again. "Richard?"

"Yes?"

"I can't talk about this any further."

Neither can he. He hangs up gently.

When Evelyn gets off the phone, she hurries to the den, where Marty watches television, the volume booming. Since he retired from Dobbs Publishing, where he was a production editor for a line of automotive trade magazines, Marty has been watching a lot of television. Right now, the business news is on full blast, chatter from investment analysts spouting "long-term" and "disconnect" and "value-driven." Marty follows the market and, though it has been booming, worries that his money isn't safe, that it will all disappear with the next crash. Evelyn is unaware of such threats.

"He's lost his job," she shouts over the TV.

Marty just looks at her.

"Where's the remote?"

Marty shrugs.

Evelyn walks to the television, bends over, and searches a row of buttons recessed below the screen. "How do you turn this thing down?" She twists her neck to look at him as he reclines on the Barcalounger. "For God's sake, you'll wake up the dead, Marty." She finally hits the right button, pokes it several times, and the sound relents. "Good God." When she straightens, she presses a hand on her hip to steady herself.

"What's wrong?"

"I can't take this noise anymore, Marty. You've got to do something."

"It doesn't seem to bother anyone else."

"That's because no one else lives here except me . . . Guess what? Now your son can't do the hearing test for you because he just lost his job. I want you to call him and talk to him. I can't anymore."

"Lost his job?"

"That's what I said." She sits on the rattan couch, settling in for a semblance of a discussion.

"What happened?"

She knits her brows and searches the wall, as if a tele-prompter might flash the answer. "I don't know, exactly; he didn't go into detail. But he said he was 'laid off'; that's how he put it."

Marty nods knowingly. "Lots of layoffs these days; you know that." He gestures toward the television. "The market goes up and people lose their jobs."

Onscreen, a young woman with a salon shag recites the details of a Dow Jones spike.

"Marty, I think he's coming unglued again."

"Why? Just because he was laid off? People are laid off every day."

"I want you to call him."

Marty turns away from the market news and looks at his wife.

"It's that Dempsey thing again," she says. "I think he's fantasizing. I'm telling you, he needs help."

Detectives Pete Burnside and Ricky Alvarez—one cynical with twenty-five years in, the other lithe and eager in his newness—stand before the door to Davis Braun's apartment. Oliver dispatched them with a pair of warrants wrangled just this morning from the Honorable Sara Leibowitz, who somehow still trusts his reputation for fair play and is probably the only judge in town who would grant both warrants, given the evidence at this stage of the Eleanor Carson case.

Burnside's knuckles hammer the burgundy door.

Braun is in the bathroom, gliding a Gillette Sensor over his cheeks, hot water running, door half-closed. He hears the knocking and wonders what the hell's going on. He turns off the spigot, puts down his razor and, with the lather still on his cheeks, walks out of the bathroom. A bath towel is wrapped around his middle, and that's it. He looks through the peephole and sees fish eyes belonging to Burnside.

"Yeah?"

"Davis Braun?"

"That's me."

"Police, Mr. Braun. We have a warrant to search your apartment. And one for your vehicle."

The door opens and Braun stands there in his sensitive-skin shave cream and enveloping bath towel, his cool reserve gone in the presence of two intrusive visitors. "What do you expect to find here?"

"We like surprises, sir," Burnside says with a thin smile. "I'm Detective Burnside; this is Detective Alvarez." He brandishes his badge and the warrants. "This won't take long."

Braun glances at the badge and doesn't bother to inspect the warrant. "This is about Eleanor, obviously," he says as Burnside and Alvarez brush past him, the younger detective's ear missing Braun's lathered cheek by a whisker.

"Sorry for the inconvenience," says Burnside, opening a closet door in the living room.

Braun stands with hands on hips. "I'm the one who's looking for her, and you guys come *here*?"

His visitors don't say anything, just go about their business. Braun follows Alvarez into the bedroom and, when the detective opens the top drawer of the dresser, says, "That's right, I put her pinkie in with the socks."

"This is just routine," says Alvarez.

"Well, it's not *my* routine," Braun says. "Mind if I finish shaving?"

"Not at all. I'll tell you when I'm ready to come into the bathroom."

"Great. Would you do that now so you don't interrupt me?"

Alvarez stops peeling through a lower drawer and looks up at Braun. The young detective's smooth, square features tighten. "No problem," he says, shouldering past Braun and into the bathroom.

Braun stands there, shaking his head, then scratching it. "Unbelievable," he says to himself. He hears the door of the medicine cabinet creak open, then the sound of Alvarez rummaging about. He steps over to the bathroom's open door and sees Alvarez finger a vial of small, white pills.

"Miss Carson has plenty of stuff in here, I see," the young detective says.

"She lives here," says Braun dryly. "Or at least she used to."

"What are these?" Alvarez rotates the vial between his thumb and forefinger.

"I don't know. Allergy pills, I think."

"How come she didn't take them with her?"

"I don't know. Maybe she switched medications."

When they return to the bedroom, Alvarez goes through the closet and the large drawers of the bureau, sees mostly female garments and underthings. "Looks like she's crowding you a little," he says to Braun.

"I travel light."

Burnside checks the living room and kitchen before going through the trash can under the sink. Braun steps in to watch. "Let me know if you find any money down there." Burnside closes the cabinet door and straightens. "Sorry," Braun says, "but this is just so unbelievable."

"Like my partner said—routine," Burnside says.

Alvarez finishes up in the bathroom and bedroom, and

he wears a blank expression as he waits for Burnside. Braun drifts back in, still wrapped in the towel, showing lots of tan and muscle, almost posing. Alvarez glances at him, shouts toward the front of the apartment.

"We're clean back there, Pete. Her stuff is still here."

The three of them stand in the narrow hallway. "I was the one who filed the report to begin with," Braun says. "Remember?"

Burnside sways back slightly on the heels of his feet. "We know that."

"Then why come here?"

"We get lots of perps who report their crimes, Mr. Braun," Alvarez says.

Braun's expression suggests that he'd like to tangle with the junior detective right here in the living room.

"Since you last spoke with Lieutenant Oliver, have you thought of anyone who might want to harm Miss Carson, Mr. Braun?" Burnside asks him.

Braun's face relaxes a bit when he turns from Alvarez to Burnside. "No, no one at all. She was pleasant to everyone. Ask down at her law office."

"We will, thanks. And again, as far as you know, she was going to visit her father for a while."

"That's right."

"The two of you hadn't had a fight."

"I've been through this with the lieutenant."

"Try it with us for kicks," Alvarez says and Braun glares at him.

Burnside glances at his partner and steps closer to Braun. "Bear with me, Mr. Braun. Please just answer the question so we can cross the *T*s."

"No fights. We got along great. That's why we set up house here."

"Sounds cozy," Alvarez says.

Braun keeps looking at Burnside. "Do most Philadelphia detectives start out with smart mouths?"

Burnside offers a small, ironic smile. "Thank you for your time, Mr. Braun. Sorry for the interruption." He turns to leave. "Oh, we need your car keys. It's in the building lot?"

Braun frowns. "Yeah, that's where it is." He gets the keys from the bedroom and returns to hand them to Burnside.

"Thanks, we'll get these back to you."

"I hope that means in about a half hour," says Braun.

"Unless we find something that shouldn't be there," says Alvarez. He smiles at Braun. "Leave 'em at the desk?"

"Fine."

Alvarez follows his senior partner out the door, closes it behind him and, as they pad toward the elevator, fires off a left uppercut like a boxer.

"Guy could use a shot to the ribs. Shit, Pete; place was spotless."

"You didn't expect the body to be gift-wrapped, did you? Look it, Oliver has a pretty good nose. He doesn't waste warrants on cover-your-ass."

"Just sayin'."

"He don't look like a nut, does he?"

"I don't know, Pete, what's a nut look like?"

Burnside presses the down button. "Good point, kid. Let's go check the car."

The call comes from Frank at the front desk. A large UPS box has arrived.

Richard leaves his apartment immediately, looks up and down the hallway to make sure Braun is not waiting to pounce on him, and takes the elevator to the lobby. Frank has propped the box—about four feet high and two feet wide—against the wall behind the counter. Smaller packages are stacked on the counter itself.

"That mine?" Richard points to the big one.

"Yep, that's yours, my man." Frank taps a pen on his UPS delivery sheet. "General Motors. What you got in there, a giant carburetor or something?"

"No. I'll tell you about it later."

"I can't wait."

"Thanks for calling me."

"Your wish is my command, brother."

Richard bends his knees and wraps his arms around the middle of the box.

"Handle that?" asks Frank. "We got a wardrobe cart back there, you know."

"That's okay. I got it." Richard grunts as he sways his back and hefts the box, but it is more ponderous than heavy. He asked Runnels to leave out all the measurement gadgetry—things like the Achilles tendon load path—and just send enough parts to approximate human suppleness and mobility. He totes the box to the elevator. "Here we go," Richard says to the box, his only traveling companion, as the elevator lifts upward. The ride is uninterrupted. When he reaches the twenty-second floor, Richard looks furtively about the empty hallway before carrying the box to his door.

Moments later, the cardboard flaps are open on his living-room carpet. Runnels's note inside: *I probably broke a dozen corporate bylaws to get you this, so make the most of it. Guts removed per your request. Send back when you're done if still usable.*

Good man, Runnels; one of the few reliable human beings on the planet. Maybe Lori Calder has joined that small circle, Richard muses as he pulls out a skull, then a neck, torso, appendages, all the makings of a crash-test dummy. An assembly instruction booklet is included, a single sheet of paper folded four times over. Richard spreads it open on the floor so that all sixteen rectangular facings are visible. He kneels and studies the diagrams: parts identified, arrows showing inserts into sockets, screws to secure, etc. Runnels has drawn thick black lines through the sections pertaining to the fancier, missing elements.

Richard is confident he can put this thing together. His Boy Scout training helped him develop reasonable mechanical aptitude.

Braun has stood under the shower's hot water for fifteen minutes in an effort to chase apprehension and renew his customary sense of well-being. It's not every day that the police toss your apartment. He could have lived without that kind of intrusion.

He turns off the water and steps out of the tub, yanks the bath towel off the rack, and flings it over his back with the panache of a matador. Just then, a rapping. It takes him thirty seconds or so to realize that it's not coming from the pipes or from some other apartment but from his own damn door. Again.

"You've got to be kidding," he says to himself, then remembers first that the police took his car keys, then that they'd leave them at the front desk. No big deal—he has a spare set.

He hollers, "Be right there," before hurrying into a pair of gym shorts. He drapes the towel around his neck as he walks to the door and opens it without prescreening.

"Hiya, neighbor," he says, a note of surprise in his voice. "Taking the day off?"

Lori smiles sweetly. "As a matter of fact, yes."

"Need something else from the pantry?" he kids.

"I do."

"Come on in, then."

"Thank you," she says and steps past him, the door drifting closed behind them. She turns and faces him. She looks like she wants to pose a question and is mulling over the word selection.

Braun smiles down at her. "So? What's the latest?"

Lori unleashes a haymaker, an openhanded round-house-right that smacks Braun's left cheek. He is a full head taller, so she has reached high for her target. Braun, who didn't even flinch, looks perplexed. "What was *that*?"

"What the hell is going on?" Lori's left eye twitches, and the right is a flame-rimmed charcoal nugget. Braun barely recognizes her.

"With what?"

"With *you*!"

"Are you all right?" He reaches out to her, but she swats

his hand away as if countering an attacker in karate class. "I'm fine," she spits out. "How is *she*? Is she here? I'd like to meet her."

In that instant, Lori believes she hears something coming from the bedroom. "You sonofabitch. Is she here *now*?" She rushes into the bedroom but sees no one, pokes her head into the bathroom with the same result, then walks back to the living room.

"Who are you talking about, Lori?"

"Your new girlfriend. You move fast; I'll give you that."

Braun reacts by instinct. Smooth it over; duck and cover. Hey, there have been no promises here. Business as usual. What's the big deal?

"Girlfriend?"

"Babe named Janet? Nice body, huh?"

"What?"

"Or just nice handwriting? Better than mine?"

"Lori, what the hell are you talking about?"

"Dick Tracy has been watching you in action." Lori twists her mouth as she speaks, and wormlike tendons mar her usually milk-smooth throat.

"Dick—?"

"Your boy Richard."

Braun sneers. "Well, *there's* a reliable source." He leans against the half wall at the kitchen threshold. "Janet Kroll? Is that what this is about?"

Lori's eyes open wider, sending out more anger.

"She's just a friend," Braun says.

Lori's laugh is scary. "A *friend*? Give me a break. I'm getting tired of your friends, Davis." She looks like she wants to spit.

"Believe what you want to believe, but that's the truth. Anyway, what are we talking about? Did I commit a crime here? It's not like you and I are married, is it?"

"That's true enough, Davis." She is turning her anger, but neither is sure in what direction. "But, you see, I'm an old-fashioned girl."

"Yeah, right."

"No, I am, in my own way. That's the difference between us, evidently."

"You've got it wrong, Lori."

"I don't think so. Richard might be a stooge, but he gets the details right."

"Oh, really?"

"My God," Lori says, not taking her gaze from his. "I was fooling myself, wasn't I? Thinking that, finally, you and me were . . ." Her voice dies, and she hates herself because she feels she's on the verge of tears.

"I'll say it again: You're wrong about this, Lori."

She regains a measure of composure. "I don't think so." Now she has regained all of it. She takes a step toward him, closing any gap of fear. "So tell me about this bitch."

Braun's nervous smile is uncharacteristic.

"Tell me the truth. I'm a big girl."

"This doesn't change us," he says.

Her cynical smile could rend flesh, but then it mellows and turns enticing. "You see"—she draws closer—"I'm not into sharing." She's right on top of him, her head at his chest. He takes a small step back, but now Lori tugs playfully at the elastic waistband of his gym shorts, and he no longer retreats. She slides her hand inside the shorts, and it doesn't have to go very far before her squared-off polished nails tease him, and now she asks, her voice in a lower register, "Did you fuck her?"

He smooths her hair back from the temple as her tongue goes to work on his breastbone. "Hardly," is his answer.

"Just a dinner date, huh?" Lori breathes into his chest, stroking as she tests him. "I guess next you'll be telling me she's a colleague from the hospital."

Braun grabs her shoulders and lowers his head. "Exactly."

The kiss is hard, consuming. Lori's hands spring free and dig into the small of his back, her wrists slender, a bracelet on the left one already making its imprint on his flesh. Their bodies press against one another. The towel slides off Braun's shoulders and to the floor like a serpent.

Eight feet away, the refrigerator lurches into a cooling cycle, and its humming fills the space the instant that Braun's hands shoot to her neck.

Richard is having some difficulty assembling his crash-test dummy. The shoulder sprockets don't seem to be sprocketing quite right, and the pelvic assembly is clearly offline. He knows this doesn't have to be perfect—it's just a simulation, a demo, after all—but he doesn't want to send Venus de Milo down the chute. He is determined to do this without calling Runnels for coaching over the phone.

Richard envisions an eventual court order to dig up a section of landfill where Eleanor Carson surely is buried. Without him, without his prompting, it never gets that far; her body is never recovered and Braun roams free. Of course, he realizes there is no guarantee that he will convince the law to act, but not for lack of effort on his part—he won't let go this time. He knows what he heard outside Braun's apartment on that night, just as he knows what he heard all those years ago through the wall of his row-house bedroom. Talk about balancing the scales: He was placed at the door of apartment 2307 at that moment to right a wrong. He could not prevent murder then any more than he could twenty years ago, but he can avenge it. This time, he will prove everything. If the universe is indifferent, man must not be indifferent. He has a choice. He must not be a stranger.

Richard is at the spine of the matter, as the abdominal assembly tests his resolve. The diagrams are maddening: part A into socket B, simple enough, but is *socket* in Figure #1 the same as *receptacle* in Step #3? Consistency of terms would be helpful. And why use both *socket* and *sprocket* but to infuriate? What kind of nefarious creatures write these instructions for GM?

He may have overestimated his mechanical aptitude.

Though there is the possibility that Braun disposed of Eleanor somewhere other than the landfill via the Dumpster and a city sanitation truck, Richard believes as strongly in his theory of disposal as in the murder itself. Right down the chute into the giant pile of moldering rubbish and flattened cardboard containers

Just like a pizza box.

Hands fly up reflexively in a shockwave of horror. Different hands—the strangler's—form a vise around the narrow neck, thumbs pressing inward as if intent on plunging through tissue and bone to meet the fingers wrapped behind. Eyes bug out, and the desperate cry summoned cannot escape the throat and, instead, turns downward like something swallowed by mistake. A convulsive movement mashes a shoulder against the right-angled ridge of the half-wall opening to the kitchen, but the impact can't even be felt, though there will be a splotchy, black-and-blue mark on the upper arm, an eyesore by the pool or on the tennis court.

Tiny blood vessels spiderweb the whites of her eyes, and her limp figure slumps against the wall before being guided to the floor, first in a sitting position, then on its side. Full control all the way—no slip and thud this time.

Later, Braun stands over the grounded body. Beneath his beach-boy locks and anatomically perfect skull, his brain goes into overdrive, simultaneously computing a series of steps to be taken to resolve this matter, weighing them against alternative actions, calculating the necessary provisions and movements; his circuitry buzzes in a neuro-electrical frenzy. Yes, the other two disposals were successful but they followed planned, rather than spur-of-the-moment, terminations. The 42s' trash pickup schedule now leaves him out of sync. It's Friday, and early morning pickup has come and gone; the next one will be on Monday. He knows the schedule, is maybe the only tenant in the building who knows precisely. Who else would care?

He doesn't want the body—even if sheathed by a body bag—sitting in that garbage heap for seventy-two hours. That's too long. This time, he needs to keep the body at bay for a while. This time, it must be embalmed.

FOURTEEN

As a boy, Richard Keene was always on the run from the noise of the universe, looking for shelter, some safe space where it all became less oppressive and he could breathe. As he matured, running became an outlet; the air whistled about his ears, creating a kind of white noise to diffuse the harsher sounds always on the attack. He grew wise to the doctors, who could never find anything abnormal about him and attributed his symptoms to neuroticism. He learned to tolerate a level of discomfort, and he discovered new channels of partial escape afforded by Walkmans, iPods, sound conditioners, and his own humming or chanting to spar with the world's rude, unceasing cascade of decibels. He learned, of a fashion, to exist.

Cindy Dempsey made his early existence bearable by giving him a sense that, in her presence, he could show his feelings. There was something precious in this understanding that was theirs alone. She had an Earth Mother's sensibility in a precocious child's body, a wisdom far beyond her years, a caring that thrilled Richard in its lack of demand.

They were children and didn't pretend otherwise but instinctively knew that their bond was special and unbreakable.

Then she was taken from him.

Herb Dempsey's madness flared that awful night, Richard believes. But that wasn't all of it. There had been something dangerously wrong all along. Was Richard the only one to see it?

Cindy's mother knew; she had to. But she did nothing.

Ever since, Richard has tortured himself, mostly over his failure to react on that night and tell the police what he heard but also for missing, or not acting on, the clues, the evidence that preceded the horror. For he was always enormously uncomfortable around Herb Dempsey, always sensed something off-kilter about this man: the dark recessed eyes, the way he'd call Cindy to come inside when she was playing in the street, hollering, "Let's go, Cindy," like a command suited for a dog, an assertion of ownership, a hurried and almost contemptuous summons. But more than that, Richard detected an unmistakable undercurrent of jealousy, a sick resentment at sharing Cindy with the kids on the block—especially the boys on the block, and most especially Richard. That's what six-year-old and seven-year-old and eight-year-old Richard Keene sensed about this man, with the same exactness that his aural antennae received the world around him.

Yet, as if it were a burden she was obligated to bear, Cindy refused to acknowledge the trouble in her life, never amplified what Richard observed for himself. Still, wasn't she strong enough, smart enough, to evade the monster and save her own life? Even at seven years old?

Or did the monster come in another form, something

unexpected and unexplainable and, thus, more monstrous?

Did the sickness belong, as some had hinted, to Richard himself, though but a child at the time? Their objectionable questions and insinuations made him sick, indeed—to his stomach. How could he possibly have gotten in and out of the home without detection at nighttime, with both parents there? Not a shred of evidence to connect him. How could they think he would ever harm a single molecule of his beloved Cindy?

The mother? Penny Dempsey—Aunt Penny—sympathetic with a tiny voice and a bashful smile, was always nice to all the kids, including Richard. No match for her husband, grown-up Richard would conclude. Rendered useless by training and temperament but hardly blameless—a mother, after all, must protect her own. No match for the horror, the worst kind of violation of nature, the hell on earth brought by a twisted man like Herbert Dempsey.

No, Richard knew where he was and what he heard that night, and no one was ever going to convince him otherwise. He knew it as surely as his own heartbeat. Knew it then, knows it now.

Even *she* sensed she was unstable but she was his mother— the father gone in two years, never to return. Dolores Braun, whose vitriol and explosive temper had chased off her husband, displayed revulsion toward most men, yet she treated her young son with all the cheerfulness and equanimity she could muster. As he grew into adolescence, she depended on him increasingly for mundane minutia, such as zipping the back of her dress, but also for companionship and other emotional attachments, though never inappropriate.

Ten years after Leonard Braun ran out on her, ten years of drink and scattered jobs, Dolores left her ex-husband's hometown of Milwaukee with her twelve-year-old son and moved back to her native Philadelphia, using money inherited from her father to buy a modest brick house in the western suburb of Havertown. She worked secretarial jobs that she would quit after a few months, a luxury afforded by her inheritance. But Dolores stayed sane and sober enough to hold onto her son. And rather than resent her shiftlessness and fits of depression, he felt protective of her and, as he matured, injected himself with greater frequency into her personal life.

Though she harbored no desire to remarry, Dolores did not lack for suitors, mostly sales types with easy patter and a forced laugh and zero interest in her young son. She was a shapely, attractive woman right into her forties, though drink and a haphazard diet thickened her body and coarsened her features. Still, she could be as selective as she wanted, since she regarded men as a mere diversion, an occasional physical release and, most importantly, objects to dominate. She could toy with affections, break a heart or two. She would get dolled up for a night on the town, make her son a sandwich for dinner, braceleted wrists fumbling with the Skippy jars, a sensual fragrance announcing her entry into a room and trailing her leaving it. The doorbell would chime, and there in the threshold would be the evening's turkey gussied up with slicked-back hair (sometimes not a lot of it) and cologne potent enough to neutralize her own augmented scent, two force fields colliding in a compact living room of lifeless furniture. Davis took it all in and, when he reached his teens, enjoyed challenging the male visitors with pointed questions about their livelihoods and personal histories. They resented his tone, his smarts—he was too sophisticated for his years—and his physicality. He was a damn handsome kid and already larger and stronger than most of them.

Dolores admired her teenage son's brashness, physical maturity, and precocious command. She often tapped him as her escort for a theater outing or dinner at a dressy restaurant. How could she have a son this old, maître d's gushed. If Davis were mistaken for her date, she'd sometimes fail to correct the impression; one waiter handed him the check while Dolores was in the powder room and said, "That's a fine-looking woman you're with."

For her son's sixteenth birthday, she made an elegant little dinner at home, complete with wine and a chocolate cake sporting sixteen burning candles that Davis extinguished with one gust from his athlete's lungs. She gave him two professionally wrapped presents: an expensive dress shirt and a set of imported cologne and body talc. "I wanted to splurge for this birthday," she told him. This night she wore a light scent, just a bit of makeup, and a calico dress that rose and bunched nicely above the knee when she crossed her legs.

Not long after that night, Dolores brought a man into her bed, which normally looked storm-tossed but on this occasion was immaculate with the lavender spread halved and creased to expose a salmon-colored blanket and color-splashed sheets. The man, nervous and youngish, obediently sat down next to her. Her hands migrated across him, and she deftly unbuttoned his shirt and proceeded to his belt buckle. The young man groped her, and she assisted his labors. Soon their pace spiked to an urgent level, and the bed reverted to its customarily disheveled state.

When they had reached that point in the second-floor bedroom, the front door opened and in walked Davis Braun, home hours earlier than expected from a party across town. The party had been a dud, and now he was to encounter a more private sort of party. He vaulted up the stairs and, ever protective of his mother, seized her bed partner and threw him onto the dresser and against its mirror, which cracked under the impact.

Dolores was upset, but in the coming days she dismissed the incident with a wave of her hand, a derisive gesture aimed at that evening's bed partner. Secretly, she was thrilled by her son's aggression in defense of her honor, which she otherwise prized as much as a dish towel.

Her victimized date had fled the house and, probably embarrassed, pursued no remedies against mother or son.

Dolores's haphazard personal life left Davis with distaste for the ways of both men and women. He vowed never to shrink from correcting such behavior.

Lori Calder always had an appetite. She was a wee girl who outdid her older brothers at the dinner table in their cramped house in Pennsauken, New Jersey, just across the bridge from Philadelphia. She was a welter of paradoxes: a tomboy for whom tears came easily, equally impelled to dive into trouble or her schoolbooks, then a blossoming teenager of enchanting sweetness and startling anger. Two people inside of her constantly battled for supremacy.

The rest of the family seemed normal enough. Joe Calder worked construction and made good money during the Atlantic City casino-building boom in the 1980s, enough to raise three kids and send two of them to college. His wife, Margie, took charge of the household and family finances; she was smart, organized, and calm—a tempering influence on her husband, who sometimes preferred a fistfight to a rational discussion. Lori inherited her scrappy genes from her father.

The boys were standard, athletic high school youth: wrestlers, footballers, average students, prom attenders. Lori made all As and was a cheerleader (as the smallest and most energetic, always out front), a gymnast until the school disbanded the sport, then a basketball player, the team spark plug. In the spring, she was third singles for the girls' tennis team, her blistering serve compromised by erratic baseline play. Her brothers marveled at the strength of her right-hand grip, comparing it to that of their quarterback noted for his large, strong hands. Lori was emotional on and off the courts, and she tended to fall rather hard for guys, but that was hardly a unique predicament among high school girls.

She had two loves in high school. As a sophomore, she dated a senior who stopped speaking to her after she had the audacity to question the accuracy of some pronouncement he spouted; he was a member of the debate team and the legal society, 1500-plus on the college boards, self-absorbed. Affronted, he just walked away from her, and that was that. It turned out that Lori was right and he was wrong about the information in question, but that just cemented the breakup. In time, she found it amusing.

Then, as a senior, Lori lost her virginity (quite late by high school standards) to a jock, a three-letter man who dumped her for someone taller and more coveted only weeks before the prom. That wasn't so amusing. Lori considered fashioning a *Carrie*-like revenge but settled for writing a letter that said she "felt sorry for" him and taping it to his school locker. An orange happy-face sticker topped his name on the envelope. At the time, she avoided any online campaign of retribution.

They graduated and went their separate ways. Of course, she didn't really feel sorry for him, but she did know the value of biding her time. For one driven largely by impulse, Lori had a great capacity for patience—another duality in her personality. That summer, at the swim club, she sat at the foot of his deck lounger as he was taking in the sun, and she made him an offer he couldn't refuse. She led him to a semi-enclosed alcove behind the clubhouse, peeled his swim trunks down, and went to work. Poised on the roof behind them, her best girlfriend trained a cell-phone camera on the action, which quickly went viral; the boy's girlfriend, the tall prom-buster, saw the rushes.

Come Labor Day weekend, Lori's ex died in a car crash, legally drunk and permanently crushed, football shoulders and all. She was dry-eyed.

In college, Lori Calder was active socially and sexually, a smart girl who studied hard but went for mindless fraternity parties and guys who offered muscles rather than intellect. Some years later in the adult world, as a career girl interested in men and money, she met Davis Braun on a casino cabana beach in Atlantic City. His body was tanned and ripped.

She was drawn to him. He reminded her in some ways of the high school jock who had jilted her—there was some unfinished business there, but she didn't quite know what. What she did know was that the future doctor was her sexual match. That was a dynamic she craved and one she sought to preserve at significant cost.

FIFTEEN

Braun sits on his living room sofa, a do-it-yourself futon he assembled in less than an hour one Saturday morning a few months ago. He is sweating and still wearing nothing but gym shorts. A twisted, motionless body lies near the door. A broken rag doll.

Now he must clean up the mess. The cell phone's insistent bleating sideswipes him. He rises and scoops it off of the ledge of the kitchen's half wall.

"Yeah," he says, annoyed.

"You really know how to make a girl feel welcome," says Janet Kroll.

Braun smiles self-consciously, emerging from hell. "Sorry, I was expecting a callback from someone."

"Someone you're not too crazy about."

"Trying to straighten out my cell phone account."

"Roaming charges?"

"Something like that."

"Well, guess what. Instead of Verizon, you've got me."

"I'll take the trade-off."

"Good. Other than phone bills, are you busy?"

"Unfortunately, I have to go in to the hospital."

"I didn't think you were on today."

"I'm not usually, Fridays. Something special; duty calls. Sorry."

"You'll miss a delectable lunch . . . and more. How about tonight?"

For a moment, Braun thinks only of Janet and how good she might make him feel. But he has business to take care of, and the timetable is uncertain. How long, for instance, will it take for a first-timer to prepare a body?

"I drew an extra shift," he says to Janet. "How about tomorrow? If it's nice, we can get some sun up on the deck. About one o'clock?"

"I'm game if you are, mister."

"You talked me into it." He hears her laugh. Nice sound.

He hangs up softly and the moment passes. The next impulse comes from another region of his brain. He must get to the hospital. The things he needs are at the hospital.

He moves the body into the bathroom and places it in the tub. No one else is due to drop by today—the police came too early for their purposes, it would seem. Timing is everything.

When a T-shirted Braun strides out of the elevator and into the lobby, he sees that Mike is at the front desk. Big, awkward, not-too-bright Mike.

"Police bring something for me, Mike?"

"Huh?"

"Set of car keys?"

"Oh yeah." Mike scoops the keys from below the counter and hands them to Braun.

"Regular trash pickup Monday, Mike?"

"Huh?"

"Trash. They pick up on Mondays?"

Mike nods his head like it's on puppet strings. "Far as I know."

Braun is in motion, pondering how he would explain his questioning Mike on this point in the unlikely event that an investigation reached that far. No sweat; he'd come up with something palatable, and chances are huge that Mike would not remember a thing about it, anyhow.

Braun stops at the convenience store, and buys a quart of iced tea and a copy of *Philadelphia* magazine. A few months back, some bullet-headed writer interviewed him at Metropolitan for a story about area med schools; Metro public relations had offered up photogenic Braun for a resident's perspective. The article should be in this issue, October. Just hit the stands.

Next door, Jay is in the booth at the parking garage, and Braun gives him a healthy wave and smile en route to the elevator. He knows his car is on L level, six floors up, on the Sixteenth Street side, where he parked it after returning with Janet last night. It's a different spot each time, nothing reserved, so one must rely on memory or write it down. Braun trusts his memory, and it never fails him.

He usually walks to the hospital on Ninth Street, but he plans to bring back a heavy load this trip, so the Fiat is pressed into action. His army-green duffel is in the trunk. He wants to be at the hospital during the lunch hour, when the morgue is . . . like a morgue.

Metropolitan Hospital sits behind a well-tended, sloping lawn and a formidable enclosure of iron spears anchored to a knee-high concrete retaining wall. A tall, brick pedestal anchors each of the right angles framing the building. Braun pulls into the main driveway and parks in the subterranean garage, his ID gaining him admittance there and into the bowels of the hospital itself. His canvas duffel is folded and tucked under his arm. Through broad swinging doors, as if to a hotel kitchen, a dank corridor leads to the morgue on the right, marked in simple lettering on the door, the holding tank for bodies headed south. Braun pushes through that door, and as he anticipated, anything living is at lunch. The long metal drawers, like oversized safe-deposit boxes, all are shut. In the corner on the other side of the room, the supply closet is locked, but Braun has the antidote: a slender, annealed metal pick that he won from some juvenile offender in a card game on the beach in Wildwood, New Jersey, many summers ago. It now finds its way to the heart of the tumbler for a delightful click. The knob turns.

The light switch is soundless, and the shelves bulge with liter jugs of all the necessary fluids. Braun knows that they don't employ inventory specialists from the Wharton School down here; they'll never miss a few items from stock. He puts into his duffel one of each: formaldehyde, mercuric chloride, zinc chloride, borax, and glycerin, along with a few others. Then he selects a packet of specialized steel instruments and places it among the fluid containers. He plucks a folded body bag from a stack on the floor and adds to the booty, then zips up the duffel.

He returns to his car within minutes without passing another human being, this even in a big-city hospital in the middle of the day. It's a question of knowing your terrain and moving swiftly in the creases. The afternoon has turned sunshine-sweet, earthy smells filtering even to the oil-stained depths. Braun keys open his trunk and deposits the duffel. Before leaving, he sits in the car for a few minutes and quaffs some iced tea while trying to locate the med-school piece amid *Philadelphia*'s bevy of body-contouring and hair-removal ads. He finally finds it, a nice spread beginning on page seventy-two, and there he is, smiling in his scrubs, outdoors in the greenery, one foot up on a courtyard ledge, forearm resting on the knee, cool and casual, the caption identifying one Davis Braun, Metropolitan Medical School resident, with the caption: *They allow you to exercise your own judgment.*

He reaches his apartment in less than five minutes. The body, dead and discoloring, is naked and stretched out in the bathtub. He draws the blood out through a cleaning spray bottle's plastic stem and straight into the drain, the makeshift intravenous hookup so deft (the stem is pinched at the point of insertion in the throat by a pencil's metal eraser band) that, so far, hardly a drop of blood has escaped.

The biodegradable cleaner stem is necessary because Braun found himself shy one duct and decided to improvise, not wanting to press his luck and return to the hospital. He does have a long, stainless-steel tube through which to draw cavity fluid, and he has made the puncture just below the breastplate. Another tube inserted at the carotid artery forces the aqueous solution of chemicals, including rubbing alcohol, into the cavities and tissues of the body. The tart smell of the chemicals mixes with the now-muted stink of the corpse. Any normal bodily scents have long since evaporated. During the entire procedure, Braun avoids look-ing at the face, which is turned downward and rests on the inside tub wall so that only part of a cheek and the hair are visible.

Braun has both the dexterity and the fortitude for this task, though he guesses he may not have the stomach for severing heads and limbs and discarding them piecemeal. He is not crude, after all, and such acts seem revolting. No, he will not descend to that level of barbarism, which is simply too messy, too gruesome. And, in this instance, unnecessary. Stick to clinical workmanship and a clean dispatch.

So he leaves his subject to its bloodletting, washes his hands with antibacterial soap pumped from a pyramidal canister, and walks into the kitchen, where he dabs mayon-naise on Swiss cheese and slices of tomato slapped between two mitts of Stroehmann's potato bread. He takes a healthy bite and chases it with Nantucket grape-cranberry juice; he's hungry as hell.

He pokes the remote, and the twenty-seven-inch TV screen produces a pristine visual. Somehow CNN is on. Braun doesn't know how that happened; it must have been an inadvertent stopping point when he last switched it off after channel-surfing. He never watches any news stations, reads a newspaper, or listens to all-news-all-the-time KYW on the radio. He lives outside of the world at large and concentrates on his personal pathways.

He jumps off CNN and onto a premium movie chan-nel. Some teen comedy, with all the girls mindless and bare-midriffed.

After a dish of fruit cocktail and a generous helping of

Sara Lee pound cake, he gets back to work. By now, a large volume of bodily fluid has been removed and is spiraling into the city's sewage infrastructure. There is a moment, as he hovers, when something ripples down his spine. It is a shudder of self-doubt, a split-second hesitancy as powerful as electric current. It might even be a frisson of regret. In the instant it happens, it possesses him. But then it passes, and in the immediate aftermath of arrogance, he knows what he must do, what he will do, to survive.

While Braun has his hands full, Richard still struggles to piece together his hard-plastic dummy for its downdraft ride. He has called Lori and left a message reminding her that she promised to witness the test. In late afternoon, he manages to click the feet into place to complete the unit, a female adult model, as he requested from Runnels. He jams it into a four-foot-long garment bag, pushing the head to the side and bending the lower legs as if the dummy kicked them upward in a leap of joy. Richard zips the polyester bag, wraps lengths of twine around it at several spots top to bottom, and ties each tight so that the bag's overall shape is no longer broad and flat but near cylindrical. A reasonable facsimile, he figures.

He's ready to go, but he wants Lori on hand as planned. He calls her apartment again, believing she's still at work. Her recorded, mellifluous voice clicks on once more: "Hi, this is Lori Calder. Sorry we're not speaking at the moment, but leave me a message, and we will be soon."

"Lori, I've got Eleanor X rigged up and ready. Call me as soon as you get in."

Directly one story above Richard's assembly site, Braun's project is taking longer than expected due to the physics of gravity and the resistance of the spray can stem he has jury-rigged for the occasion. He has never performed an embalming before and only observed one.

He calls Janet's cell, and her voice message comes on after several rings. He looks forward to seeing her tomorrow and relaxing in the sun. Supposed to be clear skies and warm. A short break here at the hospital, he says, and he was thinking of her.

She has a nice voice and a pleasant way about her. None of Lori's flash temper or Eleanor's critical barbs. If redheads are stereotyped as volatile, this one is calm.

So far.

It is five o'clock, and Richard nips at his cuticles as he sits with the loaded-up dummy at his feet. He knows he must find a way to contact Janet and warn her about Davis Braun, about the danger she may be courting. But right now, there's a greater concern, a growing fear.

There has been no return call from Lori so far and, while she's not super-late, a whorl of uneasiness eats at Richard. His mind races. He has put her in a dangerous position. He fears that she got too close to Braun, asked the wrong question the wrong way, and tipped her hand.

He stands, takes a bottle of filtered water out of the refrigerator, and drinks. He calms himself. So she's a little delayed, held up at work. So what? What's the hurry? It's early yet. Settle down.

He can't. He leaves his apartment, eyeing the hallway in both directions, still wary that Braun might jump him like a sneaky kid in a schoolyard. He walks to the stairs and up one floor, moves silently across the carpet to Lori's apartment, one door from Braun's. When he presses the doorbell button, it sends a rounded chime into the unit and out into the hallway. He looks toward Braun's door, fearing that it will open, ready to dash away if it does, then hoping it *will* open, ready for confrontation, ready for anything, damn him. He rings a second time, and it is apparent that Lori is not in, or at least that she is not answering.

He takes the elevator to the lobby and hurries out the rear door onto the loading platform. He opens the door to the Dumpster room and steps inside. The room soaks in orange-yellow light and has a faint smoky scent that seems to rise from the concrete floor. Trash droppings flutter from the overhead chute into the monster Dumpster. The whir of hidden machinery and the pulsing of embedded pipes clot Richard's ear, then clear as if from a swallow's pop on an airplane changing altitudes.

Richard stands on the eight-foot-high Dumpster's lower ledge, reaches high to grab the top one, and manages to hoist himself to a view of the contents, head and torso bobbing over the top, legs dangling down the side, hands maintaining a grip. The huge Dumpster is loaded with refuse, about three-quarters full. Scanning the broad pile is insufficient; he must explore hands-on. He rolls his legs over the top and lets himself fall onto a thatch of cardboard and paper and plump plastic bags. He slides off that tenuous platform and into the heap, his sneakered feet pedaling for traction.

He is like a kid in a bubble-ball playpen, except that there is panic rather than joy in his immersion. He digs and lifts and tosses aside, feverish and spastic, changing the shape of the mass with his two-handed tunneling. He has about six feet worth of shit to search through; thankfully, it is mostly bagged and dry. He spends nearly an hour at this task and doesn't spot any suspicious packages or human appendages.

Just as Richard decides to call it quits, a man walks in carrying several large folded rectangles of cardboard. After the man stands the cardboard up against the wall for pickup, he notices Richard.

"What the h—?"

Richard gives him a silly smile. "Threw something out by mistake. No way I'll find it in this mess, huh?"

"What was it?"

"Oh, just a—a piece of paper I need, you know, in a bag with the rest of my trash."

The man turns to leave, not interested in helping. A mildly contemptuous "Good luck, buddy," and he's out the door.

A bit of rancid orange juice drips from Richard's sleeve. He springs upward, and his knee throbs as he presses it against the overhanging top ledge of the Dumpster. He rolls his body over and out, hangs there for a moment, then eases himself down the side. He is rank and dirty.

He avoids the elevator and takes the stairs, intending to climb the full twenty-two floors to his apartment. He jerks his hand into the side pocket of his pants, panics, fishes deeper, and finally feels the reassuring metal edges of his keys.

Between floors three and four, he hears echoing footsteps growing louder, and two bodies skirt one another on the higher landing.

"Hey," he calls to the person descending, stopping a few steps below him.

"Yes?"

Cam.

"I guess you and I are the only ones in the building who practice fire drills," Richard says, startling himself with an instinctive use of humor and his ease of delivery—qualities that, until very recently, have been foreign to his adult personality.

The young man above him smiles not at all. "Guess so."

But Richard doesn't let him get away, steps quickly to his side before he can.

"I've seen you before; my name's Richard Keene." He extends his hand. Being personable seems to have its own momentum.

"Cameron," the young man says tentatively. "Cameron Miro."

In the handshake, Richard is the more vigorous of the two. "Nice to meet you, Cameron." He sees Cameron take one sniff of air, and gestures toward the dirt and stains on his shirt and pants. "Sorry. Had a little accident, so I thought I'd spare the people on the elevator. Anyhow, it's good exercise."

"I always use the stairs," says Cameron, warming up. "I'm only on the fifth floor."

"Smart," Richard says. "How do you like living here?"

"Okay, I guess."

"What do you do?"

"I'm an intern at Metropolitan Hospital."

Richard nods and, behind the nod, assimilates the connection. Why was he snooping on Braun? Does he have a thing for him? Or is there something more sinister going on?

"I'm an audiologist. So I guess we have a vocational connection, though a tenuous one." Richard smiles, laying on his newfound charm.

Cameron returns a weak smile as his body language signals he's anxious to get going. "Well, I'll see you around campus, Cameron. But I hope not down at Metropolitan."

Cameron already is two steps farther down, his head turned away. "Cam Miro," Richard whispers to himself. Does he play a role in all of this, or is he merely incidental?

The knee cooperates as Richard scales the next eighteen stories. The hallway on the twenty-second floor is clear—he continues to be leery of Braun surprising him. He showers and puts on a clean T-shirt and shorts. For a moment, he feels like the little kid he once was, snuggling into a pair of freshly laundered flannel pajamas and sliding into the warmth and protection of bed; the kid he was before it happened, before the night when the walls whispered to him, screamed to him. From that moment, there was no safety. Everything closed in on him, the world turned into a closet; a police station interrogation room turned into a phone booth; the lies, the words not said. Even the shelter of bed became a trap—no soft release of comfort but steel belts pinning him to the rack. And most other compartments of life were equally constrictive. Except for the occasional, delicious peak—hiking in Pennsylvania's Blue Mountains as a teen, the observation deck of the Empire State Building visited with his parents—where he was somehow free and in command of his nervous system.

And now here he is, twenty-two floors up but nonetheless hemmed in and scared. Yet, despite that, somehow he feels renewed determination, some kind of rod at his spine that won't let him collapse this time, a gift that arrives with the realization of last chances.

He must go to the fitness center to work out. What else is there to do? He won't be able to persuade Frank or Lieutenant Oliver or anyone else to barge into Lori's apartment. Or Braun's apartment. Figures his sanity is still precarious in their eyes.

This may be unjustified panic on his part, he concedes. Take a breath and step back. She's all right; Lori is all right. She's just a little late; that's all. Or she forgot, had to do something important on a moment's notice. A powerful distraction. Forgot even to call or text. A simple explanation.

The dummy test can wait.

Janet Kroll. He'll likely see her right now at the fitness center. Warn her. She'll be there; it's that time of day.

He laces up his cross-trainers, takes a business card from the desk drawer, and scribbles his telephone and apartment numbers on the back, places it along with his apartment key in the back pocket of his shorts, and goes to the elevator. She'll be there; Janet will be there. And Lori will be all right.

Janet Kroll is indeed there on a treadmill, her sleeveless athletic top cutting a deep V down her bare back. She runs like an anchor for a relay team, accelerating toward the finish line. Richard settles onto a stationary bike that provides a perfect view of Janet, her smooth back and fluid running form. He doesn't want to lose her when she completes her run and steps down from the treadmill.

Richard pedals lazily on the bike, conserving energy. Janet breaks off her sprint and runs like a two miler. Ten minutes later, she slows her pace further, then walks the final minute, towels off her neck and forehead, and steps down from the treadmill. As she makes her way to the weight room, Richard intercepts her. He keeps his voice low but distinct.

"Janet?"

She looks at him, curious; she recognizes him. "Yes?"

"Can I speak to you for a moment?"

She doesn't look annoyed but says simply, "I was just going next door to work out."

"It won't take long—it's very important."

She gauges him, puzzling it through. "How do you know my name?"

"I asked someone; I hope you don't mind. Mine's Richard Keene. Anyway, we're not strangers, right?"

She moves into the doorway of the weight room. "Well, come on in. I'm listening."

"No, please, in private; just give me two minutes. Believe me, it's extremely important."

He feels the understated emotion in his voice and hopes she can, too.

"Over here," he says, leading her out of the fitness area and into the deserted banquet room. Almost deserted. A young woman, collegiate and studious, sits on a ledge above a heating vent as she scans text on a laptop, her back pressed against the window. Richard and Janet walk to the other side of the large room, well out of earshot.

"Please don't get mad or think I'm spying on you or anything like that," he says.

She looks puzzled, tense. "What is it?"

"Last night, I saw you out with Davis Braun."

Janet presses her lips tightly together.

Richard holds up his hand as an apologetic gesture. "It was completely by accident; I wasn't following you. When I came into the lobby, the two of you were walking out."

"So?"

Richard's hand slices the air. "I believe that you are in danger if you spend time with him . . . alone."

"Really?" She appears composed, but her heart is beating faster than it does when she's at full throttle on the treadmill.

"I believe," Richard continues, "that he's a murderer. He murdered a girl in this building—the girl he's been living with."

Janet stifles a gasp. "Okay, you've got my attention." She runs the towel over her face again, chasing fresh perspiration. "How am I supposed to believe this?"

"Did you know he was living with someone?"

"Yes. He said it was no big deal."

"She's disappeared. Ten days."

He senses Janet counting backward in her head to place the day it happened.

"What are you thinking about?" he asks.

She blinks. "Nothing. Have you gone to the police?"

"Yes. They're investigating."

"They are?"

"Yes, they are."

"This is pretty wild, uh . . . Richard?"

"Yes, that's right. It *is* wild."

"How are you involved?"

"I heard the murder take place." He pauses. "I was passing his apartment. Strictly random."

She blinks twice and opens her mouth a moment before the words come out. "You heard, what, a gunshot or something?"

"He strangled her." He taps one ear. "I have very good hearing."

Janet shakes her head, and a strange smile shows up. She searches for equilibrium. "This is . . . Excuse me, this is—"

"Please—"

"Aren't you worried I'll think you're kind of crazy?"

"Do you? Think I'm crazy?"

"I don't know." She looks right into his eyes. "Aren't you worried I'll tell him all about you?"

"He already knows. He knows I know."

"This happened ten days ago?" There's a trace of anger in her voice, a shift in tone that Richard picks up.

"That's right." He finds himself staring at her neck, its slope and smoothness. He looks beyond her at the college student slouched against the window, then back at Janet. "Stay away from him, Janet. *Please.*" She looks like she's falling through space. "I know what this sounds like," Richard says. "I have no reason to make it up."

She places two fingers on his wrist, tentative trust. "You seem like an honest guy."

He tells her more: the way in which he heard it happen, how he believes the body was disposed of via the trash chute. He doesn't mention Cindy Dempsey or his worries about Lori; that would be too much, an overload. He reaches into the back pocket of his gym shorts and withdraws something he brought expressly for her benefit. A business card. Lieutenant Robert Oliver's.

"Look, if something happens to me," he says, handing the card to her, "this is the policeman handling the case. He's an honest guy. I think."

He looks into her eyes. "I wrote my number on the back."

Janet pinches the card between her thumb and forefinger, looks at both sides, then back at Richard. Her voice sounds nervous. "You should let the police handle it, and stay out of it yourself."

"I can't do that."

"Why not?"

"It's a long story . . . Anyway, I'm already *in* it."

He does not hear from Lori all night, and the crash-test dummy remains in his living room. He tries to sleep, inserts his earplugs as usual, but finds no respite under the covers. There are no rest stops for the mind as it spins out its excesses. Lori is dead, he fears, he believes, he convinces himself. She got too close. Her body is somewhere in that Dumpster pile; he missed it when he jumped in to search, missed it because it's been carved into small pieces.

No, it's still in Braun's apartment, primed for disposal.

Meanwhile, Janet Kroll is at risk.

Oliver. He must call Oliver.

What the hell will he tell Oliver?

Eleanor Carson. Her body. The law's corpus delicti.

Must find it, will find it. All the other elements will then assemble themselves in sharp relief in the light of day, the case built and certain. Her body must be located.

He falls asleep, or at least into what passes as sleep for him. He floats into an out-of-focus pastel world, the old row-house neighborhood tented by summer sky. Plastic kiddie pools on front lawns. They are no more than four or five, splashing in the wonderful cool water, both of them in the flimsy pool on the Keene lawn, their mothers gabbing on the patio. The heat rises in waves from street and sidewalk, and the air is breezeless and furnace-like, but the two kids in the pool don't feel it. They have the water to distract them, and each other to engage. The little girl sits in water a foot deep and smacks it with her palms, punctuating with a squeal of delight. The little boy slaps the water in response but then keeps silent, letting her be the attraction. They alternate spraying drops and water-feathers into the sunlight, agitating the pool water, then allowing it to settle and gather at their shins or waist, he standing, she sitting. There is a playful alertness, a knowing anticipation in her dark-brown eyes, even at this age. She is both unsettling and captivating, and as they measure their distance and speak with their eyes, and their mothers' words stay within the awning's shade, and boxy air-conditioners rattle and drone from second-story windows, and hundreds of other little dramas unfold elsewhere in the neighborhood, adult, barely sleeping Richard does not want this picture to change shape, does not want the dream to end. It is the hazy drift of the midconsciousness, the dreamer aware that he is dreaming but powerless to alter or stop it. And then Richard rudely falls out of his pastel world and through a white void, a realm beyond reason and memory, and from there he lands in some kind of hellhole of desperate murmurs and gasps, struggling and thrashing. A sudden shaft of light from above like a beacon from heaven, and he is fighting gravity as he climbs, panicked and clawing his way toward the light growing broader and brighter. The taste of ashes on his tongue, and the cylinder narrowing and twisting like a giant snake as he moves, trapped in its tract, its fanged mouth opening wider, the light streaming in now, but he is slip-sliding as he nears the top, fingernails scratching the sooted metal in a disturbing shudder of sound as if on a grade school blackboard. With a convulsive thrust, his arm feels wrenched from its shoulder socket, and the first digits of his fingers make it over the top of the open door of the chute. But escape is cut off; the door flaps shut, smashing his fingertips, unhinging him for the long tumble down, not through a cushioned air pocket but banging against the hard metal all the way into the yawning darkness and screaming, screaming, screaming . . .

The digital clock glows 9:06 a.m., a lot later than the time at which he usually awakens, when he has managed to fall asleep at all. Richard sits up in bed and gulps air, sweat lines staining his T-shirt. He yanks out his earplugs and reaches for the cell, her number already programmed. C'mon, answer. Water pipes groan through the walls.

"Lori, it's Richard. Where are you? Please tell me you're all right," he pleads after her voice greeting.

He is still tussling on a sweatshirt as he hurries to the elevator. A three-minute wait and then a full boat, even on a Saturday morning. He annoys them by getting on, nudging the bellies and pocketbooks. He takes a deep breath and closes his eyes as he pivots and faces front.

When he lands in the lobby, he runs past the mail room to the door of the trash bay, but he's too late. Minutes earlier, the Dumpster sent its contents into the jaws of the city sanitation department's largest vehicle after being wheeled onto the loading platform. It was lifted and tilted and emptied in a deluge of paper-plastic-garbage-throwaway—human exhaust. Richard bursts into the room, looks into the Dumpster, and sees that it has been picked clean.

Trash pickup on a Saturday?

He races onto Fifteenth Street and hears a trash truck's whine-and-grind somewhere nearby. He stands there, aggravated at himself for not getting here earlier, though he had no reason to believe that this Saturday morning would bring a trash collection.

What he does have is an unreasoning fear that Lori Calder's body is in that load.

What to do? He's certainly not going to try to stop a city trash truck and inspect it. He blew it; he was late. An overnight dump by Braun, and no morning inspection by Richard. Impeccable timing, once again.

That familiar feeling of desperation fills him up. He runs back into the building and calls Lieutenant Robert Oliver, who is at his post on a Saturday morning. His number, too, is a very recent addition to the cell's address book.

"The next-door neighbor's missing."

Oliver is working on a sizable mug of black coffee. "Are you the guardian for the whole building now?" he asks Richard. "How long's she been missing?"

"Since yesterday."

"Come on, Keene."

"I think he killed her."

"And what makes you say that? Did you hear this one, too?"

"We were working on this together."

Oliver takes a sip. Hot coffee is one of the few remaining pleasures that he derives from life, and this ceramic mug of his really retains the heat.

"You say you were working together?"

"Yes."

"Coupla PIs, huh?"

"She was casually getting more information from him. Maybe she said the wrong thing at the wrong time."

"What does *casually* mean?" Oliver's tone has shifted from flip to businesslike.

"Just friendly, sympathetic—nothing else."

"All right."

"Please, can you check it out?" Richard clears his throat to chase the wiggle of panic that has crept into his voice. He sits forward and digs two knuckles into his forehead right between the eyebrows, trying to ground a burgeoning headache.

"I had my men search Braun's place yesterday. It was clean."

"Of course it was," Richard says softly. Now it fully dawns on him what Oliver has just said, that this slow-to-act police lieutenant has taken some real action. Not his fault that, as it turns out, the timing wasn't optimal. "You say you did search his apartment?"

"Yes. And his car."

Richard feels energy gathering, feels that someone is on

his side. "Thanks."

"You're welcome," Oliver says through a coffee slurp.

"That was faster than I expected."

"No, it wasn't," Oliver says, but his voice is light. "By the way, my guys are thorough; they don't miss anything. We checked Miss Carson's car, too. Nothing special—no suitcase."

"There was no suitcase in there?"

"Nope."

Richard has no reason to believe that either Frank or Lori is lying about seeing Eleanor leaving with a suitcase. And if Frank cannot be absolutely positive that it was Eleanor Carson he saw, Lori certainly can. "What do you make of that, Lieutenant?"

"She took a cab and not her car."

"Or hurried back to her apartment to get something she forgot, taking the suitcase with her."

"Maybe, but I think she would've left it with the desk man while she went upstairs. Look, Richard, I'm in the reacting business, understand? My instincts tell me you may be right about foul play, but I need more to go on."

"That's what I'm trying to come up with," says Richard, gratified, almost thrilled that the lieutenant has addressed him by his first name.

"Suppose he killed these women right in the apartment like you suggest. What do you think he does with the—?"

"Bodies? I have an answer for that. It's so crude it works."

"Let's hear it."

"He dumps them down the trash chute."

A few seconds pass, and no response from Oliver. "Lieutenant?"

"I've never come across a body disposed of that way, but that doesn't mean it never happened. In fact, we considered it a possibility for a murder in a high-rise off Wissahickon Drive some years back. We've had bodies tossed into slag heaps, junkyards, freight cars. Dumpsters, too, but not down a high-rise trash chute."

"Like a Hefty bag," Richard says.

"Filled with body parts?"

"Maybe. He's a surgeon, or at least soon to be."

"I get your drift. That's quite a job for an apartment bathroom."

"True. Your men obviously didn't find any traces of blood."

"None."

"When did they inspect?"

"Morning. Ten, eleven."

Richard nods to himself. If she was killed, it had to be later in the day. She was at work . . . or was she?

"Lori works at Mazer National Bancorp. Can you check to see if she was there yesterday?"

"It's Saturday, Keene."

Richard lowers his head slightly in disappointment. He's back to *Keene*.

"Anyway," Oliver continues, "you're pretty good at checking up on workplaces yourself."

"I say he just sends them down intact," Richard says boldly, fighting to reclaim first-name status with Oliver.

"What, in a body bag?"

"He can get those easily enough at a hospital, right?"

"It's too bulky to get a whole body down there."

"You'd be surprised at what can fit."

"A foot in diameter?"

"It's a foot and a half here. Probably no government standard for trash chutes, huh?"

"Probably not."

"I measured it."

"I'm sure you did. Know what? You shoulda been a cop."

A high compliment—Richard smiles bashfully. "A slender woman—Lori's small and thin, and I'm guessing Eleanor Carson was the same—encased full-length in a body bag can fit," he says. "And it's a straight shot down."

"Uh-huh."

"In fact, I'm going to be testing it out today, Lieutenant, just to be sure. I've obtained a dummy that the car companies use to, you know, test for impact injuries in crashes. I've got it in a suit travel-bag, which is shorter than an actual body bag, which will make it even more difficult, since the body will group up a little. Know what I mean?"

"I get the picture. You better hope you don't wind up on the six o'clock news."

"Could the police observe, Lieutenant?" Richard senses an ally and wants to cultivate him. "Could *you* observe? I'd really appreciate it."

Oliver slurps more coffee. "I don't know exactly what good that does us, but maybe I will. I might even bring a body bag for you. No sense makin' it any harder than it has to be."

"Right. While you're here, why don't you drop in on Davis Braun yourself, Lieutenant?"

"I don't know about that. But I will try to make it over there. How's 12:30?"

"That's good, I'm ready to go. Thank you."

"I'll see if I can break away for a half hour. You know, maybe it could happen that way, but the trash chute's not the only possibility. Don't get married to that idea."

"I've got a pretty strong feeling about it," Richard says.

"Yeah, you've got strong feelings all right, but we'll need more than just feelings."

Richard smiles broadly. *We'll*, the lieutenant said. "I know," is all he can think to say at the moment.

"I like your determination, kid. You've got me thinking I might get a second warrant; bring in a forensic team for a full chemical scan."

"You're a good man, Lieutenant."

"Yeah, right."

"You ever read any poetry?"

"You say, *poetry?*"

"Yes."

"Not since high school."

"Do you know Walt Whitman?"

"Whitman? Sure. I remember he wrote a famous poem about Lincoln, and he's got some things named after him over in Camden. Lived there for a while, I believe."

"You'd like his stuff—'Look for me under your boot-soles,' he wrote. That's one of his great lines."

"That works for the police beat, all right. We wear out a lot of shoe leather."

"Well, if it ever comes to that," Richard says, "you can look for me there."

"Okay . . . ?"

"Or you can look for me somewhere way up high."

"What's that mean? Why am I gonna have trouble looking for you in the first place?"

"You'll know when the time comes."

"I don't like guessing games, Keene. What the hell are you talking about? 'Up high?'"

"That's right, but first things first."

"Don't go off on me now, kid."

"Lieutenant, you know where my apartment building is, right?"

"After thirty years, I think I can find my way around this city."

"It's the 42s on Locust."

"Thank you, Keene; I believe I already knew that."

"See you then." Richard hangs up. *Yes.*

"What the hell?" Oliver scratches his chin. He doesn't like the sound of this at all. Maybe his sanity verdict was premature.

Way up high, the kid said; look for me way up high. Oliver can't figure whether Keene was being wistful or trying to sound ominous.

Then he remembers their first meeting, when the kid told him how much he loves high places—the heights.

And wasn't that the same night he'd gone up that rickety ladder like a human fly, a little episode related the next day, when Burnside said he could finally climb the stairs without fear of falling on his face?

Davis Braun is on cleanup detail. The tubes, both plastic and stainless steel, are disconnected and stashed in paper bags ready for disposal. The white shower curtain and liner are still folded on the floor between the toilet and the vanity. A dozen ringlets sit scattered on top.

Wearing fresh surgical gloves, Braun lifts the body out of the tub and onto the body bag on the tiled floor. One side of the bag curls up against the base of the toilet and the vanity. After he eases the body down, he turns on the hot water in the tub full blast and watches the level rise over streaks of dried blood. Steam cobwebs the room, misting the mirror on the medicine cabinet. As the tub fills with scalding water, he jams the body into the body bag.

"Maintenance."

It is a muffled voice, next door, in the hall somewhere.

"Maintenance."

Braun stops dead. *The guy's in his apartment.*

The intruder shouts, "Hello."

"Just a minute. I'm in the bathroom," Braun yells and yanks off the water. "Be right there." He can only shake his head in disbelief, step out of the bathroom, and close the door behind him. The wood is a bit warped, and the door wedges itself into the doorjamb with a disconcerting scrape.

He wipes his hands on his gym shorts as he walks into the living room. Good old Orlando, who fixed the garbage disposal on his last visit, holds a stepladder. He is a small, polite man with lines radiating from his sharp, dark eyes.

"Sorry. I rang the bell; then I knocked. Guess you didn't hear."

"Guess not. What's up?"

"Smoke alarms. You get the flyer?"

"I don't remember. I might have."

"Gotta check 'em. Whole building. Got me working Saturday."

"No kidding?" Braun looks back toward the closed bathroom door and relaxes just a little. No need for Orlando to go in there.

"Just be a minute," says Orlando, who sets up his stepladder and climbs to the top rung so he can reach the smoke detector on the living-room ceiling. He uncaps it, fingers the wiring, pokes it, and raises a sharp beep. "New central system. We got to check everything out."

He gets down, walks to the alcove between bathroom and bedroom, and resets his ladder. Braun watches. It stinks back there, but there's no reason for him to go into the bathroom. No reason. Unless he has a sudden urge to use the toilet.

Orlando wrinkles his nose but doesn't say anything and goes about his business. Lots of different smells in these apartments and not all of them like petunias. The second smoke alarm offers its short, piercing beep. Braun stands in the living room, hands on hips. "Sorry about the stink back there," he says. "I got this new stuff to clean up the bathroom. Smells worse than whatever it is I clean up."

Orlando nods and gets down. "No problem. I don't need to go in there."

Braun looks at him. Damn right you don't.

Orlando closes his ladder and walks past Braun to the front door. "You're all set."

Braun opens the door for him. "Thanks, Orlando. See ya." With that, the little maintenance man pads down the carpeted hallway, ladder in tow, off to his next destination.

SIXTEEN

Richard keeps calling Lori, keeps getting her voice mail, fears the worst, *knows* the worst has happened. He is convinced she's gone, buried in the trash truck and on her way to oblivion. Unless Braun still has her, hasn't disposed of her yet, didn't have a body bag or a good substitute on hand.

Oliver will be here. He's coming to witness the simulation and, speaking of body bags, he said he might bring one. Richard wants to persuade him to look up Braun while he's here, nail him maybe with fresh evidence. There is no turning back from this thing now; the freight car is in motion, and the track is downhill.

His yellow plastic laundry basket is overflowing, socks and underwear spilled out of it and onto the carpet that extends into the narrow closet. A cup of coffee and a half-eaten piece of wheat toast sit on the desk in front of the window at the opposite end of the bedroom. Richard feels like diving into a shower and transforming himself, stepping out renewed, alchemized, both he and the past purified. If only.

The phone rings and he scoops it to his ear. "Lori?"

"Richard?"

He slumps. "Yeah. Who else?"

"Who's Lori?" asks Evelyn.

"Friend of mine." What business is it of yours?

"Oh," she says. "Hope she's nice. Listen, Richard, your father and I are concerned about you."

"Don't worry. I'm not going to—"

"We want to talk to you about your situation."

"Not now, Mother. I'm—"

"If you need some money to tide you over, you can count on us. I want you to know that."

"Thanks."

"Richard?"

"Yes?"

"I've never asked you for much—"

Richard sits on his bed. Here we go.

"—but I want you to tell me what's bothering you."

"Nothing."

She raises her voice. "Say something, for crying out loud; give me a clue. What's the matter?"

"I told you, Mother. You just didn't hear me."

"Told me what? About those noises in the hallway?"

Richard feels drowsy. "Yes, those noises in the hallway."

"Well, did you report it to the police?"

"Yes, I certainly did."

"Then it's *their* problem."

That wakes him up, and he fires it like a flare into the sky: "Why did you keep me from saying anything about the Dempseys back then?"

"Richard!"

"Why?"

"God, how many times have we been through this? I am so sick of it."

"I'm the one who's sick, remember?"

"Stop it, Richard." Her voice is defensive, nasty, scared.

"Despite what you say, we've never really been through this."

"I'm not going to spend time—"

"You asked me for a clue."

"I did, but—"

"I'm giving you one. What I heard that night, it mattered. Or at least it should have."

"Nothing was ever proven. Don't you understand?"

"You'll cling to that line for eternity, won't you? I'm telling you that what I heard that night"—his voice quavers and rises a half octave—"mattered more than anything else in the world to me."

"It wouldn't have changed anything. The imaginings of a little boy; that's all the police would have made of it."

"They weren't imaginings, and if I had told them, it would have become *their* problem. Isn't that what you just suggested?"

"You keep twisting things."

"The other night, I asked you whether you thought I was the one who somehow killed Cindy."

"Of course not. How could you—?"

"I thought I had my answer, but now I'm not so sure. I think maybe you thought it was possible—let's face it, you never could figure me out—but I think you were more concerned about what *you* would go through. Or maybe you were in denial. That's a great expression I learned when I went away. Denial about me or about your next-door neighbor; either way. You just didn't want to believe such a thing could happen in your neat, little world. Right under your nose."

"That's right, Richard. The whole thing was my fault. Just blame me for everything."

Richard clenches the phone as if it's his mother's arm. "Where the hell was Dad through all this? I can only remember *you* hovering over me, telling me what to do. That day at the police station . . ." Richard rocks at the edge of his bed in anguish and release.

"He felt the same way I did," Evelyn says. "We didn't see any point in stirring things up, in pointing a finger at a man who, as far as the police could determine, was innocent."

"I might have changed that."

"We always had your welfare in mind, and we still do."

Richard lies on his back on the bed, exhausted, no longer speaking directly into the phone, almost mumbling. "So I just sit there and answer the questions—questions that have nothing to do with anything. And all the sounds stay inside of me. And the whole time, I feel like they're trying to trap me in a corner somewhere. So after a while, *I* don't even don't know who or what to believe."

"Richard, tell me the truth. Are you all right?"

Richard's pause stretches the seconds. "That's what I have to find out."

It's the toughest cleanup that Davis Braun has experienced

in the history of his hospital duty in Philadelphia and at the New Jersey seashore. He must get rid of the stink in his place, and he doesn't want to use a fumigator and leave a clue. Plus, fumigators don't show up on demand, and he needs action now. He has dumped into the tub all of the cleaning fluid from the container whose translucent stem he utilized in the embalming. He has scoured the tub with a stiff-bristled brush, sponged the sink and floor, and wiped it all dry with rags and triple-ply paper towels. In the process, he has emptied two canisters of heavy-duty scrub foam and an aerosol deodorizer in a frantic effort to chase every last offending malodorous molecule—grounded or airborne— from the premises.

He did not plan on this.

Keene. The skinny runt. Of all the people to show up at his door at the moment of truth, he has to be the one. Super Ears, probably with no life of his own and nothing better to do than investigate other people's lives, as if it is his personal mission to be a savior, an avenger.

Is he kidding?

Braun spends an hour and a half disinfecting the bathroom and trying to restore its clean scent and harmless appearance before he decides that he's had enough, that olfactory fatigue has surely taken hold. He'll let it sit, then come back for a whiff after his nostrils have cleared. He slowly scans the tub and floor and doesn't see a drop of blood or a single shaft of hair anywhere. He vigorously washes his hands multiple times with antibacterial pump soap, which he regularly pilfers from the hospital.

The loaded body bag is on the floor in the living room,

like baggage ready for a trip. He almost trips as he steps over it, then realizes he has stepped on something small and hard on the carpet. His eyes search the area and he doesn't spot anything—drop something small on this carpet, and the damn thing disappears. He kneels and inspects, square inch by square inch, and there it is, lying flat on the carpet fibers: a gold, circular earring the size of a Cheerio. He rotates it between his thumb and forefinger, as if it were a nugget panned from a riverbed. When he unzips the body bag, the purpled, lifeless face takes one more hit of daylight. The other earring is firmly in place, and he reattaches the one he's just retrieved. The earlobe feels supple enough.

Something resembling remorse threatens to draw tears, though his feelings might be directed more toward himself and his burden than the dead girl. He gets rid of the emotion by reminding himself that some women have a natural urge to possess, backed by the compulsion to betray, should possession be denied. Some women are to be feared.

Maybe he'll be a psychiatrist after he gets tired of surgery.

He thinks of Eleanor. It was nice at first. She was warm and sensuous and rather stylish, something he didn't expect from a paralegal. She would touch his hand or thigh to elevate a humorous or intimate remark. He liked that she wasn't a high-toned chick—they met at a shot-and-sawdust bar in the shadow of the hospital. Within weeks, he invited her to move into his apartment at the 42s. Sharing the rent was a prime motivation; Eleanor was making decent money, and he was leveraged to the max with his credit cards and student loans. She went for it in a heartbeat, leaving her nearby studio apartment a month early and writing off the security deposit.

He knew that up close over time, a couple test each other's nerves. But with Eleanor, things unraveled even faster than he'd expected. After a few weeks, she started treating him like a roommate rather than a lover. She got a bump in salary, and he was still grappling with loans from his undergrad days, but she never offered to kick in a little extra beyond her half of the rent. She enjoyed his stud services, then felt no urge to cook meals or be the engaging, attentive woman who had originally attracted him. Worse, her fault-finding (always misguided, he felt) grew in frequency and intensity. He was puzzled, then peeved, then retaliatory.

She would cock her head when she was annoyed, her accompanying smug expression enraging him. As she launched into her recrimination or shifted to subtle mocking, her nose seemed to flare, and her eyes flattened so that the overall look of womanly superiority perfectly fit her tone.

It made what was to follow all the easier.

Second thoughts surfaced for him when she would try, or at least seem to try, to make amends in bed. Of course, he was pretty damn sure that she received a nice payoff for her rigors. He never doubted his potency in that regard, his ability to please a woman. He had the right physical equipment, in abundance, and an athlete's instinct for pacing. After a session of lovemaking several months into their live-in arrangement, in the combined muskiness of her sweat, perfume, and secretion, Braun understood just how the relationship would end. It was inevitable.

But if the insight owed anything to impulse, the deed would be carefully crafted.

Just like the one before.

And now, as he stares at the body bag at his feet, he

unaccountably thinks of Dolores, his mother, dead these last half-dozen years, the cancer unyielding to the protection he strove to give her.

Then his thoughts turn to Lori, so skilled in toying with Keene, who fell into her lap. How she relished the unsavory thrill of being the other woman. In his life, there will always be another woman.

Lori's bad-girl side, which attracted him in the first place, served them well in bed. Outside the sheets, she was regarded as a woman on the rise in the city's financial arena, a cool professional with smarts and polish. *She* was the one to suggest that they frisk Eleanor's bank account, perfectly situated at Mazer National, Lori's employer. When Keene happened along, she figured she could beguile him and defuse the threat.

Braun shakes his head in ironic amusement and pushes a thin stream of air through his lips. Now *that's* a partner in crime.

"Richard?" she says into the phone. "Janet Kroll . . . I've been thinking about what you told me yesterday. I'd like to speak with you."

Richard is surprised, excited. "Sure."

"Can we meet on the sundeck up on the roof in about forty-five minutes?"

Braun remembers something and unzips the body bag with a hissing flourish. Just double-checking: the body is naked, except for the attached gold earrings and—yes, there it is—the gold-and-ivory bracelet on the wrist. Dressed for the occasion. Nothing left behind; clothes and shoes are stuffed in a plastic shopping bag, its drawstring tied in a knot. Now he zips the body bag closed in slow motion, so that he sees the face gradually disappear, a kind of final good-bye. He drags the body bag across the carpet and props it L-shaped against the door.

At Richard's apartment, the phone rings again. He hopes against hope.

"Lori?"

"Can I speak to the person who handles the utility bills?"

Sinking feeling. Smile-and-dial. Richard hangs up so slowly and carefully that the receiver makes barely a sound when it is laid to rest.

He closes his eyes in utter weariness, and they remain shut for at least ten seconds before they spring back open. He picks up the phone, punches in the three digits for Information, and is treated to a computerized, vaguely female voice: "What city and state, please?"

"Philadelphia, Pennsylvania."

"What listing, please?"

"The City of Philadelphia Sanitation Department." Long shot.

The next voice is human. Barely. "Hold for that number, please."

He selects automatic dial for the sanitation department and gets through to a woman he fears may be busy mopping the floor on this fine Saturday. He explains to her that he has inadvertently thrown out a very valuable item. Can he somehow intercept the trash truck or meet it at the landfill and rummage around in the load? He'll be able to spot it readily.

To her credit, the city employee treats the call with seriousness. "No, sir. I don't know any way we can do that. It's kind of like putting a letter in a mailbox. Once you drop it, it's gone. Besides, it would be dangerous for you to do that, and we're not insured for that kind of thing, you know? What did you throw out?"

He calls Oliver and suggests a court order. Keep those court orders coming. Premature, says Oliver, who adds that he can't make it to the 42s this afternoon to witness Richard's dummy drop and won't question Braun again, at least for now. "If I interrogate him after my detectives have already done that—with no further information—it starts to look like harassment," he says. "But I tell you what. Hold off on that trash chute business 'til tomorrow, and I'll come over when I'm off duty. Just as an interested private citizen, understand?"

Richard will take what he can get, but he's growing antsy, can't bear to wait around. Janet's invitation to meet him on the deck is quite welcome. Fresh air. High altitude. She needs to confide in him. He's excited about that. He wants to protect her.

And what if *he* happens to be up there—Davis Braun. So what? Turn the tables on the sonofabitch. Show him who's pursuing who.

Richard puts on the Disney World T-shirt he's had since his middle-school trip more than fifteen years ago and leaves the apartment, looking both ways like a child crossing the street as he steps into the coolness of the hallway. He takes the elevator to the top, walks past the fitness center and the banquet room and the glass-domed swimming pool, and steps outside onto the sundeck.

September is almost gone but still offers this day of high heat, as if summer is determined to fight the calendar. The pale-green concrete deck stretches to a barrier of bulky, wooden-planked planters hugging a chest-high railing, gaps between the planters wide enough for a person to squeeze through. Azaleas sway in the breeze, and beyond their dance, the city's forest of glass and chrome looms, broad and immovable. Gauzy traces of cloud brushstroke an otherwise clear sky, and the sun warms Richard's neck, cheeks, and arms, pale skin attesting to his indoor life. There is a part of him that wants to strip off his shirt and join the scene of lounging bodies and oiled limbs, but he fears that his physique and paleness are not up to the task. Instead, he stands and receives the sun as a dose of health, hoping to store its warmth for recall when the world turns cold. Maybe at some point after Janet arrives and they're talking and relaxed, he'll remove his shirt and take in the sun, lie back on a lounge chair next to her.

She's not here yet. He walks until he runs out of deck, then wriggles sideways through the narrow space between two wooden planters to a metal railing of column-like verticals attached to a single horizontal top rail not far from the edge. To the east, the Ben Franklin Bridge seems to hang above the river, its sweeping lines shrunken by distance, sized for a wall painting. Due north, just a few blocks away, bronze William Penn squeezes through the nouveau giants that now dwarf his brimmed hat, once the highest point in the city. The lofty height and the scale of the metropolis give Richard hope for a grand scheme of things. He likes the city when he can view it from afar. He feels relaxed and powerful, a tingling of invulnerability, however temporary, spreading through him like an analgesic chasing pain.

He props his arms on the railing and looks downward.

"Long way down, huh?"

The voice chills him but only for an instant, because somehow he expected it. It has to be this way; avoidance is yesterday's curse and will guide him no longer.

Richard turns from the rail and faces Davis Braun, who is bare-chested and wearing sunglasses that turn his eye sockets into coals. "I don't know how they build 'em this high," Braun continues, moving a step closer. "Can you explain that to me?"

Richard tightens and cowers ever so slightly, the heady feeling of invulnerability dispatched by the wind. The cool he summoned during his chance encounter with Cameron Miro is inaccessible in this matchup. Still, it's time to press the issue, confront the monster.

Braun is an impressive specimen, a blunt configuration of evil in a photoplay package. He steps back, selects the lounger closest to the deck's end, and drapes his towel on the backrest. There are five additional sunbathers up here at this midday hour, four young women and one other guy, capsuled apart from one another; separate water bottles, lotions, and cell phones.

"You look familiar," Braun says to Richard, playing with him. "You live on my floor?"

Richard looks at him squarely and doesn't move. "I don't know."

"Wait a minute . . . I got it," Braun says. "Yeah, right. I saw you at the elevators that time, remember?"

"No."

"What apartment are you in?"

Richard keeps silent but moves away from the railing.

Braun sits and straddles the lounger, which is angled toward Richard and the sun. "Yeah, that's it. You're that guy right underneath me, the one who thought he heard some funny business goin' on at my place, right? Isn't that you?" He kneads sunscreen onto his deltoids. "You get off on the wrong floor that time or somethin'? Musta had one too many, huh?" He coats his neck, cheeks, and forehead. "Or maybe you were just visiting someone else on my floor; that it?"

Richard stiffens, but he is not frightened; he can sense that in his extremities, which remain limber. "I don't remember," he says, his voice low in his throat.

Braun springs from the lounger as if ready for a round of horseplay. Richard flinches a second before Braun extends his hand. "Davis Braun."

Richard puts his hand out and Braun takes it, gripping it like a sopping washrag he wants to drain dropless. "It's nice to meet people in the building," says Braun as Richard hangs on, worried about small, crushed bones at the knuckles. "Sometimes things can be pretty impersonal around here, you know?"

Braun releases him, and Richard draws his hand back as if from an electric shock. Braun smiles. "Looks like you got some kind of nervous tic there." He goes back to the lounger and lies down, a frat boy lolling in the sun.

Richard remains locked in place, absorbing the insult, weighing his options for action. Then the calculations stop and something from his gut takes over. He steps forward, approaches Braun, hesitates, passes him as if leaving the area, then stops and turns back toward him.

"I know what happened," Richard says softly, his words thinned by altitude or wind. "To both of them. Every bit of it. It's just a matter of time 'til all the evidence is in."

Braun doesn't move a muscle. "How's that, buddy?"

A tremor runs through Richard. "You want to kill me, too?" The other sunbathers are too far away to hear Richard's soft voice.

Braun just lies there, luxuriating in the sun. "Hadn't given it much thought," he says between almost-closed lips.

Frozen for an instant, Richard turns and walks away, but another voice stops him.

"Is this seat taken?"

He turns back slowly to see Janet Kroll in an aquamarine one-piece bathing suit. Funny he had not noticed her on the deck until right now; her angle of approach, his attention to Braun. Now, though, he sees her. The way she curves above, below, and through the high-cut suit.

Braun pats an empty chaise longue. "All yours."

As Janet sits down, she looks at Richard, then averts her eyes and covers them with sunglasses. Disappointment shows in his gaze, but he won't let it linger. In a moment, he is on his way. He will speak with her later. She obviously doesn't want to acknowledge him in Braun's presence. She's playing it smart.

Something stops Richard when he opens the glass door to the indoor pool and steps inside. A corkscrew twisting in his stomach, and breath that dies in his throat. *She is there expressly to meet Braun.* The bathing suit, her cool demeanor—a rooftop rendezvous. She invited me to see me squirm, to have Braun frighten me off. Served up on a platter.

No. Can't be. She wore the suit for *me*. Well, if not quite that, at least to get a nice tan. But to meet with me and only me.

He doesn't know what to think. If he could talk to Lori about it, she'd figure it out.

If he could talk to Lori.

He wants to turn back and look through the glass at them, check their body language, catch their expressions. *Hear what they're saying*. He can't resist. He steps outside again. Watches and listens from a distance.

Stretched out on their lounge chairs, Janet and Braun are close enough to smell each other's breath.

"So," she says, "how's the sun?"

"Outstanding," he says.

Her skin is already moist with sunscreen, and Braun smells it and sees its sheen. He runs a finger across her shoulder, capturing some of the moisture. "How come you didn't let me do the honors?"

"We're not quite up to that yet," she says.

"But we're getting close?"

"Close enough for me to cook you dinner tonight."

"I have to go to—"

"Let me guess: the hospital. What else is new?"

"Duty calls."

"How about tomorrow night?"

The lounger squeaks as he sits up and extends his hand toward her. "Deal."

She remains on her back, drinking in the sun, but reaches out and places her hand on his, delicate as a leaf falling onto a pond. "Bring some white wine."

SEVENTEEN

*H*erb Dempsey is pointing an empty sleeve like the Ghost of Christmas Future. His face is distorted and malleable, changing shape like pizza dough. What doesn't change are the eyes, lifeless and milky blue, eyes that you run from. Through the sleeve comes a forefinger, self-possessed and detached from the body, an alien's accessory to disengage and hunt down prey, incapacitate and kill.

And through it all, Evelyn provides a Greek chorus of fear, uncertainty, and self-recrimination. We wanted to keep you out of it. Nothing was ever proved . . . We wanted to keep you out of it . . . We wanted to . . .

If she wouldn't listen to him, wouldn't heed his warning, add the name of Janet Kroll to the list of people who have paid him no mind, have given his words no weight, to whom he has been invisible or, if visible, an annoyance. He offered her his most earnest caution. If she chooses to regard him as a nut and cast in with Braun, that's her misfortune. Lori's situation was different—*he* got Lori involved, and that's eating at him. That this guy could be so brazen as to do it again, and in a matter of days, no less—same place, same MO, the live-in, then the next-door neighbor, surrounded by people on all sides—is unthinkable. ´

Still, that's what has happened. Richard knows it like he knows the sounds he heard that night at the door of apartment 2307, and that night in his bedroom in the row house on Airdale Road.

Something else has been gnawing at him. What if Braun showed up on the sundeck neither by coincidence nor by Janet's invitation? What if Braun somehow is, as feared, tracking him, shadowing him? A familiar shudder runs through Richard from pelvis to neck, then he forces his mind to leap to another thought, to focus on what he's doing, his mission, the completion of which will take care of Braun and all the demons through all the years. That banishes the fear and paralyzing dread. He can deal with it because he sees a way to end it. There is a resolution coming.

Lori's disappearance makes it inevitable. But the case of Eleanor Carson is what Richard must master. No one to safeguard her when she lived and no one to avenge her in death. Not her father. Not the police (at least not without prodding). Not her *boyfriend*, for God's sake.

Bitterly reminiscent of an earlier case involving one little girl in an otherwise placid row-house neighborhood.

The facts and suppositions, the weight of it all, will tell. The two adult bodies will be in a landfill somewhere, under layers of refuse. If it takes a small army to find them, so be it.

If it takes Richard working around the clock with a pick and shovel, like the little boy he once was, dredging wet sand at the shoreline in Atlantic City, so be it.

If Janet was surprised by Braun on the deck, and she believes Richard, she'll let him know; otherwise, to hell with her. Meanwhile, the crash-test dummy is assembled and ready to go. Wait a day for Oliver; the man's on his side.

At the door to his apartment, Richard listens for any strange sounds from within, though reason tells him nobody's there. Still, he listens for murderous sounds. He listens for subtle sounds. Maybe Braun somehow flew down the stairs ahead of the elevator and got inside his apartment with a key from Mike.

Ridiculous, of course. Richard assures himself that he is now too smart to succumb to paranoia; too stable, this new-found composure arising from conviction. No, there is nothing sinister waiting inside; there is only the ticking of the battery-powered kitchen clock and the refrigerator's drone and all the other buzzing, slicing, and swirling sounds that saturate the hallway and the building, all swarming about his cursed ears.

Davis Braun had been thinking about Richard Keene an hour before heading up to the sundeck, wondering what to do about him. It is clear that he can no longer ignore the tenacious little bugger. He thought he could simply scare him off, but that hasn't worked.

When he spotted Keene near the edge of the rooftop sundeck, his first impulse was to grab the sucker by his shorts and boost him over the railing for an unimpeded plunge to the street forty-two stories below. As that murderous urge subsided, he realized that disposing of Keene must be as masterful a stroke as the others.

The movie, with Eleanor and with Karen before, now that was a great touch—symbolic and, in its masking of like noises of distress, tactically inspired. *Grip of Death* made an impression on him when he first saw it on cable a few years ago—not that it's any good, but the sound effects are startling. So when the time came for a well-considered, cold-blooded murder, why not embellish with that movie sound track and, simultaneously, conceal the real struggle in real time?

What disturbs him about yesterday's sudden events is that he had no opportunity for his customary orchestration. He was caught flat-footed and had to scramble to get things on track. That raised the ante for risk.

Of course, he is no serial killer, no mentally disturbed monster killing at random to quench some compulsive need. In fact, he is no killer at all. He, Davis Braun, is a man in charge of his emotions and his life, capable and clearheaded. There are triggers for certain behaviors—he knows that, as he has studied psychology—but the trick is to recognize them and be rational in response.

Murder sometimes can be rational. But it must not compromise self-preservation.

He has a compulsion for orderliness and an expectation of completion. He believes that, once started, a job must be seen through—and as tidily as possible. Leaving it unfinished is an insult. Allowing it to descend into sloppiness due to poor planning or inadequate skills is an even greater insult, such an affront to him that he often is eager to clean up another's mess or, better yet, take over the task before it gets to that stage. He will be a very great surgeon someday; he has the meticulousness and the mind-set.

And the touch of an artiste. His use of *Grip* has been ingenious, he tells himself yet again. Eliminating Eleanor was a rerun of Karen. Same movie, same outcome.

Only this time, someone is on his trail: Keene, with this crazy hearing of his, his almost unfathomable timing, and the persistence of a flea.

And there he was on the sundeck, standing near the edge of the building, an invitation difficult to ignore. But Braun is too smart for such rashness. Self-control, baby; reason. He flexed quiet intimidation in the mellow sunshine.

To be on the safe side, however, he must watch the skinny twerp closely.

Some bird-dogging is in order.

As she lay next to him that afternoon, both of them faceup to the sun, part of her felt cold and hopeless, offset by the part of her that remained alert and calculating. Now she worries that she has placed someone other than herself in jeopardy. She drew Richard Keene to the deck in order to observe Braun under pressure, to induce a reaction that would reveal more about him.

"Who's he?" she asked him.

"Nobody," Braun answered. "Just one more disposable character in the big wide world." Then he caught himself and added, "I've seen him around here once or twice."

"He looked upset," she said.

"Could be." Braun smiled broadly and jabbed the armrest of his lounge chair. "I think he wanted this spot. But I beat him to it."

She senses that Richard is right about everything. God, another dead woman and she did nothing, could do nothing, though she's been watching this man for a month now in this high-rise vault, where private worlds are all locked up. The last couple of weeks, she has maneuvered herself into his life, yet she had no inkling of what's taken place until Richard told her.

She is in her bathroom, replaying the conversation while combing her wet hair straightened and lengthened by the water. The word *disposable* is on her mind, and the ripple in her stomach is the one she feels when an airplane hits a rough patch. She touches up the color with a few lines of Clairol red. The blonde highlights are still there but not as bright. The hair and the thinned eyebrows and the aerobically contoured body have been more than enough to fool her audience of one, since they saw each other only once before and on the fly at that—a quick introduction from Karen, goodbye, nice to meet you, see you again. A matter of seconds; he never got her last name (her married name, different from her sister's) and barely got her first. Still, this has been a command performance from her, fooling him, putting herself at risk, staying with the name Janet, though, of course, there are lots of Janets in the world, the name hardly memorable.

She likes the new Janet, a much more provocative version both in appearance and manner. But that's a consideration for another time. This thing can't go much longer, she feels, and she's alert to the danger to herself and others and, moreover, the overriding possibility of failure, of coming up empty.

Richard Keene . . . what a strange story, his bizarre but precise account. What else could it be but true? Now she must stay closer on Braun's trail, step for step, or miss a chance that may not come again.

It will not come again if she becomes his next victim.

Fellow casino employees noted no warning signs prior to Karen Karpinski's disappearance. Nothing at all. She was well liked on the casino floor and in the front office, a black-jack dealer who kept the cards coming, her balances accurate to the penny, and her cool at all times.

Missing bodies were not a new phenomenon at the seashore. Atlantic City, with its lurid history, rootlessness, swampy back bays, barnacled piers, and great, lapping ocean, was a place where people disappeared. Like sand crabs.

Still, when Karen Karpinski disappeared, it made no sense to her sister. Janet saw Karen's boyfriend—a medical student, Karen told her—only once, that quick introduction at their little place (actually, *his* place) at the high-rise Oasis on the boardwalk. Afterward, after her sister was gone, Janet felt reasonably sure that the moment did not etch her face in Braun's memory, but she knew that she'd recognize him again. She believed that he knew something about Karen's disappearance. The instinct of a sister, a close sister.

Braun and Janet were each summoned to the police station on different days to answer questions. The police were as baffled as Janet. There was no evidence of foul play, not a mark anywhere. Karen's car was in its reserved spot in the parking garage. Her live-in boyfriend was a well-mannered, well-spoken medical resident on loan from his Philadelphia school to Burdette-Tomlin Hospital in Cape May County. Davis Braun.

Janet tried to reach him for weeks afterward, but he never returned a call. Finally, with no sign of her sister, and the police still at square one, she went to the Oasis to see him in person, but he wasn't there. She prodded the man at the front desk for information. He told her that Davis Braun had a six-month lease on an efficiency condo and was scheduled to move in two days.

Karen had never said a word about the impending move. *Because she did not know about it.* What other explanation was there?

My God, Janet thought, after leaving the Oasis.

A Realtor since her early divorce from David Kroll, who placed her second to his career as an investment banker with one of the old-line Philadelphia firms, Janet liked to set her own schedule, and that flexibility was about to serve her well. On the day of Braun's move, she returned to the Oasis and staked out the moving van for three hours while it was being loaded. Braun was not around, but his was the only move scheduled at the building that day. Janet followed the van as it motored west on the Black Horse Pike, through Camden, and across the bridge to downtown Philadelphia and the rear dock of the 42s building on Locust Street. The next day, she applied for an apartment there and moved into her fifteenth-floor unit six weeks later. She had no mortgage on her house in Lower Merion, courtesy of the divorce settlement, so for the time being, she could afford to make the 42s her home away from home.

He had seen her just that one time at the Oasis, he

coming in, she leaving. Seconds.

Still, she wasn't exactly a trained undercover agent, and she was taking a big chance. She turned her thick brunette hair red and let it grow, thinned her eyebrows, and attacked the fitness center, transforming her curvy figure into something sleek and stunning. She found out what she could about Davis Braun. She bided her time, then worked it so that their paths would cross. They did one day in the elevator, then at the gym, then in the mail room. He asked her to dinner.

She planned to get close to him, get him talking, her micro digital recorder concealed. She would risk her life, if necessary, to turn up something against him.

Through the microblinds, Richard sees the somber light of dusk take over the city and slow its pulse. Most of the windowed squares of the office building facing him are dark and deserted, though a couple are lit and occupied. In one of them, a man whose white-shirted midsection spills over his belt buckle slumps in his chair and stares at a computer monitor, Saturday overtime at the office. In some darkened squares, desks and shelves alternate shadow and streaks of dim light; others are dark enough to hide all traces of weekday action.

Richard paces in his living room, the rippled soles of his running shoes flexing against the low-pile carpet. He is antsy, anxious to do the demo, make the drop, and prove his theory. It is past 7:00 p.m., and though Lieutenant Oliver will not be coming until tomorrow, if at all, Richard is tired of waiting. Waiting allows bad things to happen. He wants to move now, and just in case he gets only this one chance, he wants a witness. Lori was his original choice. Lori is gone.

Frank. Frank's the one. It is time for Frank to join his team. And Frank is the only one who can get him into the Dumpster room, which is locked after hours.

"I'm busy down here, man," Frank says to him on the phone.

"You have Mike there."

Frank scoffs. "In body only. Without me in the saddle, all hell's liable to break loose, you understand?"

Richard has asked him to witness a little experiment but hasn't elaborated.

"You know Lori Calder?" Richard asks.

"Little girl on twenty-three?"

"Twenty-three oh nine, to be exact. Might want to hold her mail." He is forcing himself to get over Lori by being casually indirect.

"You got to be kidding me, Keene. Are you gonna go right down the hallway with this—every single apartment before you're through?"

"Frank, I'm giving you a chance to help solve a murder in your building. Two murders now. You'll be a hero."

Frank thinks about that and his expression suggests he likes the image.

"Imagine your picture in the paper, the chief of police pinning a medal on you in a ceremony at City Hall," Richard says. "All you have to do is go with me, open the door, and watch—nothing else for now."

"Here we go with the *for now* bit. What comes after?"

"Nothing. I'll do the rest."

"Oh, that makes me feel much better. All right, let's

hear it. What door? Watch what? What you got in mind?"

Richard explains the whole thing, the crash-test dummy, the drop down the chute, corroboration that it works, the grisly yet almost whimsical disposal right under the collective nose of the whole building, of the entire city. Talk about a throwaway society.

"I can't allow that," Frank says. "What's the matter with you?"

"What do you mean?"

"How big is this thing?"

"It fits down the chute, don't worry."

"You jam things up, Keene, it's all over."

"It *fits*. Remember, straight down, right?"

"You are too much, Keene. Too fuckin' much."

"It'll take two minutes. Frank, I'm telling you. Two murders. You can feel it that I'm onto something; don't deny it. Come on up; you can't ignore this."

"Sure I can."

Richard smiles. "Look, I'm gonna do it anyway. Now or some other time."

"You are a piece o' work."

While Richard tries to persuade Frank to witness his chute drop, Davis Braun sits on his couch, a cell phone pinned to his ear and Richard's recorded voice filling it. "I am on the line at the present time. Please leave a message and I'll call you back as soon as I'm free."

All right, he's in his apartment. Good deal. Fastidious little putz has his outgoing message distinguish between on the line and out of the apartment altogether; of course, the out message could play and he might be taking a crap, so nothing's foolproof. But if it's on the line, he's there. Unless he's not and someone else is using his phone, which is unlikely. This boy's a loner all the way.

Time for a little surveillance. See what this guy is up to. Get him out in the open, then eliminate him. Braun wonders whether he's overreacting—how big is the threat, really? But, as they teach in med school, the best cure is prevention.

Moments later in the apartment directly below, Richard stuffs the assembled crash-test dummy into a new home— not a suit travel bag but a longer wardrobe storage hanger that he inherited from one of his mother's cedar closets in the attic. He rediscovered it hidden in a corner of his apartment closet, forgot he had it. He has dismantled the squared-off top by removing its metal frame and wire hanger so that the zipped-up package is suitably rounded and scrunched and he's sure it will fit into the chute. It is flat on the floor by his feet as he sits on his couch as if waiting to be called to board a bus. Through his closed door, he hears the elevator chime and its door slide open, followed by some static and babbling from a walkie-talkie.

Richard gets up and opens the door to his apartment, and there's Frank with a this-better-be-good look on his face and a black, palm-sized walkie-talkie clipped to his belt.

"Thanks for coming, Frank."

"Yeah, sure. Let's see what you got."

Richard reaches down and lifts the top half of the wardrobe-wrapped dummy off the floor and drags it into the hallway, right under Frank's nose and disbelieving eyes. "That's it, huh?"

Frank says, as Richard moves ahead.

"C'mon Frank."

"C'mon what?"

"We're gonna drop it down the trash chute."

"*We* ain't gonna do nuthin'. I don't know a thing about this, understand? This is *your* baby.

Richard is halfway to the trash room. "This will confirm the feasibility of disposing a body via the trash chute."

"Well, that's wonderful, professor, but no way! This is exactly what I was worried about—this thing is too goddamn big."

Richard stops and gives him a level look. "It's not. I checked it."

"Well, if you checked it, what're you botherin' me for?"

"I just measured; that's all. I still have to test it. You're my witness that I didn't just heave it into the Dumpster."

Frank looks like he has an itch somewhere. "And if it gets stuck?"

"It should slide right through. I won't jam it."

"You're damn right you won't. All I need is—"

"But if it fits through . . . All the way down, right, Frank?"

Frank scratches the beginnings of a goatee. "I can't let you do this, man. Sorry."

"Look," says Richard, gripping the knob of the trash-room door. "I'll just do it on my own later; I told you that. At least now you're here if anything goes wrong . . . and you're part of the investigation."

"That's great, man. That'll look good on my termination notice."

Inside the trash room, a smoky rancidness trumps the faint rubber scent of a nest of wires and cable lines.

Richard opens the hatch. "Give me a hand," he says to Frank, motioning to the back end of the bagged dummy.

"No way. It's all yours. I'm not touchin' it."

"I promise not to name you as a coconspirator," Richard says, but he gives up on him after a few seconds and tugs the wardrobe bag into the chute himself, inching it forward by segments, until half of it is inside.

That's when he hears it.

Noises from above funneling down the chute. A thud against the wall, a grunt, exhaled sounds. Of struggle? Of *strangulation*?

Of pleasure?

Richard's mouth opens as if he's starting a yawn.

Frank looks at him. "You goin' wacky on me, Keene, or—?"

"Sssh," Richard hisses. A "Yes" jumps down the chute and into his ear. Spoken with a kind of dominance.

A woman's voice. Familiar.

Richard lets go of the wardrobe bag as if his hands were on a hot grill and bolts out of the trash room, yelling, "Don't leave."

Frank stands there, flabbergasted, as the wardrobe bag jackknifes on the chute ledge, half in and half out. "What the—?"

Richard sprints to the stairwell and one flight up and then to the trash room on the twenty-third floor. When he tries to push the door open, he finds it jammed.

"Open this door," he yells, and though he feels desperate,

he nonetheless imagines himself to be a character in a bad melodrama.

He steps back and rams his shoulder into the door but with no result other than what will soon be a sore shoulder. He pounds on the door with his fists, the banging thuds reverberating in the hallway. He stands there, breathing heavily, right up against the door. Finally, it opens slowly, rasping, and just before Davis Braun's fist shoots through the opening and collides with his jaw, Richard sees a smallish, brown-haired woman in a state of undress, facing away from him.

Lori. Has to be.

All this within seconds, and then he is kneeling on the hallway carpet, stunned, head down, the big man's hard punch having done some damage but not enough to knock him unconscious. Two bodies blur past him, but when his senses return and he looks about, he sees no one in the hallway. He gets to his feet and moves drunkenly toward the door of Lori's apartment, where he raps on it repeatedly, then bravely shifts his attack next door to Braun's apartment, each hammering to no avail.

He is convinced that he has seen Lori, but his happiness in believing she is alive yields to bitterness that she has apparently betrayed him.

He returns to the twenty-second floor, where an irritated Frank waits at the door of the trash room. "You look a little woozy."

Richard has been gone only two minutes.

"What was that all about?" Frank says.

"I don't know yet."

"What's that mean?" Frank notices Richard's reddened

jaw beginning to swell. "What happened to you, man?"

"Walked into a fist."

"Hey, Keene, what the hell's goin' on here?"

But Richard already has stepped back into the room. He picks up where he left off, lifts the half of the wardrobe bag hanging outside the chute, and sends the crash-test dummy on its way. With a whoosh and a puff of sour air, it vanishes from their midst, down into the depths like a torpedo. Richard bends from the waist to stick his head into the opening and listen to the whistling of the falling object, then straightens and looks at Frank, who watches from the threshold. "Let's go," Richard says, steps past Frank, and leads the way to the elevator, where he presses the down button. "Told you, no sweat."

"I still say my ass could be out of a job for this."

"No, it won't. You'll get a raise—you'll be a hero." He now feels comfortable with Frank; he's got a pal.

But Frank stands there, frowning. "I give you this, Keene. You don't give up easy."

Richard's face relaxes as he looks at him. "Think so?"

"I want you callin' the police if you got attacked."

"Later." Richard feels his growing anger toward Lori Calder. He mutters to himself, "Chump."

Frank leans in. "Say what?"

The elevator arrives and they get on.

Plastered against the closed door of the stairwell, one eye peeking around the edge of the alcove, Davis Braun has seen them from his vantage point at the end of the hallway. What the hell did Keene need in the trash room that required the front-desk man?

Braun's cell phone is in one pocket, a handkerchief and a hard-plastic kit containing a vial of chloroform and a hypodermic needle in the other. He rushes into the trash room to inspect and finds nothing out of the ordinary. No matter, he needs no more convincing that Keene has become a major threat. The chloroform, more product smuggled from the hospital, will come in handy.

On the third floor of the 42s, Flora Spivack, a four-foot-ten widowed octogenarian, carries a small bag of garbage from her apartment to the trash room. It is a sheer yellow pouch that was propped in a small metal frame by the sink to hold rinds and large fruit pits that she doesn't want to submit to the garbage disposal and risk a breakdown; the disposal has already received repairs twice in the last year. Flora doesn't like the little pouch to sit long with such contents, so she is headed for the trash room from apartment 311, the bag tied and knotted by her determined, arthritic fingers.

She enters the trash room, opens the chute's metal flap, and, with her other hand, swings the yellow garbage pouch in a tight arc toward the opening.

But something stops her from completing the full motion and making her deposit.

After eighteen straight hours at the station, Lieutenant Robert Oliver has returned to his apartment, where he sits on a stiff chair pulled out from the dining-room table. He has avoided the recliner angled toward the television set because he can't bring himself to relax, can't get a grip on how to spend the evening, or any evening for that matter, especially a Saturday night.

What he's doing in the larger scheme of things, he realizes, is waiting to die. He hopes that retiring from the force will speed that process.

He has lived in this walk-up on Pine Street for nearly three years, since six months after Cassie's accident. When Libby died—after the cancer had spread to her lungs and beyond, after he had given quarts of blood and urged others to give lesser amounts in her name, after she'd been cut open and sewed back up, after he'd taken a leave of absence and spent every waking moment at her bedside, after he'd found a deserted moment and cried for the first time since he was five years old, after he'd cried some more and then cursed the enemy he could not fight—after all of that, he stayed in their Mount Airy home with the big backyard where Cassie and Robert Jr. had played, where Cassie ran her tree-house club and dug for gold or oil until her mother told her to fill up the hole, where both of the kids splashed in their little kiddie pool, where the sun rose and set and the seasons changed. When Cassie was taken from him, that whole world was reduced to a photograph bleached by the sun and fading with each passing day, and part of him wanted to lie down and die right there, and that part of him was capable of making it happen, but some kind of automatic pilot pushed him forward, set him in motion to play out a string whose end he could not see, a dreary regimen that he had no power to change. Robert Jr. hied to the West Coast and a job in the movie business—a creative kid, gets it from his mother—and they haven't talked since. They were never close, anyway.

Cassie . . . well, Cassie is gone forever.

He sits on his dinette chair with nothing to do and nowhere to go, and no sense of how to change that or even a feeling of wanting to. He's a man out of road maps and out of gas but not out of time. Not, regrettably, yet.

Flora Spivack's problem, the predicament that makes her stand there, mouth agape, her little trash bag of fruit pits and rinds dangling from her hand, is that a paper bag of trash and dripping garbage has toppled out from *inside* the chute and landed at her feet. As if someone tossed it at her. Her other hand loses its grip on the metal flap and it slams shut.

"Oh my," Flora says, then puts her trash on the floor and opens the chute again. Another bag, this one plastic, copper-colored, and bottom-heavy, hurtles out of the opening and plops onto her deck sneakers. There are more bags bulging behind, itching to burst. The cylinder is ripe.

After taking the elevator to the ground floor, Frank and Richard have made their way across the lobby, Frank motioning toward Mike at the desk with, "I'll be in the Dumpster room."

"Got ya covered," Mike says.

"Sure he does," Frank says as he steps past Richard, then mutters, "Let's go see if that thing came apart like a cheap suit or what."

They walk through the mail room and down a short

corridor to the rear exit door that dumps them outside on a concrete apron fringing an alley that somehow merits the name Latimer Street. The door to the Dumpster is two steps away, and Frank keys it open, revealing a room washed with yellow light and smelling like soggy cardboard. "Sucker better be there," Frank says.

"Why wouldn't it?"

"I don't know; you're the genius."

"You're the one who knows the building inside out."

They step up onto the lower ledge of the Dumpster.

"I must be outa my mind," Frank says.

"By the way, Frank, do they usually pick up trash on Saturdays? I was down here this morning right after they left."

"They missed yesterday, so they had to clear it out for the weekend. Otherwise we'd be swimmin' in this shit. I saw those guys this morning comin' down Fifteenth Street. Probably getting time-and-a-half."

They hoist themselves onto the top ledge of the Dumpster, then swing around and sit there so they can scan the contents. "Not a whole lot here," Richard says. "Could be a lot of people went away for the weekend."

"Where is it?" Frank asks.

Richard narrows his eyes. "Good question."

They swing their legs up and around to the outside, step down to the bottom ledge of the Dumpster and off, and stand there and wait, staring at the chute. Richard remembers a neighborhood restaurant from his youth, a family cafeteria-style restaurant, cheap and full of pleasant, ordinary people and the smell of hot gravy. An oblong counter with a conveyor belt ushered orders out from the kitchen, plates heaped with home fries and hot roast beef sandwiches, small saucers of baked beans, bowls of beef barley, all moving inexorably toward the front, a nonstop procession. That's where he always wanted to sit—at the counter in front of the delivery queue—so he could lean over and look to the rear of the belt for approaching dishes, watch the parade and wait for the moment, which came at least once every visit, when the lineup was too full and a collision was inevitable, often spilling contents onto the counter.

Now here he stands in the bowels of the 42s, watching the chute opening with that same eager expectation, that same heightened sense of urgency. But nothing is happening at the chute opening; nothing is coming out.

"Shit," says Frank.

Richard waits. Though the room is silent except for the buzz of the overhead fluorescent lights, he is captive to remote sounds. He hears a medley of noises, his private, hidden, discordant orchestra: a groaning of water pipes, the buzzing of electrical feed lines, the humming of heat-pump compressors . . .

And something else. He steps closer to the chute on the far side of the Dumpster, as close to it as he can get. Frank follows him, stops, puts hands on hips, impatient.

"What?"

For two seconds, Richard blinks like a hummingbird flutters. He hears the faint creak and snap of a few chute flaps opening and shutting on different floors. The friction of something sliding on metal, then coming to rest with the sound of a light sneeze.

"Nothin' since we walked in here," says Frank. "That's just great. I knew this was gonna happen; I just knew it."

"We haven't been here that long."

"Long enough."

"But you're right—"

"No, I'm wrong. For letting this show go on. I knew I was makin' a big mistake. Serves me right."

"People are using it."

"Using what?"

"I can hear them putting trash in the chute."

"You can hear—?"

Just then, Frank's walkie-talkie squawks and sputters like a transatlantic broadcast, vintage 1930.

"Yo, Frank." It's Mike. Frank rips the walkie-talkie off of his belt.

"Talk to me."

"Somethin's wrong with the trash."

"*Tell* me about it."

"It's backed up on three. That's what they're tellin' me."

Richard peers up into the chute, listening for clues, trying to divine the source of the blockage.

"What the hell's that mean?" Frank asks Mike.

"The, uh, whad'ya call it—trash bin?—is filled when they go throw theirs out. Y'understand? It's, like, stacked up."

Frank does a little agitated wiggle. More like a shudder. "That's just great. That means three stories' worth of this goddamn chute are clogged, maybe more."

"Guess so."

"Any other floors call in?"

"That's all we got so far."

Frank turns to Richard with an accusatory look. "See, what the hell did I tell you? How'd I let you talk me into this . . . ?"

Richard doesn't take his eyes from the chute and cocks his head, as if trying to communicate with its contents.

"What? What is it?" Frank asks.

Richard's lips barely move. "There's something there."

"Yeah, your damn dummy."

"No . . . too soon."

"Too soon for what?"

"We just dropped it, Frank. It can't clog up three floors that fast."

"How do you know? Maybe it's just stuck right on that floor."

"Thought you said straight down," Richard says, standing perfectly still.

"Yeah, for *normal* stuff. I musta been out of my—"

"Sssh!"

Frank glares at him, but Richard looks only into the black cylinder of the chute, a horror hatch, another dimension perhaps, like the movie thrillers with ghosts and time warps that always entranced him.

"Frank, you still with me?" Mike's voice is flat and dull.

"Yeah, I'm here. Listen, Mike—"

Richard draws a bead on the chute like a cat on a water bug.

"What is it, for God's sake?" Frank's voice is part panic, part resentment.

Another hissing "Sssh" from Richard, so strong, so authoritative, that it startles Frank into silence.

From the chute comes a scratching sound that only Richard can hear. It stops. "Hold on, Mike," Frank says into the walkie-talkie. Richard clambers onto the top ledge of the Dumpster right below the chute opening and almost falls off as he stands and grabs at his knee in pain. Frank rushes over.

"What the hell you doin', man? Get down from there. We ain't got no coverage for this kind of craziness."

Richard ignores him—ironically, he may not even *hear* him—and looks up into the darkness. The scratching sound resumes, louder . . .

He is petrified in his bed, unable to move, as if bolted down. The wallpaper closes in on him. The cowboy on the bucking bronco can offer no help, no sign of reassurance. The cowboy's face is angled toward the wall so that his features are not visible, and the top of his head is obscured by his large sand-colored cowboy hat. A red scarf flies out from his neck, one arm is tethered to the saddle while the other reaches toward the ceiling, and his boot presses down on the stirrup. But he will ride to no rescue, Richard's wallpaper friend, because the gasps come from beyond, Cindy Dempsey's gasps, an alarm neither of them can answer. He could scream. He could get up and rouse his mother, his father. But he can't move. He might be dreaming. He prays that he is dreaming. It is the middle of the night. And the gasps keep coming, and now he knows that he is not dreaming and that life must be oozing out of her, the one who means the most to him of any person on this earth, and he knows who is doing this to her, and he is powerless to prevent it because he is molded to the warm bed, strapped down by the fear that confusion brings in the middle of the night for an eight-year-old who is smothered by it all, the wallpaper closing in on him, the sounds, the sounds . . .

He is at eye level with the chute opening, trembling as he looks inside, up and into the dark cylinder.

The scratching persists. He glances down at Frank. "Is there a broom around here?"

"A *broom*? What the hell for?"

"Pry this stuff loose."

"Great. That's just great." Frank looks around the room. Not a broom or a mop or a shovel in sight. "I can get one from the utility closet up front." He moves to the door and opens it. "Be back in a minute." Richard watches him go, then squints back into the cylinder.

The thought comes to him in the form of a command: Don't wait. Climb into it. Somehow. Defy gravity and dislodge whatever is there. Hand-to-hand combat. Enter this dark, narrow world of mysterious noise and metallic scratching and whistling drafts and muted roars like the inside of a seashell cupped to one's ear, the ocean's symphony embedded there, so goes the tale told to youngsters on the summer beach with the sun a hot lamp from above, pail and shovel waiting in the sand, all carefree scampering, the child he was, he should have been, a child intercepted, aborted.

The scratching.

He must climb into the chute, even as nausea and dizziness and panic throw up a wall to meet him. It is his penance. He must go in there like a groundhog, like a tunneler, like a prison escapee, must go to the source of it and, maybe, just maybe, he *will* escape and be a free man.

What to grab onto? Richard believes he sees the outline of something wedged into the chute a few feet up; it's hard to tell. He closes his eyes, takes a deep breath, reaches in with both arms like day-camper Richard Keene diving off the side of the pool, bends his knees, and springs upward from the Dumpster ledge. He instantly grabs hold of something, something soft but unyielding. His legs kick furiously to propel him, as if he truly is in the limpid waters of a swimming pool. He fights his panic and wriggles into the mouth of the beast, wedges himself between the curved metal and the trapped trash, and reaches up to grab the next rung. Just like on monkey bars.

Only now does he open his eyes. He operates on will-power alone. Yet, even as he fends off panic, one small corner of his brain suggests the absurdity of his predicament. What is he doing?

What are you doing? Evelyn would ask him when he'd dig a deep hole in the backyard and stick his arm into it, delighted that the rest of him was free of the trap. Digging for gold?

Enough fluorescent light from the Dumpster room feeds into the chute to give Richard some visibility right at the mouth of it but not much farther. He can't tell what he is among, this pipeline of trash he has joined. He pats nearby objects to discern composition. Paper, filmy plastic, vinyl, something sharp. He must pull it all down, whatever it is, open the clog. Which he starts to do right now, while the angle is favorable and he can still hold his position. He reaches into the dark, into the unknown.

He reaches toward the sounds. Chute flaps opening. A pile of trash above him, shifting, mounting. He inches side-ways and reaches upward, straining for leverage, torso twist-ing and arm extended impossibly from its shoulder socket, fingers splayed, the little bones and digits of the hand at maximum torque, and just then, something cool and hard and sharp and . . . *ow!* The hand yanked back with the childlike exclamation and, in the faint light straining up from below, he can tell that he has drawn blood at the base of his fingers. Something sliced him, a metal edge, glass maybe. Then the scratching sound once more, a tease, a lure. He settles himself into the groove and reaches up—he should have worn gloves—and in the instant that he touches and tugs at what feels like a *human finger*, a thread of light drops from above, all the way through the chute, and winds about a bracelet on the wrist of a lifeless arm, a golden bracelet with chunks of ivory clear to Richard in that sudden light, and the shiver that runs up his spine confirms that the piece of jewelry is accompanied by its owner, her hand and wrist a half inch from the metal cylindrical wall and bobbing there almost imperceptibly like a specimen in a jar of fluid.

The light dies and, with a convulsive last-ditch surge, Richard grips the hand he cannot now see and, as large—much too large—jagged pieces of glass fall against his shoulders and dirt powders his face, he begins to slide backward, yanking the braceleted arm down with him and dislodging the heap of trash above.

In the avalanche, the head emerges from a skewered body bag. Skewered by what? Broken bottles and the velocity of, say, a five-hundred-foot drop. There's an absurd amount of glass, as if some moron threw out a tall, skinny mirror, and it races down the chute like a guillotine. This is all split-second supposition as Richard falls the short distance out of the chute and into the Dumpster, and the hand and head follow him, though he hasn't seen the latter clearly yet. The wedge is released, and it's raining glass and debris, and at least three floors' worth of trash tumbles down the chute. Through the roar, like a giant toilet flush punctuated by shattering glass, Richard believes he hears the squawk of Frank's walkie-talkie and then Frank saying, "Look, I gotta go," and then the sharp echo of rattling metal with the last of the barrage.

Richard has plopped onto the Dumpster pile, ass-first, and has no choice but to sit there and shield his face from the torrent. It has crashed around him and on top of him, mostly plump paper bags and skinny plastic ones, scattered broken glass, a dirt-encrusted garden spade, a dozen squat batteries. Now he scrambles away from the downpour, backpedaling uphill on the shifting pile. The Dumpster is still, the chute unclogged. He shakes his head vigorously and flings his arms outward in a bid to cast off whatever flecks and gobs are clinging to him. He opens his eyes.

He feels the sting of little cuts on his neck, touches a couple, and inspects the dabs of blood on his fingertips. The smell around him, that of moldy cantaloupe and the insides of a vacuum cleaner, is not overpowering but strong enough to get his attention. For the second time in as many days, he is in a sea of trash, a giant playpen of moveable parts devoid of color and mirth. It almost makes him smile.

He looks about, trying to be methodical, steeling himself against the horror he knows will present itself in moments. A few feet away, his mother's wardrobe bag is intact with the dummy inside; she'd never guess it had made such a journey. Richard crouches and rummages through the hill of refuse, tossing cartons and bags and boxes and glop as he goes. The batteries sink and disappear like scurrying bugs. He is careful not to handle several foot-long daggers of glass that resemble stalactites. He cups less dangerous chunks of the pile with both hands and flings them away, extracts bulging wedged-in paper bags to create tiny landslides, moves about the heap as he levels it like an archaeologist sifting for artifacts. When he shifts a layer of Styrofoam packing bubbles and loose grapefruit rinds, he sees the human hand and wrist decorated by—Richard's grunt is his reaction to both the horror of the finding and its futility—the gold-and-ivory bracelet. And the head has come clear as well, sticking out of the body bag slashed at one corner.

The head does not belong to Lori.

But then, at this point, he expected that.

Nor does it belong to Janet Kroll. For that he is relieved, if indeed any sense of relief can be applied to such a scene.

The hair is blonde, the disconcertingly open eyes blue— each at variance with Lori's and Janet's coloring. Both the head and the still-sheathed body below it are too large for Lori. A tall woman, still beautiful despite the gruesome conditions. Her darkened, waxy, inhuman face looks like it's been made up for a Halloween party.

Nausea streaks through Richard but doesn't go further. A new wave of guilt takes hold of him: another young woman he failed to help. He looks toward the top of the Dumpster, a few feet above his head now elevated by the mushroomed pile of trash. "Frank," he calls out, expecting to see him smirking and pointing a broomstick.

The Stranger had it wrong. Death makes a difference— the timing and nature of it—and fate doesn't condemn man but throws down a gauntlet. Some make it out the other end; some don't.

"Frank?"

So things don't always go straight down the chute, but then human bodies aren't thrown out every day, either. Richard has a job to do. He slips to his knees and stands once more, the pile shifting around him, covering the dead woman with a thin layer of refuse. "Hey, Frank?"

He can feel someone else's eyes on him. He snaps his head around fast enough to almost pop a vertebra. There, hunched on the upper ledge of the Dumpster, looking down into his eyes and through them, then looking beside and beyond him to where a now-submerged woman in a body bag has come to an inglorious rest, is Davis Braun. His eyes have a sleepy boredom about them; his forearms press onto the scraped metal, and his hands expand a pair of skin-tight surgical gloves.

"Looks like you're in this thing up to your neck, Keene."

As Richard moves one leg, the pile shifts beneath him, and he sinks to shin depth. He feels the resurgent twinge in his right knee as he steadies himself. Fear has been knocked out of him; strange, the specter of Braun is almost welcome. It has come to this.

"Seems we have a Mexican standoff," Richard says.

Braun frowns and shakes his head. "That's not a very politically correct phrase, Keene. A fine fella like you, an upstanding citizen, should know better."

What Richard does know is that Braun intends to kill him right here, right now—there is no other option. Kill him, body-bag him, and leave him here with his newest victim, or dump them somewhere else.

"I just met your latest girlfriend. Or would that be Lori?"

Braun seems surprised. "Would *what* be Lori?"

"Your latest girlfriend."

"I thought she was *your* girl."

Richard knows that the chitchat cannot last much longer.

He backs up a step onto a higher section of the trash mound, and he looks out of the Dumpster and sees a broom lying on the concrete floor and, a bit beyond, a two-by-four pinioned at an angle between the floor and the knob of the main door. The outdoor loading/pickup dock is sealed off by an overhead garage door. Fact is, the room gets very little traffic when it's open, and virtually none after hours, when it's locked.

Braun has followed Richard's gaze.

"Where's Frank?" Richard says.

"He's around."

"You can't throw us all in the Dumpster."

"Why not? City trash removal is better than the witness protection program."

"Mike knows he's here."

Braun smiles. "We talked with Mike. He's cool."

Richard looks right at him. "What's wrong with you, Braun?"

"Just people like you, who clutter up my life from time to time."

Richard scratches his cheek and tries to look casual. "Shame she got stuck, huh?"

"Shame *who* got stuck?"

He sees something in Braun's expression: He doesn't realize. Did he know about the off-schedule trash pickup? Must have . . . Maybe not.

"Your latest girlfriend." Richard works it. He points. "She's right over there." Braun follows the pointing, and his face loses some color. Richard high-steps to the buried body bag and tugs it upward into view. The blonde head surfaces.

"All that noise, man," Richard continues. "You must

have heard it. She was clogging everything up. I took care of the clog."

Braun's shoulder twitches. He clears his throat. "You performed a fine service," he says.

"She should be on that garbage truck, long gone by now, huh? Guess it was smooth sailing for Eleanor."

"That's right."

Richard knows he has one chance to get out of here alive. Yelling won't work; the thick cinder-block walls are too far from anyone in the building. Evidently, Frank is out of commission and Mike has been duped. Once Braun gets his hands on him, it's over. Maybe he can beat him to the door somehow, but he won't have enough time to open it and get out. He looks around the Dumpster for a spray can of Lysol or something to bob out of the morass, but no such luck. Dig for something that could serve as a weapon? No time, no way.

He stands perfectly still and looks right at Davis Braun. "So?"

Braun holds up a finger. "Sorry, Keene. They keep talking only in the movies."

Richard will wait for him to make the first move. The Dumpster room is large; he's not in a phone booth. Braun will have to come in after him. Anything can happen, like a muddy football field neutralizing a superior team.

In the instant that Braun hurtles over the edge and inside the Dumpster, Richard sees it, the thing that has been right in front of him all the time: the red cylinder mounted by the door.

The fire extinguisher.

Before Braun lands feetfirst in the pile, Richard counters with perfect timing. He scrambles to one side of the

Dumpster and vaults over the top and onto the concrete floor. He yells as his knee takes the impact and stumbles as he rushes headlong toward the door, but there is no time for pain or for Frank, who lies unconscious on the floor. Without looking back, Richard mashes his shoulder against the door, rips the extinguisher free from its rubber latch, yanks the tube off its bearings, pulls the pin, and wheels to face his foe, his trigger finger in position. Twice he has let loose with foamy blasts in his apartment, salmon drippings and then ground round igniting in the oven's broiling pan. He knows the implement.

Meanwhile, Braun has torn out of the Dumpster and made a direct line for Richard, meaning to knock him senseless with the collision. But Richard meets his arrival with a sharp pivot and a propulsion of phosphates and sulfates that blinds him, stuns him, and throws him two feet off course, so that he crashes into the wall rather than into his intended target. Richard kicks free the two-by-four, opens the door, and gets the hell out of there. He runs on Latimer Street, his knee throbbing.

Braun bolts out of the Dumpster room and into the alley, looks up and down Latimer. His eyeballs did not take a direct hit from the fire extinguisher's onslaught, and his vision is clearing. And there is Richard, running toward the end of the alley at Sixteenth Street. And now Braun goes after him, with Frank left behind, chloroformed, and out for hours, and Mike under the impression Frank has an emergency at home. That's what Braun forced Frank to say into the walkie-talkie after he'd trailed him from the lobby, hammer-locked his arm just as he opened the door to the Dumpster room, kicked the broomstick inside, and taken his keys. Then the doused handkerchief, smothering nose and mouth. Frank is just a bystander, but now he, too, is a liability.

Richard, though, is the prey right now, to be incapacitated and properly eliminated.

Perfection is elusive: an unexpected delay with Maddie but no big deal. She's where he wants her to be. Tuck her back into the body bag, cover her with a blanket of trash, and let the continued accumulations bury her, no one looking. Even over a full weekend, little risk now that she's embalmed. Monday's trash pickup will cart her away, no one paying attention on either end—it's just a landslide of trash, after all—and no damning evidence, no one to finger him.

Except Lori.

But Lori will not betray him. She'd be betraying herself.

So poor Maddie got stuck. It happens, apparently—he's smiling as he runs—and Keene solved the problem for him. Perfect. Long gone, Keene said? They don't pick up trash on Saturday, so what the hell's he talking about? Doesn't matter now.

Make the chloroform dose lethal for Frank and Keene, load them in the Fiat's trunk, dump them in the Schuylkill somewhere, maybe below the banks of the picnic grove on West River Drive, where he and Eleanor went one Sunday afternoon before she moved in. Steam-clean the trunk. Several times. Not the preferred dispatch, not the way he normally operates. Risky. Or, at least, riskier.

He'll have to pull the car right up to the rear door and fetch Frank. Though it's Saturday night and a parking lot is across the way, the alley is dark. He can wait for the right moment. He's the only one in possession of the keys to the Dumpster room, other than nitwit Mike. No reason for him or anybody else to go back there at this hour.

He doesn't want to take the time to get more body bags from the hospital. Stuff the newcomers in wardrobe bags— just as good at this point. Yeah, he's got a couple of those he can spare.

It works out. He's golden.

But how does he get Keene to the car?

Braun considers all of this in motion as he runs to the end of the alley. But he feels a bit tired now. His thoughts drift, as if his brain has overheated and needs to cool down. He turns the corner at Sixteenth and Latimer, and he has Keene in his sights. His focus resharpens.

This will not last long.

EIGHTEEN

She doesn't want to call Richard and explain her behavior on the sundeck, explain everything about what she's doing. She doesn't want to join forces with him and risk compromising her pursuit of Braun.

But Richard has become part of the equation and, she fears, she understands, is in danger himself. She is more than willing to put herself in harm's way, but the last thing she wants to see is yet another victim.

She scoops her cell phone from the kitchen counter. Should she call the lieutenant whose number Richard gave her? And tell him what?

After the fourth ring, Richard's recorded voice answers, polite, apologetic even, asking the caller to leave a message. She leaves none, rushes out of her apartment, and takes the elevator seven floors skyward. Rings the bell at apartment 2207. Bangs on the door. Waits.

Suddenly she's panicky. She has used him as bait, and bait is something that gets snatched away before you can even react.

Back in the elevator and down to the lobby. "Do you know Richard Keene, the tenant in 2207?"

"Not sure, ma'am," says Mike. "What's he look like?"

"Thin, average height, dark hair . . ." She gropes for a defining physical trait but comes up empty. Then, "Intense—he's got this intense look about him."

Mike doesn't know how to translate that. He looks at the ceiling and thinks hard. "Can't say. Sorry."

"Where's Frank?"

"Oh, he had to leave."

"Damn it," she says to herself.

"First he had to go in the back. What floor you on, ma'am?"

"Fifteen. Why?"

"Were you hit by our little trash problem?"

"What?"

"The trash shot, er . . ."

"The what?"

"The thing that takes the trash all the way down and—"

"Chute?"

"Yeah, that's it. It was stuck for the first time in history, far as I know."

"Stuck?"

"Yeah, somethin' got stuck, and it was clogged startin' on the third floor at least. You believe that?"

"So it's unclogged now?"

"Far as I know."

"Frank said so?"

"Well, not exactly. But he went to check it out and now it's okay, so I figure—"

"When?"

"'Bout a half hour ago. But then he had to leave right away."

"How come?"

"Some kind of emergency at home. But I'm here, so we're okay. Don't really need two guys here most of the time, anyways."

"Where's the trash area?"

"We lock that up at night."

Janet puts her arms on the counter and leans toward him. "I'm sorry, what's your name?"

"Mike."

"Mike, I have to get back there. It's very important."

Mike's eyes seem to swim a little. "Okay, ma'am. I guess it won't hurt for me to leave the desk here for a second."

Janet has never been in the Dumpster room and doesn't know what to expect, but she's sure as hell going to have a look. Clogged trash chute. It's too soon for another victim. *She's* supposed to be the next victim.

Unless it's Richard himself.

He had this pegged, all right. Janet doesn't remember a specific reference to a Dumpster room in the official report of the Atlantic City police, but they searched all of the Oasis's public spaces; that's what it said. And found nothing. Not a trace of Karen. And nothing incriminating.

They leave the building by the rear door. Mike fetches a ring of keys from his pocket, selects one, and opens the door to the Dumpster room. They walk into the yellow light. At first, that's all that stamps Janet's retinas: the garish, numbing light.

Then she sees the big Dumpster, of course, and the cinder-block walls, and the chute growing out of the ceiling and poised above the Dumpster, and then a broom and a thick length of wood on the floor, both of them just dropped there, it seems.

And right by their feet, the fire extinguisher coated with foam. On the floor around it, more foam.

Mike doesn't know what to make of it. "What the hell?"

Then their breaths catch when they see Frank lying prostrate on the cold concrete. "Oh, geez," Mike says, his voice unsteady.

Janet moves to the body and kneels. She touches Frank's cheek; it is warm. She puts two fingers to his throat and feels a pulse, sees a slight rise and fall at his chest, looks at Mike and nods. "He's either been hit on the head or drugged."

Mike is lost. "I don't get it. What . . . ?"

Janet is afraid to look into the Dumpster. She rises and scans the room again; Mike quiet behind her, she is very much the leader on this patrol. She yanks her Android out of her hip pocket and calls 911 to report the scene and request an ambulance. Then she retrieves her wallet from another pocket and, out of that, Lieutenant Oliver's card. She runs through her mind what she'll say to him and how she'll say it.

"This is where Frank went earlier?" she asks Mike.

"That's right."

"By himself?"

Mike scratches his chin again. "Actually, he had someone with him, one of the tenants, I guess."

"Was it the one I asked you about?"

"That you—?"

"Just before we came in here, I was asking you about Richard Keene. Thin, dark hair . . ."

"Oh yeah."

"Was it him?"

"Gee, I'm sorry, I can't remember what the guy looked like. I didn't see him so good."

She makes the call. The desk sergeant tells her that Oliver's off duty. But she must speak with him, and only him; it's an emergency. The sergeant balks, suggests alternatives, but Janet is persuasive. He offers to call Oliver at home. She leaves her cell number.

"Nothin's ever happened like this around here," Mike says.

Janet knows all about the unexpected.

She slaps dust off of her jeans. Now she'll have a look inside the Dumpster.

Richard is running on Sixteenth Street and, though slowed slightly by a limp, he keeps a comfortable distance from Braun, who moves easily in pursuit, as if out for a brisk evening jog. Braun gauges how fast he must go to catch Richard before they reach the front entrance to the 42s, for that is surely where Richard is headed. He'll catch him in a few moments by turning on a burst of speed, maneuver him into the shadows, and press a chloroform-sopped handkerchief to his snout, the little shit. Then guide him like a drunk around the block and back to the rear of the 42s, hope that whoever's in the parking-lot shed isn't too observant as they pass by. It's past dusk now, and people on the street won't figure out what the hell's going on if he's smooth enough about it. No one pays attention anyhow; that's what he counts on. My buddy's had one too many, he'll tell anyone who does happen to take notice, and in fact, there's a hell-raising pub right on the corner to provide credence—he has seen police roust boisterous toughs from the place during daylight hours. He almost smiles to himself as the warm, stale, evening breeze slides past his cheeks, and he runs in the dwindling light, closing the gap.

But at the corner of Sixteenth and Locust, Richard does not make the turn toward the 42s. Instead, he continues north across Locust, running hard but laboring now, favoring his right leg. Every couple of seconds, he glances back to see if Braun draws closer. Something inside of him has resisted going straight to Mike at the front desk; he feels as if reporting this improbable matter, going through proper channels, is no longer an option. This time, he will take it elsewhere. This time will be a different story. It will be decided in the open, in the broad arena of the city, in the gaze of the public eye.

Braun is mystified. Where the hell's he going? Now he expects Richard to stop someone on the street and blurt out his story like a scared little boy. He has his hypodermic needle primed and ready if Richard tries his luck with a passerby. Excuse me, sir, I'm a doctor, this man is my patient, he's troubled; in plunges the hypo, and an arm-locked Richard is whisked away.

But Richard is simply running past people: a shining, well-dressed couple headed in the same direction toward Walnut Street; a young woman in knee-ripped jeans coming the other way; a haggard old man in a thin suit and necktie from yesteryear. Past the black-bronze figure of the man holding an umbrella against ever-threatening skies, Richard is running faster than Braun would have guessed he could, fast enough to maintain the distance between them. The light is green at Walnut, and Richard continues straight across with a backward glance, and now Braun picks up his pace but doesn't seem to gain any ground. He sees Richard accelerate, turn the corner sharply, and take off down Walnut toward Fifteenth. Damn, the little shit's pretty good on his feet. But now Richard grabs at his knee in obvious pain, and his stride becomes erratic even as he maintains his speed.

"We'll get him," Braun says to himself.

"Richard said you were the one to call, that he could count on you."

"To do what?"

"To do the right thing."

"And what's that?"

The return call came within two minutes, a long enough wait for her to see what she had to in the Dumpster. Janet stands there in the awful light, Frank lying on the concrete a few yards away, a dirty rag she placed there for a pillow. Mike wears a blank expression. The cell phone is pinned to Janet's ear. Her eyes are glazed, and her well-trained legs feel like pudding.

"Investigate and bring Davis Braun to justice," she says.

"What's your connection with this, miss?"

She doesn't hesitate. "He killed my sister."

She tells him the story—the abridged version, because time is short—with a mixture of urgency and control. She tells him about her sister, about Braun, about Richard. He is the first person she has spoken to about this, and she can feel the emotional strain of the past months, all that she has borne alone, come through her voice.

To Oliver, Janet's call mandates a response without commanding one. Not unlike the quality he found in the voice and presentation of Richard Keene. Two of them on this same case. It's enough to grab him by both shoulders and lift him out of the quicksand. These are people who need help, young people, and what are the police in business for? And this case is just quirky enough, interesting enough, to pique whatever intellectual curiosity is left in him.

There was a car once, and a boyfriend at the wheel, a young man who meant little to him but could have meant nearly everything in the reach of time—who knows? Nearly, because the one who *did* mean everything was in the next seat, and, of course, there was nothing that he could have done to save her. The utter helplessness of it all, the infuriating helplessness. Just like that, Cassie was gone, and he was left with himself, a husk of the father, the husband, the police officer who had gripped life with both hands and hid his tender regard for it.

But maybe a crueler outcome awaited his daughter, had there been no accident. Who's to say that young man would not have done to Cassie, eventually, in some apartment, in the unseemly glare of some kitchen at a mad nether-hour, what Keene alleges this fellow Davis Braun's done . . .

Oliver is up off the dinette chair and on his feet.

Richard feels like he's gliding on Walnut Street, though he realizes, of course, that he's running hard, just about as hard as he can and still leave a little something in reserve. Faces, startled or amused, pop into view, but to him they're as lifeless as the mannequins in the tony shops that flank them. Richard knows that he can run fast, even injured. He knows that Braun is maintaining the distance but is having trouble closing. Richard has run through the pain in his knee, has reached the point where he can't even feel it anymore, and right here, as his legs churn and the sidewalk treadmills below them, the world slows in front of him and grows silent.

He can't hear a thing.

He does not know what to make of it. An eerie prelude to death, or a sublime gift of relief?

When he reaches Fifteenth Street, plants his right foot, and pushes off to turn left, it all comes back: the pain in his knee, the din of the night. Pain, as a foe, is something to battle, but as a warning signal, it should be heeded. It is accompanied now by a squishiness in the knee, as if bone and soft tissue are beginning to fragment and float in gelatin. Richard gets the message, but he cannot switch off the machinery now; he'll go until the wheels come off.

The light is red at Chestnut Street, but the closest car coming toward him is half a dozen storefronts away and cruising, and his crossing is short. He bounds to safety with three loping strides and resumes the choppier gait on the north side of Fifteenth. He glances over his shoulder and sees Braun a hundred feet away, pumping his arms and puffing out his cheeks. Richard calls on whatever's left in his tank and accelerates to a sprint. The light is red at Market Street and it's six lanes across, but he checks the traffic and calculates that he can make it, an instantaneous, instinctive bet on his life.

As they run on street and sidewalk, the towering city looks down on them, two ants in a mad chase worth everything, the pursued struggling to break free of a lifelong straitjacket, the pursuer intent on his own survival and puzzled, almost panicked, by this sudden unraveling of his life, this man of prized, conventional assets compromised by terrible, inexplicable impulses. And as the chase persists, other people in the city go about their nightly business of digesting dinner, sitting in movie houses where giant celluloid images transport them from reality, shouting to be heard in noisy bars, most of them reaching out for connections, impelled by need or routine or ego, but not by the same desperation that drives Richard Keene and Davis Braun through the streets of Philadelphia on this insane night.

Richard escapes the moving cars on Market Street, missing a fender to the thigh by a yard and a stopwatch fraction—the driver has not had time to even hit the horn. Richard sprints into Dilworth Plaza in the lap of City Hall, where dank, urine-tinged air rises in shafts from the subway. He moves toward the courtyard, looking back to see Braun crossing Market, waiting for Braun a second or two now so as not to lose him, Keene now the taunter in this pairing. What has drawn him here he cannot precisely name, but he thinks he must have had it in mind all along, even before the chase was set in motion. He runs into the courtyard tunnel and is swallowed in shadow.

Braun is ten seconds behind Richard. At the outset, he thought that catching him would be a snap, and though he was wrong about that, he didn't panic. Now he's regaining confidence that he has the stamina to prevail. The true test is how you perform under pressure—not when everything is going your way. This goddamn Keene can really run. But he'll get him; it's a matter of time.

Braun follows Richard into the mouth of the tunnel. Slivers of twilight filter down about a hundred feet away, where the straightaway is interrupted and the space broadens into a courtyard of statuary, benches, and flowerbeds that brighten and soften the grim, gray confines. Another hundred feet and the arched concrete tunnel resumes, emptying finally onto Broad Street and the swerving traffic that encircles City Hall. Braun, with the twenty-fifteen vision that has always enhanced his tennis game, can see all the way through to the street, and he can tell that there are only two people in that long passageway at the moment, one coming toward him, the other walking away, neither of them Richard Keene. No way he ran fast enough to reach Broad Street—impossible. In the courtyard, which seems dimly lit as if through an indoor skylight, the flowers' brilliance reduced to grainy black-and-white, Braun sees an open door leading into the century-old building. A thick wooden doorstop is wedged between door and threshold and, just inside, a mop and a pail filled with soapy water sit unattended.

Inside, it's nondescript. A sign on the wall says City Hall Tower Elevator, pointing visitors along the swamp-colored concrete floor. Another sign sends them down an intersecting corridor to Public Works and Engineering. Braun hears the whir of an elevator.

He reaches the elevator alcove just as the door slides shut.

When Lieutenant Oliver pulls his rattling 1993 LeSabre into the alley at the rear of the 42s, uniformed officers, summoned via Janet's 911 call, are already on the scene in the Dumpster room and at the front desk, where they're talking with Mike, who opened the warehouse door at the rear loading dock before returning to his post. While paramedics lift Frank into an ambulance below the loading platform, two policemen grapple with the body of the tall, blonde woman in the Dumpster. Janet stands on the sloped driveway below the platform, waiting, as Oliver's motorized dinosaur stops near the squad cars and he gets out, the driver's side door squealing closed.

"Janet Kroll?"

She turns to him, looks into his tired eyes, and immediately feels a sense of trust. "Thank you, Lieutenant."

They watch the paramedics close the rear doors of the ambulance. "That's the front-desk man you were telling me about?"

"Yes. They say he's been knocked out with chloroform or something."

"Uh-huh."

"They say he'll be okay."

A thick-necked patrolman approaches the two of them and says, "Hey, Bob. Miss Kroll told me you'd be coming. Understand this is one of yours."

"Yeah, think it may be," says Oliver. "Another one slippery as an eel."

Beyond the stocky cop, a split-open body bag is hoisted and tugged out of the Dumpster. A head is visible. Oliver's jaw ripples. "Who's the young woman?"

"We don't know yet."

Oliver looks at Janet, who has her back to the Dumpster. "You don't know her, right? That's what you told me."

Other than a small shake of her head, she doesn't budge. No force on earth could make her look at that face again.

"Any ideas?"

She rests a hand on her forehead, as if checking for fever. "Another girlfriend would be a good guess," she says.

"Wouldn't by any chance be Eleanor Carson, would it?"

"No, I've seen Eleanor several times . . . Looks like her, though."

"And you figure Braun is going after him—Richard Keene," Oliver says.

"I do. I feel sure of it. He may already have gotten him."

Oliver's jaw ripples. He turns toward the patrolman and asks, "I hope there's nobody else in there."

"No. That'll do it for tonight."

Oliver breathes.

"These two guys'll show up sooner or later, the ones Miss Kroll named," says the cop. "Neither one's around right now. We got our eyes peeled."

"Any wild guesses?" Oliver asks Janet.

"If they're not here and not in the building"—she shakes her head—"your guess is as good as mine."

"Yeah, it's a big city, right?" He turns back to the patrolman.

"You know, Rog, I'd really like to get this guy."

"Which one?"

"Well, actually, both of them. Alive."

Inside, beyond the platform, the Dumpster sits like a giant crypt on wheels. The chute spits out a new stream of trash.

Janet's hand shoots to her mouth, and her whispered words are exhaled through spread fingers.

"Oh, God."

Up through the steel-girded, spider-webbed innards of the City Hall tower rides Richard, climbing to the heights. The backs of the luminous, golden clock dials slip into his field of vision and slowly recede below the floor of the elevator as it rises, the distance from the ground increasing by only a few feet per second. When the elevator finally stops and the door opens, and Richard steps onto the narrow circular walkway of the observation deck, a night sky greets him, dark and coarsely clouded, transformed from the tepid overhang of twilight. Airplanes crisscross in the southern sky, and below, a prairie of lights stretches to eyesight's limit.

He knew he would somehow be here at the end; he belongs here. He looks up at the massive statue of William Penn above him, folds his arms. He has the luxury of several minutes for the elevator to complete its descent and then return. All of his insides are quiet now, all the neurological circuitry unblinking; he is at ease, no heartbeat thumping the chest, no constricted throat, no grinding stomach. He is as relaxed as if he were taking a hot bath and has settled into the water's caress, a slap here, a soapy swirl there.

From the bowels comes the elevator's wheeze, the faintest of sounds only Richard Keene could pick up at this distance. Still, his nervous system does not rebel. He is calm, feels a serenity he has never felt before, yet his senses are keen and his resolve certain. He hears the elevator climbing, feels its vibration through the rubber soles of his sneakers, in his instep, and up his ankles to his shins. The rider is his nemesis, and it is here in the rippling crosswinds at the top of the city—still its symbolic zenith, despite taller, more modern buildings— that Richard will make his stand.

This time he will go all the way to the top of the statue. The route to William Penn's bronze hat is one of peril and audacity. But on the other side waits release. A free sweep of sky, and the floating kiss of eternity.

Consciously engineering this odyssey, or drawn to this precise site like the proverbial moth to the flame—which-ever, he is here.

He flexes his knees, the bad one complaining but game, and primes himself for a powerful spring upward, the kind of lift he needed for a successful high jump when he tried out for the middle school track team and didn't make the cut. It will take a healthy leap to reach the access platform so he can hoist himself onto it and get to the long ladder that cuts through the statue's cavity. There is no room for a running start. He has no shorter workman's ladder at hand.

Richard revs up his breathing and windmills his arms like some big, goofy bird readying for stationary takeoff. When he leaves the ground, the bad knee does not balk, or if it does, his will overrides it. No extraneous noises— no sounds at all, in fact—clutter his senses. There is only his body and its capacity, and the space between it and the next level. And when he flies up, and his hands and forearms thump the wooden platform, again his concentration is such that no sounds are allowed to intrude, even as he knees and elbows and scrapes his way up and over.

The base of the statue yields to an opening like a rounded, hidden fold at the mouth of a cave or an amusement-park funhouse. It leads to the statue's interior, a narrow hollow through which a ladder rises more than thirty feet through one of the massive legs, the torso, and the head, all the way to the twenty-two-inch hatch that opens Billy Penn's hat to the elements. Richard knows all this because he's read about it in an article somewhere, maybe in the *Philadelphia Inquirer*.

He waits on the platform.

The elevator arrives and disgorges Davis Braun, who eyes the empty space and walks halfway across the observation deck. Richard issues a brief, birdlike whistle from above, and Braun snaps his head upward. He smiles an I-got-you smile but one that has elements of recognition that Richard is a fellow lunatic, and even a worthy adversary. It's a smile that has all of Braun's potent charm in it, a poison Tastykake.

Richard turns from him and disappears into the statue. Inside the thirty-seven-foot bronze giant, he grabs a rung and gets his footing on the ladder. He brushes against the cast metal as he ascends, visibility blacker than tar. His serenity vanishes. Dread seizes him, the sweats of closed-in fear, but he fights it on equal terms now. He convinces himself that the darkness is his ally because he can keep his eyes open and imagine that he is on a beach whose ocean hugs the horizon, or that he's drifting in the sky, caressed by clouds. The mind rules. And now he begins to gather strength from each step up, the altitude recharging him like water aerating the gills of a landed fish tossed back into the ocean.

He knows that Braun will be coming after him. They'll finish this thing, at last.

He hears him, feels him, on the ladder, twenty feet below. Richard runs out of ladder and fits himself into the hatchway, which is snug as an MRI scanner or a blanketed bed. But the dread is gone, all gone, dismissed by adrenaline. He places both hands on the metal surface above him—the underside of the hatch itself, the very top of the statue— and feels about for a handle or latch but locates none. So he pushes for all he's worth and feels it give a bit. He lowers his hands a few inches, then thrusts them upward so that the heels hit first, and the palm and fingers complete the impact. He feels more give and repeats the motion.

This time, the hatch flies open and the night rushes into the space. A refrain of wind, a darkening sky speckled with early stars. Richard pokes his head out and breathes in the sky-cooled air.

He knows Braun is climbing toward him.

He eases himself through the opening and onto the top of William Penn's hat, now on his knees, palms down, and then up on his haunches. He rears up, gritted teeth pulsing his jaw, to a full standing position. A mountain climber at the summit. The city spreads before him, even more alive than when viewed from the enclosed observation deck, a platter of shapes and angles and lights, and he feels a literal part of the tapestry rather than a spectator. This is no oil canvas or planetarium display, no mere scenic exhibit but a fabric that has stitched him to its center.

He carefully slides onto the brim when he hears Braun near the hatchway. There is little maneuvering room here—a hop, skip, and a jump, and you're in free fall. But for Richard's purposes, there's enough. This is where intrepid city workers drape giant, sheet-like logos of the town's sports teams when a championship has been won. Bright, colorful symbols the populace can rally around. Up here at the peak of dreams.

Braun's head is visible just above the hatch, and his eyes locate Richard immediately, then scan the bronze hat, this unlikely perch he has reached. He climbs through in segments—shoulders, chest, waist—pausing at each to gauge the playing field and his equilibrium. He knees his way out of the hatch and, when he finally stands, slowly but gloriously, like a giant character righting itself on a parade float, he faces Richard on the brim, just below him and six feet away. They stand in a dancing wind surrounded by a dizzying panorama but notice neither.

"The perfect suicide," Braun says.

"Are you volunteering?"

Braun smiles. "Who will notice us all the way up here, at nighttime yet? I can always count on people being oblivious."

He takes a tiny step, six inches, and feels his weight supported. The other foot, same thing. Richard holds his ground.

"You're a crazy one," Braun says, as he sits and slides tentatively onto the brim, his words chasing through the wind to Richard's ears. Richard hears them as if through a megaphone, for his senses are ultrasharp, every nerve and corpuscle strung to the limit.

"Who's the girl?" he asks Braun, trying to sound just as

conversational. "The girl in the Dumpster."

Braun's smile chills him. "What do you care?"

"I have my reasons."

"Good for you. Tell you what—it doesn't matter now . . . Madelyn Burke. That's her name. People call her Maddie. Happy?"

"Who is she?"

"Just some girl . . . By the way, I didn't kill her. Your girlfriend killed her."

"*My* girlfriend?"

"That's right. Sweet, little Lori Calder."

Now it's Richard's turn to smile, but he doesn't. "You don't have to lie now, Braun." It's the first time that he's addressed him by name. "What's the point?"

"I'm not lying."

"Why would she kill her? And how?"

"Let's keep it simple: she's the jealous type. She killed Eleanor, too—how's that grab you? Little girl can be a terror . . . I guess you could call me a facilitator." He looks pleased with his word choice.

"A facilitator," Richard repeats softly. He can't bring himself to believe what he's just heard. "So now it's time for you to kill *her*?"

"Why would you think that?"

The wind skitters between them. Richard braces himself. "In the trash room this afternoon—"

"Yeah?"

"You and Lori—"

"That was sex, my boy. You're a little short on your education . . . But you always show up, don't you?" The wind swoops and hisses. "How does that happen?"

Richard just stares at him.

Braun is about an arm's length away, and in the fraction of a second that it takes for him to lunge at his target, Richard sidesteps with perfect economy and leaves the bigger man swatting at air currents that tease from head to toe. Richard is in his element, surefooted at the apex, but does not counter, even though Braun is off-balance and seems ripe for a shove.

They square off again, and Braun hesitates as a look of wonderment comes over him. "I'll be damned," he says.

"You already are."

"I'll take you with me," Braun says, as if offering a ride to work. Below the two of them, the broad visage of William Penn surveys his real estate, unmoved by their dance overhead. Radio-tower lights on a neighboring building blink at the sky.

Now Braun is on him, and this time Richard avoids the brunt, but not all, of the short charge; they are both down after Braun's shoulder collides with the left side of Richard's flat chest. In rising, Braun slips and then slips again, and there is no further margin for error on this unenclosed summit more than five hundred feet off the ground. He flounders on the mild slope as he scrambles to stand once more.

Richard is on his feet and silhouetted against a mass of night-white cloud. He is a step from the hatch—he could try to scramble down and take the elevator out of harm's way, but he has no intention of doing that. There is no safety in that. He has his monster on a limb, and he wants to cut it off.

And now Braun has lost his comfort level. He sees rotting bodies everywhere yet remembers that he has left a warm one at the 42s. The unbidden image of his mother takes hold of him at this precise moment, and he isn't sure what he feels—some curious mingling of embarrassment and arousal—but he does know that it's something he wants to extinguish and fast. He has a quarry to catch. He has Keene in his cross-hairs, figures he'll nail him with the next charge. But he is overheated and sweating beyond the cooling powers of the unrelenting wind. He is leaking, juices ebbing out of him.

Something is coming for him.

A gust of wind leaps up and takes him as he stands, moves him like a piece on a chessboard, right off the bronze brim and into open space on a cushion of air. Richard jerks forward at the sight, but there is nothing to do. Braun hangs there a frozen moment, like a bird seeking direction. And then he is gone, and the gust is gone, its trailing breeze just a flutter whispering unintelligible secrets fifty stories above the pavement.

NINETEEN

The news about a jumper off the statue of William Penn comes over the police radios, springing out of squad cars and echoing in the alley. Oliver is the only one to make a connection.

Good God. What he said those times on the telephone. Strange talk about that poet and all. Whitman. Under your boot soles, he said. Scale the heights, he said. *Way up high.* The words, and the way they were said, have stuck with Oliver.

A little tug at his stomach and throat. The clincher: Scaling that shaky ladder with impunity, all the way up to the second-level ceiling on the first day he came to the station.

"I hope that's not our boy," Oliver says to Janet, though he believes otherwise.

Janet seems in her own world as she leans against a strip of brick wall at one end of the loading dock. Finally, she realizes that Oliver has said something to her. "I'm sorry, what was that again?"

"Someone just jumped off the top of City Hall."

"What?"

"Or fell," Oliver adds. "We just got a report."

He places a hand on her shoulder. "I'm sorry," he says. "All kinds of things come over that radio. Can't stop it."

"Why would that be Richard?"

"Something he said to me. I have a feeling. Could be nothing."

"Do you really think . . . ?"

"I'm gonna check it out," Oliver says. There's a humming inside of him, a motor that has been started after a long period of disuse. He walks to a squad car, braces himself with one hand on the roof, and leans toward the driver. "I'm gonna see what's up with that jumper, Rog."

"Busy evening, huh?"

"Could say that."

The patrolman starts the engine and eases the car into the alley; a second blue-and-white follows. Oliver returns to Janet, who hasn't moved from her spot in ten minutes.

"You all right?"

They watch the ambulance pull away. "They're both in there?" Janet asks.

"Yep. They'll be going to different departments."

She shudders.

"Sorry. Why don't you get some rest?"

"What will you find there?"

"At City Hall?"

"Yes."

He looks away and shakes his head. "I don't know."

"*Who* will you find there?"

Oliver looks right into her eyes—beautiful hazel eyes. She is about the age that Cassie would be, maybe a couple years older. "I don't know that, either," he says evenly. "But I think our guy's comin' out of this one whole. Just a hunch."

"I want to go with you."

He balks. "Well—"

"Please."

What the hell. This kid can take it. Just like Cassie. Tough young lady.

"Let's go," he says, turning toward his battered Buick and almost smiling to himself. "I'm off duty, anyway."

It's just two turns and four blocks to City Hall, but they hit three red lights, and Oliver has no siren or emergency light for this jalopy, so Janet has time to give him a fuller summary of her sister's death and her pursuit of Braun.

"Do your folks know what you've been doing?"

"Are you kidding? I couldn't put them through that. My father would die."

Oliver looks at her with admiration. This girl's got guts . . . and character. Reminds him of someone.

It has begun to drizzle, and when Oliver switches on the arthritic wipers, they scrape the windshield and leave sagging ridges of water in their wake. Better to keep them quiet until the rain picks up.

Police sawhorses and yellow tape festoon Dilworth Plaza, and a crowd gathers just beyond—squad cars and TV-news vans angling in. Big doings: big-city swan dive to the pavement, film at eleven. Reporters clutch mikes and lean into the klieg lights. Braun's body lies crumpled beneath a sheet near the tunnel leading to the courtyard, ground he trod less than an hour earlier. The police interrogate a grizzled homeless man, who, so far, is the only eyewitness at ground level. All he saw was something fly through the air and hit the ground. "Didn't sound like much," he says. "Like, I dunno, a bag of groceries or somethin'. Only saw it for a coupla seconds, when it was gettin' to the ground—no, not from the top, y'understan', don't know what happened all the way up there. Can't see that far anyway."

The 911 call came in from a janitor in a high-rise office building facing City Hall, right across Fifteenth Street on Market. He was Windexing the tall windows and had a dead-on view. That call was the only one per this incident. If anyone else caught a glimpse, it either didn't register or the random onlooker refused to believe his eyes. A daredevil's final flight, and not much of a gallery for oohs and ahs.

Arms bracing hiked-up knees as he sits on William Penn's hat, Richard feels immobilized. The winds continue to snake-dance on high, funneling up from below the hat's brim and spinning off into the mist of night.

When he finally rises, a shiver runs through him and out into the air. The surface of the great bronze hat is slick with light rain. Five hundred feet below, a mad world scrambles for traction. Richard hunches at the precipice, looks up at the phantom sky and back down at the hard, level ground.

A new sensation weaves its way through him. He is sloughing off the fears and self-loathing that have constricted him forever, purging himself of the poison he has consistently administered to his system. All of it went overboard with Davis Braun, and there is no reason he should follow. He has no regret for the horror that transpired here at the heights. Behind his grimace forecasting tears is jubilance, a silent cry of triumph.

And so, after a while, he slips himself back through the hatch and down through the gullet of William Penn.

Lieutenant Oliver has checked in with the detectives on the scene. They are from the center-city substation and, of course, he knows them. They've already retrieved a wallet, keys, a vial of chloroform, a handkerchief, and a hypodermic needle.

"His name happen to be Davis Braun?" asks Oliver, relieved after peeling back the sheet and not seeing Richard.

One of the detectives, a fortyish man with slits for eyes and thick, wavy black hair, says, "You know 'im?"

Oliver raises his wise, weary eyes. "Second time we've met, but he looked different before."

"Interesting stuff he carries around."

Oliver looks skyward toward the City Hall tower set back from the building's lower levels, then again at the covered body. "How'd he wind up all the way over here?"

"Windy night."

"Guess so."

Oliver stands there, hands in his pockets. "How the hell'd he get up there in the first place? It's Saturday night, for God's sake."

"Custodial crew comes in Market Street East entrance after seven," says the detective. "They left a courtyard door open. Woman who mops the floor says the ammonia fumes get to her . . . Anyway, I don't know what the hype's all about—looks like suicide to me."

"I wonder," says Oliver, an ironic smile forming on his lips.

"I figure the chloroform was in case he couldn't stomach the ride down."

Janet stays outside the barricade, waiting, looking almost shell-shocked now, but striking enough to generate some heat among a couple of the officers. Oliver looks right at her as he walks across the plaza after seeing the sheeted corpse. A smile would be inappropriate, but he wants to do something from a distance to reassure her, settles for walking fast and speaking the words while still in motion. "It's Davis Braun," he says as he nears her on the other side of the sawhorses.

He can hear her breathing. He admires her doggedness and senses the end of her travail, the unplumbed tangles of personal lives. And she begins to cry.

Richard appears out of the darkness of the courtyard tunnel like a ghost. Oliver has been expecting him.

"Look who's here," he says to Janet, and she stifles her crying, looks up, and sees Richard moving toward them, limping. There is something reverential in his eyes, as if he has learned a truth that will anchor him forever. They both realize that he is looking past them with an almost hypnotized gaze. Oliver shifts so that he is directly in front of Richard, who is now thirty feet away. A flicker of recognition, and Richard's trance falls away. He walks right up to them, and Janet moves to him and hugs him, her chin on his shoulder and her eyes full of turmoil. Startled, he hugs her back. When they break, Oliver asks him, "What happened up there?"

Richard jerks his head toward City Hall and looks up the clock tower to the sky. "He chased me," Richard says simply. "He wanted to kill me."

Oliver nods, directs his eyes skyward, then back to Richard. "Chased you all the way up there, huh?"

"All the way up there."

"And?"

Only truth can come out of Richard, and Oliver knows it. "He went after me and . . . he slipped . . . He was gone."

"He's gone; that's for sure," Oliver says.

Richard turns to Janet. "I'm sorry."

"I'm not," she says. Her cheeks are tear-streaked and her facial muscles quiver. "Thank God you're all right."

Oliver places a hand on Richard's shoulder. "Something I should have realized when you came in that first time: You're a courageous young man."

"Not really," Richard says. "You see, I had no other choice."

Oliver points to Braun's covered body and the huddle of police and detectives, none of whom are aware of Richard's presence or relevance. "Time to tell them your story."

It is a riot of color and glare: the revolving red lights of squad cars and the hot, white floods for television, the machinery of accountability, of public display, the energy of it all.

"I'll be damned," Richard says.

Oliver looks at him. "What's that?"

"That's what he said up there. And he had the strangest look on his face. For the first time, to me, he looked like a human being. Tortured but human. Like he was beginning to understand himself. I can relate to that."

Oliver again gestures toward the police.

"Will you come with me?" Richard asks.

Oliver smiles and, for the first time in a long time, he feels good about himself, even if it's only temporary. "Of course."

"Thanks," says Richard, "and thanks for everything else."

"All I did was some paperwork."

The two of them move toward the barrier, but Janet stops them in their tracks. "He killed my sister," she says to Richard.

He looks at her.

"Atlantic City," she continues. "Another high-rise. They were living together. He was never even arrested."

Their subsequent silence unleashes the squawking of police-car radios and competing media voices carving out slices of the story. "I've been after him ever since. Can you believe that you and I were hunting the same man?" She starts to cry again.

Richard processes what Janet has told him and connects it to this very moment. "Parallel paths," he says, and immediately chides himself for sounding too profound. "But I have something else to tell you, Janet. Get ready for another shock . . . I have a feeling that Braun didn't kill your sister."

This gets Oliver's attention in a big way. He waits for Richard to continue.

Janet looks perplexed, with a tinge of anger. "What do you mean?"

"It may have been Lori Calder. I think it *was* Lori Calder."

"Lori?" Janet is incredulous. "Next-door Lori? . . . How is that possible?"

"He said as much before he . . . went over. Braun did." Richard looks at Oliver, then back at Janet. "He said that Lori was the one who actually killed Eleanor Carson. And the girl we found tonight. She could be quite fierce, evidently. Homicidal.

"I believe him. Why would he make it up? It's like a death confession, regardless of which one of us was to die— or both . . . I'll bet that, if we investigate Lori, we'll find that she was living at the seashore and involved with Braun at that time. Just like here."

He looks again at Oliver, who produces a strange smile.

"As for why," Richard says to both of them, "Braun said the oldest reason in the book: jealousy."

Janet lowers her head. "Why didn't they just move in together, then, and leave everybody alone?"

Richard's eyes close halfway, as if he's drifting off to sleep. "I figure it was about more than that for them."

"A team of serial killers," Oliver says, and they both turn toward him.

Richard nods. "He called himself a 'facilitator' . . . up there. Can you imagine using that word?"

"You had quite a conversation," says Oliver.

A lean, dark-haired young man approaches them, but only Richard makes eye contact.

"Why did they do this?" Janet asks Oliver.

"Young lady," he says, "that's a question that almost always runs away from answers. There is no dealing with the perverse."

The newcomer stops six feet away, as if to acknowledge a respectful distance. Richard's attention, however, returns to Janet, and he can't hide a note of disappointment. "Why didn't you tell me? We could have—"

"I wasn't trusting anybody, and, at the same time, I didn't want to endanger anybody," she says. She shuts her eyes. A derisive puff of air sneaks out of her. "Like a bag of trash." She opens her eyes and turns toward the sheet-covered mound beyond the barriers. A near whisper: "Good-bye, you bastard."

Richard turns to the newcomer, who looks stricken. "Cameron, right?"

The young man doesn't answer, but his voice quavers when he asks, "Did you kill him?"

"He killed himself." Richard turns to Oliver. "This is Cameron . . . Miro, Lieutenant. A colleague of Braun's at Metropolitan Hospital."

Oliver doesn't waste any time. "Why did you ask him if he killed him?"

"He's been following him around."

"And how do you know that?"

"'Cause he's been following *me*," Richard interrupts. "Do you know a girl named Madelyn Burke?" he quickly asks Cameron. The question startles Oliver and Janet. Cameron's answer is a reflex.

"Maddie Burke? Yeah, I know her. We're friends. With Davis, too."

"No longer," Richard says.

Oliver leans in toward Cameron. "Do you know what your friend has been up to?"

Cameron looks unbearably sad. "I don't know what you mean."

"I'd like you to come with us," Oliver says, then waves the three of them to walk toward the detectives. "We're gonna take lots of notes tonight. Might make a call to Atlantic City while we're at it." He leads them through the barricade.

"Guess you have a new investigation on your hands, Richard," he continues. "Told you, you could be a good cop."

"*You're* the good cop, Lieutenant."

"What about you, Richard?" Janet says, walking next to him. "What was this about? What was it really about?"

Richard doesn't break stride, looks somewhere beyond the covered corpse and the plaza as he answers.

"Freedom."

TWENTY

Three days later, a day after Richard learned that Mazer National Bancorp implicated Lori Calder in Braun's piddling check-fraud scheme—news that would have torn out his heart if his belief in her deadly behavior had not already done that—he stands in front of his bathroom mirror. When his reflected form stares back at him, he figures he's real enough, as tangible as his toothbrush.

He has told the police an amazing story, and they have no reason not to believe him. They have an embalmed Madelyn Burke, a chloroformed Frank Grant, Frank's testimony and that of Janet Kroll and Cameron Miro, and a still-missing Eleanor Carson.

Especially useful was Frank's characterization—seconded by Cameron—of Miss Burke as a friend of Eleanor and Davis, and one whose resemblance to Eleanor in both form and features made the two look like sisters, almost twins. Frank recalled seeing Maddie walk through the lobby and out of the 42s, and mistaking her for Eleanor on the evening that Richard Keene said Eleanor was murdered. The police soon learned that Miss Burke left for a European vacation that night and returned on the night she died.

A fateful visit, evidently, to apartment 2307 to see her good friends upon her return and tell them all about her exciting trip.

The police also have one of their own, Lieutenant Robert Oliver, backing Richard's story all the way, and a nice find by the forensic team on a return visit to Braun's apartment: traces of embalming fluid. They did ask Richard repeatedly why he raced Braun through the city and drew him to the top of the City Hall clock tower instead of seeking the protection of others on the street or calling the police. It was uncertain whether he could find immediate sanctuary with Braun coming after him, he told them, and even if he could and contacted police, Braun might have had time to cover things up yet again. Furthermore, why endanger others, with a killer on the loose and on the attack? So he took it on himself and devised a strategy on the fly. He went where his legs, heart, and lungs—and perhaps his mind—carried him. A place from which there would be no escape, only resolution. A place where fear evaporated, and monsters were at the mercy of the natural elements. A place of absolute faith, an equalizer, a place of balanced scales, under the nose of God and the city's master planner.

If he didn't get into City Hall, he told them, he'd have run all the way to the Ben Franklin Bridge.

This time, Richard Keene told the police the full story. In private, he told Lieutenant Oliver one more story, this one about a little girl who was his next-door neighbor, an enchanting girl who didn't live past her eighth birthday.

The telephone is ringing. Richard walks into the bedroom and picks up the receiver. Evelyn is on the line, breathless.

"Richard, Herb Dempsey committed suicide."

Richard lets the news seep into his skin.

"Did you hear me?"

"Yes, I heard you."

"Two days ago. Neetz Berman told me; I still keep in touch with her. She always asks about you. She found out from somebody; I don't know who. It happened in the building where he was living, somewhere in West Philadelphia. I thought you should know."

His eyes are shut. "How?"

"What?"

"How did he kill himself?"

"Neetz says he stuck his head in the oven."

Richard is embarrassed that he can't suppress a smile. "What took him so long?"

Nervous laughter from Evelyn. "I'm surprised your father didn't see it in the obituaries. Maybe he did and forgot to tell me; you know his memory isn't so good these days, either . . . So, anyway, now you can worry about something else, but you don't have to worry about Herb Dempsey anymore."

Richard's eyes are open. He hopes he isn't dreaming.

One thing he hasn't yet done, he will do now. He walks up one flight to the twenty-third floor and knocks on the door to Lori's apartment. After a moment, a voice comes from inside. A young woman's well-modulated voice. For an instant, he thinks it's Lori's.

"Yes? Who is it?"

Not Lori, but close.

Damn, they turn these units over fast. Big demand in center city.

No dissembling this time. "Richard Keene, a neighbor."

The door opens and a petite, smooth-shouldered young woman stands in the threshold. Lively eyes, auburn hair. A lovely smile.

"Hi. What's up?"

Richard eases into a relaxed stance. "Did you just move in?"

Eight floors below them, Janet Kroll is in her apartment and reordering the pivot points of her life. She will clear out of here fast and go home, she knows that much. The job is done; the investment has paid off. At great cost. The horror sticks, both here and at the seashore, where her sister's disappearance is back on the police department's front burner.

Meanwhile, she has learned some things about herself. She is a stronger person than anyone has suspected. She has been regarded as sweet, smart, healthy, and attractive—all the good things, conventionally speaking. That's how she saw herself, too.

But in dogging Davis Braun until he selected his own death, she became a different person. Sure, she was playing a role, but she has emerged with some of that persona onboard. Sex as a compeller. Guile as an orchestrator. To avenge her sister, she *became* her sister—the actress, the personality, even the morals—and she leaves the crime scene with altered chemistry.

Across town, Lieutenant Robert Oliver feels better about himself and the world around him, or at least the immediate four walls of his apartment. He feels that way for the first time in years. This morning, he could taste the sweet-sour tang of his orange juice and the fresh-brewed flavor of his coffee, elevating those beverages from rote offerings to pleasures. He shaved close and smooth and slicked a skin-conditioning gel over the sagging pouches of his cheeks and neck; it smelled great and soothed the scraped skin, even if it did nothing to firm the contours. If he's not exactly a man with a new lease on life, he is at least one whose outlook has risen above that of a galley slave. There are lots of people on this planet, he reminds himself, and he's still among them. People of strength like Richard Keene and Janet Kroll. He hasn't stepped into a church since Cassie's funeral, but he may change that. Anyway, religion is a state of mind, he believes. People are here to help one another—that is the highest calling, the rationale behind the Master Plan. It's a flawed plan, to be sure. Tragically flawed. But to turn away from it is to self-destruct. The mood for that has passed.

Last night, he even retrieved the album barricaded at the top of the closet and looked at the old photographs. Cassie at four with her blonde hair cut short, giving the camera a big gap-toothed smile, her nose wrinkled and eyes squinting under a sky radiating sunshine. Libby raking leaves in the backyard; she did all the gardening and maintenance, a strong woman—in so many ways a strong woman. Robert Jr. standing in his crib, clutching the wooden restraining bars and smiling through them.

Call him tonight.

In another part of town, desolate acreage stretches out under a tame sky like some ancient riverbed deserted by its waters. Big birds issue predatory squawks as they circle and observe from on high. The stink of decay rises as if to fend them off, but it serves only to entice them. It is the saturating smell of rot, the quotidian discards of daily life come to the dumping grounds for proper burial.

A broad pit of earth receives its payload as a trash truck rears and lets slide, then pivots and roars into traction like a tank on a battlefield. Two hundred feet away, a steam shovel unearths heaps of trash, a torrent of dirt falling away between the huge, metal teeth.

At the edge of the site, their backs to the highway and the traffic that flies past, police stand aside their squad cars on the hard-packed dirt. Based on the guesswork of the sanitation department and the trash men whose beat includes the 42s, they hope to find a body somewhere in this vicinity.

Fifty-five miles east, Atlantic City police will be going through a similar exercise designed to recover a body, probably encased in a body bag. They'll likely have many more layers of trash to uncover.

Right here, right now, on this stark flatland in southwest Philadelphia, the steam shovel attacks the mound with swiveling menace and dinosaur teeth. As police and birds look on, and dirt and detritus cascade, recurrent thumping and grinding whir dismiss the squawking from above and any radio chatter spitting from squad-car dashboards. The bulky, mechanized monster digs deeper into the earth.